COLLABORATOR

Murray Davies, the son of a miner, was born and brought up in the South Wales valleys. He won a scholarship to university and went on to do a degree in International Politics and an MA in First World War poetry. Thinking he wanted to write, he entered journalism, working on the *Daily Mail* before joining the Mirror Group as a reporter and feature writer.

Twenty-odd years later he realized that journalism and writing were not the same things and bailed out to write novels.

In his time on Fleet Street he had various claims to fame, including being the first Western reporter to visit death row in a Russian prison, when interviewing cannibal killer Andrei Chikatilo; the only man covering a war in Zaire to wear a sheepskin jacket; and holder of the longest lunch award – three and a half days before anyone noticed he was missing.

Author of *The Devil's Handshake*, also published by Pan, he lives in Greenwich with his long-term partner, when he is not hiding in Wiltshire with his border collie cross, Tip.

Also by Murray Davies

THE DEVIL'S HANDSHAKE

COLLABORATOR

MURRAY DAVIES

PAN BOOKS

First published 2003 by Macmillan

This edition published 2004 by Pan Books
an imprint of Pan Macmillan Ltd
Pan Macmillan, 20 New Wharf Road, London N1 9RR
Basingstoke and Oxford
Associated companies throughout the world
www.panmacmillan.com

ISBN 0 330 49080 X

1 3 5 7 9 8 6 4 2

A CIP catalogue record for this book is available from
the British Library.

Typeset by SetSystems Ltd, SaffronWalden, Essex
Printed and bound in Great Britain by
Mackays of Chatham plc, Chatham, Kent

To the memory of Peter Cliff

Acknowledgements

I would like to offer warm thanks to everyone who has helped in the research and production of this book, especially the staff of the reading room of the Imperial War Museum; Roger Todd for his advice with some of the German; Merric Davidson for his support and encouragement and Susannah Alexander at London's Jewish Museum. Finally, but by no means least, at Macmillan, I owe a large debt of gratitude – and lunch – to Peter Lavery and Stef Bierwerth for their wisdom, patience and friendship.

PART ONE

Yes, I understand the Prime Minister wants a report. Oh, really! And the King's anxious to know his brother's part. That's easy. No, he wasn't playing a double game. He wanted the crown for himself.

All right, I'll help set the record straight, but in my own way and in my own time.

Don't forget, I have the blood of one hundred thousand of my countrymen on my hands. My whole family has perished. I do not have a relative left alive in the world. All my friends have been murdered.

You say it's changed the war. You crow that 'England is aflame.'

Rubbish! It's in flames.

I know the Nazis are scrapping amongst themselves to get to the top of the heap. And there may be an army coup. Yes, I've heard that the Germans haven't the troops to fight Russia and still hold down a rebellion in the British Isles.

But it doesn't help my mother, my father, my sister, my young nephew. It doesn't help Roy or Matty or the rest. They are dead.

Mr Churchill forgets that the British people are Britain. Destroy the people and the notion of a sceptred isle becomes a meaningless mockery.

No, General, I don't have much respect for you or your kind. Respect has to be earned. The way England collapsed, the way the Germans walked in and then walked over us was abject. That was down to your lot.

Arrogant! I never used to be. If I'm arrogant now, it's the arrogance of survival.

I've been hunted by the Gestapo, the Abwehr, even good old British bobbies.

I've been through the flames. I feel nothing.

And don't tell me I'm safe now. You don't share my nightmares. You know I'll never be safe. It only needs one fanatic out for revenge – and God knows there are enough of those out there. Maybe I look forward to my final sleep. But yes. I'll help you.

I don't have the whole picture. Most I know. Some I can guess. The rest I'll make up. See if you can tell the difference.

Where shall I start? At the beginning, I suppose. The day I returned.

I hadn't heard from anyone since I'd been captured. I didn't know what I was returning to.

Imagine finding the Wehrmacht had seized your family home for officers' billets.

It was my sister Joan who told me what had happened, and told me where to find my mother. I hardly recognized her . . .

1

'We had such a lovely surprise this afternoon that I just had to come and tell you. Our Nick is coming home. Isn't that good news! It's such a relief, now that so many prisoners are being shipped off to Germany. Joan's opening the last tin of corned beef and making up the spare room . . .'

My mother plucked like an angry sparrow at the weeds around the earthen mound.

'. . . He doesn't know about you. I wrote in the early days but my letters were returned.' Her eyes were full of tears. She still hadn't noticed me. 'It'll be strange to have both the children under the same roof again. I'm at Joan's now as they took our home. They said it belonged to a terrorist. I said it belonged to a hero . . . but you know that, love. I've told you often enough.'

My mother, in a shabby brown coat I didn't recognize, sighed and rearranged the sodden paper flowers in the small vase. Beyond the drystone wall, Devon Red heifers were munching the grass. Galleons of clouds breasted the inland hills where, more than three and a half centuries ago, the beacon had been lit to alert England that the Spanish Armada was drawing near. Off the headland, the sea was a dull, sullen grey. The December day was drawing to a close.

When my mother spoke again, her voice was infused with infinite sadness. 'You remember Jeffrey Harding? He hanged himself with his dressing-gown cord yesterday. He'd heard he was on the *Gestapo*'s blacklist because he'd fought in the International Brigade in Spain. Joan and I have counted twelve suicides since the Germans came.'

I didn't remember her hair being so white, nor that she was so small.

'Mum.'

'Nick. Nick.' She tried to scramble to her feet.

Joan had warned me how frail mum had become, but it still came as a shock to see her thin body twisted to one side by her wounds. I helped her up.

'Hello, mum.'

'Thank God, you're safe.'

Her relief and joy burbled over me like a warm stream as we clung to each other. I didn't know what to say so I gazed at the rough wooden cross that marked my father's grave.

William Penny
July 26 1885–September 5 1940.

The ink of the handwritten inscription was already fading.

'The cross is against the rules but I'd be blowed if he's going to rest in an unmarked grave,' whispered my mother, following my gaze. 'I come up here to tell him our news. We were together for more than thirty-three years, you know.'

'I know.'

'And you're going to work in Shire Hall, or whatever they call it nowadays.'

'The Germans need translators.'

She held me at arm's length to look at me. That was when she noticed it for the first time. The blood drained from her face. She shrank from me.

'Take it off.'

'I can't.'

'Nick!'

She wrenched herself away to stare out to sea.

. . . Stare out to sea so that she would not have to look at her only son in his British Army greatcoat with the three sergeant's stripes – and the swastika armband.

'Mum, mum, listen. I didn't have a choice. It was this or be transported to Germany in the next draft. At least we're all together. I've come home to look after you.'

'You call this home?' she said.

*

New European Time meant it was still dark when I left Joan's next morning, the pit of my stomach like iced jelly. The Edwardian villas were asleep, hiding behind closed curtains. Unswept leaves still lay in red and gold mounds, blocking the gutters. I turned into the main road, my feet growing more leaden with every step. Before the occupation, this thorough-fare would have been thronged with cars, delivery vans and lorries heading for the port and the fishing harbour. Now a solitary, canvas-topped *Kriegsmarine* lorry growled past an emaciated horse pulling a milk cart. The windows of small shops that had gone out of business were covered by sheets of yellowing newspaper. The few people out on the street avoided each other's eyes.

The stigma of defeat lay like a shroud over the grey morning.

Last night I'd answered my family's questions and had asked some of my own, but it had all seemed unreal. My feet had not touched the ground since I'd been marched into the camp commandant's office and given discharge papers, a priority rail warrant, and the swastika armband. Since then, little had sunk in. The enormity of discovering that my father was dead, my mother crippled and homeless, my sister widowed – it was just too much to comprehend. It was as if I was in a familiar yet strange world and seeing it through someone else's eyes.

It was with the same sense of detachment that I

noticed a rough cross drawn on a wall, alongside a small workshop. Underneath was chalked the inscription:

John Godwin
Patriot
RIP

'Who was John Godwin?' I asked a woman wrapped in a worn coat and headscarf who had materialized by my side.

'He was a young lad who shook his fist at them as they marched in. The SS swine shot him dead. The Germans'll be here soon to rub out the cross, so don't let them catch you near it.'

'Why? What'll happen?'

'They'll take you into protective custody, and that's the last anyone will hear of you.'

The woman suddenly noticed my swastika armband. She jerked as if stung and scurried away. I heard the sound of an engine whining up the hill and hurried into a newsagent's doorway just as a half-track carrying eight *Wehrmacht* troopers hove into view.

The shopkeeper, Hubert Leech, was watching me with interest. I'd known him before the war, an unctuous little man whose humility was as hollow as it was exaggerated. He had done well during the months I'd been away. His newsagent's business had expanded into the grocer's next door, so now he sold everything from bacon to lamp oil, metal pails to bootlaces, as well as newspapers. My favourite *News Chronicle* had been banned. I picked up a *Daily Mail*.

The front page was dominated by a picture of the Duke of Windsor and his wife waving from the steps of a Junkers aircraft on their arrival at Croydon aerodrome as they were greeted by the Prime Minister, Samuel Hoare. Other photographs showed the Duke shaking hands with the Protector, Joachim von Ribbentrop, and inspecting an honour guard of SS troops accompanied by Field Marshal Busch, the victor of England.

His Royal Highness the Duke of Windsor has graciously acceded to the petitions of the people to become Regent . . .

I opened the paper to find a picture of Nelson's Column being raised in Unter den Linden in Berlin. That was enough for me. I dropped the paper on the counter and slammed out of the door, making the bell tinkle furiously.

I grew more and more depressed as I walked on. The city around me had lost its pride. It had stopped looking after itself, so that everywhere appeared grubby, soiled and in need of a coat of paint. Discarded newspapers and crisp packets lay in drifts in the doorways of the empty shops. I came to the grammar school where I'd been a pupil, and then a master for a short time. Now a German salvage team occupied the site, their crippled trucks, armoured cars and personnel carriers sitting axle-deep on the playing fields. Even the familiar sight of a local double-decker bus was marred by a sign over its destination board: *Nur für Wehrmacht*. At the top of the hill, *Feldgendarmerie* in steel helmets and with Schmeisser sub-machine guns slung over their shoulders had set up a checkpoint. Parked to one side was a British Army Bedford three-tonner, its divisional symbol painted over with a crude red 'W' for Army Group West.

A surly *Feldwebel* with a brass gorget around his neck took his time inspecting my identity card, prisoner-of-war discharge papers, residential permission and current orders. I'd got used to Germans bossing us around in the PoW camp, but to be stopped here, in my home city, riled me. The *Feldwebel* kept breaking off his inspection of my documents to stare hard at me. I fought to keep my face neutral. Don't let the bastards know that you are bitter – and frightened.

Finally, he waved me through. I was looking forward to seeing the view over the city, with its Victorian municipal buildings, old merchants' streets and winding cobbled lanes with the port and harbour beyond. But to my dismay the skyline had changed. Instead of the cathedral spire and the thicket of church steeples rising from a tumble of grey roofs, a red cloud of massive Blood Banners – black swastikas on crimson flags – floated over the city. The largest flew over the Shire Hall, or *Feldkommandantur West* as it was now called.

One huge long banner hung triumphantly across its front.

Deutschland siegt an allen Fronten. Germany victorious on all fronts.

Kurt von Glass was young to be a *Generalleutnant* and even younger to be governor of the *Westgau*, one of the six provinces of Britain. Around his neck hung the prized Knight's Cross for bravery. The coveted *Dover* on his right cuff told he had been among the very first ashore in the invasion. He wore black riding boots, polished so you could see your face in them, and the full jodhpurs favoured by élite units. There was a hint of expensive cologne. His right hand was beautifully manicured, with long tapering fingers. His left arm was missing.

His promotion to Governor was a reward for his bravery in overcoming the British resistance on the cliffs of Dover – which had opened the way for the invasion – and a compensation for his injuries.

At first sight, von Glass was the epitome of the ramrod-straight, square-jawed Prussian officer – he even had a scar that ran upwards from his left eyebrow diagonally into his sandy hair. Only the sardonic half-smile that lifted one side of his mouth hinted that there was more to him than just a humourless, tradition-bound Junker.

I was to learn that Glass could be frequently cold, was usually arrogant, and always intelligent. He believed life was a comedy for those who think, and a tragedy for those who feel. I was going to miss him when he left.

He was standing next to a blackboard on which was pinned a large-scale Ordnance Survey map covered with a surreal squiggle of red and blue hieroglyphics.

'*Schauen Sie sich das mal an.* Come and see – the Battle of Ashford. You lost an opportunity here.' He indicated with a wooden pointer. 'Fourteen hundred hours, Horne's attack against our exposed left flank. Good in theory but the way he threw his armour in piecemeal, before their recovery vehicles arrived, was criminal. That attack proved the effective end of the British Guards Armoured Brigade as a fighting force. By the time your reserves came up, we'd closed the gap, and the rest was history.' Glass turned from the map. 'I myself would have waited until evening to attack. Those five hours would have allowed the British recovery vehicles to get into position, and meant that our Panzers were even further over-extended. Those few hours could have changed history. As it was, when 18th Panzer Division counter-attacked they cut through your General Highland's Sixth Division like a knife through butter.'

'We had no armour-piercing shells for the 3.7s,' I explained in German. 'They just bounced off your tanks.'

'You were there, sergeant?'

'We were supporting the anti-tank guns, sir, but I got concussed in the first hour. I was unconscious for half the battle, and in a German field hospital for the rest.'

'I fought for just twenty minutes on British soil.'

'Sir?'

'I commanded the Brandenburgers who captured the Langdon battery above Dover before the first wave came ashore.'

'Is that where you won your Knight's Cross, sir?'

'And lost my arm. Now I fight on paper the battles I missed. The English always win.'

He resumed his study of the Ashford battle, and I took the opportunity to glance round his office. I'd been here once before, with my father when it had been occupied by the County Solicitor. The worn Axminster carpet, the chunky walnut desk, the old-fashioned swivel chair were the same. But the portrait of the King had been replaced with one of Hitler, and a pair of crossed swastika banners took up most of the far wall. A silver picture frame and a bottle of pills stood on the desk beside an empty in-tray.

Glass swung from the map to face me. 'Why did you take this post, sergeant?'

'Did I have a choice, sir?'

'You were asked to volunteer.' Glass went to rub his missing elbow, then stopped.

'That's not how it was put to me.'

'Do you want the job?'

'Yes, sir.'

'To help cement Anglo-German friendship?'

'To avoid being shipped off to Germany.'

'At least you're honest. And your German's good, although I could do without that Rhenish twang. Your year in Trier University, I suppose? Don't look surprised – it's in your *Abwehr* file. Nicholas Fricourt Penny. Fricourt?'

'An uncle killed there in the last war.'

'I too lost an uncle on the Somme.' Glass nodded. 'Graduated London University 1938. Then teacher. Volunteered 4th September 1939. Do you know why you're here?'

'No, sir.'

'I will explain. I wear two hats. Not only am I the military governor of the Western Province, I am also the regional head of the civil affairs department of the occupying power, the *Oberkriegsverwaltungsrat*. What's that in English?'

'Senior War Administrator.'

'Good. And as senior war administrator it's my responsibility to set up the *Deutsch-Englischen Kameradschaftsbund* – the Anglo-German Friendship League. It's the *Führer*'s current pet idea so everyone is very keen to have it up and running as soon as possible. The League is going to forge our two countries into one.' Glass smiled sardonically. 'Or rather, it will turn the British into National Socialists. Do you know what *Selbstgleichschalter* means?'

The word did not translate easily into English. 'A . . . self-disciplined citizen?'

'One who accepts Nazi beliefs immediately and without question. Those who cannot achieve *Selbstgleichschaltung* have no place in society. They will be removed. The *Führer* has given the creation of the League absolute priority. As he says, "We must be *friends* with the countries we conquer."'

'The speech was broadcast over the camp loud-speakers every day for a month.'

'Was it?' Pain passed over Glass's keen face like a cloud. He picked up the bottle of pills, toyed with them and put them back unopened. 'Did they also tell you that Hitler boasted *Die Länder die ich besetze, werde ich korrumpieren*. How would you translate that?'

'I will corrupt the countries I occupy.'

'We are going to corrupt England and you will help.' He glanced down at the pills. 'Others are desperate for the chance to please the *Führer*. Not only does *Reichsminister* Goebbels believe his Ministry of Information and Propaganda should run the League, but more importantly the SS will do *anything* to get their hands on it. For the moment the League is the responsibility of the German Army. In this province, I hold the chalice, poisoned or not, and from now, you are sipping from it as well. You will report directly to me. Do you understand?'

'Yes, sir.'

'No, you don't. How can you?' Glass's words cracked through the air like a whip. 'What do you know of the SS?'

'Not a lot, sir. I fought against the 2nd SS Division *Das Reich . . .*'

'That's the *Waffen-SS.*' Glass cut me short. 'The fighting troops are just a small part of *Reichsführer* Himmler's empire. Under Himmler, the SS has become a state within the state, an army within the army. More relevantly, Himmler controls all police and security forces in Germany and its occupied territories. The Reich Security Department take up the whole southern wing of this building. *Standartenführer* Stolz, *der Höhere SS und Polizeiführer,* just cannot wait to sit in this chair. If the League falters, the SS are waiting to take it over. And their power grows by the month.'

I thought it strange that, within minutes of meeting one of the most powerful Germans in England, he was warning me against some of his own countrymen. I didn't know then the deep-seated antagonism and distrust between the German Army and the SS.

Von Glass weighed down one end of a rolled-up

poster with a deactivated Mills bomb, and opened it out. It showed a little boy and girl smiling rapturously up at Hitler, who oozed avuncular kindness. The caption read:

Morgens grüße ich den Führer, und abends danke ich dem Führer.

'Translate,' ordered Glass.

'In the morning I salute the *Führer* and in the evening I thank him.'

'Good. Your translation of this poster will go up in every classroom and scout hut in the region.'

'Scouts?'

'Scout troops will form the core of the English Hitler Youth.'

There was a tap on the door. An attractive German woman brought in a large bunch of purple and yellow flowers. Glass sniffed them delicately before reading the message.

'Put them in water.'

Her tight skirt bounced away to the door. It had been months since I'd seen anything like it. Glass gave me an old-fashioned look.

'*Blitzmädchen* – known as Grey Mice because of their uniforms. They are off limits. Fraternization is allowed in one direction only. In any horizontal collaboration, the German has to be on top.'

'I'm happy to fit in with whatever position German women prefer.'

There was a flicker of a smile before Glass's eyes

went blank. 'There's an American movie phrase: "Don't get cute with me."'

'No, sir.'

'You have an office along the corridor. All correspondence with the *Feldkommandantur* must be conducted in German. You will be called to translate the *VOBIES** into English, like this one, promising there'll be a Christmas. Any questions?'

'No, sir.'

'Those flowers are a gift from one of the region's leading market gardeners. Quite a feat to grow them at this time of year considering the fuel restrictions, wouldn't you say?'

'Why don't you throw them away if they disgust you so much?'

'I enjoy flowers. You see, it's not just the occupied who have to compromise. The Friends of New Europe are giving an official lunch for me at the Golf Club. You will come along and translate. My ADC, Hauser, will show you your office.'

'General von Glass insists you are close at hand,' said *Hauptmann* Hauser as I inspected my new office. 'He really wants the Friendship League to succeed.'

'So I gathered.'

---

* *Verordnungsblätter des Militärbefehlshabers in England.* Laws and regulations.

17

'I'll put it another way – he needs it to succeed.'

It was clear that Hauser was a gossip. He had a pleasant round open face and softer hands than a soldier should. He pointed out of the window into the interior courtyard.

'You see those sentries? That's the *Gestapo* HQ. Don't go anywhere near it. In theory, as you're seconded to the *Wehrmacht*, the *Gestapo* has no jurisdiction over you. But by the time we get you back . . .'

The sentence hung in the air along with the hint of stale sandwiches of generations of clerks. Someone had replaced the desk with a trestle table set against the grimy window. A wooden chair, green metal filing cabinet, waste-paper bin and a coat-stand took up the rest of the small room. At least I was spared the photograph of the *Führer* that hung in every office. Or perhaps someone had nicked that, too.

A Grey Mouse swept in to drop a pile of papers and posters on the trestle table. She flounced out without looking at me. I picked up the top sheet.

All German orders are to be registered with the British Supreme Council, so no person can plead ignorance of the law.

If the Council refuses to register legislation, it will be promulgated by decree.

Offences against German military personnel will be tried by German courts.

𝕹𝖔 𝕲𝖊𝖗𝖒𝖆𝖓 𝖎𝖘 𝖙𝖔 𝖆𝖕𝖕𝖊𝖆𝖗 𝖇𝖊𝖋𝖔𝖗𝖊 𝖆 𝕭𝖗𝖎𝖙𝖎𝖘𝖍 𝖈𝖔𝖚𝖗𝖙.

𝕿𝖍𝖊 𝕭𝖗𝖎𝖙𝖎𝖘𝖍 𝕹𝖆𝖙𝖎𝖔𝖓𝖆𝖑 𝕬𝖓𝖙𝖍𝖊𝖒 𝖎𝖘 𝖓𝖔𝖙 𝖙𝖔 𝖇𝖊 𝖘𝖚𝖓𝖌 𝖜𝖎𝖙𝖍𝖔𝖚𝖙 𝖘𝖕𝖊𝖈𝖎𝖆𝖑 𝖕𝖊𝖗𝖒𝖎𝖘𝖘𝖎𝖔𝖓.

𝕹𝖔 𝖌𝖆𝖙𝖍𝖊𝖗𝖎𝖓𝖌 𝖔𝖋 𝖒𝖔𝖗𝖊 𝖙𝖍𝖆𝖓 𝖙𝖊𝖓 𝕭𝖗𝖎𝖙𝖎𝖘𝖍 𝖕𝖊𝖔𝖕𝖑𝖊 𝖜𝖎𝖙𝖍𝖔𝖚𝖙 𝖘𝖕𝖊𝖈𝖎𝖆𝖑 𝖕𝖊𝖗𝖒𝖎𝖘𝖘𝖎𝖔𝖓.

𝕻𝖗𝖎𝖛𝖎𝖑𝖊𝖌𝖊𝖘 𝖆𝖈𝖈𝖔𝖗𝖉𝖊𝖉 𝖙𝖔 𝖙𝖍𝖊 𝖕𝖊𝖔𝖕𝖑𝖊 𝖜𝖎𝖑𝖑 𝖉𝖊𝖕𝖊𝖓𝖉 𝖔𝖓 𝖙𝖍𝖊𝖎𝖗 𝖌𝖔𝖔𝖉 𝖇𝖊𝖍𝖆𝖛𝖎𝖔𝖚𝖗.

Flicking through the papers I found that, from Monday, fishing boats had to post a bond of 1,000 *Reichsmark* per boat and 500 *Reichsmark* per fisherman before they were allowed out to sea. The rate of exchange was 9.36 *Reichsmark* to the pound, and the catch was to be weighed and recorded in metric measurements.

From 1st January, the Court of Appeal at the High Court would sit with one German judge and two English advisers.

The song 'Kiss Me Goodnight, Sergeant Major' was declared decadent and henceforth banned, because it was degrading to *Wehrmacht* personnel.

I was still wondering at the mind of the bureaucrat who had thought that one up when Hauser came to tell me it was time for my lunch excursion.

*

In spite of the grey skies and keen wind, an open-top Mercedes staff car was waiting in the forecourt. Glass ordered me to sit in the back with him.

'Seen much of your home since you returned?'

'I've not had time, sir.'

'Apart from the docks and where there were pockets of resistance, you'll find the city's largely undamaged. Head for the port, corporal,' Glass instructed the driver.

The rusty fishing boats tied up alongside the quay were a familiar sight. The three German corvettes breasted up next to them were not. German sailors were crouching over the torpedo tube of an E-boat moored at the harbour entrance, near where divers were working to raise two scuttled Royal Navy MTBs. Glass kept up a running commentary, pointing out places I'd known since childhood. The old colonnaded fish market, the seaman's church with its crooked spire, the narrow cobbled alleys and Napoleonic warehouses.

Clouds of dust were billowing from the coal dock, where a listing Hamburg collier was being loaded. In the eastern harbour, cranes were lowering industrial machinery and machine tools into the hold of a freighter.

'We Germans are good at conquering countries. We are not quite sure what to do afterwards,' announced Glass. 'At first, we were going to deport all your able-bodied men to Germany until someone pointed out that that would leave no one to work in your factories, so how would you pay war reparations? The planners then suggested transporting England's industries to Germany and filling them with English workers. Finally someone had a radical idea. Why not leave both factories and workers in England and let them get on with it?'

'So what happened, sir?'

Glass made a see-sawing motion with his hand. 'The chemical industry in the north-east has been shipped wholesale to the Ruhr, but I've persuaded the *Reich* Economic Ministry in London to leave things alone down here. There are always exceptions,' he added drily.

On the western quay a lone ship was unloading cases of wine onto a convoy of commandeered lorries, watched by armed *Luftwaffe* guards. Across the quay, the new wharf, built only two years ago, was now a blackened roofless shell. The Georgian Customs House was pock-marked by cannon fire. A stick of bombs had fallen along a terrace of whitewashed fishermen's cottages, so the flattened homes looked like missing teeth in a smiling face. On every corner stood pubs with names like Admiral Hardy, the Galleon, Anchor and Hope, and Man-o'-War. Once they had teemed with life; now they were all boarded up.

Back in the city, German sentries paced in front of the telephone exchange and the County Hotel, now the SS Officers' Club. The Lyons café bore a sign – *Wehrmachtlokale* – and I noticed the nursing homes had become *Soldatenheime*, where German soldiers could drink coffee, play table tennis and read magazines.

Pedestrians stared openly at the Mercedes with its incongruous occupants. Glass, in his field-grey topcoat decorated with dark green and silver lapels, wearing a general's cap heavy in braid and gold, and me in my khaki greatcoat with side cap.

Suddenly I spotted my sister Joan in a long queue outside the butcher's. As we drew level, a woman nudged her, said something, and fifty women swivelled as one to stare at the Mercedes and its passengers. Joan went white.

A wave of sickness swept over me. I knew now why Glass was giving me a guided tour of my home town. He *wanted* people to see us together. I could hear the gossip now.

'Did you hear about Nick Penny in the back of the German Kommandant's car? Pally as anything, they were. He knows which side his bread is buttered.'

'Thank you. That's enough,' I said, hearing the gravel in my voice. 'I've seen all I want to see and I'm sure enough people have seen me.'

'One more place.' Glass leaned forward and murmured to the driver. We picked up speed, leaving the city centre on the London Road. The war damage was greater in the eastern suburbs. Concrete dragons' teeth, intended to stop the Panzers, still lay at the side of the road. A burned-out Beaverette light armoured car lay on its side in a ditch, no match for the Mark IIIs of the Third Panzer Division. The road crossed a bridge over an inlet. On the far side, a hastily built pillbox had been blown apart by a 88mm gun. The semi-detached houses on either side of the road were now piles of bricks, rubble and charred timber. Ragwort and rosebay willowherb grew among the debris. The car drew to a halt.

'This is where your father died,' said Glass.

'You're right. I wanted people to see you with me. For you, it is a time for choices.'

I was wondering how to reply as we swept through a car park graced with Rolls-Royces, Bentleys, Humbers and Armstrong-Siddeleys, in spite of the strict petrol rationing, and halted in front of the ivy-clad clubhouse.

'Been here before?' asked Glass.

'They didn't encourage poor young schoolteachers to apply for membership; at least, not unless you had wealthy parents.'

'In which case you wouldn't have been a poor schoolteacher, would you?'

I smiled. I was beginning to think there was a decent man hiding inside Glass's jaundiced view of the world. He hadn't needed to take me to see where my father fell, nor encourage me to spend time there. We had spent the journey from the bridge discussing how one man's resistance hero was another man's terrorist. The debate had been without rancour, and Glass had concluded by saying he hoped that he would have had the courage to fight as my father had done.

'I'm going to need your help,' said Glass, as I opened the car door for him. 'My English is only schoolboy level.'

'You're being modest, sir.' I already suspected his English was considerably better than he let on.

'Sometimes it's useful to appear more stupid than one actually is.'

The clubhouse lobby was deserted.

'This lot's learned nothing from the invasion,' I said.

Glass gave a barking laugh and went off to the lavatory, leaving me to read the wallboard listing the names of club captains stretching back sixty years. Four families dominated. Three still controlled the city's commerce. The fourth was the largest land-owner in the county. The nearby trophy cabinet, filled with silver cups and shields, deserved a police guard. I was bending over to read an inscription . . .

'Get away from there. What are you doing here?'

A small man with a porcine snout quivered in pompous indignation.

'We've . . . um . . . come for lunch.'

The man curled his lip at my sergeant's stripes. 'Really! I didn't know you were a member.'

'I'm not.'

'Only members, German officers and guests are allowed in here. Now get out before I call the *Feldpolizei*.'

'Who the hell are you?' The red mist was descending. I was about to pick up this bloated little jobsworth and bounce him over his shiny floor when Glass reappeared.

'Was is' los?'

'This . . . sack of shit doesn't think that we – I – should be here.'

'Ich?' Glass pointed his thumb at his own chest. He spun on his heel and marched back to the front door.

'No, no, please.' The man had gone white. He scuttled alongside, as if about to grab Glass's missing arm. 'This is a terrible misunderstanding. Apologize to the *Kommandant* for me. Tell him he is welcome. I'm *ordering* you to tell him.'

I held open the door for Glass to leave.

'Please . . .'

With a show of reluctance, Glass agreed to stay. The club's secretary fussed around, helping him take off his coat. As the little man scurried past, I dropped my greatcoat over his arm, too. He did not complain.

About twenty men representing the region's Friends of New Europe smirked in our direction as we entered the deeply carpeted bar, panelled on three sides with oak and hung with golfing cartoons and old golf clubs. Tall windows looked out over the pristine eighteenth green. The secretary made the appropriate introductions among the assembled businessmen, worthies, aldermen and landowners, led by the Lord Lieutenant, Sir Reginald Launcestone, and Horace Smeed, owner of the marine engineering works. The majority of the men sat on the Region's Supreme Council which had supplanted the County Council to rubber-stamp German decrees.

The next hour was to pass in a blur of tweed suits, whisky-mottled faces, malt Scotch and strident bonhomie. The defeat had not touched these men, who still spoke with loud confident voices, unlike the furtive whispers I'd grown used to in the camp. They were taking it in turns to buttonhole Glass as Hector Trevellian, who owned most of the property between the harbour and the High Street, drew me aside.

'Just wanted to say how sorry I am about your father. Brave man. If there's anything I can do . . .'

'Thank you.' I was touched and grateful.

Delicacies appeared. It had been rare to see a spread like this even *before* the war. Tray after tray laden with angels-on-horseback, prawn vol-au-vents, goujons of sole, chicken drumsticks, cocktail sausages, small beef olives.

Between mouthfuls, the Friends of New Europe brayed loudly.

'It was all right for that drunken warhorse Churchill to tell us, "You can always take one with you." What did he do? Fled to Canada. And who did he take with him? His wife. Pah!'

'Business is business. We should never have gone to war with Germany. For what? For some bloody country no one's ever even been to . . .'

'Hitler's our bulwark against Communism. No more shop-floor agitators bleating about conditions and wages. Productivity's up fifteen per cent since I had those troublemakers deported . . .'

'There must be scrupulous obedience to the occupying power. We have to be grateful for German forbearance . . .'

'I'd like to see the Regent on the throne, myself. He's always got on with the Germans. He and the Duchess visited the *Führer* in Berchtesgaden in 1938 . . .'

As Glass broke off conversation to take two pills washed down with whisky, a ruddy-faced man sidled up to him. 'Did you get the flowers, *Kommandant*?'

'Thank you,' replied Glass. 'They must be difficult to grow in December.'

'That's why I'd like a word about getting allocated more fuel.'

'I've only a fixed amount of coal for the whole region. If I give you more to heat your greenhouses, there'll be less for people's homes. You don't want people to go cold in winter, do you?'

'Of course not, although we are blessed with a mild climate down here. I am hoping to supply flowers to the Party's London headquarters.'

The others continued in their confident voices.

'Of course we're English – patriots to the core. But we must practise what I call *passive patriotism* . . .'

'Heard about that boy caught cutting telephone wires? Deserved to be shot, bloody little vandal.'

Glass turned severely on the speaker. 'The *Führer* is considering banning the word "vandal" as disrespectful to our ancestors.'

'Oh, quite.'

'Absolutely.'

'I was joking, gentlemen.'

At the end of the hour, the braying was grating on my nerves. Glass let it all wash over him. He was polite and courteous, listened carefully, and promised nothing.

My stomach lurched, to remind me it was not used to such rich food. I was closeted in the lavatory cubicle when two men came in.

'Who's that sergeant with the *Kommandant*?'

'His name's Penny. It was his father who made the last stand on the bridge – bloody fool.'

I recognized the voice of Hector Trevellian.

'I wasn't here then. What happened?'

'The stupid man managed to rally the retreating troops and a few locals. Pointless! They didn't have a cat's chance in hell. I wouldn't care a damn except they chose some of my properties to fight from. Cost me four good houses. Still, if young Penny is going to be matey with Glass . . . get my drift?'

I was silent in the car on our way back to the *Feldkommandantur*.

'So, what do you think now of your countrymen?' demanded Glass after a while.

'What do *you* think of them?'

'Last week, I received visits from fifty of them: politicians, local dignitaries, councillors, business-men. Forty-nine wanted favours only for themselves – things like extra petrol rations, travel documents, a relative released from some camp. Only the fiftieth spoke of England. And he was a Jewish baker and café owner.'

'Jacob Jenner?'

'You know him?'

'He was our next-door neighbour. He was the one who encouraged me to learn German. He can quote you Schiller from dawn to dusk.'

'I'm glad he didn't,' said Glass drily. 'Instead, he asked me to allow the fishing boats to go further out, so that part of the larger catches could go to the schools. He's worried that children aren't getting enough protein. When I pointed out that diesel is precious, he suggested the boats rig up sails. You see, not everyone is totally selfish.'

'I know. It's short-sighted to believe that the face presented to you at any given moment is the true face of society. You never know what potential lies deep and dormant in the hearts of the people.'

'That's very profound. Schiller? Goethe? Mann?'

'Me.'

'Sis, that was lovely. My first square meal in four months.'

I couldn't tell her that I was still full from the clubhouse lunch. Joan had queued for an hour, used up a week's meat ration, and then still had to grovel to the butcher – all for a shoulder of mutton. I had forced it down; now I thought I was going to be sick.

'I hope you don't mind eating here in the kitchen. It costs too much to heat the rest of the house.'

Day-to-day life in Joan's large Edwardian villa had become compressed into the kitchen with its blackened old range, oilcloth-covered table, and the airing rack suspended under the ceiling. Incongruously, the room was packed with photographs in heavy silver frames.

'I'm just glad to be here. Is there any news of Roy or Matty?'

'I saw Roy Locke yesterday,' said Joan.

'Brilliant. How is he?'

'Fine. He's been back a while but I've not heard anything of Matty Cordington.'

Roy and Matty were my oldest friends. We'd been to school together, grown up together, did everything together. We were known as the Three Musketeers. We'd even joined up and fought together, until we'd been separated by the fog of war.

'I'll go and see Roy now.'

'You don't have time to get to the Three Horseshoes and back by the eight o'clock curfew,' warned Joan.

'I'll go straight there from work tomorrow, then.'

Joan glanced at her young son pushing a pile of mashed swede around his plate. 'David, stop playing with your food and eat it.'

'I'm not hungry, mum.'

'We can't afford to waste food. Nick ate all of his.'

'But I don't like swede.'

I sympathized. I hadn't liked swede either when I'd been thirteen. I still didn't at twenty-three.

But Joan was determined. 'Please, love. There's a good boy. Finish your food, then you can go out.'

David accepted defeat and set about clearing his plate. He was tall for his age. He had his mother's straight fair hair but his father's strong features were already coming through. So was the determination – although, at David's age, Joan called it stubbornness.

'What about your homework?' demanded mum as David went to put on his coat.

'There's only German, gran, and Uncle Nick said he'll help me with that later.'

'You're not learning German!' My mother was outraged.

'It's compulsory – instead of French.'

'Make sure you're back well before curfew.'

As David pulled on his school raincoat, I saw just how much he'd grown during my time away. The coat was far too short in the sleeve, and Joan had said he was demanding long trousers. Perhaps I could buy them for him for Christmas.

Mum waited until David had closed the door before holding up the morning's newspaper. 'The Duke of Windsor's got no right coming back here, or bringing that American trollop with him,' she declared. 'He should have done the decent thing and gone to Canada, like his brother the King. I think he and that Simpson woman *wanted* to be captured by the Germans.'

She spoke freely now that David had left. Joan had warned me not to discuss politics or the occupation in front of the boy. Everyone had heard terrible stories of children unwittingly betraying their parents. You could never be too careful, she said.

'The Duke's going to become another Nazi puppet, just like those yes-men on the British Supreme Council,' predicted Joan.

'At least Sir Oswald Mosley will have nothing to do with them. They say he's in the Tower.' The leader of the British Union of Fascists had risen in my mother's estimation by refusing to cooperate with the Germans.

'They reckon this Amery's barking mad. And we all know about Hoare. He and that Laval tried to sell those poor Ethiopians to the Italians, like slaves. They make fine bedfellows.'

'The whole lot are sucking up to Ribbentrop. Calling himself The Protector, indeed!'

My mother was winding herself up into an anti-Nazi frenzy. My sister was more pragmatic. She and I shared the ability to make the best of anything. She had already confessed to me her worry that she did not hate the Germans as much as she should. She comforted herself that our mother hated them quite enough for the whole family.

'I'll tell you one thing,' continued my mother. 'I'm not having a son of mine wear that disgusting arm-band in this house. The moment you do, Nick, I leave.'

'I won't, mum.'

'I don't know how you can even bring yourself to put it on.'

'I don't have any choice.'

Joan signalled to me that it would be a good idea if I disappeared. I went upstairs to the spare bed-room to reorganize my very few possessions. I had stored my things with my parents when I'd joined up. Consequently, all my clothes and books had been lost when the Germans evicted my mother from her family home of thirty years, giving her less than half an hour to get out with only what she could carry.

Sitting on the narrow bed I felt alone and frightened. Left to itself, my mind wanted to ignore the war and the upheaval; to pretend that nothing had happened. But when I removed this mental barrier, the reality hurt like hell. My mother had become a bent, querulous shell of the woman she had once been. Dad was dead. We had never been close. He could bring too much of the headmaster's study into the home – but he was my father, and I was proud of the way he had died.

I reassured myself that I hadn't known he was dead when I'd agreed to work for the Germans. Objectively, my decision made sense: it meant I got home. If I'd refused, the Germans would have found someone else for the job and now I'd be in some camp in Germany.

I tried to justify my actions to myself – and didn't make a very good job of it. How much of my decision had been compromise, how much expediency – and how much cowardice? At the end of the day I had to face the fact that, dress it up as I might, I was a collaborator.

In the chest of drawers I found a Fair Isle pullover and some shirts belonging to Joan's missing husband, Ted. I put on the pullover and went downstairs. It was a mistake. Pain flashed behind Joan's eyes as she recognized it.

My mother rose painfully. 'I'll take my tea upstairs and have a lie-down.'

'Mum always has a rest after meals now,' said Joan, too quickly.

I opened the door for mum to shuffle through. It hurt me to see how a vigorous, jolly woman had been reduced to a bitter and literally twisted cripple. It hurt even more that she would not look at me directly.

'Mum'll come to understand,' Joan said quietly. 'She's glad you're here.'

'Maybe I should stay somewhere else.'

'Don't you dare. Are you sure you won't have anything more to eat? You're as thin as a rake.'

My older sister was still trying to look after me – as she always had done. But she, too, had changed: she was less substantial somehow. She had always been slim with mum's good bone structure, but now her face was gaunt – eroded by grief and uncertainty. The rolled-up sleeves of her cardigan revealed pitifully thin forearms. I wondered if she had been eating enough.

'How have you been managing for money?

Joan's honesty overcame her pride. 'It's been tight, Nick, I'll be honest. And now David's got his heart set on a bike for Christmas but I don't know how I'm going to afford it.'

'It'll be easier now I'm back.'

'Neither mum nor I get any pension. She's banned from teaching, not that she's well enough to. If I could get my hands on that Messerschmitt pilot, I'd cut off his balls with a rusty knife.'

It was rare for Joan to show her feelings – even rarer for her to be so crude. Things really had changed.

'Anyway, as you say, things should be easier now. How does it feel being back?'

'I can't get used to seeing Germans on the streets,' I admitted.

'It was so quiet when they first arrived.' Joan motioned me to the chair by the fire. 'Everyone stayed indoors, watching from behind the curtains. I had this queer, hollow feeling, an ache in the pit of my stomach. I imagine we all felt much the same. There was a little white dog who walked round and round the tree outside the house. Its owners had left him behind when they'd fled. I tried to bring him in but he wouldn't come. He'd gone next morning.'

'It must have been hell.'

'It was . . . unreal. With one or two exceptions, like the SS swine who shot John Godwin, the Germans behaved very well. They didn't impale babies on their bayonets. They didn't push people off the pavement. They bought the food and drink they could easily have plundered. Most German soldiers were eager to be friendly and the younger ones were so homesick that they'd do anything to get invited into someone's kitchen for a cup of tea. The first time a German asked me politely for directions, I didn't know what to do. It would have been rude to ignore him. I thought about sending him the wrong way, but in the end I helped him. It was impossible to make myself hate this one man. Instead I hated myself, once he'd gone. *They shouldn't be here.'*

As she spoke I looked around the kitchen, filled with photographs charting her life since her engagement to Lieutenant Edward Pendleton RN. She'd been just eighteen and he'd been twenty-two. They were married the following year, in 1928. The photograph of the bridal couple emerging from a guard of honour of raised swords had pride of place on the dresser. I was there in short trousers in the family group, our father in a high collar, everyone looking old-fashioned and frowsty. Then there was David as a baby, David being christened, David batting in a house cricket match. And photographs of Ted's ships – HMS *Exeter*, *Warspite*, *Orestes* – of Ted and Joan during their three years on the China station. Finally, Ted's last command, the destroyer HMS *Greyhound*.

'Then the *Gestapo* came along with their blacklist,' continued Joan. 'The editor of the newspaper, the dockers' leader and the secretary of the local Communist party were put in protective custody within the first week.'

'What happened to them?'

'No one knows. There's not been a word of them since. Not knowing what's happening is part of the numbness of living under an occupation. You can't think, you can't feel. You're frightened to talk to anyone. There's a sort of clamp on top of you. In the end the argument for not rocking the boat becomes such a powerful one that it's tempting to do nothing at all.'

She finished putting away the dinner plates and, with a sad smile, picked up her wedding photograph.

'Cheer up, sis. Ted may be safe in Canada with the fleet. You never know.'

'No.' She sighed. 'Ted's bosun came to see me. The *Greyhound* had been crippled by eight-inch guns and it was a miracle that she was still afloat. E-boats were closing in to finish her off with torpedoes. Ted was last seen firing a Lewis gun at them from the flying bridge. If only those bloody French hadn't allowed the Germans to get their hands on their fleet . . .'

As I couldn't get over to see Roy, I settled for a pint in the nearest pub. The quickest way to the Victory, a nondescript place on the main road, lay through the alleys running past the backs of the gardens. It was a cloudy night. The street lamps had burned out and hadn't been replaced but I wasn't worried about finding my way there. My concern was whether I'd still enjoy a pint. Beer is an acquired taste and I hadn't tasted any for four months.

That night I never did find out.

I heard the sob of pain first, then swearing followed by the thud-thud of a fist striking something softer. Men were scuffling in the deep shadows by the wall of the pub's outside lavatory. Or rather one man was holding another, while his mate was beating the shit out of him. The victim was too far gone to defend himself.

I don't know why I interfered. I had no idea what the quarrel was about. I suppose the odds of two to one offended my sense of fair play. I should have known better.

'Leave it.' I dragged the hitter away. 'Fucking leave it.'

He took a wild swing and missed me by a country mile. I tapped him on the nose.

Now I'd acquired my own fight against the odds.

The back door of the pub opened, and in the light I saw that the victim wore field grey with black patches on his collar. Hell, not just a German but an SS man!

The door slammed shut again. Whoever it was had more sense than to get involved. Whistles blew from the main road nearby and hobnailed boots crunched over the gravel towards us. The yobs scarpered the way I'd come. I knelt down by the side of the battered German. He looked in a bad way.

A bright light flashed into my face and a German army boot sent me flying.

2

The pile of orders and paperwork on my desk had grown since yesterday. I was struck by a new poster showing a handsome German soldier holding a laughing little girl in his arms. She was munching on a biscuit while a little boy stood to one side, obviously wanting to be part of the happy scene but still doubtful.

'I see you're coming to terms with our German love of bureaucracy.' Glass stood in the doorway behind me. I jumped to attention.

'Am I supposed to translate every *VOBIE*, sir?'

'God, no! Only the relevant ones. This one, for example, will be pinned up in every church and chapel.'

He handed me one proclaiming that the Protector had graciously decided to allow divine worship in Christmas services, as long as they contained no anti-German propaganda. A single infringement would mean the closure of *all* churches in the parish.

'Remember that *your* main task is to nurture

Anglo-German friendship,' said Glass. 'Well? What ideas have you had?'

You could go back to Germany. 'Um . . . what about concerts? The English find Wagner a bit heavy-going, but composers like Liszt or Mendelssohn go down well.'

'There are four things wrong with that idea,' replied Glass coldly. 'Firstly, it is not at all original. Secondly, it would attract only the upper classes who enjoy such music. Thirdly, Liszt is Hungarian and fourthly, Mendelssohn is banned in the *Reich* because he is Jewish.'

'Oh!' I tried to think of something else. 'Football. Put German teams in local football leagues.'

'Ye – es.'

'Better still. Have the best German players join our existing clubs.' I was warming to my idea. 'Integrate them. Everyone likes a star.'

'What happens if no one will give them the ball?'

'Pass a law to force them.'

'Football. Hmmm. Yes, I like that,' he conceded. 'Now tell me about the fracas last night.'

My heart did a somersault, lost its bearings and landed in the pit of my stomach.

'Sorry.'

'The *Geheime Feldpolizei* say you stopped two ruffians beating up a drunken SS *Unterscharführer* outside a pub. Why?'

I didn't like to admit that I hadn't known the

victim was German when I had intervened. 'If they'd killed him, you'd only have taken reprisals.'

'You let the attackers escape. In fact, the patrol commander believes you deliberately sent him in the wrong direction.' I did not reply. 'You cannot even be bothered to lie?'

'It's one thing to stop a fight, another to hand over one's own countrymen.'

'You've been away too long, my friend,' mocked Glass. 'Most of your *countrymen* would have handed over those men for a packet of Woodbines.'

'Ahem.' A thin man in pinstriped trousers and a high wing collar cleared his throat with a sound like the rustling of dried leaves. 'Excuse me, *Kommandant*, the CID have arrested the two criminals involved in last night's attack. They were hiding in a house in Fore Street. They're being handed over to the SS for punishment.'

'Shouldn't they be tried first?' I said without thinking.

'Let me introduce you,' said Glass. '*Herr* Tickell, Secretary of the Province's Supreme Council. Sergeant Penny of the Anglo-German Friendship League.'

Percy Tickell removed his pince-nez and put his head on one side. His action dislodged a drift of dandruff that rolled down over the shoulders of his black jacket. He replaced his pince-nez.

'We've met,' I said. 'You and my father used to

play bridge together when you were County Solicitor.'

Tickell cleared his throat again, now in a hurry to leave. Glass put out his arm to detain him.

'Taking the sergeant's point, can you legally hand over those two without trial?'

'Oh, yes, *Kommandant*. An assault on SS personnel or damage to SS property has to be dealt with by the *Feldgericht der SS* under Article Ten, Section Two, of the Declaration of Occupation.'

'But who will try them?' I demanded.

'They will be court-martialled under SS regulations, where they will have the chance to defend themselves. You will be called to give evidence, sergeant.'

'It was dark,' I said.

The narrow black and white frontage of the Three Horseshoes gave the impression that it was a small public house. It lied. Although Northgate was now a back street, centuries ago it had been one of the city's main arteries, and its inns had been built accordingly. The Three Horseshoes – with its maze of flagstone passages, enclosed cobbled yard, stables and bowling alley – extended back all the way to the next street.

The pub had been in Roy Locke's family for four generations. Here I had tasted my first pint of beer, first got drunk and first been sick from too much

booze. I'd celebrated exam successes and New Years'
Eves, kept wicket for the pub's cricket team, and
occasionally turned out for euchre matches. It was
my second home. But as I pushed open the door to
the public bar, conversation faltered and died. My
smile of greeting faded as I realized I didn't recognize
a single drinker among the dozen men staring coldly
at me. For a second I thought I was in the wrong
place. But no, there were the beer barrels still racked
up behind the bar, the familiar elm-block floor and
mismatched chairs and tables, and the old stuffed sea
bass in its cracked glass case.

'Is Roy here?' I asked a barman I'd never seen
before.

'Who wants him?'

'Nick Penny. I'm an old friend.'

'He's not here.'

'Any idea when he'll be back?'

'Nah.'

'I'll have a pint while I'm waiting.'

Four men at the table by the window began muttering together. A large man in a shapeless jacket and
corduroy trousers held up by a thick belt was staring
hard at me as he leaned against the wall by the fire. I
kept my eyes firmly on my beer.

'There's an unpleasant smell in here,' said one of
the men in the window.

'You rub against shit, you're going to smell of
shit.'

The colour surged into my cheeks. It seemed Glass was succeeding in making me an outcast in my own town. I was working out that I had three options – I could walk away, I could try to explain or I could thump the big mouth who was stirring up the bar – when the bruiser by the fire straightened up.

'Hey, you.'

I ignored him.

'I'm talking to you.'

The bar fell silent as the brute lumbered towards me. I put my back against the wall and took a deep swig of beer. It seemed a shame to waste it, seeing that I was about to throw it in the man's face and follow it with my broken glass.

'You said your name's Penny?'

'Yes.'

'Your mam's a teacher?'

'She was.'

'Right, listen, everyone.' The man glowered around the bar until everyone's eyes were on him. 'When that fucking Nazi pig machine-gunned the school playground, this bloke's mother threw herself on top of our Gloria. She saved my daughter's life and got crippled for her pains. His mam is the bravest woman in the world. And I mean the fucking world.' He pointed a finger at me. 'It's not his fault he's got to work for the Krauts. We all have to do things we don't like nowadays. He's all right in my book. Now, if anyone thinks different, say now so I can hear it.'

Everyone suddenly found their beer mugs fascinating.

'Mr Penny, Med Tibby.' He held out a huge hand. 'You'll have a pint with me?'

'I'm honoured.' Relieved would be more accurate. Med Tibby was a bear of a man with heavy brows, apple-red cheeks and wire wool for hair.

'You said you're a mate of Roy?' murmured Med as we stood at the bar.

'I practically grew up in this pub.'

Med glanced round conspiratorially. 'He did a bunk when those two boys were arrested for beating up the SS man – just to be on the safe side. He's on his way back now the boys are dead.'

'Dead!'

'Within half an hour of being arrested. At least they wouldn't have got much out of them in that short time. Cheers.' Med handed me a pint. 'Tell your mam she's no worries about food now I'm back.' He saw the enquiry in my eyes. 'I've been staying with His Majesty for a month, following a disagreement with some gamekeepers. I'll not let the bastards take me again. Here's your mate now.'

I turned around. Roy stood in the doorway, a huge grin of pleasure and surprise spreading across his broad face.

'Nick.'

'Hello, mate.' Our friendship went too deep for us to shake hands.

'How's life?'

'Fine – and you?'

'Ay. You've lost weight.'

'*You* haven't.'

'Living on the fat.' The others in the bar were regarding us with open curiosity. To look at, we could not have been more different. Roy was dark, stocky, cheerful, whereas I was taller, thinner, more thoughtful. 'Let's go into the snug.'

'I didn't know anyone,' I said as Roy led the way across the passage into a tiny bar and lit the gas fire.

'It's a different crowd. Most of the old regulars are still prisoners of war.'

'How did you get out so soon?' I asked.

'I caught some shrapnel in my back. A British doctor laid it on thick that I was going to kick the bucket, so I might as well do it at home and save the Germans the trouble. You're looking at a miraculous recovery. But what happened to you? The last I heard, you'd come back from Intelligence to be with Matty in C Company.'

'Any news of Matty?'

'I was hoping you were going to tell me. I heard the daft sod won the MC in the field, for leading a counter-attack.'

'Roy, you should have seen him. There were blokes from the Cornwall Light Infantry, Devonshires, Wilts, SLI, all mixed together. Matty was the only officer left. He got them in order, commandeered an armoured car from somewhere, and caught Jerry totally by surprise. We pushed their infantry back to the Stour before their bloody Panzers came up, and then we were going backwards again.'

'What was your part in all this?'

'I helped him.'

'To Matty.' Roy raised his glass.

'To Matty.' As I toasted our friend, the hot summer day returned to me so clearly that I smelled again the warm earth and the dry grass. And felt again the prickles of fear and the forlorn sense of hopelessness.

We drained our glasses. Roy rang a bell and ordered two pints, whisky chasers and a jug of water.

'He saved my life, you know,' I said.

'That's Matty for you. What happened?'

'It was the next day – or was it two days later? Anyway, we were accompanying the 3.7s. It was a dead loss. I saw a shell literally bounce off the front armour of a Mark III at two hundred yards. We tried to make a stand at Cheeseman's Green. The Panzers came down the Roman Road, blasting everything in sight. I was blown out of this foxhole. A tank was about to roll over me when Matty dragged me clear – inches from its tracks. The last thing I remember was this tank clanking past. I woke up in a German field hospital. Dave Fairlight – in the next bed – said

Matty had been trying to set up a strong point with a couple of Bren guns and a Stokes mortar. Anyway, I hope he's all right.'

'Matty'll always be all right. He's a survivor. Remember that time we went scrumping apples?'

'Which one?'

'When you and I got caught and got a hiding, and Matty escaped scot-free.'

'Oh, yes. And that time we were almost done for being drunk and disorderly. Matty was making more noise than either of us but he ducked down the alley . . .'

'Matty.'

'Matty.' We raised our glasses again. 'We could go and see Matty's father. He might have heard something.'

Roy sucked his teeth. 'I should have gone myself by now but I can't stand the way the Major looks down his nose at me.'

'Don't be daft. Anyway, he drinks enough . . .'

'You know what I mean. You can see him thinking, what's gentry like Matty doing hanging around with a publican's son?'

'Or a teacher's son.'

'Your dad was a headmaster. He was respectable.' Roy passed his whisky glass over the water. 'The King.'

'The King.' Roy was the only person I knew who had stood up for the National Anthem at the end of the nightly Home Service programmes. 'How did you cop it?'

'The few of us left were crossing an open field by a railway line, falling back on Ashford, when their guns caught us. Percy Poughill and Bill Tremaine bought it there, I got wounded in my lower back. Not pretty but not serious. I was evacuated as far as Maidstone. I was still there when the Germans arrived. As I said, a doctor persuaded them I was a lost cause.' He poured two generous slugs of whisky. 'To the doctor.'

'The doctor.'

It was easy to slip back into old ways. Already, we were comfortable with each other. It's hard to define good friendship. You just know when it's there.

We drank steadily, catching up with each other's news. Roy's parents were well, although his uncle in Bristol was poorly. There was no word from his two brothers in Australia.

'I'm sorry about your father,' said Roy. 'He was a very brave man. And your mum, too. I'd heard you were back.'

'How?'

'You broke up the fight outside the Victory pub last night,' said Roy, to my surprise.

'How did you know that?'

Roy gave a slow wink.

'I didn't tell the Germans, but the attackers were

those two London kids who used to clean dad's car on Sunday,' I said. 'They lived in the Warren.'

'They said they recognized you,' admitted Roy.

'You saw them?'

'They came here. They used to carry messages for us.'

'Us?'

'Come on,' whispered Roy. 'It's not like you to be slow on the uptake.'

'You mean . . . You're involved in the . . .'

'The Resistance,' said Roy softly. 'Yes.'

'I didn't know we had one.' Rumours and half-baked stories about a resistance movement had done the rounds at the PoW camp. When my train home had broken down near Saltash, passengers had winked to each other that it was sabotage, but I hadn't believed it. This country was not ready for such a movement yet. It was still suffering from the shock of defeat.

'So what's this about you working in Shire Hall?' asked Roy.

I explained about my post with the Anglo-German Friendship League, unable to mask my sense of embarrassment and betrayal.

'Couldn't be better. You'll help us?'

'Me!'

Why was everyone trying to make me choose sides? Glass had compromised me so I would be driven into the German camp. Now Roy was assuming that I would become an active member of the Resistance. It was all happening too quickly. I needed time to think.

'Oh, sorry.' A short man of military appearance had begun to enter the snug, then saw me and backed out. Behind him, I glimpsed a pretty young woman with cropped fair hair. The man closed the door.

'How did you get involved?' I asked Roy.

'Someone's got to do it. And I was here.'

'So you helped those two boys who attacked the German?'

'I told them where they could hide.'

'But they were found.'

'Perhaps they were careless.'

'Perhaps they were betrayed.'

'Nick, beating up that SS man was exactly what we don't want. Uncoordinated, spontaneous attacks against pinprick targets will only generate reprisals against the civilian population.'

Those words weren't Roy's; he was quoting someone else. I didn't want to know any more.

'I've just started working there, Roy. I can barely find my way to my office. Give me time.'

'No problem, Nick. You'll come through – I know you will.'

Once Nick had left, the stocky man reappeared.

'A friend of yours, Roy?'

'My best friend – or, rather, one of my two best friends.' The pleasure on Roy's face was plain to see. 'We joined up together, but Nick was transferred to Intelligence. He made it back to the battalion in time for the last rites, so to speak.'

'Tell me about him.'

'What do you want to know, colonel?'

John Mills held up his hand. 'No ranks. You don't know who might be listening.'

'Sorry.' Roy blushed, then embarked on a rambling account of his friendship with Nick that had begun at the age of five when they'd sat next to each other in their first primary-school class. 'Of course, he's much brainier. He became the German master in the Grammar School before the war.'

'And you'd trust him?'

'With my life – him and Matty Cordington both. Sometimes I felt privileged to be their friend.' Roy gave a small chuckle. 'Someone once said that if we were horses, Matty'd be a polo pony, finely bred and nimble, and Nick'd be a hunter, full of intelligence and stamina.'

'What were you?'

'Can't you guess? A dray horse.'

'Strong, with a lovely, honest nature.' The woman he knew as Coral Kennedy was listening at the doorway. 'You're too modest, Roy. The success of the Western Line is largely down to your efforts.'

'Canada is delighted with your work.' Mills

sipped at a glass of lemonade. 'Which reminds me: two Norwegian politicians are due here soon. They're hiding up north but we hope they'll make the rendez-vous with the next submarine on Christmas Eve.'

'I'll be ready.'

Roy's eagerness made Mills smile. 'Now tell me about Nick's job with the Germans.'

He listened with his head on one side as Roy repeated all Nick had said.

'We must use this friend wisely and sparingly. He's too important to be a simple courier,' judged Mills. 'That is, if he's willing to be used at all.'

'Of course he's willing,' exclaimed Roy. 'Just give him a day or two to come round.'

When Roy had left the bar, Coral Kennedy shut the door. 'I'll organize a leaflet to blame the boys' murder on the *Gestapo*,' she told Mills.

'You're sure there's nothing that can be traced back to you?'

'Nothing at all.'

3

'Mrs Pendleton, I hope you don't mind me popping around . . .'

'Mrs Harper.' Joan failed to keep the coldness out of her voice.

'I've brought this duffel coat for your mother. It's hardly been worn.'

'That's very kind of you.' Joan, schooled by countless naval receptions, locked a smile in place. I knew what she was really thinking: *You patronizing, nosy, two-faced old bag. You'll do anything to get into this house.*

'Hello, Nick, I heard you were back.'

I swallowed a piece of toast. 'Good morning.'

Already Mrs Harper's sparrow-like eyes were flickering around the kitchen as she counted the cups on the draining board. It was hard to keep secrets in this road.

Joan winked at me. *Too late. The birds have flown.*

She had told me about the two escaped prisoners of war whom she'd hidden in the attic for a week. She'd been terrified that David might let something slip out but what else could she do? The chief petty officer had served with her husband on HMS *Warspite*. You looked after old shipmates.

You did if you were a patriot.

But Mrs Harper was not a patriot. She was an informer.

Joan would not have allowed her over the doorstep if the two men had still been hiding there, but they had moved on the day before I'd arrived; gone to join the bands of fugitives up on the moors.

Mrs Harper sat with a cup of tea on her lap, head cocked for the slightest unusual sound. I knew Joan would have liked to tell her to take a running jump, but it did not pay to cross informers. An anonymous tip-off that guns were hidden here would bring an SS search squad to wreck the place.

'You must find things very different now, Nick?' Mrs Harper wrinkled her nose at the weakness of the brew. Most people declined a cup, knowing how scarce tea was, but Mrs Harper had no such scruples.

'Indeed. And how's Mr Harper?' The husband had a chronic back problem that prevented him working at any settled job – although it did not stop him visiting the bar of the Conservative Club every lunchtime. He described himself as a trader.

'Suffering, as usual. He's a martyr to pain.'

'Is he still ... trading?' Joan could not resist asking.

'Oh, yes. He's busier than ever. The Germans

need so many things. But how's your mother? That operation to remove the bullets wasn't really a success, was it? I thought, at the time, the surgeon had his mind on other things. Of course with the Germans about to march in ... She's still ... incapacitated?'

'She doesn't complain,' said Joan, shortly.

'Just like Mr Harper,' smirked Mrs Harper.

Joan's patience was wearing thin. 'I wouldn't say they were the—'

'Nick,' interrupted Mrs Harper sharply. 'Your name's not up behind the door. You know how the Germans like catching people out on little things like that.'

Sharp-eyed bitch. Under Occupation law every home had to have a list of occupants pinned up behind the back door.

To give Joan time to cool down, I asked after Mrs Harper's daughter Vee. She and I had been an on-off item before the war. *On* when she couldn't find a man with a car or loads of money to spend on her; *off* when she could.

'She's quite the independent young lady nowadays. She's living in digs off the Point,' replied Mrs Harper. 'I'll tell her you're back. I'm sure she'd like to see you.' At the door, Mrs Harper laid a conspiratorial hand on Joan's arm. 'Don't worry about those two escaped prisoners. I won't say a word.'

'What prisoners?'

'There's talk you're hiding a couple of prisoners.'

'Mrs Harper, I give you my word that I'm not. But if I were, I'd only be helping my fellow countrymen – just as I know you would.'

Mrs Harper gave her a sick smile.

'General von Glass is in a meeting.' Hauser ran his new Parker pen down the open desk diary. 'If it's urgent, I can give you fifteen minutes with him between the City's Chamber of Commerce and the Regional Director of the *Reich*'s Labour Service.'

'Thanks.' Glass had insisted that I kept him informed of my progress with the football idea.

'You don't want to go in there now, anyway.' Hauser's official visage cracked and the helpless chatterbox popped out. 'He and *Standartenführer* Stolz are having a furious row over the deaths of the two youths, but don't say I told you.'

I'd yet to meet Stolz who, as the region's security chief, was in charge of the *Gestapo* as well as the Nazi Party's own secret police, the SD. As far as the English were concerned, *all* German secret police were called *Gestapo*.

'Don't they get on together?' I asked casually. Knowledge was power, I realized, and Hauser was just bursting to tell me. One day he'd gossip himself into a torture cell.

'Chalk and cheese. The general's from an old

military family – he's the nephew of Field Marshal Busch's chief of staff. Stolz is a Swabian policeman who joined the Nazi Party at the right time.' Even in the privacy of the Military Governor's office, Hauser could not help but glance over his shoulder to make sure that no one was eavesdropping. The German look, it was called. 'He models himself on Himmler.'

'So, what's the row about?'

'The *Gestapo* claims the boys were poisoned. Glass reckons the *Gestapo* beat them to death. The *Gestapo* deny it but when Glass suggested releasing photographs of the bodies Stolz blew a fuse. Of course the *Gestapo* couldn't resist giving those boys a smacking.'

'And were they poisoned?'

'That's what the post-mortem says.' Hauser's cheeks glowed with the thrill of sharing such news. I liked Hauser but couldn't help wondering why he was so frank with me. I wasn't his type. I hoped he recognized it.

'Would the *Gestapo* have poisoned them?'

'Too subtle.' Hauser tutted at the idea. 'They must have carried suicide pills.'

I doubted it. Those lads had fled down here from the East End during the Phoney War to scratch out a living with odd jobs and petty thieving. A year later the juggernaut of war had not just caught up with them, it had rolled over them. But if the *Gestapo* had not killed them, who had? The telephone rang.

'He's here now, sir.' Hauser looked up at me with eyebrows raised. 'You can go on in.'

Glass sat at his desk. A man in a black uniform, bristling with anger, hovered near the window. God! Stolz was the spitting image of Himmler. Hair cut to the bone, the same steel-rimmed glasses, feeble moustache, weak chin and spiteful mouth.

The air crackled with the tension.

Glass held up one of the Resistance leaflets that had magically appeared overnight on walls or in shopping baskets all over the city. I'd even seen one stuck on the side of a *Wehrmacht* lorry. 'Sergeant, translate this for the *Standartenführer*,' he ordered.

> *Liberation*
> *The Voice of Free Britain*
> *Share this with a Friend. Pass it round.*

The strain of masquerading as part of the civilized human race has proved too much for the Nazis. They have revealed their true colours. They have shown us that they are the bullies and cowards we always knew they were.

Two teenage boys, Dennis Green and Harold Hopkins, were set on by a mob of drunken SS thugs outside a pub on Monday night.

The lads defended themselves. Although outnumbered, they fought back so bravely that one Nazi bully ended up in hospital with a fractured skull.

Being unable to overcome the boys by fair means, the SS resorted to foul. The heroes were arrested and handed over to the Gestapo.

Within thirty minutes they had been beaten to death in revenge.

Dennis Green and Harold Hopkins did not die in vain. They will be remembered.

Next time a German offers you a smile, ask yourself what lies behind that shallow mask. Do not help with directions. They are not tourists. They are unwelcome invaders. Scorn them.

Do not despair. We have lost a battle – not the war. Our Fleet is intact. Our colonies and Empire are still with us. All freedom-loving nations of the world think of us constantly. It is not the end, nor the beginning of the end. It is the end of the beginning.

Take courage. The fight will be a long one, but one thing is certain. We shall prevail.

God Save the King.

I was reading out the second paragraph when Stolz began ranting, his face purple with rage. 'Lies, filthy lies. I'll rip the bollocks off the bastards who wrote this shit.'

'You have to find them first,' said Glass.

'You stick to your duties and I'll stick to mine. I do not need lessons in police work from some army officer.' Stolz snapped to attention and threw out his right arm. *'Heil Hitler.'*

There was a perceptible delay before Glass lifted a hand. *'Heil Hitler.'*

Stolz glared at me. I came to a semblance of attention. His lips narrowed and for one terrible moment I feared he would order me to give the Hitler Salute. He brought down his arm and swept out. I exhaled.

'While we battle to win minds, Stolz poisons hearts,' said Glass softly. 'Mark him well and do not cross him.'

I had no intention of doing any such thing. I became aware my hands were shaking as Glass picked up another sheet of paper. 'You've asked permission for the Salvation Army band to be allowed to play Christmas carols in the city centre. Don't you know they've been banned as a paramilitary organization?'

'The Sally Army?'

'I think someone in Berlin must be worried about their initials.' Again that mocking half-smile. 'All right, as it's Christmas their band may play at certain fixed points, but traditional carols only.'

'Thank you, sir.'

'Don't sound so surprised. We Germans love Christmas as much as the next man. I've already ordered the special release of extra fats, flour, dried fruit and sausage meat. *Wehrmacht* lorries are fetching Christmas trees into the city this afternoon. The tallest ones will be erected in public places, the next in size will go to hospitals, orphanages, old people's homes. The rest we'll give away to the public.'

'Why not sell them cheaply and give the money to a charity for the war-wounded?'

Glass thought for a moment. 'No. People wouldn't believe we'd pass the money on. Maybe next year when we're better trusted.'

The casual way Glass mentioned the following Christmas under German rule made me shudder. I took the opportunity to explain that the City Football Club was only too pleased to hold a game that brought paying fans through the turnstiles. They had no problems about a German playing for their team. They would prefer him to have two legs, but one leg and a crutch would do if it meant money in the bank.

4

The wind from the north-west whistled down from the moors, carrying the icy threat of snow that already lay on the higher ground. I thought of the ragged bands of escapers hiding there and wished them well as they strove to keep warm in their shepherds' stone huts and grass burrows. They wouldn't be able to get through the winter up there. The occupying forces knew this. They were watching the lower pastures.

The shops were full of Germans hunting for presents and souvenirs to send home. The tall Christmas tree in the market square was festooned with coloured bulbs and lights were strung across the main shopping streets. The Salvation Army band was playing carols on one corner, yet the festivities seemed hollow. Few shops had bothered to decorate their windows, the goods inside were limited, and people's hearts were just not in it. How could they be, with most of the menfolk still in prisoner-of-war camps and no hope of early release?

Joan and I assumed our mother would ignore the festivities, but she surprised us, saying that our father would have wanted her to make the best of it. Mum and dad had always shopped for Christmas presents together. This year, mum was alone. I volunteered to meet her, in the middle of her shopping excursion, at Jenner's Tea Rooms.

She was already at her favourite table, a pot of tea in front of her. She looked tired, but she was full of how she'd snubbed a German soldier who had offered her his seat on the jam-packed bus into town.

'I'm getting David some long trousers,' she announced. 'I've bought a pair of leather gloves for Joan. Her best pair are getting old. If I can find one, would you like a silver cigarette case – to replace the one you had stolen in that German hospital?'

Four scones accompanied by dollops of cream and raspberry jam appeared in front of us, as Miriam Jenner lowered herself onto an empty chair.

'Miriam, we didn't order . . .'

'Tsk, look at the pair of you. Nothing but skin and bone. Eat. It's Christmas. Eat.'

'You're very kind.'

'Who knows how much longer we will have anything left to share? It's good to see you, Nick.'

Miriam was small, round and homely, and a mother to everyone she met. Even though she had arrived in Britain in 1901, the year after her husband Jacob, she still kept the speech patterns of Middle European Jewry. Jacob Jenner had taught me to play chess; I'd borrowed my first German books from him.

When I'd chosen to study the language at university, a delighted Jacob had presented me with an early edition of Goethe. Under his wing, I'd written my dissertation on Schiller.

'How's Jacob?'

'He'll be better for seeing you. Did I tell you that Simon's moving back down here with Anna and the children?'

'For Christmas?'

'For ever. In London the Germans are making all the Jews live and work in the East End. Two hundred doctors for just two hospitals! It's crazy! Our son is going to try to buy a practice down here, so I'll get to see Rachel and Ruth more often.'

'How old are the twins? Two?'

'Three last September.'

'You're going to have a houseful.'

'Ach, I enjoy it. And Anna's bringing a Polish friend, Barbara, who's due to have a baby next month. The poor girl spent some time in one of those terrible camps in Poland, although she refuses to talk about it.'

'Poor thing. Where's her husband?'

'Husband!' Miriam threw up her arms. 'Bad luck follows her. The waif arrived in England in March, next month she's married to a farmer near Deal and she's expecting. Then comes the invasion. He was killed, and the farm burned down by the Germans. Now the poor girl has no one else in the world.'

'So you're looking after her?'

'Someone has to.' Miriam glanced round. 'We're getting busy, so I must go. Will you call in on Christmas morning?'

'I don't think I could,' said my mother slowly.

'I will,' I volunteered.

'Thank you, Nick. Jacob will love to see you.'

That afternoon I found a pile of copies of official orders lying on Hauser's desk. I liberated one to show to Roy later. It made chilling reading.

Orders for the Organization and Function of the Military Government.

1. The main task of the military government is to make full use of the country's resources for the needs of German fighting troops and the requirements of the German War Economy.

2. Law and order must prevail as an essential condition for ensuring efficient use of labour. Administrative measures will not violate international law unless the army has been given cause for reprisals.

3. Armed insurgents of either sex will be punished with the utmost severity. Hostages should,

if possible, be taken from that section of the population connected with the insurgents.

4. Laws of the country prior to occupation will be upheld unless they are contradictory to the purposes of the occupation. English authorities may be allowed to function, if they maintain the correct attitude.

5. The welfare of the inhabitants will be considered insofar as they contribute directly or indirectly to the national economy, as defined by the Reich Economic Ministry.

'Can I show this to Mills?' asked Roy that evening when he'd finished reading it.

'Sure. You know these orders aren't worth the paper they're written on, without English bureaucrats to see they're carried out.' I snorted in disgust. 'It doesn't seem to matter to Tickell and his snot-gobbling clerks who they work for.'

'You're being a bit hard, Nick. It can't be easy for him.'

'Pah! Listen, this afternoon Glass complained that the Germans were desperately short of electricians, plumbers, carpenters, cooks, cleaners and laundry-women but English people were unwilling to come forward. Do you know what Tickell suggested? Halving the benefit of every unemployed man or woman who refuses to work for the occupying forces.'

I'd only been back a week but I was quickly learning that Tickell's policy of 'dignity and courtesy to the Germans' actually meant peace at any price. Tickell didn't realize, or perhaps he didn't care, that by enforcing such regulations he was helping run the German occupation for them.

At the same time, black marketeers were becoming *Reichsmark* millionaires, while the poor and the old went hungry. Already tales were doing the rounds of spivs eating steak hidden under a fried egg in restaurants while sitting under signs proclaiming 'No Meat'.

I was still ranting on about the injustice as Roy and I arrived in front of Matty's family home, an imposing honey-stone Queen Anne residence.

Roy held back. 'You go in. I'll wait here.'

'You're not scared?'

'Shitless.'

I pushed Roy ahead of me down the gravel path. The house appeared to be in darkness but I knew better. I knocked on the kitchen door.

'There's no one in,' muttered Roy.

I knocked again, louder this time. Behind the farm, the ancient hills were fast retreating into darkness, the first stars emerging bashfully around a waxing moon. The door flew open to reveal a faint light shining from a passageway leading into the cavernous kitchen. A thin irate elderly man in a thick cardigan and a cravat glowered at us.

'Yes? What do you want?' Whisky ballooned on his breath.

'Hello, Major. We wondered if you'd heard any news of Matty.'

'Oh, it's you two. You made it back, then – got home safe and well.' He made it sound like an accusation of cowardice.

'Only a few days ago,' I said. 'Is there any news of Matty?'

'News! News! Of course there's no bloody news. He's in one of those camps. They keep officers there longer, you know.'

'Can we write to him?'

'He's only allowed one letter a month.'

It wasn't clear if the Major wanted to keep that letter for himself.

'Matty saved my life, Major. If there's anything I can do to help.'

'Help! What on earth could *you* do to help?' The door closed in our faces.

'Peace on earth and goodwill to all men.'

Roy swore under his breath. 'I hope the bastard drinks himself to death.'

We returned to our push-bikes. Across the lane, cows were being milked in a dilapidated barn under a single naked light bulb. The farmhouse had sunk back into darkness.

'Let's go and see Bert and get some milk.'

'You mean, let's go and see if we can cadge some of Bert's scrumpy,' corrected Roy.

It was good being with Roy again. We'd slipped back into a mutual understanding just as we would have slipped on an old, well-fitting jacket. We even knew what the other was thinking.

'I haven't time to talk to you young tinkers. I'm a busy man.' Old Bert Latcham looked up from the stippled flank of the cow he was milking. 'If you'm be after milk, take it from that pail. It's still warm.'

'Thanks, Bert. We've been up to see the Major. He wasn't exactly . . . friendly.'

'He don't have much time for anyone nowadays, does the Major. Did he tell you his last letter to Master Matty came back unanswered?'

'No.'

Pleased that he knew something we didn't, Bert unwound. 'If you be wanting something stronger, you know where it is. Try the jug on the left.'

'Why was the Major's letter sent back?'

'Dunno. Perhaps Master Matty wasn't there any longer.'

'But if he'd been transferred to another camp, the letter should have followed him.'

Bert shrugged his old shoulders. 'It upset the Major badly. I know that.'

A cock pheasant called from the walled-in wood on the neighbouring estate of Sir Reginald Launcestone. Bert returned to his milking, murmuring his own special litany to each cow. It was a timeless scene: something from a Christmas card, with a sense of serenity and peace.

Roy shattered my contemplation. 'Does the fact that you've passed on those orders mean you're now in with us?' he murmured.

'Roy, I'm not ready yet. My feet have hardly touched the ground. Most people already regard me as a traitor.'

'Don't matter what people think. It's what you do that's important.'

'Easier said than done.' Children taunted me, women cut me dead, men insulted me, one had even spat on the pavement in front of me. I didn't blame them. I was only surprised that no one had yet tried to pick a fight with me.

'Try some of that stuff on the top shelf,' called out Bert.

Bert's cider tasted like a harmless apple drink – until you stepped outside and your knees gave way under you. After half an hour, I knew I'd had more than enough.

The cock pheasant called again – and Roy's nut-brown face split into a mischievous grin.

'This is madness. If Ransome catches us—'

'We'll take the old sod's cudgel and beat him around the head with it,' said Roy. 'All we're doing is redressing the balance of nature. No one's allowed to shoot pheasants any more. If we don't do something, the country will get overrun by the bloody things.'

The cock called again – an alarm call this time to warn others that there were intruders in the wood. Roy spotted the outline of a hen roosting on a low branch. A flurry of movement, a quick wrench of its neck and the bird hung limp and dead in his hands. Silence fell again over the dark shadows.

A twig cracked. I held my breath. Twenty yards away, someone was creeping towards us through the undergrowth. Ransome, the vicious head gamekeeper, who regarded poachers as vermin. Four years ago he'd shot and killed a gypsy he'd found in Home Covert. As he'd been defending the Lord Lieutenant's land and property, he was acquitted. Now he delighted in preying on the increasing numbers of amateur poachers who hoped to eke out their meagre rations with the odd bird. After a beating, they were handed over to the constabulary to be tried by land-owning magistrates – who locked them up as a deterrent to others.

I stood stock-still, trying to place where Ransome was hiding. A sour odour drifted past my nostrils. The gamekeeper was growing complacent. He was upwind and I could smell the stale tobacco smoke on his clothes. I put my hand on Roy's arm and slowly pointed to the solid shape some fifteen yards away. I bent down, felt for a pebble, and flicked it to my left. Ransome, taken by surprise, spun around. I lobbed another pebble further to the left. We began moving quietly away.

He heard us. 'No, you don't, you scum.'

We crashed through the wood, knocking aside branches, giggling uncontrollably. Creepers and brambles snatched at our legs. I stumbled and fell. Roy was alongside me, hauling me to my feet.

The wood grew denser until we were confronted by a high brick wall. Roy hurled the pheasant over it, then bent down and put his hands together. I put my foot in the makeshift stirrup. Roy hurled me up. I scrambled the last couple of feet to the top, lay astride the wall and reached down. Ransome came crashing through the wood, swearing blue murder. I grasped Roy's hand and heaved. We dropped to the other side, breathless with laughter and excitement.

'I'll get you buggers, you see if I don't,' called Ransome.

'Not yet, my lover,' Roy called back in his broad West Country burr. 'Not ever, in fact.'

5

The soldiers hidden in the back streets were not
needed after all. The cathedral itself was packed full.
The Anglo-German carol service was a tremendous
success not only among the Golf Club set but also
with ordinary people who wanted to remember it
was Christmas. Afterwards, worshippers filed out of
the great West Door onto the Cathedral Green, where
Germans dressed up as Santa Claus stood behind
white-covered trestle tables decorated with holly and
yew. Storm lanterns cast a mellow glow over plates
of hot mince pies and steaming cauldrons of *Glühwein*. Nearby a twenty-foot-tall Christmas tree was
strewn with white lights and topped by a bright star.
Glass disengaged himself from the attentions of Horace Smeed to join me.

'Well done. The way the ushers organized Germans and English to sit next to each other was
masterful. I liked the way the schoolgirl read the
lesson in German, and the battalion doctor the one in
English. And the joint choir ... You know, Penny,
you should become an impresario.'

COLLABORATOR

He put his hand on my arm in a familiar gesture.
I didn't know if the gesture was genuine or whether
Glass was again deliberately compromising me in
front of the crowd, many of whom were taking this
opportunity to have a close look at the one-armed
Kommandant.

'Are any of your family here?'

'Yes, my sister and her son.'

'I'd like to meet them.'

There was no sign of David but I caught sight
of Joan on the edge of the scrum around the
Glühwein. I beckoned to her but she shook her head.
I beckoned more urgently. She shook her head more
determinedly. Glass, watching the pantomime, murmured to Hauser who sidled up to Joan and, taking
her by the elbow, led her towards us. She blushed
scarlet.

'*Generalleutnant* von Glass, my sister Mrs Joan
Pendleton.'

Glass gave a formal bow. 'You have a very talented brother, Mrs Pendleton. Not only was this carol
service his idea, but he organized it in such a short
time. To be that efficient, I think he must have
German blood in his veins.'

'Oh, I hope not,' exclaimed Joan. There was a
moment's terrible silence. Joan clapped her hand over
her mouth. 'I didn't mean . . . what can you think?
I'm . . . I'm . . .'

'Honest?' Glass gave a chill smile. 'Honesty is

refreshing, sometimes. Are you planning a family Christmas?'

'Yes, General.'

'Christmas is a time for families to be together.' The mayor and senior aldermen were shuffling their feet, trying to catch Glass's attention. 'I hope to meet you again soon, Mrs Pendleton.' With another formal bow, he turned to greet the mayor.

'Why did you do that?' hissed Joan.

'He asked to meet you. What else could I do?'

'I really put my foot in it.'

'He probably found it amusing. Glass's got no time for toadies. But it's hard to make out what he's thinking – and he is *always* thinking.'

I turned away and was about to head off to the Three Horseshoes, when my heart missed a beat. There was Vee Harper – she had her head back and she was laughing, showing off her white teeth. I couldn't remember if we were still speaking or not. She'd chucked me for a RAF navigator with an MG tourer that last August before the war, but it was such a long time since I'd been near a woman that I was willing to forgive her anything. Vee could be a million laughs. Other times, she was a right cow. I had thought about looking her up but I wasn't ready to ride the inevitable rollercoaster of affection and rejection.

She was peering up towards the West Door,

searching for someone. Then she saw me and pushed through the crowd, waving vigorously.

'Nick, darling, how perfectly lovely to see you.' She offered her cheek.

'And you. You look good.'

She did too. While most women's clothes were becoming increasingly shabby, Vee could have stepped straight out of a fashion magazine. She was dressed in a tightly belted Burgundy coat with a grey fur collar, and a tiny hat was perched roguishly on one side of her head. Her hair looked blonder and more waved than I remembered but her skin was still satin-smooth. The elusive hint of warm damask brought back memories of our naked bodies and murmured vows of togetherness that turned hollow by daylight.

'I saw you talking to the *Kommandant*. You must be important.'

'No . . .'

'Oh, come on.' Vee swept me along on a wave of chatter and laughter. She linked her arm through mine and strolled us through the throng until I found myself perilously close to Glass, surrounded by the usual ring of worthies. I dreaded being summoned to interpret, so veered away.

Vee squeezed my arm. 'Someone said you were his right-hand man.'

'I'm afraid not. Anyway, he's already got a right hand. I'd have to be his left-hand man.'

Vee was staring intently at Glass as if willing him to look her way.

I tried to distract her. 'Would you like a drink?'

'Can't we meet the *Kommandant*?'

'Why?'

'You introduced your sister to him.'

'That was his idea, not mine.'

Vee sensed she was not going to get her own way. 'I've heard the Great Western Hotel's popular.'

'Only with Germans.'

For a moment I thought Vee was about to throw one of her tantrums. Then she relaxed.

'*Glühwein* will be fine, darling.'

We sipped *Glühwein* under the Christmas tree as I learned that Vee now worked in Horace Smeed's private office. But, for once, she didn't want to talk about herself; she wanted to hear about my job in the *Feldkommandantur*.

'You must be able to get hold of anything you want.'

'Don't be daft. I've only been working there a week.'

'You never push yourself forward, Nick. You let people take you for granted.'

Her criticism stung me. 'Actually, Glass has just complimented me on the carol service. It was my idea.'

'Wow!' Her face lit up. 'Get close to him and you'll be surprised how many friends you'll have.'

'Are they the sort of friends I'd want, though?'

'Don't be silly, darling. I know, why don't we go back to my place?' she said brightly. 'I've got some booze there and my landlady's going to be out. There's no curfew until midnight tonight, remember. It'll be really cosy. What d'you say?'

As we were walking away I thought I heard someone hiss, 'Jerrybags.'

But I wasn't sure if I'd heard right.

Christmas Eve had a winter tang to the air, as if snow was not far away. There were queues of women and older men standing outside bakers, butchers, grocers and fishmongers. The fishing fleet had been allowed extra diesel, so many families were having cod or haddock for Christmas dinner. I'd found a bag with a cock pheasant and a Christmas card hanging on the scullery door. With the pheasant and a piece of boiled bacon we were going to have a feast. Shoppers were wishing each other Happy Christmas. No one said anything to me. I blamed the swastika armband.

As usual I'd left buying presents to the last minute. Hauser had agreed to get me a box of chocolates from the *Feldkommandantur*'s commissariat to give to Joan. I'd chanced upon a fountain pen and some good stationery for my mother. I had wanted to get David an air rifle, but they had been banned. Instead

I hoped the binoculars and book of British birds would be acceptable. David could use his bike, bought second-hand by Joan, then freshly painted and hidden by me at the Three Horseshoes, to go birdwatching.

I thought about buying Vee something but then again, her room last night had been like an Aladdin's cave with tins of meat and packets of tea stacked up alongside bottles of whisky and sherry.

Vee had sat on the bed and began unrolling a silk stocking down one long leg.

'If you hear of any stockings you'll think of me, won't you?' She proceeded to unroll the other one, holding my eyes with hers, before rising to press her body against me. 'Aren't you going to help me undress?'

Afterwards she had been in a hurry for me to go. I wasn't even allowed a post-coital cigarette. Her landlady might come back at any moment, it now appeared. Vee had stuffed a bar of chocolate in my pocket as I did up my bootlaces.

'A Christmas present?'

'You've just had that.'

In that case, so had she.

I was on my way back to work, just entering the square in front of the *Feldkommandantur*, when I spotted Roy walking ahead of me, flanked by two strangers. Both wore long dark coats and felt hats and somehow they looked out of place. Maybe it was the coats, or the fact that none of the three was carrying anything. I was intrigued.

I was hurrying to catch them up when three troop carriers of *Feldgendarmerie* appeared, racing down the hill from Corunna Barracks to seal off the square in a snap identity check. Anyone who didn't have their documents on them would be spending Christmas in the detention camp at the old racecourse. Bloody Germans! Just when you thought you could relax. The carrot last night. The stick today.

The strangers had spotted the approaching Germans. They stopped and began arguing with Roy as the troop carriers slewed in position, soldiers leaping down to set up barriers across the roads and the pavements. A *Feldwebel* was already dragging one protesting woman towards a covered Opel lorry.

Two sharply dressed men carrying suitcases were hurrying away towards a side street. I could have told them it was too late. The Germans always quietly sealed off the back streets first, then lay in wait. Rat runs became rat traps.

'Trust in your papers,' Roy was saying.

'They are not good enough,' protested the older man, in a foreign accent. Fear made his voice sound as taut as cheesewire.

'The longer you stand here, the more noticeable you're becoming,' I warned, joining them.

'That's what I'm trying to tell them,' muttered Roy, relieved that I'd arrived.

'I can't do it. I know I can't,' insisted the stranger. His eyes widened as he caught sight of my swastika armband.

I took stock. The Germans had now sealed off the square, with us in the middle. The stranger had turned grey, clearly too panic-stricken to risk trying to get him past the checkpoint. His younger companion was not reacting much better. There was only one thing to do. We'd have to brazen our way through the *Feldkommandantur*.

I pulled the swastika armband off my British Army greatcoat and handed it to the older man. It was no good trying to do things on the sly. We had to appear so natural that we were invisible. I slipped one arm out of my coat, pulled the swastika off my battledress tunic and slid it up the other man's sleeve. Now that both foreigners were wearing swastikas, the coats appeared right. I realized it was because they were cut in a Continental style.

'Take these packages,' I said. Nowadays everyone carried a bag with them in the hope of finding a shop with an unexpected delivery. 'You see that gap over there between the large building and the smaller one on the right – under the archway? That's where we're going. Remember – act confidently. You have every right to be here. Avoid eye contact, but don't look at the ground.'

The nervous one was muttering to himself, his eyes zooming around like two mad pinballs.

'Shut up. Just talk to your colleague. Be natural. What time are we having a pint tonight, Roy?'

'I don't mind. Around eight. Mam and dad have gone to Bristol. Uncle Oscar's taken a turn for the worse.' Our conversation sounded false and leaden but at least we were trying.

'Come for Christmas dinner if you're by yourself. Joan would be delighted.'

'Are you sure? I could weigh in with a few things.'

'Of course.'

We were approaching sentries, with closed hostile faces, who goose-stepped twenty metres in one direction and then twenty metres back again across the front of the *Feldkommandantur*. They were just for show: the real security began when you tried to enter the building – and I had no intention of doing that. I waved familiarly to a Grey Mouse returning from last-minute shopping. She ignored me.

Glass was arriving in his staff car, pennants flying from the wings. The guard doubled out of the main entrance to present arms.

'Now,' I ordered.

We walked through the archway and into the central courtyard where a platoon of German infantry was standing around with piles of kitbags, waiting for transport. We could not walk through them. Instead we were going to have to pass close to the SS guards outside the *Gestapo* wing. The strangers would have to hold their nerve.

Two sounds filled my ears: the ring of our boots on the stones, and the pounding of my heart. An SS lorry, canvas top tightly fastened, growled into the courtyard to stop directly outside the *Gestapo* doorway. Fighting to stop myself breaking into a run, I led the party around the lorry and towards a small archway at the far end. I felt hostile stares boring into my back and expected every second the command to halt. I held my breath – then we were through the archway and out onto the rear perimeter road. Shallow steps led down into a small park. We were beyond the cordon. As casually as possible, I took back my swastikas.

'Thanks, mate,' breathed Roy.

There was an unpleasant surprise waiting for me at the security desk inside the *Feldkommandantur*. Instead of waving me through, the big *Feldpolizei* sergeant planted a firm hand on my chest.

'The *Kommandant* wishes to see you immediately.'

Hauser's face was a carefully composed blank. I put down my Christmas presents, not knowing if I would ever see them again. Hauser picked up the phone and muttered a few words.

'Go in.'

Tickell stood in front of Glass's desk. Stolz was again pacing by the windows.

'Threaten to demolish the home of everyone who listens to it,' the *Gestapo* boss was saying.

'How am I supposed to enforce that?' demanded Glass. 'Even if I had the manpower, it would take days. In the last weeks, the 56th Fusilier-Regiment and two Engineers companies have been recalled to Germany. Carry on like this and the English will have to occupy themselves.'

'The *Führer* knows what he is doing,' said Stolz, stiffly.

'Of course.' Glass saw he had overstepped the mark. 'Sergeant, your King George intends to broadcast from Canada at three o'clock Christmas afternoon, local time. We are discussing how best to prevent people listening. Make sure *Herr Sekretär* Tickell understands.'

I did my best not to show the relief that was flooding over me. 'Of course, sir.'

'You can make it illegal to listen under Article Eight of the Occupying Forces Regulations, which follow from the Declaration of Occupation,' suggested Tickell, once I had explained. 'It can be ratified by the Supreme Council in special session. Or you have Extraordinary Powers under Article Four, dealing with enemy propaganda.'

'We could not enforce such a ban,' snapped Stolz, slapping his cane against his jackboots.

'Can't you jam the broadcast?' asked Tickell.

'It's not as easy as it sounds, and this region's especially difficult to jam because of its terrain, say the experts.'

'Do we even know exactly who owns a wireless set?' asked Glass.

'No, that's part of the problem,' barked Stolz.

Tickell ran a finger under his wing collar. 'I'm afraid the electoral lists and council rating schedules are out of date, sir. Many men are still . . . away, but on the other hand we've had a huge influx of refugees.'

'We need a comprehensive household register detailing information like name, age, sex, occupation and religion.' Stolz's eyes burned with enthusiasm. 'Together with possession of things like a wireless set or a car.'

'That still doesn't solve our immediate problem.' Glass opened a small gunmetal container and put two white tablets side by side on his desk. 'Sergeant, write this down. *Reichskommissar* von Ribbentrop has been pleased to grant a seasonal gift to every residence as a token of Anglo-German friendship: a Christmas present of ten cigarettes or a bar of chocolate, a kilo of potatoes and one hundred grammes of tea per household – to be collected at the nearest junior school. Got that?'

'Yes, sir.' I scribbled desperately in my notebook.

'All I have to do now is to get it approved by *Militärbefehlshaber London*,' muttered Glass, almost to himself. 'Sketch out a poster announcing the gift, Penny. They'll be printed this evening and put up throughout the region overnight. The announcement will be read out tomorrow morning on BBC Western Region .'

'That's very kind, sir.'

'Remember to call von Ribbentrop "The Protector" – not *Reichskommissar*.'

'Yes, sir.'

'One last thing, sergeant. The offer is open only from three to three-thirty tomorrow afternoon.'

The Germans could be terrifyingly efficient when they wanted to be. Within an hour, supply staff at *Zufuhrstelle* food depots were beginning distribution to the main *Nebenstelle* and far-flung *Außenstelle* across the Province.

I had a rough outline of the poster ready for approval by the time Hauser delivered Joan's chocolates.

'What do you think of the general's idea?' he demanded. 'Clever, eh?'

'Very.' I kept my views to myself.

'He knows you never win over people by terrorizing them – only by kindness. That man'll go right to the top, as long as he remembers to bite his tongue about the Party.' Hauser was a big fan of the *Kommandant*. Perhaps he hoped to rise on von Glass's coat-tails. He'd have to learn discretion first. As if to prove the point, he started to tell me about how much pain Glass was in.

'His missing arm hurts like hell, all the time. That's why he takes those tablets. Mind you, he shouldn't be washing them down with cognac. That doesn't do him any good. Is this the poster? Good. I'll show it to him. Don't go away yet.'

I wasn't going anywhere. I began to wrap my presents. Images of Christmas drifted across my mind. Crisp snow on deep starry nights, carol singing, crowded pubs full of happy laughter, the midnight service, the last goodnight kiss and fumble, creeping home to the scent of resin from the Christmas tree. Images – that was exactly what they were. Images. You seldom got snow in this part of the country. There hadn't been any carol singers this year. It was almost indecent to laugh nowadays, and the tree I'd taken home was still out in the garden. Joan wasn't interested in decorating the house. And I wouldn't be getting a goodnight kiss from Vee. She was sorry, but she was tied up visiting her parents all over Christmas.

I made a dog's dinner of wrapping my presents. I'd usually been able to call on the help of a girlfriend – or even Roy's mother one year. Now I had to do them myself. I couldn't understand why a rectangular box of chocolates ended up looking like a wrapped pullover.

The door opened and Glass came in, carrying a bottle of cognac and two glasses. I leaped to attention. He kicked the door shut with his heel, perched on the edge of the table and poured two measures. He'd been drinking continually since I'd last seen him.

'You did a good job with that poster. Have a drink. It's the season of goodwill.'

'Thank you, sir.'

'Why didn't you tell me about your King's speech?'

'You knew already.'

'Actually, I didn't. *Reichssicherheitshauptamt London* only put out a priority signal at midday. So?'

'No one told me either.' It hurt that no one I'd spoken to while shopping had trusted me enough to tell me.

'I thought that must be why you looked as if you had a guilty secret when you came in.'

Christ! Had it shown so clearly? 'Everyone looks like that in the presence of the *Standartenführer*, sir.'

Glass laughed. '*Prost.*'

'*Prost.*' I coughed as the liquid flowed down my throat, setting my empty stomach alight.

Glass drained his cognac in one. 'Stolz doesn't like you. I've told him I understand your loyalty to your country, but as long as the country lacks a focus for opposition, people like you are harmless. That is why we must stop people listening to the broadcast.' Glass held out the half-empty bottle. 'I envy you, Penny.

You're home. You have your family, friends. Was that attractive blonde I saw you with outside the cathedral your girlfriend?'

'Not really, sir.'

'No?' Christmas was making Glass nostalgic. 'Tonight, at home in Prussia, my mother will give dinner for the estate workers. My father was killed in November 1918, just one week before the armistice. On what you call Boxing Day, relatives and neighbours will hunt boar and gather for drinks in front of the fireplace.' He sighed. 'Do you know, Christmas is the only time of the year when I wish I had children. The satisfaction of sneaking into my son's room to hang his stocking at the foot of the bed and, in the morning, see the wonder in his eyes.' He took another gulp. 'I fear I am being romantic.'

'Are you married, sir?'

'No. My second cousin Emma and I have known each other all our lives. The family expects us to wed, but I do not want to marry in wartime. It reeks of desperation.'

This was getting embarrassing. I did not want to listen to Glass's half-drunken confidences – especially as there would be the inevitable reaction when he sobered up. But I sensed he wasn't acting this way just from drink. Maybe his pills were reacting with the alcohol? I was saved further awkwardness by Hauser returning with a finished poster.

'Very good,' announced Glass. 'Just put *Merry*

Christmas on the top. Now, how many do you think will take advantage of our generosity, Penny?'

I did not reply.

'All right, how many will fall for it? How many will give up the chance of cigarettes, chocolate and tea just to listen to a broadcast from their departed King, which we'll do our best to jam anyway?'

'I don't know, sir. I really don't.'

'Nor do I, Penny. What will you do?'

'Me? Well, they say one can't live by fine words alone . . .'

'Yes?'

'But a man without a soul is a beast of the field. I'll be very close to the wireless.'

'I rather thought you would be.' He poured himself another drink.

Glass did not say so then but he had a very unpleasant surprise in store for me.

I was a little drunk when I arrived home. Joan had not put up the Christmas decorations. The tree was still leaning against the garden shed.

'It just doesn't seem right,' she explained. 'It's been a bloody terrible year. What's there to celebrate?'

'Just being alive, sis.'

'That's the point. Some aren't.'

I put my presents in the front parlour. I'd promised

to take young David to the pictures as a Christmas treat. I was worried about the boy: he was too quiet, staying in his room for hours on end. He used to be so boisterous and outgoing. He was obviously grieving for his father but he never said a word. Instead he bottled up his feelings. He was tucked away in his room even now. The old David would have been badgering me as soon as I walked in. I called up to ask if he still wanted to go to the cinema. Yes, he said, but he did not sound that enthusiastic.

Cinemas had been allowed to reopen a month ago although the national anthem was still forbidden. The German forces' cinemas – *Soldatenkinos* – were strictly segregated, and British films were heavily censored. Any story touching on Britain's military or imperial history was banned, leaving us harmless comedies and Westerns. Tonight the Odeon was showing *Stagecoach*, along with a couple of Laurel and Hardy shorts.

David laughed aloud at their antics, then bounced up and down as the Indians chased John Wayne across the desert. I suspected he had seen the film before but it cheered him up nonetheless. Afterwards I bought us a penny's worth bag of chips and a fried patty each to eat on the way home.

David used to be so easy to talk to. Now I didn't know what to say to my nephew. 'How are you getting on with your German studies?'

'All right, thanks. I've got some prep to do over the hols. Will you help me?'

'Of course.'

We munched our chips in silence until David asked suddenly, 'Uncle Nick, why did you learn German?'

'Jacob Jenner got me interested. He used to help me with my homework and lend me his books. He had a magical knack of making German sound wonderful, the language of poets and philosophers.'

'And Nazi invaders.'

'And Nazi invaders. But Jacob only spoke of the good side.'

'He's the man who owns the bakery and those cafés in town?'

'That's right. We used to live next door.'

'Until the Germans took your house away.'

'Yes.'

'Why did we go to war?'

'To protect Poland.'

'But we didn't. The Germans conquered Poland.'

'We had to do the decent thing.'

'Why did we lose the war?'

'Basically, we weren't prepared. We didn't have enough aeroplanes or tanks. The Germans caught us on the hop by invading before they'd made peace with France . . .'

'All Frenchmen are cowards,' declared David.

'You can't really say that.' Although, God knows, I'd heard the same sentiments expressed in far more forceful ways during my time in the PoW camp. If the Frogs hadn't run . . . If they'd pulled back into the Breton bastion . . . If they hadn't handed over their fleet.

'The Fifth Column blew up the radio detection finding station on the Isle of Wight, so we couldn't see the invasion coming. We were stabbed in the back.'

'Who said that?'

'A boy at school. His father was in the RAF.'

It was a popular rumour but I doubted it was true. It was hard for a nation to accept defeat so it made up excuses. Ironically, most Germans believed that they had lost the First War by being stabbed in the back. That myth had led directly to the Second War.

'German planes destroyed the RDF stations and the airfields,' I replied carefully. 'I've not heard of saboteurs.'

'*We* need saboteurs to blow up the Germans. If we kill enough of them, they'll go home.'

'What happens if they take reprisals and shoot innocent people here?'

David crumpled up his chip paper and drop-kicked it along the road, as if testing me to tell him to pick it up. 'I don't care about innocent people. I want to kill Germans.'

*

The current regulars in the Three Horseshoes were largely made up of those who had stayed behind. Unlike the old bunch, they did not buy rounds or share cigarettes. I didn't pretend to like them but at least I could have a pint here without being made to feel a traitor.

'Thanks for your help today,' said Roy as we sat by ourselves in the snug. 'I thought that one bloke's arse was going to fall out.'

'Who were they? Or shouldn't I ask?'

Roy leaned forward. 'Norwegians on their way to set up a government in exile.'

I shouldn't have asked.

In exchange, I told Roy of the handout designed to lure listeners away from the King's speech. For good measure, I threw in something else Glass had said. 'What do you think the *Gestapo*'s number one priority is?'

'Dunno. Crushing the Resistance movement?'

'No. They're desperate to find the Crown Jewels. They think they're down here in our neck of the woods. Shit, are you all right?'

Roy had gone white – literally white.

'Say that again.'

'What? The *Gestapo*'s priority is to find the Crown Jewels.'

'How do you know?' He was staring at me in a mad way.

'Glass told me this afternoon, when he was half cut. He hasn't much time for the *Gestapo*.'

Roy chewed his lip, a sign that he was thinking hard. 'I won't be a minute.' He got up.

'I'll get us a couple of pints,' I volunteered.

I was standing at the bar when Med strode in, bringing the cold in with him. He warmed his hands in front of the small fire.

'There's a frost out there. Might even have snow.'

'Thanks for the pheasant.'

'Don't mention it.'

'My mother loved the card.'

'Gloria did it all herself. Spent ages on it. Mind you, it's a funny world when a six-year-old draws Messerschmitts on a Christmas card.'

'It's got reindeers, too.'

'Ay.'

Roy reappeared. 'Nick, let's go down the smoker. There's someone I want you to meet.' When we were in the corridor, he whispered, 'Just to prove to you the resistance movement *does* exist . . .'

The smoker was a small, intimate room with a bare wooden floor and a low nicotine-stained ceiling, tucked away among the pub's nooks and crannies. A stocky man in a sports jacket stood by the chimney breast. I'd seen him before, on my first visit here. Roy closed the door behind us.

'John Mills, Nick Penny.'

'I've heard a lot about you,' said Mills, extending a hand. 'You're Roy's oldest friend.'

'One of them.' I put Mills in his late thirties. He had a firm jaw and dark slashes for eyebrows. 'Army officer' was stamped through him like a die.

Mills regarded me with an uncomfortably direct gaze. I held his stare.

'You put your neck on the line for Roy today . . .'

'It was nothing.'

'In spite of saying you weren't interested in joining the Resistance.'

'I didn't quite say that.' I didn't know whether Mills was deliberately twisting my words or if Roy had misreported me. 'I said I'd not been back here long. Everything's changed. I need time to get my bearings.'

'And once you've got your bearings?'

'Then I'll plot my own course.'

Mills smiled. It was a cold smile but it lifted his heavy features and made him look younger and more approachable.

'You're rather a belligerent young man, aren't you? Willing to meet trouble head-on. Not at all how Roy described you.'

'Am I?' I was surprised. Roy's usual description of me was along the lines that I was the bright one who could sometimes be as daft as a brush. Maybe war had changed me.

'Roy's been on to me to meet you ever since you got back.' Mills's smile seemed genuine this time. 'Your actions today rather show where your loyalty lies, even if you don't want to admit it.'

I said nothing, thinking it was a strange world when I could confess my patriotism to the German Military Governor but not to this man.

'Roy says you mentioned the Crown Jewels,' continued Mills. 'Can you remember what Glass said – as precisely as possible.'

I described how Glass had brought the bottle of cognac into my office, the talk about loyalties and the King's broadcast.

Then, out of the blue, Glass had asked, 'I don't suppose you know where the Crown Jewels are, do you, Penny?'

'I'm afraid not, sir.' I wondered if I'd heard him correctly. 'Don't *you* have them?'

'No. Your country's gold reserves and securities were shipped to Canada . . .'

'Really!'

'The cruiser HMS *Emerald* left with the first 900 gold bars and 500 boxes of securities on 23 June. By the end of August your Government had transferred £637 million in gold and £1,250 million in negotiable securities. The gold is in Ottawa and the securities in the vaults of the Sun Life Insurance company in Montreal. But someone slipped up with the Crown Jewels. They're still here in England.'

I hadn't known about the gold reserves. I kept the smile off my face.

'Two days ago there was a Triple-A signal from *Reichssicherheitshauptamt Berlin* to *RHSA London* and the six provincial *Gestapo* HQs, setting out the seizure of the Crown Jewels as an absolute and total priority over all other operations. There are unconfirmed rumours that they are hidden down here in the West Country. There's a £10,000 reward for any information leading to their discovery. You could be a rich man, Penny.'

'I prefer to be a poor patriot, sir.'

When I finished, Mills was quiet for a long time. 'I wonder how Glass knew about that signal? You are in a unique position to gain inside information, Penny, you know that, don't you?'

'As I told Glass, I'm just a poor patriot –' the room held its breath '– who will do his best by his country.'

'I always knew . . .' Roy put his arm around my shoulders.

'Good man.' Mills shook my hand. The room became a warmer and friendlier place.

There was a tap on the door. Roy flung it open. The young woman with short sandy hair and elfin features, who'd been with Mills before, stood in the doorway. She wore a pale raincoat and was playing with a cigarette holder. She made a silent enquiry of Mills with raised eyebrows.

'Fine. Everything's fine,' he reassured her.

'Good.' She looked at me, as if taking a mental photograph, before turning abruptly away, her footsteps fading towards the back gate.

'Nick, let me explain a little of what we do.' Mills pinched the bridge of his nose, as if his sinuses were painful. 'When it became clear that the battle for England was lost, the War Office decided to put in place the skeleton of an underground Resistance. A handful of us stayed behind and went undercover. At the moment, most of our work is concerned with smuggling people out to Canada, where they can help continue the fight. We're at the end of the Western Line escape route here. The two men you helped past the Germans this afternoon will board a British submarine later tonight.'

'Do the Germans know about this Western Line?'

'They know that it exists. They don't know *who* runs it or *where* it runs. We have other escape lines but this one's the most successful – largely due to Roy.'

Roy looked suitably bashful.

'The more lines we have, the more flexible we can be. The Germans turn up the heat on one line, we switch operations elsewhere. The *Abwehr* penetrated the Lancashire Line just last week. Winter now means that the line through the Highlands has become increasingly perilous so the Western Line must carry the brunt of the traffic in the months ahead. The Germans are desperate to destroy it.'

Roy was bursting to say something but Mills shot him a warning look. I was trusted, but not that much – and not yet.

For the rest of the evening I felt curiously elated. I had a sense of belonging, a sense of importance; as if I'd been initiated into a strange cult, yet didn't know or understand all the rules. It was only as I drunkenly rode David's bike home, dodging German patrols at one o'clock on Christmas morning, that I began to feel very scared indeed.

6

I found it hard to sleep on Christmas morning – although it had more to do with the amount of beer I'd drunk the night before than with any excitement. I wrapped myself in Ted's dressing gown and, after going to the lavatory, decided to make a cup of tea to take back to bed. The lie-in would be my Christmas present to myself. It was still dark as I crept downstairs but a light was on in the kitchen. I opened the door to find Joan, with tears in her eyes, struggling to push a drawing pin holding a red and green paper chain into one corner of the ceiling. She finally succeeded and climbed off the chair, sucking her thumb.

'Happy Christmas.'

She leaped in the air.

'Nick! Don't do that. You'll give me a heart attack.' She turned away to wipe her tears with her pinafore.

'What's wrong, sis?'

'Nothing – nothing now. Come and help me.' She carried the chair to the diagonal corner and pinned up the other end of the paper chain before, together, we fastened a blue crêpe streamer across the room. I delved in the decorations box and pulled out a Father Christmas with a cotton-wool beard, who had seen better days. Who cared! We hung him on the mirror over the fire and looped silver and gold tinsel along the walls. Joan put the few greetings cards on the dresser. The Germans had banned Christmas cards but a few people had made their own and had given them out personally. The room was beginning to look festive at last.

The fire was in two minds whether to stay in or go out. I encouraged it to stay in with a precious stick. Household coal was in short supply, and of poor quality. All the best went to Germany.

'The Christmas tree.'

'I'll get it.' The morning was raw with cold. A smear of grey on the eastern horizon and a handful of bedroom lights heralded the start of Christmas Day. I used the coal shovel to fill a metal pail with earth, and carried it inside. The tree was difficult to pick up, even harder to carry. Its branches jammed in the doorway, but together we wrestled the tree into a bucket. Joan damped in the earth around the stump, and miraculously the tree stood upright.

'I almost let them beat me, Nick.' Joan had a wistful look. 'Do you remember the parties we used to have?'

'God, yes.'

Ted and Joan's last big Christmas party had been in 1938, the last year of peace. Handsome naval officers in uniform, wives and girlfriends in posh frocks. Waiters in black ties had circulated with trays of pink gins, horses' necks, champagne and canapés. A magnificent tree had stood in the hall, surrounded by presents. The church choir had sung carols by lantern light in the garden. David, on his best behaviour, had been allowed to stay up for the first hour; dad wrapped in discussion with a rear admiral about the obsolescence of battleships; mum making sure everyone was at ease. Matty had got off with a captain's daughter from Plymouth. I hated formal parties so I'd stayed in the kitchen with Roy and got drunk.

Joan was wrapping the bucket in red crêpe paper when she stopped dead.

'What's wrong?'

'I was thinking of our last party. I could see it all in my mind's eye, but I realized I hadn't seen Ted. His friends, shipmates, dad, mum, you, David were all there – but not Ted. I'd erased him from my mind.'

'It's your way of dealing with the pain.'

She smiled: a faraway smile that grew lovelier and sadder as I watched. I knew she could see her husband now – see him as he had been that night. Tall, weather-beaten, with deep blue eyes and wavy brown hair. She had been so proud of him. She still was.

'Oh, Ted, darling.' She blew a kiss into the Christmas morning air.

I busied myself in dressing the tree with tinsel streamers, little packages, miniature candles, and a star at the top. Joan joined me and when we stepped back to regard our handiwork we both felt better. Better for the crying, better for the kiss, better for making the effort.

The carriage clock softly chimed eight.

'Not many years ago David would have been up by now, desperate to see his presents,' Joan said. 'I'm worried about him. He's just lost interest.'

'Have you tried to get him to talk about Ted?'

'Endlessly, but he doesn't respond.'

'He'll come through. At least he's got the bike. He'd set his heart on that.'

'And I've draped his new long trousers over the bottom of his bed.' Joan put on the kettle and began peeling potatoes.

A few minutes later the stairs creaked and David appeared around the kitchen door. He was still half asleep. He wore his new trousers with his pyjama jacket.

'Thanks, mum. Happy Christmas, Uncle Nick.' His eyes opened wide as he saw the tree and the decorations.

'The good fairy.' Joan picked up a cylinder wrapped in brown paper from behind the tree. 'We'll open our presents later but here's something for you now.'

David tore off the paper to reveal a bicycle pump. He regarded it with suspicion.

'That's no use without a bicycle, is it? Why don't you look outside?'

David's joy as he saw the bike for the first time made Joan forget her worries, her fears, and the ghosts who crowded around her like guests in a wedding photograph.

Seeing my old home hurt me more than I'd expected. It hadn't really registered on me on my first day back, although I'd got the shock of my life at the new sign on the gate:

Nur Deutsche Wehrmacht. Eintritt Verboten.

But that whole first day back in my home town had been spent in a daze.

Now this Christmas morning, the front door opened to release a bellow of laughter. An artillery captain strode out and glowered at me.

'What are you doing here?'

'This used to be my home,' I replied in German.

'Well, it's not your home now. Be off.'

Resentment surged inside me like a spring tide. I had the urge to rip down the sign and beat the arrogant bastard over the head with it. It meant that

I was starting to wake out of my trance. My blood was pulsing through my veins again. I was beginning to hate Germans.

I walked up the short drive to the identical Victorian house next door, to find four urchins crowding around the side door.

Miriam Jenner was saying, 'One bag of broken biscuits each. Here, wait. Have a piece of cake as well. There . . . Happy Christmas.'

She blushed when she saw me, as if I had stumbled upon a guilty secret. 'Ach, they are poor. Christmas is like any other day for them. What's a few biscuits? I baked some extra just in case. Come and say hello to Jacob.'

As usual, the house was filled with the warm homely smells of baking. Miriam asked after mum and Joan, and explained that I had just missed Simon and Anna who had taken the twins for a stroll with their friend Barbara.

'How are you managing now with rationing?'

Miriam took that to be an enquiry about running the cafés. 'We manage. We picked plenty of fruit in the autumn so we could make our own jams. I don't know what'll happen next year. The farmers let us have cream on the quiet, but it's getting difficult to find tea and coffee – even from our special suppliers.' Miriam led me into the drawing room. 'Jacob, look who's here.'

A gnomelike man with grey curls and kind eyes rose from a deep leather armchair, an almost completed *Times* crossword by his side.

'Happy Christmas, Nick. It's good to see you again.'

'It's good to see you, too.' I went over to shake his hand.

But Jacob held it up. 'Forgive the glove. I've developed a skin infection that's taking a time to heal. The glove stops me scratching it.'

'There was a German soldier who brought us some ointment, but then he was posted away. It's a shame,' said Miriam, returning with a plate of mince pies.

'If I have any of these I won't be able to eat my dinner.'

'Ach, you need feeding up.'

'Christmas gives Miriam the chance to press even more food on even more people,' Jacob smiled indulgently as she went back to her kitchen.

I liked this spotless room, cluttered and over-furnished in a heavy Middle European style, with framed photographs of the extended Jenner family filling every inch of the polished tables, the mahogany sideboard, the upright piano and the mantelpiece. There was something solid and permanent about it all.

Nothing better illustrated Jacob's broad religious beliefs than the sight of a Christmas tree standing in the corner and the two lighted candles of the Chanu-kah lamp on the windowsill.

'Did you know Simon's going to take over Dr McIlvaney's practice?' asked Jacob.

'Miriam said Simon and Anna would have had to move to the East End, if they'd stayed in London.'

A cloud passed over Jacob's face. 'From the first of January, all London Jews have to live in a ghetto in Whitechapel. There's a rumour that the Germans are going to build a wall around it to keep them in.'

'But why?'

'In Poland, the Nazis have persecuted Jews terri-bly. They've destroyed their synagogues and seized Jewish businesses. They've even put Jews into camps. I know because Barbara was in one, but she will not speak of it.'

'That won't happen in England. The people wouldn't allow it.'

'I hope you're right. Luckily, we Jews are a resili-ent race. We've had to be.'

'You're not a practising Jew.'

'I'm not a practising Christian either. I pray to any God who'll listen that Simon, Anna and the girls will be safe down here.'

At the gate, I met Simon and Anna coming back from their walk. We wished each other Happy Christmas, as the twins peeped at me from behind Anna's coat and pretended to be shy. Simon intro-duced Barbara. Pale and tired, she stood with her hands supporting her bulging belly, quick to drop her eyes to the ground, and slow to smile.

Until the day she was executed eight months later, Margaret Penny could not forgive the Germans for taking away her son in the middle of the family Christmas dinner.

She had been woken early by her pain to lie alone on that cold Christmas morning, hating her twisted, sick body – but hating more the Germans who had killed her husband, and wounded her.

When the lone plane had first flown over the city, the children had jumped up and down with excitement, crying out that it was a Spitfire. It was only when it dived on their school and opened fire that they found out their mistake.

What sort of man strafed a playground full of children?

She could not understand why Nick had to work for these Germans. Surely he could find himself another job. Maybe back teaching at his school? And why did he have to wear that hateful swastika? She knew he took it off when nearing home so as not to upset her, but she had heard he wore it openly around the town.

Joan eventually brought her in a cup of tea and drew back the curtains. Margaret sipped her tea and looked at her hands, gnarled and bent, claws rather than hands, with dark age spots spreading over the increasingly pronounced tendons and sinews.

It was only when Margaret saw how Joan had decorated the kitchen that she made an effort to stop feeling sorry for herself, reminding herself that this was what Bill would have wanted.

So she shared in David's delight with his new bike, and helped Joan lay the table as they listened to the morning carol service from Westminster Abbey on the wireless. At half past one, Nick and Roy dashed in, carrying parcels.

'I was despairing of the pair of you,' said Joan.

'It's my fault,' said Roy. 'It took time to get the regulars out and shut up the pub.'

Nick produced a small Christmas cake. 'From Miriam and Jacob.'

'They *are* kind,' said Margaret. 'When your father and I first knew them, they had just one small café near the harbour. They work very hard.'

'I've got some presents to put under the tree,' announced Roy. 'But here's a bottle of sherry for now and a bottle of peach brandy for after.'

'Roy, you shouldn't have.'

'It's the least I can do.' Roy poured the sherry. 'Now I don't want you getting tiddly, Mrs Penny. No singing until after the meal.'

'Roy!' Margaret giggled like a schoolgirl. She had always had a soft spot for Roy. A nice, uncomplicated boy, she called him. Joan preferred Matty for his looks and charm, but he was too smooth for Margaret's taste. Give her Roy any time. 'Have you heard from your parents?'

'They've run away,' joked Roy. 'Normally it's the children who leave, in my case it's my parents. They couldn't wait to get away from me.'

'I hope you don't mind me laying the table in here,' said Joan. 'It's so cold and empty in the dining room.' She had found a box of crackers, and even a bottle of claret from somewhere. And if the bone china, cut glass and best silver appeared incongruous on the old kitchen table under the airing rack – who cared?

Margaret sat by the fire and read aloud snippets from yesterday's newspaper as Joan made last-minute preparations. 'The Duke of Windsor and his American hussy are having Christmas dinner at Buckingham Palace, as guests of the Protector,' she announced.

'Does it say what they're having?' Joan was curious despite herself.

'A traditional European dinner: goose, carp, duck and a baron of beef. The American ambassador, Jack Kennedy, will be among the two dozen guests including Field Marshal Busch and those toads Amery and Hoare.'

'*They*'re not going to go hungry, are they!' Joan began mashing the swedes. 'Nick, open the wine and call David in before he disappears off on that bike again.'

'I'll do it,' volunteered Roy, returning shortly with the boy.

'Start carving, Nick. What are you doing, David?'

'Looking at a man looking at us.' He stood in the window, peering out through his new binoculars.

'Where? What sort of man?'

'Just a man.'

'Is he in uniform?'

'Yeh, German. He's gone now.'

Roy and Nick were still staring at each other in alarm when Margaret remembered a photograph she had found that morning. 'You two and Matty when you were sixteen,' she explained, handing it to them.

The three boys were on a beach, crowding together to grin into the camera. Roy couldn't remember it being taken. Nick did.

'That was the day we carried on playing cricket on the sand while the tide was coming in. We only gave up when the wicket was three inches under water.'

'You dropped your sandwiches into the sea,' Margaret recalled.

'It was Matty's fault but I got the blame as usual.'

'Matty's like his mother there, you know,' mused Margaret. 'His father defied the family to marry her. There was some talk that she was unsuitable, but the

Major had made up his mind. She died when Matty was little, and the Major's not been the same ever since.'

'Mum, please put that photo away,' called out Joan. 'Nick, start carving or the vegetables will get cold.'

'*Jawohl, Herr Gruppenführer.*'

'Nick!' exclaimed Margaret. 'Not here, not on Christmas Day, not even as a joke.'

'Sorry, mum.'

At last the family sat down for their Christmas meal.

'I don't like cabbage,' wailed David.

'If you knew how long I had to queue for it ... just you eat it up.'

'If you don't eat it, I'm going to take your bicycle pump and stick it up your nose,' threatened Roy.

'Then what'll happen?'

'All the snot will come flying out of your other nostril. Whoosh!'

'Roy!'

'Sorry.'

David chuckled with delight, and Margaret thought how good it was to see him laugh.

'Wasn't it nice of Mr Tibby to give us this pheasant.'

'He's a rough diamond,' observed Roy.

'We'll be finished in time to hear the King speak.'

'If they don't jam the broadcast.'

'Let's pull a cracker, David.'

David got a rubber spider on an elastic band in his. He bounced it towards Roy who swatted it with his own cracker. Everyone put on paper hats and Nick proposed a toast.

'To us.'

'To us – and absent friends and loved ones,' enjoined Joan.

Suddenly, there was a heavy knocking on the front door. Ponderous yet urgent. Everyone froze – sharing one unspoken thought.

Gestapo.

The knocking was repeated. More urgent and even angrier.

Roy's eyes flickered to the back door.

Nick took a quick gulp of wine. 'I'll go.'

The others waited in tense silence. They heard Nick open the door and caught a rough, demanding German voice. Nick, by his tone, was trying to be reasonable. The German kept repeating himself, growing more and more angry.

Finally Nick came back. 'I have to go.'

'Why?'

'I don't know. Don't worry.' He put on his army greatcoat over Ted's slacks and jacket. 'It shouldn't take long, whatever it is. Keep my food warm.'

'But it's Christmas Day.'

'Take care,' said Roy.

'Take care,' echoed Margaret.

I had made myself sound a lot more positive than I felt. Was this the backlash to Glass's tipsy bonhomie yesterday? Over-familiarity one day and hell to pay the next? Or had the *Gestapo* found out about the Norwegians? About my conversation with Mills? My agreeing to join the Resistance?

I was still reviewing my recent transgressions as we drove into Corunna Barracks and pulled up alongside a small grey Morris van with two loud-speaker trumpets fastened to the roof. A signals major came strutting out, still wiping gravy from his chops.

'This is what you'll read out. Speak clearly. Now get going. The corporal knows the route. We'll be listening.'

The major turned on his heel, not wanting his dinner to get cold. I looked aghast at the script he had handed me, urging people to leave their wireless sets and take advantage of the Germans' Christmas offer. Hell, I was supposed to broadcast *this*?

The driver, a corporal, was regarding me with undisguised loathing for spoiling his Christmas. Tough. It was nothing to what they were doing to mine.

Sentries raised the barrier as we drove out of the

barracks towards the new pebble-dashed council estates above the Point. The loudspeaker van had been cobbled together in a hurry. Twisted wires fell from the speakers, through a hole in the roof, to an electrical box humming away in the back. I dropped the bakelite microphone deliberately. Sadly, it still worked.

'Do you know where we're going?' I asked the corporal in English. So far we had spoken only German.

'*Was?*'

'Do you know the route?'

'*Deutsch. Sprich Deutsch.*'

Good, he clearly didn't speak English. I slipped lower in my seat.

'*Remember to collect your free gifts of cigarettes and chocolate, tea and potatoes from your nearest junior school at three o'clock,*' I read out. '*Chocolate, cigarettes, tea and potatoes, all free at three o'clock at the nearest junior school.*'

'Louder.'

I repeated the message time after time as we crawled through the new estates, around the older streets surrounding the harbour and out along the coast road with its small square bungalows. It was almost three o'clock as we climbed towards Joan's neighbourhood. By now I had dropped my voice half an octave, and was doing a parody of a German speaking bad English. '*Chocolate, cigarettes, tea and potatoes, all free at three o'clock at the nearest junior school. Tell your friends in the army and the air force. Above all, tell the Marines. Remember, tell it to the Marines.'*

My body prickled with sweat as we drove into Joan's street. I sunk even lower, wishing I was invisible. As we crept past our house, I saw Joan pressing her head against the glass pane of her bedroom window. We did not acknowledge each other.

Mrs Harper was coming out of her front gate, a shopping bag over one arm. She looked neither right nor left but scuttled defiantly towards the school. Others were coming out of their homes – not many, just one or two here and there; mostly women. I noticed that no one greeted anyone else, no one wished another Merry Christmas. It was as if all believed themselves to be invisible. As many emerged from the slums of The Gut as from the semi-detached suburbs. They had one thing in common: they all looked guilty, and ready for a fight.

By half past three my voice had grown genuinely hoarse. I was expecting to be allowed home then but instead we drew up at the Sea Scouts drill hall where the region's response to the offer was being correlated. I was given the chore of logging the number of recipients from each city ward, and expressing it as a proportion of the population. It was a task any German clerk would have cherished – except they cherished having Christmas Day off more. Those on duty looked unhappy and took it out on me. Only the fact that I reported directly to Glass stopped them picking a fight. I only wished they'd try.

All the time, I wondered about the King's Speech. It was not until much later that night that Joan was able to tell me they'd been able to hear only parts of it through the interference. She had written it down for me. *'People of Britain . . . in this black hour . . . carry on the fight on land and by sea . . . right will prevail. The free countries of the new world . . . from under the monstrous darkness of Nazi rule . . . Now, there is only one way . . . We shall not give up. The fight is only just begun. God bless you all and keep you safe.'*

Joan told me how she, mum, Roy and David had stood for the National Anthem, feeling immeasurably proud. She didn't say how she felt about me.

'Christmas night is traditionally a time spent at home with one's family,' said Glass. 'So it'll be interesting to see how many people turn up.'

Lots and lots, I thought, remembering the clamour from the Friends of New Europe for invitations to Christmas Night drinks with the *Kommandant* and senior German officers at the Golf Club.

'Indeed, sir.'

Glass picked up on my irritation. 'You're a soldier on duty, Penny. Anyway, what else would you have done tonight?'

'Stayed with a friend, sir.'

'That girl I saw you with outside the cathedral?'

'No, sir. An old school friend.' Vee had gone to spend Christmas with her parents. I'd understand, she'd said. I wasn't sure I did.

A welcoming committee in evening dress stood in the entrance to the Golf Club. I wore the same slacks and Ted's old sports jacket that I'd put on when I'd left our house at lunchtime.

'I'm not dressed for this,' I blurted out.

Glass seemed to notice my clothes for the first time. 'Oh dear, what will they think, my aide being incorrectly dressed for the occasion.'

Under his urbane façade, Glass seemed to possess a strong streak of sadism. For all his professed love of England and the English, he was never happier than when humiliating them – or, in particular, me.

'We won't stay long. It's my privilege to arrive last and leave first. Ah, at least this time they are waiting for me. Not a very attractive bunch, are they? They're the type who'd do well in any situation. I'm glad you aren't like them, Penny.'

Glass possessed the ability to throw me off balance. One moment, I wanted to throttle him. The next I was blushing under his compliments.

'Thank you, sir.'

The car drew to a halt, the honour guard presented arms, and Sir Reginald Launcestone and Horace Smeed stepped forward.

'*Kommandant*, on behalf of the Friends of New Europe, we wish you a merry Christmas and a prosperous New Year.'

Then they saw me. If looks could kill, I'd have been a corpse. I discovered for the first time how it was possible for a group of short men to look down their noses at someone taller. As we climbed the stairs, the Lord Lieutenant snapped, 'What do you mean coming here dressed like that? You're a disgrace to your country.'

'I didn't know I was coming here,' I hissed back. 'I have better things to do than spend time with the likes—' I bit my tongue.

The elegant dining room was crowded with Englishmen in black tie and tails, their wives in their best pre-war frocks, and German officers in immaculately tailored dress uniforms. The dove grey of the SS, the brown of the Nazi Party, blue-grey of the *Luftwaffe*, the deeper blue of the *Kriegsmarine* mixed among the *Wehrmacht* field grey. Waiters in white ties glided through the throng, carrying trays of champagne flutes. A large new oil painting of Adolf Hitler illuminated by spotlights held pride of place on the far wall.

My stomach churned.

'May I present my wife Lady Launcestone and my son Henry.'

A plump, over-powdered woman with a huge diamond brooch on a dramatic bosom bobbed a curtsy in front of Glass. Behind her, the young Henry Launcestone's Adam's apple bounced up and down like a nervous yo-yo.

'The fat cow's got more snow on her face than the Eiger.' Glass muttered so rapidly that I only just caught what he said. His polite smile was still in place.

I cleared my throat. 'The *Kommandant* says it is a pleasure to meet such a charming and beautiful lady. She must be proud to have such a fine son.'

Lady Launcestone simpered.

Horace Smeed pushed forward. 'My wife Phyllis and our daughter April.'

England's fall had not troubled Mrs Smeed but her weight had plummeted when she'd discovered that her husband had bought his mistress a house by the harbour. Now her crushed velvet gown hung from her shoulders as if from a coat hanger. She wore a majestic triple string of pearls, far too opulent for her scrawny neck, to stop the mistress getting them.

April had horn-rimmed spectacles and the kind of frizzy mousy hair that made hair stylists give up and become shop assistants. I already knew her from the tennis club. She possessed the unnerving ability to play an intense game of mixed doubles while talking endlessly to her female opponent about the previous night's party. Maybe that was why she won so often.

'Did you avail yourself of our Christmas gifts this afternoon, Mr Smeed?' inquired Glass.

Smeed smirked. 'I sent the cook. Too good an offer to pass up.'

'So you heard the King's speech?'

'Hardly a word through the jamming.'

'But you tried to?'

Smeed rolled a Romeo y Julieta cigar nervously in his fingers. 'Ahem. Just wanted to see what claptrap they were coming out with, you know.'

I translated. Glass jerked as if he had been stung, and I wondered if I had made a mistake.

'Here! What did you say to the *Kommandant*?' Smeed snarled at me. 'If you're trying to land me in it, by God, I'll make your life such a bloody misery.'

'*Was sagt er?*'

'He thinks I'm deliberately mistranslating to land him in trouble.'

'And he threatened you?'

'Yes, he threatened me.'

Glass looked down at Smeed in a way that sent shivers up my spine. He spoke very slowly in English. '*You* will not make his life a misery. Only I can do that, understand?'

'Y – y – yes, *Kommandant*.' Smeed was already mopping his brow.

'*Komm*, Penny. You see, I protect you. I am your friend.'

If you were really my friend, you would not have brought me here, I thought, feeling the resentment of the others in the room swirl over me like waves. The

125

dignitaries were not only angry that a scruff like me had been allowed into their posh club, but more, they were jealous that I had the ear of the *Kommandant*.

Stuff them. I hooked two glasses off a passing tray.

'More champagne, sir.'

'Thank you, Penny. Isn't that the same girl I saw you with outside the Cathedral?'

The bitch! Vee, glowing in a tight-fitting little black number, escorted by a portly Supply Corps major. So much for Christmas night at home with her parents!

'Did you know she was coming here?'

'I didn't know *I* was coming.'

'It looks as if the Germans have won again.'

Vee gave a gasp when she spotted me. A succession of emotions flew across her face: surprise, guilt, irritation and, finally, feigned pleasure.

'Nick, darling! How good to see you. I didn't know you'd be here.'

'Obviously.'

'My parents insisted I came when Ludwig – Major Stresemann – invited me. It was very much a last-minute thing.' She glanced at Glass, now five feet away.

I hadn't seen the dress before. It looked expensive. By the care she had taken with her hair and make-up, I reckoned she must have been getting herself ready since breakfast.

'Enjoy yourself.'

'Don't get in a pet.'

'I won't. Excuse me.' I bowed stiffly and returned to Glass's elbow.

'Aren't you going to introduce me?'

'No. That's what she wants.'

Glass gave a bitter laugh. Percy Tickell, even more cadaverous in an old-fashioned dinner jacket green with age, hovered nearby to pay his respects.

'May I wish you a Merry Christmas, *Kommandant*?'

'You may indeed, *Herr* Tickell. You may also announce that as from tomorrow curfew will begin at seven p.m. New European Time in all areas where less than fifty per cent of the population took advantage of our Christmas offer.'

'That will cover the whole region, sir.'

'It will teach them not to be so ungrateful.'

'Indeed, sir.'

'I think SS *Standartenführer* Stolz wants your help, Penny.'

I had been doing my best to avoid Stolz's increasingly impatient gestures. Reluctantly I went over to where police superintendent Norman Bearup was nodding gravely – not understanding a word – as Stolz expounded on the newly proposed population register.

Well over six feet tall and built proportionally, Bearup had once been known as a hard man, but now his paunch pressed against his waistband, his ruddy face had turned puffy, and tufts of hair grew out of his ears.

'It'll be a pleasure,' he replied once I'd translated. 'You can't have too much information on people. You might be a good citizen today, but who knows what crime you'll commit tomorrow. Good records are vital, absolutely vital.'

'Don't forget to include the possession of wireless sets,' ordered Stolz. 'And religion.'

'That's no problem. I can colour-code and cross-reference the categories. It's straightforward.'

Those two seemed to share a common language. April Smeed reappeared. 'Sergeant Penny, will you ask the *Kommandant* if he'll be so kind as to come and speak at one of my ladies' mornings? We'd all be so grateful.'

I dutifully translated.

'Do I have to? I'd be bored stiff with such a bunch of stupid, plain girls,' replied Glass, once again displaying his knack of appearing to be pleasantly civil while in fact being utterly rude.

'His Excellency would be honoured. He cannot wait. The sooner the better.' Two could play at that game.

'Do thank him.'

'*Danke*.'

'*Ihr könnt mich alle mal am Arsch lecken*.'

'What did the *Kommandant* say?' April thought she recognized a familiar word.

'He was quoting Goethe.'

Glass snorted and turned away.

'You're so lucky being able to speak German. I mean, it's such an advantage nowadays, isn't it?' April leaned closer to me so I could smell her scent. Her eyes, catlike green behind her thick lenses, burned brightly. 'Roy says you'll be a great asset to us.'

'What!'

She gave a peal of laughter, as my jaw dropped in astonishment. 'What you see isn't always what you get, you know. We'll have you on our side yet.'

I didn't tell her I'd signed up last night. Instead we carried on chatting as Vee fired a machine-gun belt of hatred at us from across the room, jealous that this millionaire's daughter and I were laughing together like best friends. Vee's sour looks, and the champagne, made me feel better. I was on my third glass when the Lord Lieutenant's braying caught my attention.

'The beggar counted on everyone being tucked up at home, Christmas morning, but Ransome and the keepers were waiting for him. God, he put up a hell of a fight. Ransome's in hospital with a broken collar-bone. This time I'm going to make sure the magistrates send Tibby away for a long stretch.'

'Get the police to charge him with assault.'

'Good idea. I say, Bearup . . .'

'Sir Reginald?'

'My keepers have just had a set-to with the poacher Med Tibby. I want him charged with assaulting Ransome. No more pussyfooting around, d'you hear?'

'I'll attend to it, Sir Reginald.'

'I can't stand much more of this, Penny,' murmured Glass.

'It'd be impolite to leave before the food is served.'

'I do not need a lesson in manners,' he bristled. 'Hold my champagne while I get my damned pills.' He shook two tablets from his gunmetal holder. 'I shouldn't really take these with drink – but you are right, I should stay. No more than ten minutes, though.'

The sound of a knife striking crystal announced that the hot buffet was about to arrive. We all turned to face the doorway as the head waiter entered, carrying the boar's head on a great platter. He marched majestically down the length of the room, as a line of waitresses in black skirts and white blouses followed behind with salvers of meats and fowls. The third waitress to enter, bearing a large capon, was my sister Joan.

7

The man's body lay on its back among tussocks of grass still white with frost. He wore a *Wehrmacht* jacket, rumpled up around his middle, and he was naked from the waist down, apart from grey socks. The first thing to catch the eye, even before his battered face, was the man's balls: bruised black, blue and yellow and swollen to twice their normal size. Not something you want to see on a Boxing Day morning – but then, Boxing Day 1940 was a working day.

Glass curled his lip in distaste and walked back to the edge of the cordoned-off area where *Feldgendarmerie* and local CID officers stood in separate clusters. To one side, *Standartenführer* Stolz was dictating orders to an aide.

Detective Superintendent Bearup cleared his throat. 'The body was found at eight o'clock this morning by a postman, John Bolly.'

'Time of death?' inquired Glass.

'That's difficult to say, sir. The doctor's not willing to commit himself, but he's certainly been here overnight. We don't know if anything's been taken because we're not allowed to examine the body.'

'Any incident involving German personnel must be investigated by German authorities,' confirmed Glass. 'You understand that, superintendent?'

'We're here to offer whatever assistance *Standartenführer* Stolz requires, sir.'

Glass dismissed him and called over the *Feldpolizei* lieutenant. 'Well?'

'*Oberschütze* Tristan Braunbaum, aged thirty, from Leipzig. Failed to report at 08.00 this morning. Last seen at his billet in Ropemakers Yard at 19.00 Christmas Eve. He was off duty yesterday.'

'And no one's seen him since Christmas Eve?'

'Apparently not, sir.'

'What's been taken?'

'Trousers, underpants, paybook, wallet and watch. We don't know what else he had on him. His pockets are empty. Identity discs still present. Cause of death appears to be multiple head wounds, but we'll know more after the post-mortem at the German hospital this afternoon, sir.'

'This soldier was murdered by English terrorists,' announced Stolz.

'English terrorist' sounded much the same in both languages so Bearup got the gist. 'That's not right, sir,' he protested. 'For my money, it's a queer-bashing that went over the top. That public lavatory over there is a well-known meeting place for queers.'

'How would a German know that?'

'Queers have a way of finding each other.'

'You're wrong,' snapped Stolz. 'I've been expecting a terror campaign for some time.'

'I can't see any evidence to suggest—' began Bearup.

'Our police methods are different from yours.'

Something about the *Gestapo* man's determination to pin the killing on the Resistance worried me. I raised the subject in the car on the way back to the *Feldkommandantur*. 'With respect, sir, this murder's got nothing to do with the Resistance. Why would they take away his trousers? Why kick his balls to bits?'

'Penny, you are too logical,' yawned Glass, closing the subject.

I wondered how much of Stolz's anger had been caused by the posters that had appeared overnight, topped by a V-for-Victory symbol, reporting the King's speech in full. They had been stuck on shop windows, post boxes, walls, even on parked German cars and lorries. Many people had been very busy – and very brave – during the hours of darkness.

First thing this morning, Tickell had ordered the Shire Hall's cleaners out onto the streets to peel and scrub them off. The women went on deliberate go-slow. When the *Wehrmacht* had been drafted in to help, the women stopped work completely and began catcalling and jeering instead.

The poster blitz had unsettled the Germans inside the *Feldkommandantur*, making them surly and suspicious. I was glad when I could get away for my lunchtime sanity stroll.

As I returned, I ran into Simon Jenner, in a homburg and dark overcoat, coming down the steps.

'Hello,' I greeted him.

Simon walked straight past me. There were snubs, and snubs, and I'd become a master at receiving them, but this was special – it really hurt. I didn't understand. Despite our seven-year age difference, we'd always got on, and Jacob and Miriam had been like second parents to me. I went after him.

'Simon. Dr Jenner.'

'What! Oh, hello, Nick.' It seemed as if Simon wakened from a dream. 'Forgive me, I was miles away.'

'Are you all right?'

'Yes, um, I've just had a bit of a . . .' Simon shook his head slowly. He looked pale and kept blinking. 'I've just left the County Solicitor, or whatever they call him nowadays.'

'Tickell?'

'Yes, Percy Tickell. I went to register my taking over of Dr McIlvaney's practice. But apparently I can't.'

'Can't what?'

'Can't practise. There's going to be a new law, from the first of January, banning Jews from public service and from practising as doctors, lawyers or teachers.' Simon spoke in a disjointed way, as if not believing what he was saying. 'He said it wasn't worth me starting.'

'But they can't stop you being a doctor. That's not right.'

'It's happened in Germany.'

'What will you do?'

'I don't know . . . I haven't had a chance to think.'

'If there's any way I can help.'

'Rewrite my family tree?'

Back in the *Feldkommandantur* I was still trying to work out the ramifications of Simon's news when I was summoned to translate at a meeting in Glass's office. I was not made to feel welcome. Tickell eyed me coldly, obviously resenting my friendship with Glass, and Bearup ignored me, while Stolz's little eyes glittered with suspicion.

'SS *Oberführer* Professor Dr Six demands ten hostages . . .' Stolz was saying.

'*Militärbefehlshaber London* has asked for only five,' countered Glass.

'All right, five hostages – as long as the English

realize that acts of violence against the German Armed Forces will not be tolerated. The killer has twenty-four hours to give himself up.'

'Then what happens?'

'We shoot the hostages.'

'What do we know about this Braunbaum's movements?' asked Glass.

'He was seen drinking by himself in three public houses not normally used by German troops, on Christmas Eve,' replied Bearup. 'Two of them, the Crown and the White Swan, are known to be frequented by queers. The Swan is only three hundred yards from where the body was found. We could try to track down drinkers who were there that night. Maybe some of them saw something.'

'Don't waste your time,' sneered Stolz.

'Was there any evidence of sexual activity?' I inquired.

'These things do not concern you.' Stolz swung savagely towards me. 'Braunbaum was murdered by terrorists, I tell you.'

Stolz's venom shook me. I looked to the other Englishmen for support. No one was prepared to meet my eye, although Bearup tried again.

'There's a gang of hoodlums who go in for queer-bashing around the St Austell Road public urinal, where Braunbaum was found. I could pull them in for questioning.'

'Superintendent, you are not listening. The terrorists have twenty-four hours to give themselves up – then we will shoot the hostages as a lesson to others.'

'How do you know *Oberschütze* Braunbaum was not killed by fellow Germans?'

Stolz ignored me. He did not want to catch the murderer. That was why he was refusing CID help. He just wanted an excuse to kill five Englishmen.

'Is this legally proper, *Herr Sekretär* Tickell?' inquired Glass.

'Oh, yes. Both Articles Five and Six set out the option of reprisals in the event of sabotage or hostile acts against the occupying forces.'

'*Herr* Tickell, you must learn the language of occupation,' sneered Stolz. 'In theory we do not take reprisals. We conduct *Vergeltungsaktionen . . .*'

'Retaliatory measures,' I translated.

'. . . And we do not take hostages. We have *Sühnepersonen.*'

'Expiators.'

'Very well,' said Glass. 'Braunbaum will be buried with full military honours at midday tomorrow. If the killers have not come forward by then, we will execute the hostages.'

'You can't just shoot five innocent people,' I protested.

'Who says they are innocent?' it suited Stolz to reply. 'Here's a list of prisoners in the city jail. Super-intendent, choose five of them.'

'Some of these are on remand.'

'Just choose five.'

Bearup produced a fountain pen from his inside pocket. 'These two broke into an old lady's home and strangled her, although we can't prove it. They'll be no loss to society.' He warmed to his task. 'This one's a hit man for a London gang – one born to be hanged. This one's been in trouble all his life, never going to go straight.' He scanned the list, pen poised. 'And this poacher – include him and you'll be doing the Lord Lieutenant a favour.'

'That's agreed, then. Until tomorrow afternoon,' said Glass.

Four British *Freikorps* volunteers, with the cross of St George on the shoulders of their field-grey uniforms, were hogging the bar of the Three Horseshoes. I moved on to the snug.

'Why didn't you tell me about April?' I asked when Roy and Mills joined me.

'Security,' replied Mills. 'April shouldn't have said anything.'

'What shouldn't I have said?' She appeared from behind the door and grinned at me.

'Anything,' Roy repeated, putting his arm around her.

'Why? He's a friend, isn't he?'

The buzz of conversation from the public bar grew

louder as a whole evening's drinking was crammed into the hour before curfew.

'One day, young lady, you'll tell someone who's not a friend, and then we'll all be in trouble.' Mills sounded deadly serious and April blushed.

'Sorry, I promise it won't happen again.' She gave Roy a kiss on the cheek. 'I've got to get those posters onto the milk lorries before curfew. See you tomorrow. Bye, Nick.'

'How long have you two been . . .?'

'Not long,' replied Roy. 'She's invaluable. A spy in the enemy camp, so to speak.'

'Just like me.' I brought out two curfew passes I'd lifted from Tickell's office. 'You'll have to pretend to be a council workman on an emergency job – gritting the road, something like that.' Mills and Roy inspected the passes like schoolboys who had just found the one cigarette card they needed to complete the set. Then I went on to tell them of the five hostages and how Bearup had included Med Tibby on the list.

'Stolz's itching to teach us all a lesson. He insists that the killing was the work of the Resistance.'

'It wasn't,' said Roy, shortly. 'I promise you it wasn't.'

'Can we free Med in time?'

'If you mean an armed raid on the prison? No.' Mills dismissed the option out of hand. 'It would just provoke more trouble.'

'Can we bribe a prison guard?'

'There's not much time. Do you know anyone working inside the prison?' Mills asked Roy.

Roy shook his head. 'Could we put out the word for the real killers to come forward?'

'They're not going to do that, are they? No one's ever going to offer themselves up for execution.'

'Maybe if they tell the Germans it was a queer-bashing—'

'Stolz would suppress it.' I cut him short.

'You and the *Kommandant* are very matey. Can't you use your influence?'

'What influence?'

A policeman held up the traffic to allow a convoy of three furniture vans to rumble past, heading towards the docks. Each van had a *Luftwaffe* driver and guard on board. They were escorted by two motorbike-sidecar combinations and a scout car. I wondered what local art treasures had taken the eye of Fatty Göring.

'Fancy meeting you.' Vee Harper materialized alongside me, smart in her red coat and pillbox hat.

'Hello.' I was still cross with her over last night. 'Where's your Ludwig, then?'

'He's not my Ludwig.' Vee pouted. 'I only went because my parents nagged me. Please don't be cross. I don't like it when you're cross.' She threaded her arm through mine, determined to keep bright and cheerful. 'We could go for a drink?'

'Sorry, haven't got time.'

'This curfew is the pits. How's a girl expected to enjoy herself when she's locked in by seven o'clock?' She giggled. 'Mind you, it depends who you're locked in with.'

Despite my resolutions to be distant, I couldn't help smiling. It was hard not to enjoy the envious glances from passers-by.

'It's a shame you haven't got a curfew pass, or you could come back to my place.'

'Never mind.'

'*Don't* you have one?' Vee sounded incredulous.

'No.'

'Mr Smeed's got a pass and so has April.'

'Can't Ludwig get you one?'

'You know he can't. The Germans are being terribly strict.' She gazed up into my eyes. 'Think of the fun we could have if we *both* had passes. We could go out for dinners, then back to my place. I'd be ever so nice to you – and it wouldn't matter what time you went home, would it?'

The first thing I noticed, as I took off my greatcoat, was one of the precious curfew passes on the sideboard made out in the name of Joan Pendleton, valid for the following week.

'The Golf Club's pulled strings.' Joan busied herself sweeping up pine needles that had fallen off the Christmas tree. She was uncomfortable talking about her new job. During married life Joan had grown accustomed to being waited on; now she was doing the waiting, though I hadn't understood why.

'Money, Nick. We need the money, simple as that,' she'd explained on returning home late last night.

'But you've got my army pay to help.'

'It's not a lot, is it? Oh, please don't think me ungrateful. God only knows how much longer we'd have coped if you hadn't come home. The little savings Ted and I put together have long gone. But, even with your wages, we're living hand to mouth. I had to borrow the money to buy David's bike.'

I discovered later that she had pawned her diamond earrings – a present from Ted to celebrate their fifth wedding anniversary.

'But why a waitress?'

'I have to take what I can. I'm not qualified as a teacher or secretary, or anything like that. Shops are closing down, and I don't fancy factory work. Anyway, being a waitress shouldn't offend your socialist principles.'

'Sis, I think you're wonderful.'

I was tucking into my Boxing Day tea of leftover pheasant with boiled potatoes and beetroot when mum came down from her room, wringing her handkerchief.

'Nick, you are going to have to do something for Mr Tibby,' she said. 'He's been very good to us. He gave us that pheasant you're eating. You must speak to the *Kommandant*.'

'It's not that easy, mum.' The shed door opened and closed as David put away his bike. He made a beeline through the kitchen to the hall door.

'Don't you want any tea?' Joan called after him.

'I'm not hungry.'

'Look at your shoes – and your trousers! David! It looks as though you've been rolling in the mud. Come here and let me see.'

'I'm all right.'

'Turn around.'

Reluctantly, David did so, to reveal the finest black eye I'd seen for years.

'I fell off my bike,' he muttered sullenly.

But Joan's maternal antennae were twitching. 'You've been fighting. Your lip's cut, too. What have I told you about fighting! Who was it?'

A silver star slipped off the Christmas tree and rolled across the kitchen floor.

'No one you know.' David scuffed his feet on the linoleum.

'Why were you fighting?' Joan bent to retrieve the star from under the table.

'Doesn't matter.'

'It does.'

'Mu-um.' There was a tearful quality in David's plea for his mother not to persist.

'I want to know why you were fighting?'

'They said Uncle Nick was a Nazi collaborator.'

8

 **Vergeltungsaktionen.**

Militärbefehlshaber London has announced that five expiators will be executed at noon today, 27th December 1940, if those responsible for the death of the German soldier found murdered on rough land off the St Austell Road yesterday morning do not come forward.

Further acts of cowardly violence against the German Armed Forces, in violation of the Declaration of Occupation, Articles V and VI, will be met with similar swift and decisive action.

The people have only themselves to blame for their misfortunes.

Let this be a lesson.

Heil Hitler!

It was almost mid-morning when I intercepted Detective Superintendent Bearup lumbering down the corridor towards the front hall, his green tweed suit out of place among the German uniforms.

'Has anyone been arrested for the killing?'

'Why do you want to know?' He made no effort to stop.

'Med Tibby's a friend.' I fell in beside him.

Bearup regarded me through watery blue eyes. 'Then choose your friends more carefully.'

'Are the Germans making any efforts to find the killer?'

'Why would I know? I'm only in charge of CID here. Don't waste my time.'

'They can't just shoot Med.'

'Why not? He's been a thorn in the side of law-abiding citizens for as long as I've known him.'

'You mean a thorn in the backside of the landed bloody gentry.'

Bearup ground to a halt and pointed a truncheon-like finger at me. 'You watch your tongue.'

'He's been good to my mother.'

'If Tibby ever gives her anything you can bet it's been stolen. She should know better.'

We reached the top of the stairs, where the enormous painting of Hitler glared belligerently over the foyer.

'You can't just stand by and see an innocent man shot.'

'It's nothing to do with me. This is up to the Germans.'

I grabbed him by the arm. 'You put Med on the death list.'

'So I did.' Bearup removed my hand with a bear-like paw and slowly descended the red carpeted stairs towards the armed SS guards.

I got to see Tickell at eleven o'clock. He was drinking tea from a fine china cup. Three Marie biscuits sat on a matching plate on his desk.

'You can tell the *Kommandant* that the women cleaners have been disciplined,' he began. 'The ring-leaders have been dismissed and the rest will lose three days' wages.'

'It's the hostages I wanted to talk about.'

It was as if a portcullis dropped across Tickell's face. 'We have to let the law take its course.'

'Where in the law does it say you can take inno-cent people hostage and shoot them whenever it suits?'

Tickell nibbled at a biscuit, his little finger jutting at an acute angle. 'They wouldn't be in prison if they were innocent.'

'Med Tibby is there on remand. He's innocent until proved guilty, remember.'

Tickell's mouth snapped shut, then opened. 'You forget yourself.'

'Maybe *you* do.'

'The local people are themselves morally respon-sible for the deaths of these men. We agreed to lay down our arms. We have no right to strike the

Germans in the back. If that soldier had not been murdered, they would not now be obliged to punish us. This is a matter for the Germans and the Germans alone.'

'Except that the Germans are murdering your countrymen in cold blood.'

Tickell bit into the biscuit with such force that crumbs spilled onto the cream carpet. As I left, he was down on his hands and knees, picking them up.

My hands were shaking as I got back to my office. I tried to tell myself that the Germans were only bluffing. No one could be that barbaric. Then I glanced out of the window into the central courtyard, and my stomach lurched. Workmen were breaking up the cobbles to insert five wooden stakes. Lengths of rope lay ready beside each.

Hauser cocked an eyebrow as I hurried into the outer office. 'The general has to go out in two minutes. Is it urgent?'

'Very.' I tapped on the door and went in.

Glass was scanning a document, his pen speeding over the lines. 'Yes?'

I took a deep breath. 'With respect, sir, I'd like you to spare the life of Med Tibby.'

'Indeed!' Glass began initialling a pile of papers. 'I'm told he is an inveterate poacher, and also part gypsy – the very sort of antisocial element we should be eradicating.'

'He's got a wife and young daughter.'

'So had many other men who have died. Do you know this Tibby?'

'He helped my mother when times were hard for her. Before I returned.'

Glass finally looked up to find me still standing stiffly to attention. 'All right.'

My eyes closed in relief. 'Thank you, sir.'

'You want me to substitute another man for Tibby?'

'Ah, no, sir . . .'

'We need five expiators. Five's the minimum that London will tolerate.' Glass picked up his hat and single glove from the corner of his desk. 'I must attend Braunbaum's funeral. Tell Stolz I have agreed to replace Tibby on the list of those to be executed.'

I left Glass's office feeling physically sick. I did not want to sentence another man to death; I just wanted to save Med. My legs grew heavier with each step towards the *Gestapo* wing. The SS sentry shook his head curtly at my pass. 'That's not valid here.'

This was my way out; my way of doing nothing. I rejected the thought. The minutes were ticking by. Already it was eleven-forty. Twenty minutes to the execution.

'I need to see *Standartenführer* Stolz. It's a matter of life and death.'

Surprisingly, Stolz agreed to see me. It was quiet

in this wing, with none of the hustle and bustle of the main building. I remembered that Glass and Hauser had both warned me against coming here.

Stolz was standing in front of a roaring fire, hands locked behind his back. The carpet was thicker than in Glass's office and there was the lingering smell of fresh paint. Huge photographs of Hitler and Himmler stared down from the walls. A smaller, signed one of Himmler stood on a Hepplewhite side table.

'With respect, *Standartenführer*, *Generalleutnant* von Glass wishes you to release the expiator Tibby.'

'Does he!' Stolz strutted behind his desk. He held out his hand. 'The order.'

'He was just leaving to go to the funeral, sir. He asked me to tell you in person.'

'Indeed! What's your interest in this matter?'

Reluctantly, I confessed that Tibby was a friend.

'How do I know you're not making up this reprieve?' Stolz peered at me through his steel-rimmed spectacles.

'You'll be able to verify what I say when the *Kommandant* returns. You'll still hold Tibby in custody. I'll still be here.'

He nodded. 'Very well. If you are found to be lying, you will be punished and this man Tibby will be shot anyway.'

'Yes, sir.' I'd be damned if I'd let him see how frightened I was.

Stolz picked up a sheet of paper. 'Here is the roll of prisoners currently in the City Jail. Pick one.'

'What!'

'Choose one to take the place of your friend.'

'Me?'

'Yes, you – you decide.'

'That's not fair.'

'It's called responsibility.' Stolz was enjoying watching me squirm.

I regarded the alphabetical list with loathing. 'How do I know which of these has committed what?'

'Does it matter? Murderers, rapists, wife-beaters, drunks, thieves – they are all there.'

'I can't do it.'

'Then Tibby dies, and you are wasting my time.'

I looked away and jabbed with a finger. 'Edwards, Jasper.'

Stolz consulted another list. 'Stole two loaves of bread during curfew.' He went to pick up the phone.

'No, no. You can't kill him for that.'

'I'm not about to – *you* are.'

'Let me do it again, please.'

'Your conscience will be the death of your friend.'

I closed my eyes and jabbed again. 'Strong, Trevor.'

'Better,' announced Stolz. 'Assault on a police officer. Has a string of convictions for violence. So you think *he* deserves to die.'

The only man I felt deserved to die at that moment was Stolz. Why was he doing this, playing out this charade?

I didn't know what to say. I was still searching for words when a volley of gunshots echoed from the courtyard.

Ten minutes to twelve?

'I ordered the executions brought forward,' said Stolz. 'Didn't anyone tell you?'

I said a silent prayer for Med Tibby, and another to give myself the strength to get out of this room without throttling the smirking midget in front of me.

Notices announcing the executions were put up all over the region. By next morning, they had been ripped down. New ones were quickly pasted up and policemen ordered to keep an eye on them. Most of these were again destroyed overnight; others were found with poppies stuck to them. The Germans were forced to step up patrols around the spot where John Godwin, the boy who had shaken his fist at the SS, had been killed, to prevent it becoming a shrine.

This test of wills between conquerors and conquered was the first collective act of disobedience from a population that, up to now, had been cowed and quiescent.

The initial phase of the occupation, when humiliation had been perversely welcomed, was passing. It had been the Time of the Ostrich – pretend nothing has happened – and it was drawing to a close. Resentment was taking its place.

Glasgow, living up to its reputation as a hard town, was soon to become locked into a spiral of protest and violence, until fifty civilians – mostly communists and dockers' leaders – were executed following the massacre of a five-strong *Wehrmacht* patrol.

Glass did not mention Tibby's death, and I did not raise it, but I kept my anger tight inside me. I blamed my fellow Englishmen more than I blamed Stolz. You expected that sort of behaviour from the *Gestapo*, but I'd thought that Tickell and Bearup would do the decent thing.

A little piece of me died that day. There would be greater blows and greater betrayals, but Med's death was the start of a hardening process.

'You did your best,' Roy comforted me the night of Med's execution as I got morosely drunk. Roy locked me in the Three Horseshoes to stop me attacking the first passing German patrol, promised that Med's wife and daughter would never want for anything, and encouraged me to drink and rage until eventually I passed out.

New Year's Eve was hardly noticed because of the seven p.m. curfew. Only the birth of Barbara's healthy baby daughter, weighing six pounds two ounces, on New Year's Day 1941 provided any reason for cheer. It was very much a family affair, with Simon delivering the baby and Anna acting as nurse. Miriam, ever mother to the whole world, was delighted, and fussed over Barbara as if she was her own.

The baby was named Hope.

Jacob produced bottles of champagne from somewhere and we celebrated. Even our mum made the effort to come and see the new baby, although she could not help wondering aloud what sort of world was this to bring a baby into.

'Let's pray that it's one which will get better as Hope grows stronger,' replied Miriam.

9

The late-January afternoon was crackling with frost as we left the Chapel Hill football ground, part of the good-humoured crowd still buzzing with City's 3–1 victory over Bristol Rovers. It was just like the old times, spending a winter Saturday watching soccer, except our unexpected win had been due to the brilliance of Otto Klein as City's centre forward.

Still discussing the game, Roy, David and I sauntered down the middle of the road, David in the red and white scarf Joan had knitted.

'Give Klein his due,' I argued. 'That run from inside his own half to score that second goal was something special, eh, David? And the way he headed that third goal.'

'Yeh, suppose so,' he said begrudgingly.

The problem was that Klein was a corporal in a local *Wehrmacht* signals unit. He was also Germany's international centre forward whose skilful passing and dribbling runs had won reluctant applause from the home crowd, and enthusiastic cheers from the German troops on the Tump behind the goal.

The game was the result of my suggestion made before Christmas. Glass had promised that if today was a success, he would recommend restarting a limited football league across England. Both Roy and David were totally against the idea of including Germans in English teams.

'Come on, David, Jim Macksey couldn't have scored those goals. Klein won us that game.'

'I don't care.' David started nibbling silently on his Cornish pasty. He loved football – and hated the Germans. Germans being good at football confused him.

At the crossroads, David set off in the falling dusk to climb the long hill home to Mountroyal, while we two headed for the Three Horseshoes. Once we were alone, I handed Roy a piece of buff cardboard.

'This is the new curfew pass due to be issued from Monday.'

'It's not too different from the present one so it shouldn't be too hard to forge,' Roy decided. 'What we really need is one of Glass's personal stamps.'

'We've been through this already. If it was ever found, it'd be bloody obvious who'd nicked it. *You* go and be interrogated by Stolz, if you like. He scares the life out of me. He's sinister.'

'What do you expect? He's German.'

We rounded the corner into Water Street. The winding cobbled street was normally a picture-post-card scene of low Georgian houses and old shops with bowed mullioned windows. But now that postcard had been defaced. *Jewish Business* had been scrawled in white paint across the glass windows of Jenner's Tea Rooms, while a banner stretching across the top of the building proclaimed: *This shop is owned by Jews*.

Two burly SS men were waving a mother with a pram away from the café doorway while other pedestrians were crossing the road to avoid the bullies. Only one elderly woman with a walking stick confronted them.

The larger of the men shouted at her. *'Gehen Sie. Gehen Sie, schnell.'*

'I don't understand a word you're saying but there's no need to shout.' The woman motioned for the SS man to move aside. He shouted at her even louder. She put her hand on his burly chest – level with her white hair – and gently pushed him away. She was followed into the café by a tirade of foul-mouthed abuse. In spite, the SS men shoved the next woman shopper who passed them sprawling into the gutter.

'Fuck this.' Roy strode towards the café doorway. I hurried after him. It was not often Roy lost his temper, but when he did, he took no prisoners. I'd been there when he'd single-handedly cleared the bar after strangers had insulted his mother. But now was not the time for fury.

'Cool down,' I hissed. 'You can't afford to get into trouble.'

The nearer SS man waved us away, pointing towards the painted message.

'*Nein. Verboten.*'

'What's this Kraut saying?'

'He says you're forbidden from going in.'

'You fucking watch me, sunshine,' spat Roy at the German.

Oh Jesus! Any second, there was going to be an explosion. And, whatever happened in the short term, there would be only one long-term winner. It would not be Roy.

'Under the Agreement of Occupation you have no legal right to prevent us entering this shop,' I told the SS man in German. 'If you try to stop us, I shall report your conduct to the *Befehlshabern der SS.*'

Before the startled German could reply, I pushed Roy on through the doorway. Half a dozen waitresses with white starched pinnies were huddling nervously together behind the counter. The neatly laid tables were empty apart from the old lady who had just entered.

'You shouldn't be here.' Miriam Jenner bustled up to us. 'You will get into trouble.'

Typical Miriam, worrying about everyone but herself.

'Us!' exclaimed Roy. 'What about you?'

'Ach! Do not worry about me. The Germans do not like the Jews, it's as simple as that.'

'I thought it was the Nazis who didn't like the Jews.'

'The Nazis rule the Germans. It is the same thing.' Miriam held up a plump finger. 'I will fix you a special *Jägertee* but don't tell anyone I have spirits here or they will close me down.'

There was something pathetically noble in the way she bustled bravely around, making an effort not to let the waitresses see how frightened she really was.

'When did all this happen?' I asked.

'About an hour ago.'

'While many people were at the soccer match.'

'What could I do? A lorryload of SS men came and started painting over the windows. When I asked them to stop, they threatened to pour paint all over me. They want to drive us out of business.'

'Swine!'

'Ach, Jacob and I are old. It doesn't matter to us. But what will happen to Simon, Anna and the twins? They've already stopped Simon practising as a doctor – what's he supposed to do if there's no family business to run? How will they live?'

'Why didn't you call the police?'

'Sergeant Hupple stood there and watched them do it. When he knew I'd spotted him, he slunk away. He's had his last free piece of *strudel* at my back door.'

'I expect he was powerless,' I suggested.

'I expect he was,' agreed Miriam, with her usual kindness.

'How can he be powerless?' demanded Roy. 'Come on, Nick, you reckon the Germans are keen to show they respect the law, yet those bullies are breaking the law and getting away with it. That can't be right!'

'They follow the letter of the law only when it suits them,' I explained.

Late the next afternoon, I stood outside the Jenners' home, smelling the damp evening air, and listened as two violins and a piano played a Mozart sonata inside. The notes spoke of sad, unfulfilled dreams, and made me yearn for times past. Next door, all the lights were burning in my old home. Stars were beginning to twinkle in the gloom as a party of worshippers hurried home from Sunday evensong. I waited, until the last tremulous note of the violin had faded, before knocking. It sounded intrusively loud in the twilight. Anyone knocking at this time of night was likely to be a policeman or from the *Gestapo*. I knocked again. Softer this time.

'It's me. Nick Penny.' I called through the letter box.

Jacob unlocked the door, violin still in one hand. 'It's good to see you, Nick. Miriam told me what a brave thing you did yesterday. Thank you.'

'I just wanted to make sure you were both all

right.' By now I knew that the Jenner bakery and their other two cafés had also been daubed with paint – together with businesses like Rosenthal's Bon Marché, Bloom's sweet shops and Greene's second-hand furniture store. Until the SS got to work with their paint pots, I had never thought of these places as being owned by Jews.

The drawing room was crowded. Simon stood by the piano, violin in hand, Miriam on the sofa next to Anna, while Barbara was sitting in the corner, murmuring gently to her baby daughter Hope, clasped to her chest.

What surprised me was the tubby German army private who rose from the piano and bowed to me shyly.

Jacob introduced us. 'Nick Penny, Hans Bleicher.'

'Honoured to meet you,' he said. 'I've heard a lot about you.'

The German wore thick spectacles and the green *Waffenfarbe* of the motorized infantry. It was difficult to imagine anyone who looked less like a front-line soldier.

'This is our friend who brought the ointment for my hands when I had that rash,' explained Jacob.

'Now I'm back here, I'll get you some more from the *Wehrmacht* pharmacy,' said Bleicher. 'It is a small token of my gratitude. When I'm in this house, I am reminded of my loved ones in Germany. Making music here helps me overcome my homesickness.'

It was a pretty speech but later I learned that ten years previously Bleicher had been promoted to a post that enabled him to learn English only by denouncing his two Jewish superiors in an Augsburg printing plant.

'It was very kind of you to escort me home last night, Nick. At one point I thought Roy was going to hit that nasty man,' said Miriam. 'I don't want him to get into trouble with the Germans.'

'Please, do not lump all of us Germans with the SS,' cried Bleicher. 'I am mortified at what they did to your shops.'

'What will happen when you reopen tomorrow?' I asked Miriam.

She shrugged. 'The brave will come in. Others won't.'

'Mother and Joan will call in for morning coffee. And I'll be down at lunchtime.'

'You are too good.' A tear welled in Miriam's eye. 'My little old ladies are a match for any SS man but I worry about our suppliers. If the Germans – sorry, the SS – get to them . . .'

'How is Hope?' I smiled towards Barbara.

'She's fine, thank you,' said Barbara shyly. It was difficult to get the girl to say more than two words.

'She's the spit of her mother, aren't you, my precious,' said Miriam, gently pulling back the shawl so that I could see the baby's tiny features. 'She's got Barbara's mouth and eyes.'

'She cries a lot,' muttered Barbara, rearranging the shawl.

'All babies cry,' reassured Miriam. 'You're a sweetheart, aren't you? We have to watch the twins, mind. They think Hope's some sort of doll.'

'May we play Mendelssohn next?' requested Bleicher. 'His music is banned in Germany so it'll be a treat for me.'

'Come.' Miriam gestured to me, and patted the sofa beside her.

I had plenty of time before I was due to meet Roy off the train so for the next half an hour I listened as the three musicians played the Jew Mendelssohn's first sonata. There was Jacob, grey head nodding in time with the melody; Simon, intense, technically more correct than his father, but lacking the deeper insight; and Bleicher, holding it all together with understated artistry on the piano.

It was a memory that I would cherish in the times ahead.

The once-proud station was begrimed with soot, and sorely in need of fresh coats of brown and cream paint. The waiting room was locked and the chocolate machine rusty from disuse. A one-armed porter was half-heartedly sweeping the platform with a broom while the few remaining weak overhead lights washed the scene in a depressing monochromatic dullness.

'Any idea when the London train's due?' I asked the ticket collector.

'It's running about three-quarters of an hour late.'

'That's going to be close to curfew.' Roy and I would have to run to reach the Three Horseshoes in time.

'Tell that to the Germans.'

The train pulled into the station one hour late. A khaki haversack over his shoulder, Roy alighted from a third-class carriage. He was taking his time. I noticed Vee Harper stepping down from a first-class compartment with a small overnight bag and vanity case, her hair looking blonder than ever. I quickly hid behind a crowd of *Wehrmacht* soldiers returning from leave with their kitbags and rifles. Once Roy was satisfied we were not being watched, he came over and handed me an oilskin packet. I dropped it into the pocket of my greatcoat with its all-protecting swastika armband.

'How's your uncle?' It was important to try to sound normal.

'Not too good,' replied Roy. 'I don't reckon he's much longer for this world.'

The *Feldpolizei* at the ticket barriers were picking on random travellers, making them open up their cases on the platform. One flustered young mother with a little boy was finding it impossible to refasten her bulging case so Roy went to help her. Mills had impressed on us that we should do nothing to attract attention, and here was Roy doing his Knight Errant impression. There was only one thing for me to do – go and help as well. I sat on the case after the blushing woman had poked her underwear back inside, while Roy used his strength to push the two clasps together. God knew how she was ever going to carry it, but we had our own problems.

While I was waved through the checkpoint, Roy was made to empty his haversack.

'We are going to have our work cut out to get to the pub before curfew,' I grumbled once he had been cleared.

'No problem,' reassured Roy. 'There'll be no one around on a Sunday night.'

We stepped out into the forecourt to find a platoon of German infantry, standing at ease next to three Great Western Railway lorries. Two of their officers were conferring over a street map.

'Shit! Why did you have to open your mouth?'

It was our rotten luck that the Germans had chosen tonight to flood the town with troops to catch curfew breakers. The late arrival of the London train would be no excuse. Anyone caught out on the streets after seven o'clock faced five nights in the detention centre. If I was caught and searched, I reckoned I'd be facing a hangman's noose.

'We're not going to make it.'

'We'll do our best.'

We jogged down Station Road towards the town.

It had started to drizzle, the fine stuff you didn't really notice until you were soaked. Already it was misting my eyelashes.

'You wouldn't mind telling me what I'm risking my life for?'

'Plates.'

'Plates?'

'Hang on, I'm getting a stitch.' Roy slowed to a walk. 'Printing plates for 50-*Reichsmark* banknotes. A chap from the Royal Mint's been copying them. Now they're going to Canada.'

There was the sound of motor engines behind us. We ducked into a shop doorway as two lorries packed with German infantry growled past. Three hundred yards ahead, one turned right up Liskeard Road – our direct route home. The other stopped to drop off five soldiers. The Germans were swamping the city. We were going to have our work cut out ever to reach the pub.

We headed up behind the drill hall into St Mary's Hill – a rectangle of long, sleepy terraces. By tacking through the backstreets we would be travelling along two sides of a triangle, but at least we'd be safe. Or so we thought! We'd only gone a few hundred yards when one of the *Wehrmacht* lorries crossed a junction ahead of us. Roy swore under his breath.

We needed a hiding place fast. I pointed to a Wesleyan chapel, remembering that houses of worship were allegedly never locked. This one was.

'Even God's turning his back on us,' panted Roy.

It was almost seven o'clock.

'What about Matty's flat?'

To get away from his father, before the war, Matty had rented a flat in a smart new block on the drive overlooking the harbour. We had enjoyed a number of wild parties there, until the neighbours started complaining and the landlords had pointed out a morality clause in the lease. Anyone other than Matty Cordington would have been slung out on his ear.

'Can you run a mile in four minutes?'

'No one can.'

We dashed across Commercial Street, an empty glistening ribbon beneath the amber street lamps, as the town clock began winding up to strike the hour. As if on cue, a patrol emerged from a side street not two hundred yards ahead. I wiped the rain off my brow and tried to think fast. The Germans began marching purposefully in our direction. We had to get rid of the printing plates.

There was a post box on the corner, its top still coated in yellow chemical reactive paint, to detect gas. We could post the package to ourselves.

'Do you have a pen?'

Roy fumbled around in his coat. 'No.'

Neither did I.

The sound of a car made us turn. An old Riley was speeding towards us, the driver trying to get home before curfew. Nothing ventured, nothing gained. I put out my thumb.

The Riley braked harshly. The passenger door was thrown open while it was still moving. We sprinted towards it as the clock began striking.

'Get in,' a voice commanded.

Roy dived in the back. I fell in after him as the car screeched into a side street and accelerated away.

'Thanks.'

'That's all right. What are friends for?'

It was Matty.

The three sat around the gas fire in his flat as Matty dispensed whisky and savoured the effect of his *coup de théâtre* on his friends.

'I don't believe it. I just don't believe it,' Roy kept repeating.

Even Nick was impressed, and it took a lot to impress Nick.

'It was lucky I saw you.'

Matty was slight compared to Roy's barrel-like bulk or Nick's six feet, but he possessed the nervous energy of an orchestra conductor. He had a small well-bred face with neat compact features that some would have mistrusted as too handsome were it not for his roguish air, which older folk said he had inherited from his mother.

'Lucky? It was a miracle.' Roy shook his head in wonder.

'When did you get back?' demanded Nick.

'I arrived earlier on this afternoon, liberated the old jalopy from the farm without the Major knowing and I've been running to stand still ever since,' replied Matty. 'I was going to look you both up first chance I got, honest.'

'What are you doing back here, then?'

'I'm going to run the estate. It's all part of Jerry's plan to increase agricultural production. I was released from PoW camp on parole to manage a farm in Suffolk. I made a success of it and I thought if I could do it there, I could do it down here. I applied for a transfer and here I am.'

'We called on your father. He said he hadn't heard from you.'

'I kept escaping so they put me in the bad boys' camp on Canvey Island for a while. You don't get any mail there.'

'How were you captured?'

Matty pulled a face. 'We were almost surrounded and out of ammo so I told my lads to split up and try to make their own way back. He who fights and runs away lives to fight another day, and all that. Finally six of us crashed out in this hayloft, absolutely knackered. I woke up to find a German bayonet at my throat. I reckoned someone must have shopped us.'

'Bastards.'

'Anyway, why were you two out and about so close to curfew?'

'We'll show you.' Roy unwrapped the oilskin parcel to reveal two metallic plates. 'These are used to print 50-*Reichsmark* notes.'

'Christ!'

'They're on their way to Canada.'

'You're not . . . you're not involved?' demanded Matty, as if fearful of the answer.

'Afraid so,' grinned Roy cheerfully. 'Up to our ears, and now you're back, the Germans had better look out. The Three Musketeers take on the Third Reich – and win.'

'Me!' exclaimed Matty.

'I've told the chief all about you . . .'

A key turned in the door.

'Quick,' whispered Matty. 'Put these away. And don't say a word about . . .' He thrust the plates into Roy's hands, as a dark-haired woman entered the room. 'Ah, Sara, you managed to duck the patrols, then? Let me introduce you: Roy Lock, Nick Penny, Sara Burskin. These are my best friends, Sara. You remember I've spoken about them.'

'Many times.' Sara extended a hand as though to be kissed. 'It is an honour to meet you.'

'And you,' said Roy with a broad grin.

'A pleasure.' Nick rose.

Matty watched Nick weigh her up as he did

everyone he met. He wondered what his friend was making of her. Pale, almost translucent grey eyes that were never still, arched eyebrows, a solemn smile. Not the warmest woman in the world – but then, she had her reasons.

'Sara's Polish. Burskin's not her real name but it's as close as I can get,' explained Matty. 'She's a refugee with not a soul in the world so she's come home with me. Which brings me to a favour I have to ask. Father's not going to take at all kindly to me coming back to run the estate, over his head . . .'

'You mean, he doesn't know?'

'I still have to break the news to him. Will one of you come with me, on Tuesday evening?'

'Why not tomorrow?' asked Nick.

'I've got to go to Exeter – more German paper-work,' replied Matty shortly. 'If I see him on Tuesday, we can have a proper reunion afterwards. I'll really need a drink by then.'

'Not me,' said Roy. 'He scares the life out of me.'

'I'll come,' smiled Nick. 'One good turn deserves another. Though it'll be the bravest thing I've ever done.'

10

Glass stood staring at the map on the blackboard showing the German advance around Basingstoke. This time he had set himself the problem of repelling 7th Panzer Division's left hook that had broken through the GHQ line. The British forces – Pollock's 43rd and Montgomery's 3rd Infantry Divisions – were relatively fresh and the 3rd was a regular division, but their frontages were too long and the 3rd had only sixty per cent of its artillery. I was learning more about the collapse of Britain's army from Glass's war games than I'd ever understood when I'd been part of it.

'I'm bringing the Fifty-second Division out of reserve in East Anglia,' he announced. 'The remaining Matildas of the Second Armoured will be dug in hull-down on the Hog's Back, to take 7th Panzer in the left flank. That'll give Rommel a nasty fright.'

'But you committed 2nd and 3rd Royal Tank Regiment at Petersfield,' I objected. 'There's hardly anything left of them.'

'There's enough.'

I suspected Glass was cheating.

He made sweeping marks in blue pencil on the map before turning to face me.

'Your football match was a great success. There were six thousand, four hundred spectators at the game, making it the largest Anglo-German function held in the whole country so far. And not one arrest. *Militärbefehlshaber London* are now considering the idea of re-forming football leagues with German players in every team. I'm putting the curfew back to ten o'clock as a reward, and I've promoted Klein to sergeant for his outstanding performance.' Glass played with his pill holder before putting it down unopened. 'I've also had an idea for a series of Valentine's Day dances across the region with a week's curfew pass for everyone who attends.'

'There'll be no problems filling the dance halls, with that incentive.'

'The offer is for English girls only. The *Wehrmacht* will supply the men – handpicked for their ability to speak some English. You seem sceptical. Don't you think it'll work?'

'We'll have to see, sir.'

'Work on some posters. It'll be particularly good for German morale.'

'Only if the girls turn up, sir.'

'Quite.' Glass turned away. Then, 'One more thing, sergeant. Jenner's Tea Rooms are off limits to all army personnel, and that includes you.'

'Why? I'm not in the German Army.'

Glass's voice cracked like a whip. 'Are you questioning my orders?'

'No, sir.'

Glass picked up a manila folder. 'Your file is getting thicker by the day. The latest is a report on how you not only defied the SS, but threatened their troopers for breaking the law . . .'

'I didn't quite put it that way, sir.'

'You are too well known to get away with a stunt like that. Stolz is after your guts. I won't ask the name of your friend, but he'd better keep his head down, too. Neither of you will get off so lightly again. *Gestapo HQ London* is on Stolz's back. They're still picking up rumours that the Crown Jewels are hidden somewhere in our area, but Stolz can't find them. He'd love to take out his anger on someone – preferably you.'

'But the SS have no right to stop people entering the tea rooms. *They're* the ones breaking the law as it stands, not me. Why don't *you* stop them?'

Anger and frustration in equal parts crossed Glass's face. 'I warned you on your first day here about the SS. Himmler's using the SS to extend the *Reich*'s Race Laws to England. It comes from the top – the very top. In these matters I am powerless. What happens to the Jews is outside my jurisdiction. And that's the way I want it to stay.'

'I gave my word I'd go to see Miriam Jenner at lunchtime.'

'And I have given you a direct military order. Now I am giving you another one. Draft those notices about the Valentine's Day dance, then get a car and a driver and take them straight to the printers. At the printers, collect the new posters on the Labour Recruitment Drive and deliver them to Northern and Western *Nebenstelle* personally, so they can start distribution tomorrow.'

'But that'll take all day.'

'Quite. And Penny . . .'

'Sir?'

'Just believe I'm on your side.'

Outside Glass's door, I stopped dead. Hans Bleicher was seated in the ante-room, waiting to see the *Kommandant*. He looked the same tubby, self-effacing man as last night – except that he had become a sergeant in the *Abwehr*.

'I thought you were an infantry private?'

'Sorry.' Bleicher gave an indifferent shrug.

'Why have you been spying on the Jenners?'

'I wasn't,' he protested indignantly. 'I give you my word I wasn't. What I said last night was the truth. I feel at home there. They remind me of what was good and solid in old Germany.'

The buzzer sounded and Hauser waved for Bleicher to go in.

Bleicher took off his spectacles and rubbed his

eyes. 'No, no,' he murmured. 'You mustn't think such a thing. They have been very kind to me.'

The long drive did me good. I made the driver stop at the first phone box so I could call Miriam Jenner. He'd report the call, of course, but she had to know that I'd tried to keep my word. Typically, she was more concerned about me getting into trouble.

It was the first time I had been to the westernmost part of the region since my release, and I was surprised how few Germans there were here. Only in the towns was there any real evidence of the occupation, with checkpoints on all the main roads and swastikas flying over every town hall. The countryside was so empty that it was possible to drive for miles and miles without seeing a motor vehicle, apart from a few old lorries. Petrol rationing had driven all privately owned cars off the streets unless you were a doctor, industrialist or a 'Friend of New Europe'. From the numbers of horse-drawn carts and buggies around, you'd think you had slipped back into the previous century.

Seeing Vee at the station last night had reminded me of her charm offensive that had been short-lived but fun. We'd spent a whole Sunday in bed, much of it giggling at the springs that squeaked so much that we'd finally moved the mattress onto the floor. But once Vee had found that I couldn't or wouldn't get her a curfew pass, and I didn't greet her every time with stockings and chocolates from the commissariat, she'd started to stay in 'to wash her hair'. Other times she claimed she had a headache. She was not amused by my suggestion these were caused by the frequency with which she washed her hair. So that was that, but I missed the sex – and the laughter.

At the same time, April Smeed was becoming a fixture at the Three Horseshoes, throwing herself into Resistance work and her love affair with Roy with equal enthusiasm.

I wondered about the pixie-faced girl I'd seen briefly the night I'd agreed to join the Resistance. I'd tried to ask Roy about her but he'd been surprisingly reticent. I took the hint and shut up.

It was dark when we finally got back to the city. In the snug of the Three Horseshoes, I found Mills dressed in a tattered blue fisherman's jersey and oily trousers, and sporting three days' growth of beard. I reported on the gossip and mood inside the German HQ, then passed on Glass's warning for Roy to keep his head down.

'There's a new *Abwehr* sergeant called Bleicher . . .'

Mills halted in the middle of tying the laces of a sea boot. 'Around forty, plump, thick spectacles, brown hair, speaks good English?' he ventured quickly.

'That's the one.'

Mills paused, very still. 'It was Bleicher who broke the Lancashire escape line. How do you know him?'

'I met him on Sunday night at the Jenners.'

'What was he doing there?'

'Posing as an infantry private and playing classical music with them.'

'Bleicher's ten times more dangerous than a mindless sadist like Stolz any time. He's here for a reason.'

'Glass claims that Stolz is angry because *Gestapo London* keep picking up rumours that the Crown Jewels are hidden somewhere in our area, but he can't find them.'

'Do you think Bleicher's here because . . .?' Roy stammered to a halt. 'I'm sorry, colonel, but I think you should tell Nick.'

Mills thought for a moment, as I picked up on his rank.

'Very well. Nick, I'm telling you this because it'll help you recognize scraps of relevant information inside German HQ – trifles you might otherwise think worthless. Being privy to this operation carries a terrible risk – not only to you, but to your family. You understand?'

'They'd want me to help.'

'On your head be it. We intend to smuggle the Duke and Duchess of Windsor to Canada . . .' Mills waited for his words to sink in. 'Accompanied by the Crown Jewels.'

'So the Duke and Duchess aren't Nazi puppets after all?'

'They're just biding their time until they can get out safely.'

'It's incredible.' So my mother and sister were wrong about the Duke. Annoyingly, I could not correct them. 'Is Bleicher's return a coincidence?'

'I don't believe in such coincidences. But if we pull this off, it'll be the biggest slap in the face for the Germans since the invasion.'

'What can I do to help?'

'For the moment just keep your ears open for any mention of the Crown Jewels, or of the royal couple.'

'Is there a code word for the operation?'

'Operation Windfall. It's planned to take place in about a week's time, at the next full moon, when the tides are right. The Duke and Duchess will arrange a social event to keep them overnight this side of London. Timing is vital: we must have them on that submarine before the Germans find they're missing. Then we batten down the hatches and weather the storm. The *Gestapo*'ll turn the country upside down. It'll be hard but worth it.'

'Are you in, Nick?' asked Roy.

'He's in.' Mills replied for me, grimly. 'He's in or he's dead.'

Next morning I hadn't even taken off my army greatcoat before Hauser, a-twitter with excitement, burst in to tell me that Glass had received Protector von Ribbentrop's personal congratulations on the success of our football match. The *Führer* himself would hear how well the Anglo-German Friendship League was progressing in the *Westgau*. In addition, the Protector had noted how there had not been a single act of anti-German hostility in the region since the hostage executions, that dairy production was above target and the fishing industry was picking up following Glass's decision to allow the fleet to sail further offshore. An excellent performance, General.

'Glass is walking on water,' smirked Hauser. 'He wants to see you.'

'Come in, Penny, come in.' Hauser was right: I'd never seen Glass in such a good mood. 'I've decided the Friendship League needs a captain rather than a sergeant in command. An officer will give the operation more status. What do you think?'

I could see his point, but I didn't like the idea of having a German officer watching my every move. I'd become used to being more or less my own boss. 'If you say so, sir.'

'On the coat-stand behind you.'

I turned to see a British officer's jacket with three pips on the shoulder.

'Try it on.'

I felt my face redden. I was all fingers and thumbs as I undid my battledress tunic and put on the new jacket. It fitted perfectly – Glass had done it again. Just when I thought I was getting his measure, he did something to throw me off balance.

'Congratulations, Captain Penny.' Glass poured us two measures of brandy.

'Thank you, sir.' I did not know what else to say.

'You deserve it.' He swallowed his brandy in one gulp. I followed suit, trying not to cough. 'What's happening about the Valentine's Day dances?' he continued.

I brought him up to date with my plans, and told him how the school competition for the best German essay, with a fortnight's holiday in the Fatherland for the winners, was developing.

'You're doing a good job, better than you know.' He topped up our glasses. 'But there are clouds on the horizon. The region's food quota is being cut so that more of it can go to the industrial areas. The *Reich* Economic Ministry wants to keep factory workers and miners happy, in the hope that it'll bring greater productivity from them.'

'Our region's self-sufficient in dairy products and fish, aren't we, sir?'

'Until London demands their share,' Glass replied sourly. 'They also want us to recruit more men and women to work in Germany. Look at this poster.'

I opened it out on the desk. It showed a smiling mother with two happy children while in the background a worker in overalls was giving the thumbs-up. The caption read: *It's all right now. Dad's earning good money in Germany.*

'There's a fifty-*Reichsmark* bounty for every worker who volunteers.'

'I've heard that volunteers will be exchanged for our prisoners of war, sir.'

'I've heard the same rumour,' said Glass wryly. 'Your Prime Minster Hoare is trying to haggle with *Reichs* Director of Labour Saukel over how many workers equal one prisoner. Hoare wants two to one. Saukel's insisting on ten to one.'

'I may be naive but why develop arms and munitions now that Europe's at peace?'

'You *are* naive. Have you not read *Mein Kampf*?'

'Only bits of it, sir.'

'That's the only way to read it, but never say I said so. In *Mein Kampf*, Hitler sets out his vision for a Germany that must expand if it's to stay great. The German people need their *Lebensraum* in Eastern Europe and the Ukraine. The German–Soviet Non-Aggression Pact of August 1939 ensured we didn't have to fight a war on two fronts as we did in 1914. The pact won't last, however. Soviet Russia is Germany's natural enemy. Wait until the spring thaw sets in – then you'll see the start of the real "war to rule the world", mark my words.'

*

'It suits you.' Bleicher sat in my office, smoking a cigarette. From the way he'd moved the chair to one side, I guessed he was watching the courtyard entrance to the *Gestapo* block while not wanting to be seen.

'How did you know?' I couldn't help glancing self-consciously at my pips.

'I provided the jacket.' Bleicher still made no move to get up.

'Thank you. But why didn't you tell the Jenners you were in the *Abwehr*? Are you really a sergeant?'

'They'd have been nervous. And, yes, I am a sergeant. I don't get promoted as easily as you obviously do. I am highly regarded professionally, but jealousy, envy and the wrong social class conspire to leave me a non-commissioned officer. Did you know I own a sweet shop at home?'

I later found out that Bleicher had acquired it when working in the German foreign postal censorship bureau in the Thirties. Its owner had been indiscreet in references to Hitler in a letter sent to his sister in America. In exchange for the return of that letter, he had sold Bleicher his shop cheaply. At the price, it was better that than Dachau concentration camp.

'No. But regarding the Jenners . . .?'

'The Jenners are intelligent, cultured people. Jacob and I quote Schiller to each other, and we play Bach, Mozart and Mendelssohn together. Please do not spoil that for me.'

A Mercedes had drawn up close to the *Gestapo* block entrance. Two agents in long leather coats dragged a broken figure across the cobbles into the doorway. Bleicher shook his head in distaste.

'So I have your word that you are not spying on the Jenner family?'

'Why should I spy on them? I am military intelligence. I give you my word.'

'But you work with the *Gestapo*?'

'I tell those I capture that it's easier to talk to me than to the *Gestapo*. I am truthful in that. Maybe that is why I'm successful. The *Abwehr* disapproves of acts of needless violence. I believe I am a humane man who tries to convert my captives to my own cause. I do not desire the death of a sinner, but rather that he transfers his wickedness and continues to live.'

I began to see why Bleicher was so dangerous. 'But what happens if they won't transfer their allegiance to you?'

'Then I am sorry. I have to hand them over to the *Gestapo*.'

'Just as a judge uses the services of a hangman.'

The cordiality went out of Bleicher's eyes, as if a blackout curtain had been drawn.

'So you're a captain. Congratulations. I only ever made it to second lieutenant.'

'Don't take the mick,' I told Matty as we stood at the end of the gravel path leading to his home.

'You must be doing something right.'

'Matty, if it's right for the Germans, then it's wrong for England. This is merely recognition of my treachery.'

'Rubbish. At the moment we all have to do things we dislike doing. Anyway, as Roy says, you're perfectly placed inside the German HQ to help the Resistance.'

'Still . . .' I could not help feeling guilty, convinced it was part of Glass's scheme to make me choose sides – the German side.

'You know your trouble, Nick? You care what others think about you. This is a time of compromise. What are you supposed to do, refuse the commission and march yourself into a detention camp?'

'I'm not that brave.'

'No one is,' said Matty. 'I'd do exactly the same as you're doing.'

'No, you wouldn't.'

No one could ever question Matty Cordington's bravery. Both Roy and I were intensely proud of the way he had been awarded his Military Cross in the field. What Matty had done was extra-special. But now he was about to demonstrate bravery of a different kind. He was about to go and face his father.

*

'What do you mean, you've come back to manage the estate? It's a strange world when a son grabs his inheritance while his father is still alive.' Major Cordington took a brutal gulp of his whisky. He had received us in the dining room, heavy with the musty damp of disuse, the striped Regency wallpaper peeling away in one cold corner. 'You cannot wait for me to die?'

'No, sir.' As always, Matty was tongue-tied in front of his father. 'I assure you, this is not my idea. The Germans insist that we step up our agricultural output. With the farm manager still away . . .'

He withered into silence under his father's baleful glare. The old man had never lifted a finger against Matty. He had never needed to. He could flay Matty alive with the knotted lash of his tongue – and he knew it.

'The Germans! The Germans! Who the hell are the Germans to tell me how to run my own land? The last German I met was in Peronne in 1918. I put a bayonet through him. And why have you brought *him* here?' He waved imperiously at me. 'Not man enough to speak for yourself.'

Matty ignored the jibe and ploughed on. 'They asked for volunteers with some knowledge of farming. It was a way out for me. Otherwise they were going to send me to a punishment camp in Germany because I kept trying to escape . . .' Matty paused, waiting for some acknowledgement of his bravery.

Instead the Major refilled his glass, his gaunt face immobile in scorn.

'Better men than you have served time behind the wire. Might have done you some good.' The Major's face had acquired a deeper shade of mauve since my last brief visit. Either he was drinking even more heavily, or Matty's announcement had sent his blood pressure soaring.

'I doubt it.' Matty came as close to losing his temper as he could with the old man. 'I, too, held the King's Commission. I, too, hold the Military Cross. Just the same as you.'

'You are *not* the same as me. You come here to do the invaders' bidding.'

'You'd rather I was in Germany?' When his father did not answer, Matty continued. 'I've brought a Polish refugee with me. I'll put her up in Meadow Cottage for a while. I'd like to introduce you sometime.'

'That will not be necessary.'

'I'll move into the Dower House. Perhaps you will come over to dinner.'

'I think not.' Major Cordington turned on his heel and left the room without another word. Matty gave me a wan smile. I sympathized.

Sara was waiting for us in the car, her pale grey eyes now hooded and still. 'How did it go, darling?'

'Bloodily, as expected. Thanks for coming with me, Nick. Tell you what! That old BSA you used to ride should still be in the barn. Take it, if it's any use to you.'

'Thanks.' I was very fond of the 250cc Empire Star. I'd already sort of inherited it in 1938 when Matty had graduated to cars. I'd never been able to afford a car of my own so I did my courting on two wheels. 'Are you still on for a reunion pint this evening?'

'Is that all right, Sara?'

'Of course. I can live without you for a few hours.' The lack of any inflexion in her voice was disturbing. I couldn't tell if she was joking or not.

'Master Matty. Master Matty.' Bert Latcham came limping over from the cowshed, cap in hand. 'It does my heart good to see you, Master Matty. It really does.'

'Bert, how are you?'

'The missus will be ever so pleased when I tell her you've come home. You have come back to stay, haven't you? You're not going away again?'

'No, I'm here now. I've come to help on the farm. This is Sara Burskin, Bert Latcham. Bert's been the cowman ever since I can remember.'

'Since *before* you can remember. Forty years, I've been here. I remember Master Matty when he was a nipper, miss. Always into mischief, him and Nick Penny, both. It's good to see you together – like old times.'

'You mustn't embarrass me by telling those old

stories, Bert. I'll see you again soon. We've got lots to talk about.'

'Indeed we have, Master Matty.'

'He seems very fond of you,' said Sara as Bert limped away. 'Hero-worships you, even.'

'We're just friends.'

'You're too modest, darling. You attract loyalty. You're a natural leader, and you must use that gift. Mustn't he, Nick?'

'Yes, please. Three more pints.'

The beer was flowing fast and freely as we celebrated Matty's homecoming and talked of old times together. Roy especially had been indulging in long walks down Memory Lane. Like the time we'd swum naked into a flotilla of Portuguese men-of-war.

'I've never seen Nick swim so fast.'

'You'd swim that fast if you had one of those things six inches from your bollocks.'

'And we got back to the beach to find the girls had hidden our clothes . . .'

'Remember that fishing trip. The mackerel jumping into the boat . . .'

'And Roy jumping out of it, pissed.'

'I was not pissed. I just lost my balance.' Roy's dark rosy face glowed with drink. 'So who's this Sara?'

'I told you already, I met her when I was managing that farm in Suffolk. She's a Polish refugee.'

'You always were a jammy sod.'

'Are you still seeing Vee Harper, Nick?'

'Not really.'

'You're better off.'

Roy suddenly leaned forward. He spoke in a low voice. 'I'll tell you what, Matty. You've come back just in time for the big one.'

'What are you on about?'

Roy gave a huge wink. 'You're in time to give those German bastards a bloody nose. It's going to be the Resistance triumph of the occupation.'

'I'll have to see,' said Matty hesitantly. 'I'm still at sixes and sevens.'

'That's what Nick said at first.'

'All right, but promise me you won't say a word about this in front of Sara. She's been through a hell of a lot. She couldn't stand being questioned again by the *Gestapo*.'

'Who could?' agreed Roy. 'On to the Red Lion?'

Out on the street, he began singing a popular anti-Hitler version of 'Colonel Bogey'.

'Hush. There's a German patrol ahead.'

We cut through Sea Coal Alley to Water Street, and stopped dead. Half a dozen men were smearing something over the windows of Jenner's Tea Rooms.

'It's Ricky Gregan and his blackshirts,' said Roy.

'We once banned them from the pub for making trouble.'

'Let's stop the bastards.'

It was too late. Even as we watched, a small bundle of fury flew at the thugs.

'Stop it. Stop it. Why are you doing this?' Miriam Jenner knocked the sack of manure out of Gregan's hand.

'Fuck off, you Jewish cow.' He smashed his fist into Miriam's face. She collapsed into the gutter, whimpering in pain. The gang closed in, some kicking her mercilessly as others taunted and jeered.

We were running – running as fast as we could. Matty arrived first. I followed close behind to plunge into a maelstrom of fists and boots. I had hurled one thug away from Miriam, kicked another in the groin, and head-butted a third before a blow to the side of my head sent me reeling. Someone booted me in the back. They were getting on top, then Roy waded in – a one-man battle tank oblivious to the blows raining down on him.

He grabbed Gregan in a neck lock, and slammed his head hard into the brick wall. Once. Twice. Gregan shrieked in pain. I clambered to my feet and rejoined the fray.

One of the gang had Matty down, trying to gouge his eyes out. The Nazi screamed as my boot shattered his cheekbone.

Then suddenly it was over. The gang fled fifty yards to safety before halting to hurl abuse.

'Bloody Jew-lovers. We'll get you.'

A police whistle blew in the distance.

'Yeh.' Roy strode towards them. 'Fucking try it, scum.'

A second whistle blew, this time in the next street. 'Time to get out of here,' said Matty.

My hand holding the glass of whisky was shaking. The adrenalin was pumping and we couldn't stop talking.

'Who *were* those characters?' Matty dabbed at a deep bruise on his cheek.

'British Nazis.' Roy wore his black eye like a badge of honour. 'Basically, thugs and small-time criminals. Before the war, Gregan used to run an extortion racket. Now he thinks wearing a black shirt gives him the right to do whatever he likes.'

'I've never met him before,' said Matty.

'You're lucky. He's a nasty piece of work.'

'He's going to have a hell of a headache in the morning. You could have fractured his skull, Roy.'

'Hope I did.'

We had escorted the trembling Miriam Jenner home and were now conducting a post-mortem in the snug of the Three Horseshoes. We were in the middle of reliving the battle for the third time when Matty's Sara walked in, looking cross.

'I suspected I'd find you here.' She saw Matty's injuries and her expression changed. 'Have you been fighting?'

'We stopped a bunch of Nazis beating up an old lady,' explained Matty.

'The Three Musketeers?'

'That's right. All for one and one for all.'

'You mustn't let Matty be so brave. He's not as big as you two.'

I was trying to like Sara but there was something cold and haughty, even shifty about her. I put it down to her bad wartime experiences and made allowances. Maybe she would loosen up when she got to know us better.

'He can handle himself,' insisted Roy.

'Look at that bruise.' She stroked Matty's cheek with her fingertip. 'You must be careful, darling.'

'You wait until you're in the Resistance,' said Roy. 'Then you'll have the chance to have a crack at the Jerries themselves.'

'Matty's joining the Resistance?'

'He's playing hard to get,' said Roy.

'Of course you must fight the Germans, Matty.' She turned to Roy. 'If you know someone he can talk to, I will see that he joins.'

'Oh, I know someone he can talk to,' grinned Roy.

Matty managed a weak smile. 'Don't go into details now.'

Roy raised his glass. 'All for one and one for all.'

11

I saw the headlights when the vehicle was still a good three miles away. Then they disappeared into a dip in the rolling countryside, and all was dark again. We'd selected the changeover point on the crest of a ridge deliberately so I could spot any prowling German patrols or tell if any approaching vehicle was being followed. A tawny owl hooted from a nearby stand of elms. Another answered from near the village nestling in a hollow off the main road. The night fell still, again. I shivered with the cold and the excitement.

It was exactly a week since I had first learned of Operation Windfall. Even though Matty and I were newcomers, Roy had successfully begged Mills to have us in on it. I didn't know whether to be honoured or terrified. There was the faint growl of an engine, the driver double-declutching with a crunch of gears as the van strained to take the gradient. Overhead, on the westerly breeze, I caught the sound of a light aircraft. I craned my head to see but it must have been flying without lights. Even as I searched, the clouds parted, their tattered remnants drifting clear of the moon to reveal fields lying white under a blanket of frost. Stars began twinkling. The Plough lay low in the northern sky.

An unmarked blue van coasted to a halt. Muffled against the cold, the driver climbed down.

'It looks set to be a fine day tomorrow,' he remarked in a Somerset burr.

'And the day after, and the day after.'

We shook hands. 'Everything all right?' I found myself whispering.

'Ay. There's nothing on the roads. I've had a clear run.' He lit a match under the outward transport movement order and placed the new one, covering his journey back to Honiton, in his top pocket.

'How are the passengers?'

'Haven't said a dickie bird. Apparently they moaned about the conditions on the first leg – I suppose they're used to better – but they've been as quiet as church mice since they've been with me.'

I flung open the back of my own van to reveal sacks of potatoes and crates of cabbages stacked almost to the roof. I had just finished removing enough crates on the left-hand side to make a gap when I turned to see the muffled shapes of the Duke and Duchess of Windsor shuffling stiffly towards me. The duke had a tartan travelling rug wrapped around the shoulders of his top coat and a soft trilby pulled down over his face. The duchess, in slacks and a mink coat, wore a blanket like a cowl to cover her head against the piercing cold. They looked just what they were – refugees.

'We've lined the space next to the cab with rugs and cushions, your highness.' I was struck by how slight they were. 'There's a thermos of tea, a flask of brandy, ham sandwiches and a torch. If you do wish to use the torch, please tap on the cab wall. If it's safe, I'll tap back once. If there's danger, I'll tap twice.'

The duke and duchess gave no indication they had heard me.

'If you'll use this crate as a step, sir.' I helped them up, the duchess reeking of cigarette smoke. The rear of the van was pitch black, perishingly cold, and redolent of damp earth. I shone a torch over their secret lair. As one, the couple slumped down with their backs to the engine, drew their knees up into their chests and pulled the blankets tightly around themselves. I replaced the crates, buttressing them with sacks of potatoes.

'The phone's down the lane, and I've checked it's working,' I told the other driver.

'Best of luck.' We shook hands again.

I let in the clutch, wrestled the gear lever into first, and set off on the empty road to the west. It was a momentous night. The duke's arrival in Canada would strip the Germans of the fig leaf of respectability his presence as Regent gave them, and show up the occupation for what it really was. Something inside me expanded at the thought. Here I was, Nick Fricourt Penny, driving the Duke and Duchess of Windsor on the last leg of their journey to freedom; taking them to a beach a few miles from my home town, where they would board a submarine. I wondered if I'd get a medal when it was all over.

It was also the start of Roy's adventure. He was going with them to Canada to learn sabotage techniques and the tradecraft needed to run a large resistance circuit. When he returned in two or three months, he would train others. As far as anyone else knew, he'd gone to Bristol to care for his sick uncle.

Now the clouds had cleared, I could make out sleeping villages and ancient church steeples casting long moon-shadows over the glistening landscape. I began to relax. The lights picked out the bright eyes of a fox watching from the hedgerow; two badgers scurried across the road in front, and for a magical moment the ghostly white shape of a barn owl kept pace in the headlamps. I kept checking my rear-view mirror. Once a powerful German staff car came from nowhere to materialize ten yards from my tail. I was still trying to stop my stomach from doing somersaults when the car overtook me in an impatient flourish, and sped on ahead. A handful of milk lorries rumbled eastward towards the cities.

The towns were all shuttered and sleeping – and potential death traps. I expected to get stopped around Plymouth but I sailed through safely. In

Saltash, I ignored a solitary policeman flashing his torch at me.

The German patrol that got me was waiting at the bottom of the hill outside Lostwithiel. I was already on the bridge over the Fowey when a soldier wrapped up in a greatcoat, rifle over his shoulder, stepped out of the shadows, waving a red lamp in front of him. I tapped twice on the back of the cab to signal danger and slowed down.

'Papers.'

One soldier held up the lamp to let the other inspect my identity papers, curfew pass, driving licence and traffic movement permit. All except the curfew pass were genuine. My real one detailed my new rank and position. Even the densest soldier would want to know what the British liaison officer to the *Feldkommandantur West* was doing transporting a load of cabbages and potatoes in the dead of night. The van, bearing the legend *Horace Yapp & Son Wholesale Greengrocers*, regularly made the journey to the west, supplying the German garrison there with vegetables. The van was genuine. The driver was not.

'Why are you out so late?'

Shit. The German spoke English. 'The van broke down. *Kaputt.*'

'What are you carrying?'

'Potatoes and cabbages.'

'I look.'

'Sure.' I made myself stroll calmly to the back of the lorry. 'The fuel pump packed up. Sorry, I don't know what "fuel pump" is in German.' I spoke loudly in the hope that the fugitives would hear. Just to be sure, I made a production of rattling the door handle. 'It sticks sometimes. There you are, corporal.'

He held up the lamp near a crate of cabbages and pointed. 'In English?'

'Cabbage,' I replied, praying the royal couple would not move a muscle.

'Cabbage,' repeated the soldier. '*Kohl* in German. Cabbage good?'

I realized the German wanted one. He could have a whole bloody crate. 'Here, take one. And one for your friend.'

'Thank you.' The soldier offered a cigarette. 'It is a cold, *ja*?'

'Bloody right.' I took the cigarette, surprised that my hand was not trembling. The risk of discovery was growing with every second. 'I must go. I'm late. The *Feldwebel* at the *Zufuhrstelle* is . . .'

'*Ja.*' The Germans laughed.

The engine fired first time and I pulled away. Despite the cold, my shirt had stuck to my back with sweat. A wave of euphoria washed over me. I was safe! I'd got through one checkpoint and it would be bad luck to find another between here and the rendezvous.

I even started humming to myself. I was living in a footnote to history.

Near the rendezvous, I slowed down. The signposts had not been replaced since the invasion, but I knew the route well. At the crossroads on the ridge I wended through sunken lanes down towards the sea. On cue, a hooded torch flashed twice from the depths of a hazel bush beside a lonely telephone box. A half-mile on, I turned in through a gap in the hedgerow and pulled up outside a small pebble-dashed bungalow.

Roy was waiting to greet me at the doorway. 'Okay?'

'Yeh.' I turned off the engine. 'No sign of the others?'

'They're running late. There are German patrols to the north. What about the . . .?' Roy gestured to the van.

'Leave them there. We don't want them wandering off.'

'I must get back to man the phone. Help yourself to some tea.'

As I followed Roy into a low sitting room lit by a weak oil lamp, the phone began to ring. Roy leaped for the receiver, listened without saying a word, then replaced it.

'Five minutes.'

Silence settled again, my nerves growing as taut as a violin string. 'I wonder who owns this place?' I said, making out a chintz-covered three-piece suite in the gloom.

'It's a brilliant location, hidden away near the sea. Must be a smuggler who lives here.'

'It'll have to be one who collects china shepherdesses.'

'There's no accounting for smugglers' tastes,' said Roy.

The crunch of tyres sent us flying to the window. A Post Office van was pulling up. Matty and Mills got out, dressed as postmen. From the back of his van, Matty and I transferred two wooden cases to the vegetable van, while Mills, accompanied by Roy, went indoors to make a phone call.

'These are the Crown Jewels?' I asked Matty, pointing at the cases.

'That they are,' he replied.

'Have you seen them?'

'No, they were like this when we picked them up – but you'll never guess where they've been hidden. At Fred Worsnipp's old barn in Merricombe.'

'Never! You're joking!' As boys, the three of us had spent happy summer holidays with Fred and his wife at Pear Trees Farm, part of the Cordington family's scattered holdings.

'It's nice to know the tenants are on the right side,' grinned Matty.

'How are Fred and Hilda?'

'Positively blooming. The excitement's doing them good.'

'I'm glad someone's enjoying it.'

'Get on with you. We're only here because Roy pleaded to have us along.'

'Yeh, but he made sure April's well out of it in London.'

I suddenly remembered Roy's request for a cup of tea. There were ten minutes left before we were due to move down to the foreshore. Plenty of time for a cuppa. What did you do in the war, daddy? I made the tea, my son.

The gas flame burned blue and low and I doubted whether I'd get the kettle even warm, never mind boiling, in the time. The tea caddy was decorated with little girls in hooped crinoline skirts playing with lolling-tongued spaniels – which put another nail in Roy's smugglers' theory.

I was spooning tea into the pot when I felt the draught on my neck. For a second, I stood stock-still, only my eyes moving as I searched for a kitchen knife within reach. There wasn't one. I spun around, expecting to see a grim-faced German with his Schmeisser aimed at my stomach. Instead a pretty, slender young woman in black slacks and black leather coat stood just inside the kitchen door.

'We've met before, remember?'

'You were at the Three Horseshoes one evening . . .?'

'The night you joined us.' She grinned, looking like a mischievous elf as her smile drew the skin tighter over small fine bones. A handful of freckles, scattered high on her cheeks, combined with an upturned nose and wide mouth to give her a humorous yet pugnacious look. 'I'm bloody frozen – I've been on watch for hours. The sight of you making tea was too much. I'm Coral Kennedy.'

'Nick Penny – as I expect you know.'

'Yes.' She crinkled her blue eyes into mine. 'Milk, if you have any. No sugar.'

Mills, hearing her voice, came into the kitchen to investigate.

'There's nothing stirring for at least half a mile,' she reported. 'I've got some kindling and tarred driftwood together on the beach, ready for the fire. I've been wondering how much luggage they have with them.'

'None,' I informed her.

'None?' echoed Coral. 'The duchess will have her jewellery case with her, if nothing else.'

'Honestly, they're empty-handed.'

Coral was looking thoughtfully at Mills when Roy called out. 'Excuse me, sir, the Plymouth house isn't answering.'

We hurried into the sitting room. 'They shouldn't have gone to bed until they'd signed off with us,' said Mills. 'We have to make sure there's no German activity down the line.'

'I've tried them twice, sir. I even got the exchange to try. They can't raise them, either.'

'Get the exchange to try Honiton 547.'

Roy repeated the number to the operator. There were a number of clicks before the number dialled out. We waited.

'There's no reply,' he finally announced.

Mills frowned. 'Strange. Try the previous leg: Salisbury 891.'

Again there was no reply. Mills's frown deepened. When yet another number near Reading also failed to answer, he began to look a very worried man.

'I don't like this.' Mills produced a small revolver from his jacket pocket and inspected the cylinder. 'Let's get outside.'

'Here you are.' Coral held out her hand towards me. 'I expect you can throw this further than I could.'

I eyed the hand grenade. 'Um, yes, I expect I can.' I checked the pin was safely in place and slipped it in my pocket. The adventure was turning deadly serious.

'Aren't you forgetting something?' she demanded as I started out of the door.

'What?'

'Turn off the gas.'

Outside, the night seemed to hold its breath. Even the owls had stopped hooting.

'Come on, Nick,' said Coral. 'We'll go and get the signal fire ready on the beach.'

I followed her over the stile towards the cove a hundred feet below. It was from this lonely foreshore that the three of us had once swum naked into the Portuguese men-of-war. Coral led the way through a gap in a drystone wall and began to descend the diagonal track leading down the cliff face. She moved as confidently as a mountain goat over slabs of rock and loose shale. I possessed the agility of a mountain troll, clinging nervously to tufts of coarse grass and stumbling through the dry water gullies. By the time I reached the shelving beach, Coral was already busy adding driftwood to the signal pyre.

The tide was on the turn, the sea hissing through the pebbles with every retreating wave. Further out, the long slow swell slapped hollowly against the headland. Drifts of sand appeared ghostly silver in the moonlight. From the dark horseshoe of cliffs above us came the whine of the van's engine in first gear, as it crawled down along the precipitous, pot-holed track.

A light flashed out to sea.

'Quick. Get the fire started.'

'What are they sending?' I couldn't make out their Morse signals.

Coral looked up, a box of matches in one hand. 'Nothing I can read.'

'They're early.'

'And further inshore than I'd expected.' Coral lit paper under the wood. 'That's good. The sooner we hand over the duke and the jewels and get away from here, the better. We're like rats in a trap down on this beach.'

The van lurched into sight just as a cloud slid across the moon and the world went dark. Matty and I lifted one crate, Mills and Roy the other. Stumbling and slipping, we hauled them to the water's edge. The faint phut-phut of an outboard motor carried towards us. Seconds later, an inflatable loomed out of the blackness. A Royal Navy officer, pistol in a canvas holster at his waist, jumped ashore. He and Mills had a murmured conversation as we passed the crates to a seaman.

Then it was the turn of the royal couple, who were standing helplessly by the van. They advanced gingerly over the beach, heads down against the cold, to the line of seaweed that marked high tide. The officer gallantly picked up the duchess and carried her the few feet to the inflatable.

'A piggyback will keep you dry, your highness,' suggested Mills to the duke. 'If you don't mind not standing on dignity.'

'Not at all.' It was the first time I'd heard the duke speak. He had a strangely thin, strangulated voice.

Roy shook hands with me and Matty, then began wading into the sea. The officer seemed surprised.

'He's under orders to go to Canada,' explained Mills.

'I see. Of course.'

'Take care, you old bandit. Have fun,' I called softly.

'Take care,' echoed Matty.

'I'll be back soon.' Roy was already climbing into the rubber craft.

The inflatable surged away into the darkness, leaving a trail of luminous bubbles. As the moon peeped from behind a cloud, I made out the submarine's conning tower out in the bay.

A number of things happened all at once. A light began flashing further out to sea, and a German corvette rounded the point, its speed creating a high bow wave, its searchlight playing frantically over the surface. Coral ran to kick sand over the fire. A green Very light went up, followed by a red one. In the ghastly light I saw Roy and the others scrambling up onto the hull of the submarine. A seaman was hacking at the inflatable to sink it. The crackle of machine-gun fire echoed over the bay.

'Back to the van.'

With Mills driving, Coral in the cab and Matty and me clinging to the running-boards, we lurched back up the zigzag track.

The submarine begin to disappear beneath the surface, even as the hatch was closing. The corvette, further out to sea, kept its searchlight playing crazy patterns on the water.

We split up on the clifftop: Mills driving the vegetables back to Horace Yapp & Son while Matty set off with the Post Office van. Meanwhile, Coral took charge of me.

'We'll follow the clifftop path back to town. I did a recce yesterday.' Her face was glowing with excitement. 'It's this way. Just follow me.'

'You can be seen from miles away on the cliff path. There's a parallel track about a hundred yards inland. I've lived in these parts for twenty-three years. Better follow me.'

'Yes, sir,' she grinned.

We had been going for less than ten minutes when we heard the sound of an aero engine approaching low from landward. We hugged the stunted hedgerow lining the edge of the field and pressed on. Half a mile further on, we rounded a gorse hedge to spot pinpricks of light moving towards us, and caught hoarse shouts nearly lost on the rising wind. There came a shot, followed by another. Then a ragged volley.

'They're shooting at something in the valley,' I whispered.

'Get down.' Coral rolled into the ditch beneath a bramble bush. I followed her.

Coral put her mouth to my ear. 'Germans on the ridge above the cliff path.'

More shouts. Two figures rose from the gorse, fifty yards ahead, to crash towards us. I pressed my face into the damp earth. The soldiers thudded past. When I opened my eyes, Coral's face was six inches away. She was smiling.

'Why did you shut your eyes?'

'If I can't see them, they can't see me.'

'Fool.'

We rose slowly to our feet. The cordon had swept over us, hunting something or someone further down in the valley.

Coral was holding a small automatic pistol. I had totally forgotten about the hand grenade she'd given me.

I was woken by fierce whispers. I opened my eyes and stared blankly at the pink flowered wallpaper. Ouch! I was awake but my left arm was still asleep. I flexed my fingers, feeling them tingle as the blood seeped back. For a second, I wondered where I was. Then I remembered I'd consigned myself to the drawing-room sofa. I heard David's voice.

'Honest, mum, there's a strange lady in Uncle Nick's bed.'

'David!'

'No, really. I told her, "*You*'re not Uncle Nick."' David was getting a bit scrambled under his mother's scepticism.

'And what did she say?'

'"That's true", so I gave her his tea anyway.'

I announced my presence with a cough.

'Sorry, sis,' I said quietly as she peered into the

darkened living room. 'It was very late when we got back. I didn't want to wake you.'

'I heard you. It was nearly five. But I didn't know there were two of you.' She glanced over her shoulder. 'Little vessels have big ears.'

'It's not what you think, sis.'

'Maybe it's exactly what I think.'

I could not meet Joan's eye. *Sippenhaft* was one of Himmler's more barbaric inventions. It meant that the whole family was punished for the deeds of just one member. By bringing Coral here I had put my loved ones at risk of imprisonment, losing their home, or even being executed. But it had made sense at the time, when it had seemed that half the German army was out on patrol. We had had to get off the streets. It would have been too risky to try to get to Coral's place at the far end of town. Joan's house was much nearer – although it had taken us three hours to get here. We had almost been caught twice. Once we'd been forced to lie on one side of a low garden wall, while a patrol had shared out cigarettes on the other. Thank God the Germans wore heavy hobnailed boots so we could hear them coming.

'Someone once said that for evil to flourish all it took was for one good man to do nothing,' said Joan quietly. 'I'm proud of you.'

Coral was brushing her hair when I tapped on her door.

'I seem to have drunk your morning tea.'

'Come downstairs and have another cup.' I introduced Coral to Joan, and to a blushing David.

'I'm sorry for—'

'It's not a problem,' said Joan quickly, throwing a worried look at her son. 'Have you got your books ready for school, David?'

'Are you two courting?' David found his tongue.

'Not really.' I didn't know how to explain Coral's presence.

'Then why was she in your bed?'

'David!' Joan went the colour of beetroot. 'You know Nick slept downstairs. Go and see if your gran wants a cup of tea, then get ready for school.'

There was a knock on the kitchen door and Mrs Harper appeared. The woman had a sinister knack of turning up *exactly* when she was not wanted.

'I heard your mum's chest was bad, so I brought her this ointment. My husband swears by it.' Mrs Harper smiled at Coral, waiting to be introduced.

It was all Joan could do to be polite. 'Thank you,' she managed. 'Though I'm not sure how it'll help with a bullet wound.'

'Nick, can't you get something better for your mother from the Germans, now that you're a captain?' Mrs Harper pressed on.

'He wouldn't ask.' Joan spoke for me. We both shared the fear that at any second David would come bursting in and blab something about Coral staying the night – against German regulations.

'I don't think we've met.' Mrs Harper gave up waiting to be introduced.

'Amy Bradstreet.' Coral sipped her tea elegantly.

'How do you do. You're up early. Come far, have you?'

Joan could not stand it any longer. 'David, hurry up. What is keeping the boy?' She scurried out of the kitchen.

'Just from the town.'

'Do you work with Nick, Miss Bradstreet?'

'We're . . . in the middle of something at the moment but we're not allowed to speak about it.'

'Of course. Do you come from around here?'

Joan bustled back in. 'David's the Natural History monitor this week, so he has to get to school early to feed the animals.' She began busily slicing bread.

'How's Vee?' I asked, to try and put Mrs Harper off the scent. 'Is she still seeing that German supply corps major?'

'I really couldn't say.' Mrs Harper ran her hand through her hair. 'She's keen to further cultural exchanges. Of course, that's the future, isn't it?'

'What is?'

'German culture. The future.'

*

213

There was a buzz of excitement in the air as I walked through town to the *Feldkommandantur*. People had heard the gunfire in the night and seen the German troops on the streets but no one knew yet what had happened. I called in for a newspaper, and found Leech refusing to sell his under-the-counter blackcurrant jam to an old-age pensioner.

'You've got to put up with what you're given,' Leech was lecturing the old woman. 'We've all got to make sacrifices.'

'But this jam is full of water.'

'I can't help that.'

'I'll leave it, thank you.' Head held high, the pensioner marched out of the shop.

'Stupid old bag,' muttered Leech. 'She can't expect the same as the Germans get. Did you hear about last night? They're saying the Germans sank a British submarine off the coast.'

He announced the event with such an air of satisfaction that I came close to hitting him.

'Where did you hear this?'

'The postman told me.'

I marched out, noticing that his spelling had not improved: *Margerine* now cost 6d, while *potatos* were 2½d a pound.

The morning turned out to be an anticlimax. I'd pictured lorries full of German soldiers careering out of Corunna Barracks, the drill halls full of rounded-up suspects, roadblocks, house-to-house searches, hostage snatch squads – but all seemed quiet. Glass had flown to London at first light, and there was no sign of Bleicher, so I got on with planning the Valentine's Day dances, and the programme of Hitler Youth films to be shown in schools.

At lunchtime I met Coral at a nearby pub. She had worrying news: they had failed to raise anyone up-country. Mills had gone off to investigate. We were analysing the night's events, puzzling at the presence of so many German soldiers, when I saw Matty enter with Sara. I waved to them.

Matty introduced Sara as the two women sized each other up.

'You're Polish, I believe?' asked Coral.

'Sara's father was professor of applied mathematics at Breslau University, until the Nazis came,' boasted Matty.

'My parents and my brother were killed in the invasion,' added Sara.

'I'm sorry,' sympathized Coral. 'Your English is really very good. So, I imagine, is your German?'

'Why do you say that?' demanded Sara, suddenly very alert.

'Most people in Silesia speak some German.'

'I refuse to, on principle,' declared Sara.

'You ran into no problems last night, Matty?' I asked, to defuse the growing tension between the women.

'Piece of cake,' he said shortly. 'You all right, too?'

I started to tell him when Sara burst in.

'So you two were out somewhere last night as well?' She scowled at Matty. 'Why didn't you tell me?'

Matty shrugged and looked uncomfortable.

'Well! What were you all doing?' Sara demanded.

'It doesn't matter,' muttered Matty.

'It *does* matter. You know it does.' She was giving him a strange look.

'It was no big deal,' I said.

'No big deal,' she mimicked. 'If it's no big deal, why can't *I* be involved? You all do worthwhile things. Why can't I?'

'It can get dangerous,' I murmured.

'So.' Sara glared at Coral. 'That doesn't stop *her*.'

'We'll see,' said Matty, shooting me a small warning signal. I shut up.

That afternoon, the atmosphere inside the *Feldkommandantur* was electric. German officers, clerks and Nazi party officials were talking excitedly together. They paused long enough to cast suspicious glances at me as I passed. I shut myself away in my office, and wondered what had happened.

From my window, I noticed SS storm troopers setting up a machine gun on the roof of the *Gestapo* wing. Others in full battle gear had been deployed to cover the entry to the forecourt. Whatever had occurred, the Germans were taking no chances.

I watched as a first covered lorry arrived. Two handcuffed prisoners were pushed off the tail to sprawl on the cobbles like sacks of potatoes. They were hauled roughly to their feet and dragged through a doorway to the cells. The next lorry carried three women and one man. It was followed by another, and yet another. A stretcher was handed down from a tailgate. The guards let it drop and the man who was strapped to it screamed in agony. The guards laughed.

The knot of fear in my stomach grew tighter with each new arrival. There'd obviously been a massive round-up, but I told myself that surely Mills or Coral would have heard if any of their Resistance colleagues had been arrested. I was wondering what to do, when a Duisberg saloon with curtains covering its windows drove into the courtyard. The back door was flung open and a stocky young man, his hands bound behind him, slumped onto the cobbles, his body doubling over in pain. As he was dragged to his feet, Stolz appeared and slashed him across the face with his whip.

Defiantly the prisoner straightened up. His face was bruised and bloody, and swollen almost out of recognition. He slowly raised his head.

Roy!

Our eyes met.

'They just couldn't wait to start working on him.' Bleicher stood behind me.

217

I pressed my knuckles into my mouth to choke back the rising vomit.

'I'm sorry,' said Bleicher softly. 'I tried my best.'

Subsequently, Bleicher loved recounting the shock on Roy's face when he found he was on a U-boat and not a Royal Navy submarine. Bleicher claimed he had actually been holding the King's Royal Sceptre in one hand and the Orb in the other as he broke the news. Though Bleicher did his best not to gloat, the magnitude of his triumph overcame his modesty.

Bleicher also told me chapter and verse of his interrogation of Roy. The only reason I enjoyed hearing it was because it made me even prouder of Roy. It also explained why Bleicher had failed to get Roy to talk. Bleicher did not know his mistake – and I never told him.

It seemed that Bleicher had treated Roy well, escorting him to the Marine Hotel up on the cliffs where the two had had a breakfast of scrambled egg and sausage in a first-floor bedroom. Bleicher began while they were still eating. He asked nothing about Operation Windfall, but instead looked at the past, considered the present, and explained the future. All the while, he probed Roy's character and motives, circling his opponent, searching for a weak spot. And woven into the monologue were constant variations on the same theme – *work for me and all will be well*.

'Germany is the future. Whether you like it or not, we have won the war.'

'You've won a series of battles. The war's not over.'

'But it is.' Bleicher was patient. 'Who will ever come to England's help? Her colonies and empire aren't strong enough by themselves, especially now the French fleet's in our hands. America clearly doesn't care what happens to you. They're going to have to confront Japan's aggression in the Pacific one day soon. Anyway, it's simply not in America's interest to fight Germany. For the next decade at least, England will remain occupied. Accept that you are whistling in the wind.'

That morning Bleicher resembled a provincial bank manager in his grey suit and silver tie. Only his chain-smoking indicated a deeper tension, the pressure to get a result.

'As soon as the *Gestapo* find out that you are here, they'll want to get their own hands on you – and I mean that literally. We in the *Abwehr* despise such violence, so if you help us, we'll protect you. If you don't, then I'll have to hand you over. It will not be something I'll enjoy doing.'

'Then don't do it.'

'I have no choice.' Bleicher opened his arms in a gesture of apology. 'Listen to me. I don't want you to

inform on your friends and comrades. I'm interested
only in the future. At the moment, more fugitives are
leaving this country by submarine than arriving – but
soon the opposite will be true. I'd like your help in
tracking those coming into Britain from Canada. You
see, I'm not asking you to betray a friend.'

The hours passed. At lunchtime, trays of pork
chops in paprika sauce were brought to the bedroom.
Roy and Bleicher ate knee to knee across a small, low
table.

'Your leaders could not resist the bait of the duke
and duchess. They really thought they were pulling a
master stroke. Instead, we've destroyed your Western
Line and recovered the Crown Jewels, too. We were
ahead of you at every step of the way. We even laid
on a submarine for you. This must be the counter-
intelligence coup of the war – in which I played a not
inconsiderable role. How many do you think we
arrested last night? Two, three resistance workers?
The drivers? The odd back-up man? The keepers of
safe houses? Roy, we arrested everyone. *Everyone.*'

It was almost the turning point.

'How can I go back? They'll know I was captured.'

'It can be arranged so that you'll escape. That's
not a problem. Only we ourselves know what really
happened last night.'

'You really have *everyone*?'

'We picked up Duggie Fox and Don Gunn this
morning. The last pieces in the chain.'

That had been Bleicher's mistake. Duggie and Don had played no part in the operation. Roy had persuaded Mills to let me and Matty take their places. It told Roy that Bleicher did not know everything. It told him we were still free.

From then on, Roy grew stronger. His sheer bloody-mindedness carried him through. By mid-afternoon Bleicher was becoming frustrated.

Roy told him firmly, 'I could not live with myself if I agreed to work with you.'

'My friend, you will not want to continue to live at all when the *Gestapo* get hold of you. You will end up telling them what they want to know.' Bleicher held his gaze. 'You'll betray everyone, including yourself. Not only will those you name suffer, but everyone even remotely connected to you. Your parents own the Three Horseshoes pub, don't they? Not after tomorrow. The *Gestapo* will seize it. You are placing a handful of men you've never met ahead of the well-being of your parents, your family and your friends. I'm trying to help you, trying to make you see sense. I'm offering you a no-lose deal.'

He sighed. 'Because you will break under torture. Everyone breaks. The brutal stuff, the beatings are just for starters, to show you they are in control – to humiliate you, to demonstrate that they can do with you whatever they wish. The real tortures are more subtle. Maybe electrical, maybe chemicals that make you lose your mind so you do not even know if you have told the truth or not. But do you know what will finally get you, as it gets everyone – I mean *everyone*? Lack of sleep. After forty-eight hours, sixty hours, seventy-two hours without sleep, the mind starts playing tricks. You'll be able to think of only one thing – sleep. It will consume you. Your loyalty to your friends and colleagues will seem nothing compared to one hour's sleep. Ultimately you will beg them to let you tell the truth, you'll embrace your torturer as a brother, love him as a father, be grateful for his caress.'

Bleicher took off his glasses and rubbed them on his tie. The skin around his small, deep-set eyes furrowed with the effort of focusing. Bleicher knew this was his last chance to convince Roy.

'I offer you salvation: the chance to do the honourable thing by everyone. Your parents will keep their pub. They won't be thrown into a concentration camp. Your friends will not be tortured and hanged. Your own life will be safe. I guarantee all this. In exchange I ask only that sometime in the future – and who knows the turns of fate, it may not even happen – you will help me to identify those who arrive from Canada. They are men you have never met, men to whom you owe no allegiance. Doesn't that make sense?'

'No,' said Roy.

*

We both watched as Roy was dragged into the *Gestapo* building. Then Bleicher gave another deep sigh and left me alone, with my world crashing down around me. Once the shock wore off, my first instinct was to flee. To get out of the office, get out of the building, and run. It would be an obvious admission of guilt, but at least I'd be out of this vipers' nest.

I forced myself to stay.

The next hour passed like an eternity. I spent much of the time trying not to throw up. Any second, I expected the *Gestapo* to burst in on me. Every minute my eyes were drawn to the wing where Roy and the others were currently being tortured. I just could not help myself. By half past four I could stand it no longer. I put on my coat and set off down the long corridor. Tickell and the senior county architect strode past me as though I was invisible.

I knew I must spirit Joan, young David and mum to a place of safety. I'd take them first to Matty. They could hide in an estate cottage overnight and tomorrow I'd move them up to Fred Worsnipp in Merricombe. Then I realized that if Roy named Matty, the Germans would search there first. I couldn't think straight. I needed most to talk to Matty. Together, we'd work something out.

But how much time did we have? How long could Roy hold out?

I was out of the building and hurrying across the

forecourt when the sight of Bleicher coming towards me, one hand plunged deep in his pocket, brought an abrupt halt to my intentions. There was nowhere to run. This was the moment of truth.

Bleicher withdrew his hand. It held a bottle of pills. 'For your mother. Simon Jenner asked if I could get them for her.'

'Thank you.'

Bleicher squinted at something over my left shoulder, his eyes screwed up behind his thick lenses. I turned to follow his gaze.

A head was slowly inching up a sash window in the corner of the top floor of the *Feldkommandantur*.

Even at that distance, I knew it was Roy.

His hands must have been tied behind him, because he had his head on one side, forcing up the window with his temple. When the gap was a foot wide, he began wriggling through. His chest was clear when his actions suddenly became desperate. He pushed, twisted and slithered until he was balancing on his stomach with nothing below him but the cobbles, sixty feet down. A hand appeared, grasping at his waistband. The sash was thrown up. Gestapo men crowded into the window, reaching to grab him.

But Roy was determined to die in his own way.

He drew up his knee, kicked back once, twice. His foot came out of his shoe. He was free.

He fell without a sound, his body turning a somersault in the air.

A woman screamed.

I reached Roy before the sentries did. I dropped beside him on the cold stones and cradled his head in my lap. He was still alive – but only just. He tried to speak, his lips moving, almost in a smile. A priest arrived from somewhere.

'Can I help, my son?'

'Roy's not a Catholic, father.'

'That doesn't matter.'

The priest knelt by Roy's side and began intoning quietly. I stroked Roy's hair. I didn't know what else to do.

A whirlwind crashed into us. Stolz, black with fury, hurled the priest aside. 'Get away from him.' Stolz struck me on the head with his whip.

'He needs absolution,' protested the priest.

'I don't care what he needs.' Stolz raised his whip again. 'Move away from him, Penny.'

Ice formed inside me. It numbed me against fear. I knew only that if I were made to abandon Roy, I would kill Stolz with my bare hands.

'No, Nick.' A bare whisper. Roy smiled up at me. Then he died.

PART TWO

We never did get Roy's body back. Hauser informed me that it had been cremated that evening – February the sixth. The Germans didn't want to provide the public with a martyr's grave. For a while wreaths appeared nightly on the spot where Roy had died, but the Germans swept them up each dawn. Daring patriots began painting V for Victory signs on the pavement, until the SS caught a schoolboy, Larry Draper, paintbrush in hand. Larry, along with his parents and his ten-year-old sister, was transported to build roads in eastern Poland.

Matty and I swore we'd put up a memorial when the war was over. Until then, our Resistance work would be Roy's memorial . . .

No, General, I don't know how we escaped from the beach. I think the U-boat simply surfaced too soon. The Germans were keeping well away so as not to scare us off, and then they closed the net too late. If the U-boat had appeared even five minutes later, we'd all have been caught there like rats in a trap. The Abwehr knew only a few of the identities of the Western Line when they began rolling it up. But by following the Windsors – if indeed it was them at all – the Abwehr turned the escape route into a line of dominoes. The capture of one Resistance man led to the next. The domino chain only broke on the beach. I assume that because Matty and I were new, the captured underground workers did not know our names. Roy getting into the U-boat was an unexpected bonus for the Germans. He was the only one who could have named me or Matty, and he deliberately sacrificed himself for us.

Of course, I was subsequently questioned by Bleicher, and I admitted my friendship with Roy. But Bleicher's heart wasn't in it. He'd already received the triumph he craved. Hauser warned me that the Gestapo wanted to question me, but Glass intervened.

What Bleicher had forecast only partly came true. The Three Horseshoes was commandeered as an SS drinking club, but Roy's parents miraculously escaped Sippenhaft. Again, I didn't know why – although now I can guess. They went back to Bristol to nurse Mrs Locke's sick brother, and I never saw either of them again.

I'm sorry. Am I boring you? You did ask for the whole story. And this story is about ordinary people who were in places they didn't want to be, and at times wished they were elsewhere.

Yes, Matty was questioned as well but they just went through the motions.

I was devastated by Roy's death, but it did not do to show one's emotions. I thought of him all the time, wept nightly and swore – Christ, how I swore – that one day I would personally kill that bastard Stolz.

COLLABORATOR

That's enough now, General. I don't wish to talk about Roy any more.

The next month or two were the most unpleasant of my life. I'd rather have been in a PoW camp. At least people would talk to you there. No one spoke to me – at least, no one I wanted to. I was scum, despised by those I respected, and fêted by the likes of the Friends of New Europe. I had a standing invitation to dine at the Golf Club, and to start with I was never short of a tin of ham or a bottle of whisky. I gave them away to war widows, and I never set foot in the Golf Club. Most of that set hadn't even noticed that we had lost the war. For others, defeat simply offered new business opportunities.

I saw much less of Matty. He was busy on the farm and Sara was always there to keep him company. Coral kept her distance, too. My calls went unanswered. I saw her once on the street but she ignored me. Mills had disappeared completely. Of course it suited the Resistance that I was considered a pariah. And when they really needed me, they used me again. But if Mills had known how I really felt, he wouldn't have dared risk it.

Why? Because I constantly felt like killing myself. And taking Stolz and a few of his Gestapo shits with me.

12

You couldn't have got the triumphant smile off Leech's face with one of his own scrubbing brushes. He was bursting to tell me something. I deliberately put off going to the counter, instead going round his shop correcting his spelling mistakes so that 'cabage' became cabbage and 'potato's' lost its apostrophe.

I was disliking the man more and more. Leech had become a parrot spouting the Nazi line. When three schoolboys had been shipped off to Germany for chalking 'V for Victory' signs on walls, it was all they deserved, he reckoned. When the Germans halved all of Nettleford's rations after a staff car skidded on cowshit in the village street, it was the locals' fault for not keeping it cleaner. One day soon I was going to have to stop calling in or else, as God was my witness, I was going to bounce him round his bloody emporium on his head.

Outside, a *Freikorps* platoon goose-stepped past, with SS runes on their collars and the cross of St George on the sleeves of their field-grey uniforms.

These brave men had ignored calls to defend their homeland in 1939. Now they were falling over themselves to fight for their conquerors.

I scanned the newspapers. The *Daily Mail* had a front-page picture of the Crown Jewels on display in Berlin. The collection was attracting record crowds. To think I'd held them in my hands. Well, I'd held in my hands the crate they were in.

Leech scuttled over, still impatient to tell me his news.

'I've bought the Jenners' businesses,' he announced in a voice halfway between a whisper and a victorious bellow.

'What!'

'The Government's going to outlaw Jews from owning or running any businesses.'

'From when?' It was the first I'd heard of it.

'There's due to be an announcement this weekend. But I was given a tip-off.' He winked slowly and heavily. 'Even the local Marks and Spencer will be up for sale. It's a good time to expand, if you have the wherewithal.'

'Who sets the price?'

'The Independent Arbiter for Jewish Affairs but most Jews are selling in advance. It's always better to do something before you're forced to.'

'I suppose so,' I replied bleakly.

'Of course, *in theory*, I'm only holding the Jenners'

business in trust.' Leech sniggered. 'Jacob insisted I sign an undertaking that allowed him to buy his business back on three months' notice.'

'Did you sign it?'

Leech shrugged. 'Yeh, for ten per cent off. That Jacob's mad. He still thinks the English will finally win.'

I wished I had Jacob's faith in ultimate victory. I handed over some coppers for a newspaper and prepared to leave, but Leech had more news.

'Did I mention that I've joined the Friends of New Europe?' he asked coyly.

That explained the tip-off.

'Congratulations.'

The Golf Club set was choosy about who they allowed into their circle so they must have seen Leech as someone on the way up.

'I trust it'll mean an invitation to the *Führer*'s birthday reception.' Why didn't Leech say 'that bastard Hitler', like most other people? 'The invitations come from the *Kommandant*'s office, and as you're in charge of the Anglo-German Friendship League . . .'

I was saved by the arrival of two *Wehrmacht* artillery captains. Leech could not allow one of his mere assistants to serve such honoured clients. I was making good my escape when he pranced after me, clutching a paper parcel.

'This is for Joan. Tell her I've just had some

chocolate liqueurs come in. They're really for the German trade, but she's welcome to a box with my compliments if she cares to pop in.'

It was the first I was aware that Joan and Leech even knew each other. I would not have thought that the two of them would have had much in common.

With barely concealed loathing, Hubert Leech watched Penny disappear up the hill towards Mountroyal. Toffee-nosed git, looking down his nose at a shopkeeper astute enough to make the best of a difficult situation. Who did the Penny family think they were, with their airs and graces? They didn't have a pot to piss in nowadays. At least the Germans treated one with respect, and paid top prices without haggling or complaining. You knew where you were with them. Leech smiled ingratiatingly at the German officers inspecting some McGill postcards but, under the surface, the memory of Nick Penny's slights and put-downs made his blood boil. More than once Leech had been on the verge of giving him a piece of his mind, but had held his tongue.

Leech didn't understand someone like Penny. They should have been allies. After all, Penny worked alongside the Germans. In fact, he was said to have the ear of the *Kommandant* himself. If Penny played his cards right, he could have anything he wanted, but Leech's new friends at the Golf Club had warned him off trying to buy his way into Penny's favour. Penny either refused gifts outright, or just gave them away to spongers or widows.

Well, pride went before a fall, they said. And there were enough good folk in this town waiting for Penny to take a tumble.

'Thank you.' Leech took the postcards from the Germans and bowed. 'Will there be anything else? I have a few pots of fresh clotted cream. *Frischer Rahm.'*

The Germans appeared sufficiently interested for Leech to signal to one of his assistants to fetch them a pot from the cool larder. One officer scooped out a fat blob with two fingers and licked it off before handing the pot to his comrade. The Germans spoke rapidly among themselves.

'Two.'

'Of course.' The Germans were so easy to do business with, while Penny's mother had the temerity to whine about the price of margarine going up by a halfpenny a pound.

But then everyone had a price – even Penny's sister, Joan hoity-toity Pendleton.

Leech bowed his German customers out of the shop and briefly glanced up the hill. He had once dreamed of living up there, on Mountroyal, but now he had his eye fixed on the manor house in a nearby village. The Pennys and Pendletons were yesterday's people. The future belonged to supporters of the *Reich*.

David was out riding his bike and mum was resting when I got home. We were getting increasingly worried about mum. Frequently Joan found her lying on the bed, hands folded across her chest as though laid out and waiting for death. Her deformity had grown worse so that her whole upper body was now twisted. Joan often heard her talking to someone in her room. We guessed it was to our dead father.

'This is for you from Leech,' I told Joan, placing his package on the kitchen table.

Joan coloured, and carried on slicing turnips into the stew. I thought how pale and washed out she looked. In her flat slippers and no stockings, her legs appeared thin and very white. Her pinafore was wrapped round her like a sack.

'Aren't you going to open it?'

'It's a box of biscuits,' Joan said shortly, somehow resentful that I had brought the parcel.

'I didn't realize you knew Leech.'

'He gives me a lift home from the Golf Club occasionally. He's been trying to become a member there.'

'I'm surprised you give him the time of day, knowing he's a two-faced profiteer who waters the butter and keeps all his best stuff for the Germans.'

'That's easy for you to say,' snapped Joan. 'I can't afford to turn down bribes like you do, in your high-handed way. When Leech gives me a lift home, I sometimes find the odd bar of chocolate in my pocket or he presses a tin of something into my hand.'

'Does David know about this?'

'Of course not. Anyway, there's nothing to know. Every shop has its favoured customers. Leech is just being kind to us. He even found that box of crayons for David.'

'I didn't know they came from a collaborator.'

'He's only just as much of a collaborator as you are.'

'He's doing it by choice. I'm not.'

'No?'

We were saying things to deliberately wound each other – and a brother and sister really know how to hurt. It was like reliving one of our childhood spats. Somehow it hurt more now, though.

'I'm sorry, sis. I didn't mean to get on my high horse.'

'I know, Nick – I know.' If we had been a more tactile family we would have hugged each other; instead, Joan stopped preparing the stew just long enough to face me. 'I do not encourage Leech. God, do you think I can stand the thought of that man touching me? *Any* man touching me? He's been kind, and he's asked for nothing in return. If it goes on like that it'll be fine.'

'Of course.' *If* was a big word. I couldn't see Leech giving something for nothing.

'Don't ever tell David. He wouldn't understand. You know how he feels about the Germans.'

I was beginning to suspect that David was putting those feelings into action. Yesterday, before breakfast, I'd seen David scrubbing away to get something like paste off his hands. Then, on my way to work, I'd found Leech's shop windows plastered with 'V for Victory' posters. Both mother and son had their secrets, it seemed. And they both concerned Leech.

'Nick, the writing's on the wall.' Jacob Jenner watched his wife break off the head of a freshly baked gingerbread man for inspection. 'We had no option but to sell. Anyway, Leech has agreed to give us back the businesses once the Germans leave.'

'You think the Germans will be beaten?' I moved out of the way as Miriam went to place the baking tray at one side of the oven. No kitchen was spacious enough when Miriam was baking.

'Don't you?'

'Try this one.' Miriam had given the gingerbread man cross eyes and a Hitler moustache. She could have made a fortune out of these until the *Gestapo* caught her. 'Nick, giving up running the tearoom means I won't have to put up with those SS goons hanging about all day. They were driving me crazy.'

'What about Simon?'

'He understands the situation. He's busy helping poor children in the slums down by the docks – unofficially, of course. He's been getting cheap medicines from our friend Goldblum the chemist. Anna goes there with him. I am proud of them.'

'And Barbara and Hope?'

'She dotes on her baby daughter, absolutely dotes on her. She won't even let her out of her sight. Barbara's been through so much, and Hope is all she has.'

At that moment, Barbara herself walked in, cradling her baby. On seeing me, she was about to scuttle away, but when I asked her about Hope, her pale face lit up and she held up her daughter so that I could see her better.

I never know what to say about babies. 'Isn't she growing?' I ventured. 'How old is she now?'

'Twelve weeks today.'

'You're beautiful.' I gave the child a big smile and was rewarded by a gummy grin.

'She likes you,' murmured Barbara.

'I bet you like everyone?' I held out my index finger. Hope grasped it in her fist and I marvelled at this tiny person, perfect in miniature.

'No. You're honoured,' called Miriam. 'She usually only has eyes for Barbara. Don't you, my precious?'

13

I remember the next morning very clearly. You didn't normally get the Horst Wessel Song, anthem of the Nazi Party, blaring out of your wireless at the start of the eight o'clock news.

This is the Home Service in London on Thursday, 27th March 1941. At 0200 hours, New European Time, German troops crossed the border into the Soviet Union in an act of self-defence following repeated Bolshevik provocation. German forces, inspired by the Führer *Adolf Hitler, are advancing deep inside Russian territory in a crusade to eradicate the Communist bacilli once and for all . . .*

I listened closely, thinking how the German High Command had caught the Russians napping by striking ahead of the spring thaw. The invasion explained why so many front-line troops had been returning to the Fatherland over the past few months.

Luftwaffe squadrons have systematically destroyed much of the Russian air force on the ground. Leading Panzer units are already over one hundred miles inside the Soviet Union.

'What does it all mean?' Joan had turned into a

statue – Woman with Toasting Fork – as she had listened to the news.

'Hitler has bitten off more than he can chew.'

'How, Uncle Nick?' asked David.

'Because of the sheer size of the Soviet Union. If the Russians can avoid being sucked into a pitched battle, which they'd lose anyway, they can withdraw for hundreds of miles and keep their armies intact, while the Germans'll have ever-lengthening lines of communication to safeguard. It's, what – three hundred and fifty miles from Dover to Land's End? The Russians have *forests* that big.'

'But how's it going to affect *us*?' asked Joan, ever pragmatic.

'Less food, and more pressure to get people to go and work in Germany. We'll all have to make sacrifices for the noble German army battling to save the world from Communist enslavement – or some such tripe.'

Life was already hard enough. Sugar and butter had all but vanished. For weeks we had been carefully re-drying our tea leaves so they could be used over and over. The only meat we'd seen for two months was offal or gristle, and then only 200 grammes a week. The weekly ration of fats per person was down to 100 grammes. But recently things had seemed to improve. Joan had actually produced a rasher of bacon each for breakfast last weekend. Her shopping skills seemed to be improving.

The announcer began telling us about a battalion of SS British *Freikorps* leaving Dover to join the Great Fight against international terrorism.

'Their wives and families will be well cared for while they are away. Double rations and access to special SS shops will mean that they will not want for anything as their brave menfolk face the Bolshevik scum.'

The rest of us could go hang.

It was one of those fresh spring mornings that made you inhale deeply and taste the air. At any other time it would have bucked me up but now I hated every day, however glorious. I set off to walk to the *Feld-kommandantur*, deep in thought about the implications of the Russian invasion. In theory, all attention would switch to the east, so we should become a forgotten backwater. In practice, I was sure that life would get even harder.

'I hope they're worth a Pfennig.'

Coral Kennedy was grinning up at me. I hadn't seen her since the day Roy died, almost seven weeks ago. She had lost weight – not that she'd had much to lose. Her skin seemed stretched even more tightly over her high cheekbones, and she had more freckles than I remembered.

'Not really. Just thinking about the German attack on Russia. Is that why you've popped up, or is it just a coincidence?'

I was still cross at the way she'd dumped me after Roy's death. I'd felt very alone during the past weeks, and I couldn't even fall back on my friendship with Matty. The few times we'd met, Sara had always been there with him. It wasn't the same somehow.

'No such thing as coincidence.' Coral hooked her arm through mine. All of a sudden we were best mates.

'Who are you today, if we're stopped? Coral Kennedy or Amy Bradstreet, or is there another woman I've yet to meet?'

'I'm Coral.'

'Is that the real you?'

She winked. 'Just think of me as your guardian angel.'

'All right, I'll call you Angel.'

She pretended to consider this. 'As long as I'm a little angel and not a great big one with huge flapping wings like Gabriel, or a fallen one like Beelzebub.'

'Wouldn't you rather rule in Hell than serve in Heaven?'

'We're getting the worst of both worlds at the moment. We're serving in Hell.'

A man in a grey flat cap and grubby muffler cleared his throat and sent a gobbet of phlegm onto the pavement just ahead of me. I stepped over it. I was used to the local heroes taking liberties with me that they dared not take with the Germans.

Angel squeezed my arm. 'Things can't be easy for you.'

I shrugged. 'I survive.'

'If it's any comfort, it's perfect for us.'

'Us?'

'You know – the Resistance.'

'Still going, is it?'

'Nick, the *Gestapo* have been keeping tabs on you. You've been followed regularly, your mail's been opened and probably your phone calls at the *Feldkommandantur* have been monitored. It wasn't safe to contact you. We think they've stopped now, but the German invasion of Russia . . .'

'Means you're willing to take the risk.'

'We're not asking you to compromise yourself by doing anything like running messages or distributing leaflets.'

'So what *do* you want me to do?'

'Just keep your eyes and ears open: troop movements, ration strengths, *Freikorps* recruitment levels. And not just military but economic stuff as well – any new quota set by the *Reichs* Labour Department, how much material is being sent to Germany, even the levels of fish catches. They're all pieces of the jigsaw that'll get fed back to Canada. We're moving into intelligence gathering. Knowledge is power.'

'And I'm a spy in the enemy camp.'

'No one will know except me, Mills and Matty Cordington.'

'Matty!'

'He's been under orders to keep you at arm's length because you were being watched.' Angel was clearly enjoying my surprise. 'Mills is training him up for a command role. By the way, you're expected at Matty's house for dinner tonight.'

'Will Sara be there, too?'

'You get Matty, you get Sara.'

'You two girls getting on all right?'

'We can't afford petty squabbles. To begin with, I thought there was something about her but that's all in the past. She frequently seems more enthusiastic about our work than Matty is. Anyway, I'll peel off here.'

We were approaching the fixed German checkpoint on the hill.

'Will I be seeing you tonight?'

'I'll be there.' She swung around to look me in the eye. 'I'm really sorry about Roy. He was a good man.'

'Yes, he was.'

And I carried on to walk past the spot where he had died, as I did each and every day I worked for the Germans.

Not much work was done in the *Feldkommandantur* that day. Everyone was too excited about the invasion of Russia. A military band played in the forecourt from midday to two, and most of the German personnel took advantage of the fine weather to listen to it. Glass and Hauser were at a special meeting in London and, as I had nothing to celebrate, I buried myself in work.

The Valentine's Day dances had been a great success, with Vee Harper making herself the star of the City Ball. I was now busy with the Anglo-German reception to mark the *Führer*'s birthday, the exchange between local journalists and Westphalian newspapermen, and the scheme to fold the Women's Institute into the German Mothers' Union.

The Nazi Party was tightening its grip on every aspect of life in its efforts to turn England into a good totalitarian state. Every trade union and professional association had to be registered and approved. Even our free time was being controlled, with cricket, football and bowls clubs being forced to affiliate to Nazi governing bodies. Every boy aged sixteen to eighteen was to attend Party camps during the next summer, where indoctrination would be mixed with adventure sports in equal measure. The Scouts had already become the English branch of the Hitler Youth, known now as *Führer* Scouts. David, predictably, was refusing to join. It was even rumoured that membership of the Nazi Party itself would be open to selected Englishmen.

There was only one way to think, one way to do things now – the Nazi way. A single wrong word and you lost your job, and maybe your home. Newspapers, wireless programmes and films were all heavily veined with Nazi propaganda. Indoctrination into the *Führerprinzip* began at the age of five: producing a generation of little Nazis ready to serve and die for Hitler.

At midday the Protector, von Ribbentrop, announced that the exchange rate for prisoners of war was to be reduced from eight-to-one to five-to-one. That meant five workers would need to volunteer to go to labour in Germany to gain the release of just one British prisoner of war. I calculated there weren't enough workers in the country to deal with the equation.

At the same time, under a German amendment to the Geneva Convention, PoWs held in the Fatherland were to be allowed to work for the *Reich* in return for better rations and the chance to live out of the camps but still in barracks. Both proclamations showed how desperate the Germans were to man the industries vital to keeping their armies in the field.

On the way home I'd taken to stopping at the George for a drink. It was a small pub with a regular clientele of just one – me. At least there I could take off the hated swastika armband and the beer was surprisingly good, even if the guv'nor made a bear with a sore head seem like Charlie Chaplin. That suited me. I enjoyed sitting at the corner table, reading the paper and listening to the old clock heavily tick away my life. Just what I needed after another day in my personal hell.

Today, I got to read about a new 'partnership' between Morris Motors and Volkswagen, whereby Morris moved its main car production to the Ruhr. Two *Luftwaffe* policemen had been recommended for the George Cross for diving into a swollen river to rescue a toddler. A street trader, found with 300 gallons of petrol in his garage, had been sentenced to five years' hard labour by Judge Werner von Kloss at the Old Bailey. There was no mention, however, of yet another collision involving German troops; this time a *Wehrmacht* lorry had smashed into a bus full of schoolchildren in Plymouth, killing six of them. Collisions involving Germans were common, because they forgot that they were meant to drive on the left, but these never got reported.

Just then, two Irishmen came in. Before the war we'd had a sizeable Irish population here, most of whom had worked in the docks and few of whom had ever ventured further than the Irish Club in Dock Road, where Roy and I sometimes had a drink. I nodded a greeting. The dark, square-built man was Phil Finn, no more than five feet four tall and about the same across the shoulders. The one behind, with the red hair and vacant face, was Kelvin Fitzgerald.

'Can I be getting you a pint, Mr Penny?' asked Finn.

'I'm fine, thanks.'

'Do you mind if we join you?' asked Phil Finn, sitting down opposite me.

'Not at all.' I made an effort to sound pleased. 'What brings you up here?'

'You.' Fitzgerald sat to one side, where he could see the door. 'Here's to the memory of your father and my brother Pat, who fell alongside him fighting the Nazi tyrants.'

Most of the relatives of the men who had died with my father would not speak to me any more. I raised my glass. 'To brave men.'

'Brave men,' chorused Finn and Fitzgerald.

They both took hefty draughts of their Guinness before Finn continued, 'Mr Penny, did you know the Irish are still fighting the Nazis?'

'I know the whole of Ireland is under martial law,' I replied carefully.

'The Nazis are latter-day Cromwells. No, I tell a lie – they are worse than Cromwell.'

'Worse than Cromwell,' repeated Fitzgerald.

'Do you know what the Huns did last Sunday? They blew up the town of Skibbereen in the County of Cork. The bastards threw hand grenades into a Sunday school and then torched it. Eight women and thirty-three little children were killed. Did you know that, Mr Penny?'

I shook my head, wondering where this was leading, and what it had to do with me.

'Can you imagine, a fucking Sunday school.'

'A fucking Sunday school,' repeated Fitzgerald.

'Why did they do it?' I asked.

'Because they claimed Skibbereen was harbouring terrorists.' Finn leaned close to me across the table. 'Now, Mr Penny, you work in the German HQ so you know the *Kommandant*'s comings and goings.'

'Not really. I only have dealings with him when it involves the Anglo-German League.'

It was *not* the answer they wanted. 'But you'd know when he's going off on an official visit – to inspect something, say – or you could find out.'

'I suppose I could.'

'Good man. We'll be off now but we'll be back for another word sometime soon.'

Matty surprised me that evening by picking me up in the estate's Chrysler shooting brake. He looked every inch the country squire with his sports jacket, check shirt, wool tie and corduroy trousers. He came bearing gifts of half a dozen eggs and a bowl of cream. Joan and my mother competed as to who could fuss over him the most.

'I'm exhausted,' he confessed, as he drank the obligatory cup of tea. 'I'm on the go from dawn until nine or ten most evenings. The Germans think they can bully nature like they do everyone else. They have a formula for everything. So much fertilizer per acre, so many cows per acre, all irrespective of what the soil's like. There's a joke that their agriculture minister, Darré, was a childhood prodigy who taught himself everything he knew about farming by the age of four – and hasn't learned anything since!'

Matty finally extricated himself from the women's attentions by explaining apologetically that we had to go or the food would be ruined, and he would catch it in the neck. 'If someone's kind enough to cook me a meal, the least I can do is make sure I turn up on time.'

God! He knew how to get round women.

'You're a sly devil,' I said once we were in the Chrysler.

'What do you mean?'

'Not telling me *you*'re working for the Resistance.'

'I'm sorry, old chum. I was ordered not to. Do you mind if we go somewhere else first? I have to call in on the newspaper.'

'What paper?'

'Our paper. *The Free Briton*.'

'You sod.' It showed how deeply he had become involved. And how I had been very much left out of things.

A newspaper had to be the priority of any underground movement. The occasional Resistance leaflets had grown into *The Free Briton* that every week found its way onto the streets and into shopping bags, buses and bars, with news of the Government in exile, accounts of German atrocities and exhortations not to lose faith in final victory. It drove the Germans wild.

We drove into the yard behind the *Western Daily News* offices.

'You print it *here*?'

'It's like hiding a tree in a forest, but we can't stay anywhere for too long before the Germans start sniffing around. We're about to move the press to the old oil refinery. Here's our circulation manager.'

Pip Cartwright, the teenage son of the estate's imprisoned farm manager, was pedalling madly across the yard, an empty newspaper satchel flying over his shoulder.

'Pip?'

'He was desperate to help.'

'Isn't it rather dangerous for the boy?'

'He was already going to get into trouble the way he was going – pouring sugar into German petrol tanks. I've merely found better ways of using his considerable energies.'

The gangling teenager leaped off his bike and saluted. 'I've put twelve dozen papers on the mail train, chief. The sorters will drop them off at the stations up the line.'

'Good man.'

Pip swelled with pride before dashing into the building, to return seconds later with a full sack of papers.

'These are for the bus drivers,' he announced.

'Got one to show Nick? Thanks.'

The main story was a warning to anyone tempted by my own advertisements to go to work in Germany.

The Germans tell you they are offering a workers' paradise. The truth is very different. In Germany, out of touch with your loved ones, you will be crammed into camps and forced to work twelve hours a day. The Germans invent huge fines and taxes so you will never have money to send home to your family. You are fed thin soup and black bread. There is no freedom. Working in Germany is worse than being a prisoner. Still want to go there?

'Be careful,' called Matty as Pip mounted his bike. 'And get straight home afterwards.'

'Yes, sir.'

'Mad as a hatter,' murmured Matty fondly as Pip disappeared from sight, in a blur of pumping legs. 'Let's go and pick up Coral.'

We followed an infuriatingly slow convoy of 88mm guns being towed behind Ford lorries, until we headed off down to the river. Matty double-declutched and swooped into the smaller road, before accelerating around the chicane over the railway. I'd forgotten what a good driver he was.

'Do you ever think about Roy?' he asked quietly.

'All the time. Do you?'

'I find myself talking to him. If something funny happens, and God knows that's rare, I store it to share it with you and Roy. Then I remember. He did it for us, you know?'

'I know.'

'I wish he was here. I wish this bloody awful war had never started and we were back in the summer of 1939 – the three of us having a good time.'

'We've grown up.'

'I wish we hadn't.' We fell silent, locked in our own thoughts of Roy.

Matty halted on the humpback bridge, opposite a figure sitting cross-legged on the stone parapet, oblivious to the tumbling waters forty feet below.

'You need a pointy hat with a bell on top if you really want to become a Cornish pixie,' I said, as Angel climbed in the back.

'Another word from you and I'll turn you into a toad.'

'Great. Then I get to kiss a princess and come back a prince.'

'Only in your dreams.'

We climbed in the dusk towards the small sharp hills and deep wooded valleys hidden in forgotten folds. Low white farmhouses lay up uneven tracks off the road and a small herd of Devons straggled across the road from milking, a corgi snapping at their heels.

The Dower House, a small square Georgian building of perfect proportions and treacherous plumbing, stood by itself a quarter of a mile away from Home Farm, where the Major drank and brooded in crepuscular solitude.

At the door, Matty paused. 'I know I've said it before, but please don't talk about the Resistance in front of Sara. She's very keen and all that, but Mills insists we work on a need-to-know basis. We have to be very security conscious, especially after . . .'

'Of course.'

The walnut table in the dining room sat twelve comfortably. Four places were laid at the end nearest to an enormous fireplace blackened by the smoke of two centuries. Two standard lamps stood behind the table. The rest of the large room was in gloom.

'That's the trouble with this bloody house,' explained Matty. 'We either have to eat in here or in the kitchen.'

He poured whiskies, and the three of us stood around the fire listening to the gurgling of the central heating's intestines. Angel made a show of interest in the old paintings and ancestral portraits. Matty moved a lamp to illuminate the two Stubbses. The rest, he claimed, were worthless. I thought I remembered a previous mention of a Constable, but I didn't say anything about it.

'How lovely to see you. It's so nice to have guests.

We hardly ever see anyone.' Sara at last emerged to make the point that she was not at all pleased to see us. She wore a café au lait silk gown with a pearl necklace and earrings. No one else had dressed for dinner, so someone had got it wrong. From Sara's glares, it was us.

Matty went to refill our glasses.

'Not too much, Matty. We have wine still to come.'

I'd expected Matty to make a joke and pour larger measures to show whose whisky it was. Instead he poured us small ones, and said nothing.

'We're honoured. We're having one of Matty's precious chickens tonight,' said Sara. 'Fewer eggs in future.'

'She'd already stopped laying,' said Matty, defensively.

Sara was not going to let go. 'She might have started again.'

'So what do you think of the German attack on Russia, then?' asked Matty, as he put Elgar's *Enigma Variations* on the gramophone where it competed with the Stravinsky coming from the radiator.

Sara answered. 'The Germans will walk all over them. Stalin decimated the Russian officer corps in his purges, their tanks are old-fashioned, and they've no answer to the *Blitzkrieg*.'

'If the size of Russia could defeat a military

genius like Napoleon, it'll defeat a megalomaniac ex-corporal,' said Angel.

'That ex-corporal had no problems conquering France and England,' snapped Sara. 'Times have changed. Now you have tanks instead of horses.'

'The supply problems are the same. Tanks drink petrol. Horses eat forage,' reasoned Matty. 'German lines of communication will soon become over-extended and vulnerable.'

'If the Germans are clever, they'll use the Ukrainians' and White Russians' hatred of the Bolsheviks to get them on their side,' I ventured.

'No chance. The Nazis regard all Slavs as lesser beings,' said Angel.

Mrs Haskell brought in the chicken and vegetables and we sat down. The carver chair at the head of the table was left empty. Matty opened a bottle of pre-war Fleurie.

'We should toast the Soviet Union, now that we're officially allies,' I said. The British government in exile had signed a mutual defence treaty with the Russian ambassador in Canada within twelve hours of the German attack.

'You always were a bit of a leftie, Nick,' said Matty.

'To us.' Sara lifted her glass towards me. 'I assume we're celebrating something, since Matty's killed the fatted chicken.'

'No,' he said, maybe too quickly.

'Come on. The last time I saw the three of you together, you'd been out on a Resistance operation. It didn't work but—'

'No.' The way Sara dismissed Roy's sacrifice made my hackles rise.

I expected Matty to join in my denial but he was concentrating on carving the chicken. He looked tired and worn. The long hours he was working were ageing him.

'You will not tell me?' Sara kept her tone light-hearted but there was no mistaking the message.

'Nothing's happening,' I repeated. 'We haven't seen each other for a while. That's all.'

'Matty, darling, make them tell me.'

She was watching Matty as she spoke. She was a watchful person, I realized. She had been observing me earlier to see how I felt about the German attack. Now she was watching Matty because he had annoyed her, and she wanted to see if she was annoying him back.

'Here you are.' He handed her a plate of meat.

It was not an easy meal. Matty was unusually quiet and listless, Sara was embarrassing in her persistent questioning, Angel was amusing but did not initiate conversation.

Sara did not exactly sulk, but she got her own back. When she spotted that Mrs Haskell had forgotten to put out the salt, she ordered Matty to go into the kitchen and fetch it. Then she found a smear on her wineglass. Matty had to replace it.

In the end, she came straight out and demanded to know if Angel and I were going out together.

I let Angel decide how to play it.

'Sort of,' she managed over a forkful of chicken.

During a dessert of apple pie and cream, Sara tried to quiz me about my work in the German HQ. I denied that I had access to any secrets, and digressed by recounting the rumour that Winter Relief – the Nazi Party charity to help the poor – was going to be introduced into Britain.

'It's not as if the money goes to the needy. The Nazis keep it for themselves,' said Angel. 'And you have to give otherwise you're deemed anti-social, and that's the first step towards the concentration camp.'

Matty began yawning even before we'd finished pudding. It gave us an excuse to leave early. As we were getting our coats, Sara whispered to me. 'You *can* trust me, you know.'

'What!'

'I *know* you're in the Resistance, just like Matty. It would be impossible for such a man as you not to do the right thing.'

I don't know how it would have sounded in Polish but in English it came over as heavy-handed flattery. It made me stick even closer to my story. I took both her hands in mine.

'Sara, I'm sorry to disappoint you but I've had my fingers burned once. We were very lucky we all weren't arrested and tortured. That's enough. I'm not a hero.'

I wanted a post-mortem on the evening, so I volunteered to walk Angel home from the bridge. It turned out that she was living in rooms at the top of one of the tall old houses on top of Breech Hill.

'She's very persistent, isn't she?' We both knew who I meant. 'All the subtlety of a sledgehammer. Are all Poles like that?'

'She feels excluded.'

I was surprised at Angel's charitable interpretation. 'Matty told me to deny everything, and I did.'

'Is he always so, um, docile with women? He lets her bully him rotten.'

'No. Usually he charms them around his little finger, but he's tired. Everything's getting on top of him.'

'Including Sara.'

'You've a dirty mind.'

'I didn't mean it in that way.'

'Shame. Anyway, what's this about us "sort of" going out?'

'A cover story. Don't get ideas.'

'I've never made love to an angel.'

'You wouldn't enjoy it. The feathers get every-where.'

Angel was looking at me from the corner of her eye. I burst out laughing. She giggled and then we were holding each other.

She gave a rueful smile. 'Nick. It wouldn't work. It'd make life even more complicated. And it's complicated enough already.'

I gathered she was turning me down. I said nothing.

'It never works, working with someone,' she murmured. 'You worry about the wrong things, your priorities are skewed. We can be friends?'

'Of course.' What else could I say. 'But are we now an item, as far as Sara's concerned?'

'Sort of,' she said.

The Irishmen were waiting for me when I arrived at the George the next evening.

'We've been thinking about what you said, about knowing the *Kommandant*'s movements in advance,' began Phil Finn.

'Yes,' I said warily.

'Can you tell me by tomorrow night what he'll be doing the day after, like?'

'I can tell you now. He's going to inspect the new coastal firing range at Mare Tail Sands in the morning and from there, he's going up to the town library in Podmore where he'll announce the sixth-form winners of the German essay competition.' I was not betraying any secrets. It was all going to be announced in tomorrow's *Western Daily News*.

'You're Bill Penny's son all right.' Finn leaned back and folded his arms across his barrel chest. 'Another drink. Kelvin.'

Kelvin rose obediently.

'What are you thinking of doing, exactly?' I didn't like the way this conversation was going.

'That's no concern of yours. The less you know, the better. Now, tell me, will Glass have an escort? You know – an armoured car or a lorryload of troops with him?'

'Not usually.'

'And is there a bodyguard in the car?'

'Just the driver.'

'Will you be with him on Wednesday?'

'I'll be meeting him at Podmore. He's going to the firing range first, and that's nothing to do with me.'

'I take it he'll go to Podmore along the coast road.'

'Suppose so.' The inland route would add fifteen miles to the journey.

Kelvin came back with more drinks and the Irishmen gulped greedily at their Guinness. Their eyes were aflame with fanaticism. I had to try to quench it.

'Glass may be a German, but he tries hard to

protect this region from some of London's madder excesses.'

'The only good German is a dead one,' growled Finn.

'You kill Glass, and the whole West Country will pay for it,' I argued.

'Then *you* people will find out what it's like to fight and suffer.' Finn was staring hard into my face, unhappy with what he was hearing. 'We know the English are patriots – they tell us so all the time – but I don't see many of them dying in the struggle. In Ireland we are tying down six divisions that could be fighting in Russia. In Ireland the roll-call of martyrs grows by the hour. In England you make sure your front door is closed and bolted before you wave your Union flag and curse the Germans.'

'I think it would be a mistake to try to assassinate Glass.' It sounded weak; milk-and-water rationalism evaporating in the white heat of the others' fanaticism.

'Oh, you do, do you? But you wouldn't be thinking of doing anything to stop us now, would you?'

'Glass is not an ogre,' I persisted. 'Believe it or not, he's the best you're going to get.'

'It sounds as though you're quite a fan of his,' said Finn.

'Of course not. But kill him and he'll be replaced by someone far worse, someone like that *Gestapo* bastard Stolz, for example.'

'And that would be such a terrible thing?' Finn was openly mocking me now. 'It's a dangerous game you're playing, Mr Penny – running with the hare and hunting with the hounds.'

I stood up to leave, angry at being mocked, and helpless against their fury. They rose as well.

'You stay and finish your pint. But a word of caution, Nick boy. Don't go riding with His Excellency too often in the future, and whatever you do, don't think of repeating this conversation to anyone.'

'What do you take me for?' I hoped I sounded indignant.

'I don't know yet, Nick boy, I don't know.'

I felt I had been run over by a ten-ton lorry. I couldn't wait to get out of the bar. I went to pay a visit to the outdoor lavatory when I heard Finn's voice.

'He's like the rest of the bloody English, afraid to get his hands dirty. It doesn't matter. We've got what we want. I know that coast road from Mare Tail Sands. There's a blind bend before the wool bridge at Cheddleton, stone walls either side. Block the road in front and behind and they're as good as dead. A good old IRA ambush. If it did for Michael Collins, it'll do for *Generalleutnant* von Glass.'

'The idiots. The bloody idiots.' I'd never seen Angel so angry.

'I think they want to see this city burned to the ground like their own Skibbereen.'

'Phil Finn is the local head of the Irish Republican Army. He'd really love to see the Germans and the English slug it out. A plague on both your houses.'

It was the first time I'd been in Angel's attic, one large room with a sloping roof so low that I couldn't stand upright in the corners. It had stained floorboards, rag rugs and a huge brass bedstead. It was a world of its own, reached by ladder; very isolated, very romantic and the perfect spot to receive wireless messages from Canada.

I'd surprised Angel washing her hair. She had stuck her head through a window and tossed down a key, after I'd impressed through mime that I had to talk to her. I'd arrived up in the attic to find her in slacks and a green woollen shirt far too big for her, which revealed the tantalizing valley between her breasts when she leaned forward. A white brassiere was draped over a Chinese screen.

'You'll have to tell Glass,' she decided, fixing the towel like a turban on her head.

'Great! Excuse me, *Kommandant*, but if you go to Mare Tail Sands tomorrow, some nasty men will try to kill you. He might just ask how I know . . .'

'Yes?'

'Is Mills around? Perhaps he could—'

'*I* can deal with this.' I suddenly glimpsed an altogether different woman: one with steel and purpose. Then the hard edges melted, as if they should never have been on public display. 'Poor Nick, you do find yourself in the middle of things, don't you? You'll be damned if you do, and damned if you don't. And now you've come to your guardian angel for help.'

No one likes to be laughed at, and I expect that it showed in my face. I didn't think it was at all funny to be caught between a man with the power of life or death and a gang of fanatical killers.

'We have links with the IRA. I can probably get the attack called off, but I'm not sure I can do it in time.' Angel was looking thoughtfully at a sewing box. 'Phil Finn – dark-haired, barrel of a man?'

'More of a slab than a barrel.'

'I know him.' She stepped behind the screen, the shirt flew over the top and the bra disappeared. She walked across the room, doing up the bra, to a wardrobe where she selected a cream blouse. It was done so naturally that it was incredibly sexy.

'Where're you going?'

'The Irish Club. In case I fail, get Glass to take an alternative route.'

It was easy to get to see Glass. He wanted to see me. The map of England had now been replaced by one of the Eastern Front, with the German armies in black and the Russians in red. Black arrows indicated the three-pronged attack towards Leningrad in the north, Moscow in the centre, and south through Bessarabia towards the Ukraine. Hauser said that Glass had been talking to old friends at OKH – the Army High Command in Berlin – in the hope of getting command of an army corps in Russia.

'Some of my Brandenburgers had been behind Russian lines for three days before the German attack, you know,' he said, carefully drawing a bulge in the line towards Minsk.

There was no fire in the grate and the room was cold. Glass had ordered that the heating in the *Feldkommandantur* should be turned down, to save fuel.

'You wanted to see me, sir?'

'Ah, yes. A funfair has asked permission to spend three days on Rathdry Common,' he continued with his drawing. 'They claim it's the local tradition.'

'It's always held every Easter and on August bank holiday, sir,' I said.

'You know the *Reich* does not encourage gypsies?'

'These aren't gypsies, sir.' I didn't know if they were or not, but I liked the funfair. 'Just travelling show folk. There's usually a whirligig, dodgems where you're supposed to avoid the other cars but every one tries to crash into each other, a merry-go-round with horses . . .'

'Thank you, Penny. We *do* have funfairs in Germany, too. I suppose it can't do any harm. Might even cheer up the troops. I'll let the first night be open to both locals and Germans. If there's no trouble, it can run for the full three days. Is everything ready for me tomorrow at the library?'

'I sent the librarian a list of the banned books last week, and I'll check the shelves myself before you get there.' I couldn't be sure that no author on the blacklist – which included writers as diverse as Thomas Mann and Dennis Wheatley – was not tucked away somewhere in the library. I *had* to make sure that Glass would not be embarrassed by being photographed in front of a shelf of anti-Nazi books – as had happened to the German Governor in the North.

It had been a brave but costly gesture. The librarian and his staff had been taken from their homes when the censor had spotted the picture in the *Manchester Guardian*'s first edition. They were never heard of again. It was the first use of *Nacht und Nebel* in Britain.

Literally, *Nacht und Nebel* meant 'night and fog'. The decree, signed by Himmler himself, gave the *Gestapo* the powers to make someone vanish. The accused did not appear in court, and relatives could never trace them afterwards. The poor Accrington librarians were later believed to have died in Mauthausen concentration camp.

'Who chose the winners of the essay competition?'

'You did. They get to spend a fortnight at a Hitler Youth camp outside Cologne during the summer.'

'I've had a signal from London on that.' Glass waved vaguely towards his cluttered desk. 'The winners are now going to be accompanied by their own school captains of sport. The whole lot will be enlisted in the Hitler Youth while they're in Germany, and when they come back, they'll be made section leaders of the *Führer* Scouts.'

Glass went to rub his missing elbow, a sure indication that he was in pain. He'd be reaching for his painkillers and brandy soon. I had to talk to him before his next mood swing but I couldn't think of an easy way to begin the conversation. In the end, I decided that there wasn't one.

'Do you still intend going to the firing range before visiting the library tomorrow, sir?'

'I don't need to be at the library until one o'clock, do I?'

'No, sir, but I'd heard they'd found an unexploded land mine by the side of the coast road between Mare Tail Sands and Podmore.'

'It'll be cleared by then.'

'Have you ever been along the moors route to Podmore, sir? It's very pretty.'

'And takes longer.'

'But if the other route's closed . . .'

'It won't be.' Glass referred to a sheet of paper on his desk, and continued to mark the German advance on the map.

I stood there, not knowing what to do or say. In

the end I had to come right out with it. 'I really do think you should go over the moors instead, sir.'

For a moment I thought Glass had not heard me. Then he turned very deliberately to give me the same type of look that he'd given Horace Smeed. It was a look that made shivers search for a spine to run up.

'Why?'

'It'll be different. The people up there don't get the chance to see you like those on the coast do. I'll get pupils from the village schools to line the street. You could give away sweets.' I ran out of gabble.

'You're not trying to lead me into a trap, are you?'

'No, sir. I give you my word I'm not.'

I think Glass could tell from my face that I was telling the truth. 'Then why are you so keen for me to take the moors road? If I told you that I was determined to go along the coast, what would you say?'

We stared at each other for what seemed an eternity.

'Don't.'

'So you're trying to save me? What exactly do you know?'

I shook my head helplessly. At this rate I was going to be seeing the inside of a *Gestapo* cell before sunset. But Glass let me off the hook, and my admiration for him rose accordingly.

'All right, I remember you telling me you're not a traitor. I'll take your advice, but you'll come with me.

It's fairly impossible to attack a car and kill only one passenger while leaving another unscathed. Just tell your friends that.'

'They're not my friends,' I said.

That evening I didn't stop at the George or anywhere else. Instead I went home and worried. The change of route would seem bad enough, but if Glass got himself an escort then it'd be obvious that I'd talked. I'd nailed my colours to the mast, and there was a swastika flying on top of it. The IRA would come after me for betraying them. No one would grieve for me, except my small family and Matty.

Would Glass give me a German military funeral? Over my already dead body!

Next morning I had the pupils of three junior schools lining the streets of their various villages, waving little Union flags and swastikas. Glass stopped at each and handed out gobstoppers and humbugs. I noticed the kids were fascinated by his one arm. An armoured car preceded us and a troop carrier followed in our wake.

In fact, Glass needn't have bothered. Phil Finn and half the Irish Club had gone down with a violent attack of food poisoning that laid them out for the week and left them concentrating on nothing more pressing than how far they dared go from a lavatory. When they were next able to take an interest in life, they neither knew nor cared which route Glass had taken, and by then Dublin had passed on the word that the time was not ripe for political assassination on the mainland. Not yet, anyway.

'Where're we going?'

'To see a man about £50,000. You're always complaining I don't let you do enough for the Resistance.'

'You're just using me to pretend we're a courting couple on our day out.' We sat astride the BSA as Angel consulted a hand-drawn map.

'Clever boy.'

'I want to do something really useful, like robbing a bank.'

'It's Sunday and the banks are closed.' Angel rolled her eyes in mock despair. 'And no you don't. No one's robbing any more banks for the time being. That's why we're going to see this man.'

Matty had led a successful bank robbery in Plympton but two other recent raids had ended in disaster. In Taunton, two Resistance men were shot dead when they found the National Bank they tried to rob full of German soldiers, while in Penzance another team had bumped into a patrol as they'd fled with bags of banknotes. Matty, who had been the getaway driver on that occasion, escaped only by the skin of his teeth.

With bank raids on hold, Angel had to find another way to raise the money the Resistance needed to grease palms, buy petrol and food and make sure the relatives of the unlucky were looked after.

But, while Matty was risking his neck in undercover operations, I'd done nothing more hazardous than keep my eyes and ears open inside the *Feldkommandantur*. My complaints had finally led to my current role of acting as motorbike chauffeur to Angel.

'That one.' Angel pointed. 'Very nice, too.'

The white villa with its cornflower-blue shutters peeping wantonly over luxuriant pink and red bougainvillaea bushes would have been perfectly at home on the Côte d'Azur. It looked out of place beside the choppy grey waters of the English Channel. The glint of a wire running through the shrubbery caught my eye. A radio aerial?

Peregrine Gawain Gown, art historian, fine-art collector and dealer, had done well out of the Germans. He had been quick to capitalize on Hitler's hatred of decadent French impressionists and his love of the stolidly bourgeois. What the *Führer* admired, Germany admired; with a few exceptions among rich deviant Berliners. Gawain Gown provided connoisseurs with what they liked, and the Party faithful with what they felt they should have – and took a percentage from each. But to bank large amounts of *Reichsmark* would attract German fiscal officials demanding to know their provenance. And the last thing Gown wanted was to embarrass his clients and his patrons, as Angel was aware.

A slender Indian boy in a gold turban showed us into the morning room, where my untutored eye took in a Corot and a Degas racecourse scene. Pride of place went to Manet's *Déjeuner sur l'herbe*. If Peregrine Gawain Gown wished to impress, he had succeeded. He had also shown he had money aplenty.

'Miss Sherbourne.' A thin voice, reedy and sounding infinitely bored.

I'd forgotten to ask Angel who she was today. 'Mr Gown, this is my colleague Peter Carpenter.' So that was who *I* was.

'I must say, Miss Sherbourne, I was expecting someone, shall I say, a little older. In his letter Lord Robertson indicated . . . well . . .' The effort of continuing was clearly too much. Gown rang for coffee and offered round an ebony cigarette box inlaid with silver and mother-of-pearl. 'Turkish, French, German.'

If Gown's voice was languorous, his eyes were vital, darting around like a robin's. They missed nothing. I bet that without looking, he could have described us down to the number of freckles on Angel's nose and the double knots in my shoelaces. The boy brought coffee – real coffee – and wafer-thin dark chocolate biscuits.

'The Manet intrigues you,' he said to Angel.

'I'm trying to remember where I saw it last,' she replied. 'Was it in the Louvre in Paris?'

'Was it?' Gown's mouth crimped in disdain. 'I

was surprised to receive a letter from Robertson. I'd thought him in Canada with the Ashmolean collection.'

'He is,' said Angel.

'Ah!' A long exhalation of rarefied air.

'Shall I continue?'

'If you mean can you talk safely, the answer is yes. There is no one to overhear you. But do I want to hear what you have to say? It is, after all, a dying echo from another country.'

'It's to do with money,' said Angel bluntly.

'Pray continue.'

'You have an embarrassment of cash. Please don't deny it. I have friends who need *Reichsmark*. If you wish to give me 500,000 *Reichsmark*, the equivalent sum will be placed in an account in Ottawa at a rate of eight *Reichsmark* to the pound sterling. As the official rate is 9.36 you will have made more than £9,000 immediately. The account will pay five per cent interest and the money returned at the cessation of hostilities.'

'Aren't you rather asking me to put my money on an outsider in a two-horse race?'

Angel rose to the bait. 'Outsiders sometimes come in, you know.'

'Not often, my dear.'

Gown's patronizing superciliousness grated on me. 'You're being offered a no-lose bet, a *pari du*

Pascal,' I said. 'It's an opportunity for you to put a foot in both camps instead of being up to your balls with the Nazis.'

He professed to be shocked. 'A rather direct young man, aren't you?'

You could see his mind working. The half a million *Reichsmark* was probably stuffing a mattress in his attic. Not only would it be a good investment, but also an insurance in the event of an improbable British victory.

He took time, sipping his coffee delicately. 'This really is a preposterous suggestion: coming in here with your fairy stories, seeking to suborn an honest citizen. Anyway, how do I *know* you can deliver what you promise?'

'Give me a phrase known just to us three. Listen to the Voice of Free Britain a week from now, between six and seven in the evening. You can pick up the Voice of Free Britain?'

Gawain Gown nodded. With that hidden aerial, he could pick up the Voice of Free Tibet. It occurred to me that he must use a long-range radio to strike deals with his clients in Europe.

'I shall not ask Jean Jacques Rousseau whether birds confabulate or no,' he said.

What a strange phrase, I thought.

*

Angel made the best use of my services by picking up wireless crystals from a loyal Marconi dealer in the next town who'd had the good sense to hide his stock when the Germans had arrived. There were more crystals than Angel had expected, which put her into an even better mood. We decided to celebrate our successful day by having a picnic on the way home.

'We need some sand to roll our hard-boiled eggs in,' I said as we shopped for bread, cheese and a flagon of cider.

'What?'

'Every picnic I've ever been on has involved hard-boiled eggs falling onto the sand as soon as they're shelled.'

'You had a very strange upbringing.' Angel eyed me as if I was mad. 'Anyway, we can't get any eggs.'

'Well, it's no good just having sand by itself.'

We settled on going to Crown Haligan, a well-known beauty spot on a ridge, with the sea off in the distance and rolling blue hills inland. It had been a favourite with picnickers before the war but now no one had the petrol to get there. That was one advantage of working for the Anglo-German Friendship League – I was never short of fuel. We rode along tracks leading deep into the copper beeches until we came to a clearing set amid drifts of bluebells, with here and there small hosts of daffodils. It was unseasonably mild, almost like a summer's day.

'Do you think Gown is likely to play ball?' I asked as I laid out the food on a sawn-off tree trunk.

'I think so. He's shrewd enough to know that he's nothing to lose. But some of those paintings!'

'Thinking of liberating one or two?'

Angel grinned. 'I might do if he doesn't cooperate.'

'The Corot would go nicely in your living room, next to that print of *The Haywain*.'

I passed her slabs of Cheddar cheese I had hewed off with my jackknife, then attacked the cider. It slipped down a treat, making me bolder.

'It's a shame we're working together,' I said after a while.

'Why?'

'Because you said it never works when you're working with someone.'

'Oh, that.' She laughed. 'I have been known to be wrong, you know.'

I listened to the birds having singing competitions as I digested her words. A nuthatch was making its way down a chestnut tree, pecking away at insects in the bark. Angel noticed it, too.

'If you could come back as a bird, what sort would you be?' she demanded.

'A peregrine falcon.'

'Typical *man*,' she sighed. 'Are you really sure you want to sit on someone's wrist with a hood over your head?'

'A bittern – then I could go "boom" all day. Boom. Boom.'

'If you really want to sound like a foghorn . . .'

'A raven – then people will quote me. What about you?'

'I've always loved the mating displays of the lapwings, the way they tumble through the air.'

'Only the displays?'

'Well, I don't think birds have much fun *doing it*. The very few times I've ever seen them at it, it's over before it begins.'

'Swifts do it on the wing,' I informed her.

Angel spread her arms and pretended to fly. She shook her head after a moment. 'No, I think I'd be airsick.'

'Be a chicken, then you wouldn't have to fly.'

'I don't think I like the idea of laying all those eggs. Perhaps I'll just be my own type of bird.'

I pulled out a notebook and pencil. 'I'll show you this flying machine I designed.' I drew a rough sketch and handed it over.

'That looks more like a wardrobe.'

'Do you enjoy flying?'

'No. I hate the vibration and I usually get airsick. Anyway, it's dangerous.'

'Quite. And have you ever seen a wardrobe crash?'

'No . . .?'

'I sat inside one for four hours yesterday, and didn't feel sick at all.'

'Fool.' She flung both arms around my neck and kissed me.

But, even as we smiled into each other's eyes, a cold feeling grew in the pit of my stomach. Some primeval instinct told me that we were being watched.

Angel felt me tense up. 'What is it?'

'There's someone . . . shit.'

Two men, with an air of heavy menace about them, appeared from behind a tree. Bizarrely, they wore swastika armbands around the sleeves of their shabby jackets. I rose to my feet and moved in front of Angel. The larger of them was carrying a huge old Webley pistol. It could knock down the side of a barn – but he'd have to hit it first.

'Papers.'

'And who are you?'

The man pointed to his armband. 'Auxiliaries.'

'Auxiliary what?'

'Don't be smart, sonny. Get their papers, and their wallets, Joe. Come on, or I'll shoot.'

I held out my wallet. Joe snatched it out of my hand and scooped up Angel's shoulder bag in one movement. As he was opening her bag, I casually picked up the cheese and my jackknife.

'Where're the keys to that bike?'

''Ere, look at these.' Joe held up two of the crystals.

'Put those down, they're valuable,' I protested.

Angel had not said a word. She stood with her hands in the side pockets of her jacket, seeming curiously detached from the scene.

'They're for a wireless set. I reckon we'll be in for a nice little reward when we hand you over to the Germans.'

'You're not actually going to turn us in! You're Englishmen.' I opened my arms wide in feigned amazement. I knew they'd have no scruples, but I wanted him to get used to me waving my hands around – especially the one holding the open knife.

'"You're Englishmen",' he mimicked. 'Fuck off and grow up.'

I stepped forward suddenly and kicked up at his gun hand. My foot caught it a glancing blow. The cannon went off with a roar that sent flocks of birds rising in protest from the tree tops. I moved in and slashed at his face. He raised his arms to cover his eyes, I cut open his knuckles instead. With a scream, he dropped the gun.

There was a second shot. We froze.

'Move away, Nick.'

Angel had a small automatic pointed at the man. I quickly picked up the Webley and retrieved the radio crystals. The Webley weighed a ton. I cocked it.

'Nah, nah, we didn't mean no harm, mate,' snivelled the one called Joe, while the other one clutched his bloody hand and glowered at me from under dark brows.

'Nick, put everything in the haversack,' ordered Angel. 'We don't want to leave any trace here. Then go and get the bike started.'

'What are you doing?'

'I'm going to take these two deeper into the woods and tie them up to make sure they can't get word to the Germans before we're well clear.'

'We wouldn't do that, missus.'

'Too true, you won't. Undo your belts, and bootlaces – now march.'

I kick-started the bike and waited. After a few minutes I heard a shot, closely followed by another. I had just begun riding towards the shots when Angel came hurrying through the trees towards me.

'Are you all right?'

'The big one tried to go for the gun so I shot him in the leg.'

'But I heard two shots.'

'That was to warn the other not to get ideas.' She swung her leg over the pillion. 'Shame about our picnic.'

As I rode back, I brooded about those shots. Our prospective robbers had seen the incriminating crystals; they could also describe us and the bike. The clincher was Angel addressing me by name. She wouldn't have done that unless she had already made up her mind about what was going to happen to them.

The two men were shifty, good-for-nothing traitors who, for the sake of a few quid, would have seen us in a *Gestapo* torture chamber. Maybe they deserved to die. It made perfect sense to kill them, but I never did ask Angel, either then or in the months to come when I got to know her so much better, how she had felt when she'd murdered two men in cold blood.

14

Matty pulled back the rubber band, closed one eye, and let fly. The duck fell with a metallic quack, and Matty punched the pair in boyish pleasure.

'The deadliest catapult in the west,' he crowed.

'Men,' sniffed Sara.

'We only need another three ducks to win that purple rabbit.' I pointed out the stuffed toy.

'Don't you dare.' Angel was already carrying an indecently leering monkey that Matty had won earlier on the hoopla stall. Sara had refused to have anything to do with it.

Matty was a regular winner of trophies at funfairs. One summer we'd kept a whole aquarium of goldfish he'd won by rolling pennies, knocking over coconuts or throwing darts. My own contribution had used to be the shooting gallery, but now guns were banned for civilians and I wasn't much good with a catapult.

Roy's speciality had been tossing ping-pong balls into jam jars to win toffee apples all round. Implicitly, Matty and I had avoided that booth.

Other than that, we were behaving like kids.

Around us, the scents of damp, trodden earth and fried food wafted on the night air as the merry grind of barrel organs competed with the cries of the stall-holders. We'd been almost sick on the whirligig, tried to loop the loop on the swingboats, poked fun at each other in the hall of mirrors, and crashed our dodgems into each other so aggressively that we'd been banned.

I caught sight of Pip Cartwright furtively slipping copies of *The Free Briton* into a shopping basket. The fair was crawling with *Wehrmacht* and *Kriegsmarine* – some escorting local girls – as well as numbers of police and German *Feldgendarmerie*. If Pip's mother, a pale consumptive worrier who doted on her only child, knew the risks he took . . .

Pip grinned at us and disappeared behind the waltzer.

'Let's go and have our fortunes told.' Angel pointed at a small booth with golden stars painted on an ink-blue background. *Madame Isadora knows your future. Cards. Palmistry. Crystal Ball.*

'Do we *have* a future?' demanded Sara.

'St Augustine said that the only difference between a sinner and a saint was that every saint had a past and every sinner a future,' I volunteered.

'How do you know I'm a sinner?' Angel poked me with her monkey.

'Don't you covet your neighbour's ox?'

'Daily.'

'There you are, then.'

'Fortune-telling is just childish nonsense,' insisted Sara.

'It can't do any harm,' coaxed Matty. 'Come on.'

For once Matty got his way. As Angel pushed back the heavy hessian curtain, the fumes of a paraffin heater swirled around us. If you peered closely, you could see that Madame Isadora was only one coat of paint away from having been Gypsy Rose Lee. It didn't pay to be a Romany princess under the Nazis.

'Cross my palm with silver,' instructed Madame Isadora, who might have changed her name but hadn't got round to changing her costume. She still wore a gypsy bandanna, flamboyant gold earrings and a brilliant red sash over a long, black skirt.

Angel gave her a sixpence.

'Hold out your left hand,' the woman said in an Essex accent. 'Ah, I see you have travelled far to be here. You have come from over the water.'

'The Scilly Isles,' whispered Matty, and Madame Isadora shot him a foul look.

'You are loyal to your friends but you expect much in return – sometimes too much. You have love to give but you do not like to show your true self. You are adventurous and secretive and . . .'

There was more about how Angel accepted responsibility, was generous, and travelled a lot. I was impressed despite myself. Where did it say all that in Angel's hand?

'. . . There is a man. He is tall and fair. He cares for you but will not reveal himself.'

I caught Sara staring at me, and coloured.

Madame Isadora concluded by telling Angel she would have at least two children and live to old age.

Then it was my turn. Madame Isadora stared at my palm for so long that I grew uneasy. 'Yes, yes, I see it now,' she whispered. 'You hate what you are doing, don't you?'

I nodded in amazement. I was dressed in civvies, and I'd never met the woman before. How could she know?

'It's something to do with a talent you have. But what you are doing now does not last for ever. Not that much longer, in fact. Your life is about to take an unexpected turn.'

'Where does it say that?' Sara pushed forward.

'I see it.' The fortune-teller looked me in the eye. 'Keep your faith. Many will depend on you.'

Madame Isadora indicated my head line, heart line and life line. There was a bit about fulfilling my creative instincts, ending my days far from here, and marrying someone with a double 'N' in her first name – so that ruled out Coral. But, like her, I was going to have at least two children and live to a ripe old age.

'Matty, your go.'

I was watching Madame Isadora's face as she inspected his palm. She did not like what she saw there.

'Yes, yes,' she kept repeating. Finally she met Matty's eye. 'You have the hand of either a saint or a murderer.'

'Frequently the same thing,' Matty muttered.

'I see blood, but it's not clear if it's yours. I see a sacrifice.'

'It's that chicken we ate,' murmured Sara.

The fortune-teller glowered at her. 'Death is near you, young man. You, more than most, have choices to make.'

Matty stiffened. He and Madame Isadora stared at each other in alarm as if discovering that they shared a dreadful secret. Matty withdrew his hand swiftly.

It had grown colder in the tent. 'Come on, Sara. Your turn to be told your murderous potential.' I tried to lighten the atmosphere.

'No. This is a lot of mumbo-jumbo. She's not even a true Romany.'

'That's true, dear,' said Madame Isadora. 'I'm from Walthamstow, but I do have the gift.'

She motioned towards the curtain. Angel peered outside, then turned back and nodded. She and Madame Isadora leaned towards each other.

'The Germans are mining the south Irish Sea, off Wexford, against submarines,' whispered the fortune-teller. 'Their shore batteries in the Scilly Isles have only ten rounds per gun. There are only two AA units west of Southampton, at Bristol and Plymouth. Two more infantry regiments, the 167th and 92nd, and units of the 5th Light Division are going to the Eastern Front next week. There's talk that auxiliary German policemen will replace regular troops here.'

'Anyone there?' A prospective customer called from outside.

'*Moment mal.* That's all,' she hissed. 'We're at Plymouth next.'

We left the tent to find a German corporal waiting with a plump English girl.

'What was that about?' demanded Sara, a moment later.

'Madame Isadora's superb at snapping up unconsidered trifles,' explained Angel. 'She's also bilingual. By telling the Germans their fortunes, she gets to ask them questions.'

'And *does* she have the gift?' I asked.

'She thinks so,' said Angel – as I racked my brain for a girl with a double 'N' in her name.

They were amateurs, the lot of them, although Sara had to admit that the fortune-teller's operation was a rare touch of class. Madame Isadora had unsettled Matty. Poor little Matty.

'Sorry, Nick, but I need to get rid of all this cigarette smoke.'

Sara wound down the car window. It would be windy for Nick in the back, but he would not complain – he never did. She reflected that even the woman calling herself Coral Kennedy was making an effort to be nice to her. That was the weakness of these people: they wanted to be liked. You did not win wars by being liked.

'That's all right. What did she mean you had the hand of a saint or a murderer?' Nick asked Matty. 'Do murderers all have similar hands?'

'Search me.'

'If they did it'd be easier to get convictions. You'd just hold up an accused's hand and pronounce guilty or not guilty.'

'That's more or less how the Nazis decide on guilt,' said Coral Kennedy. 'They believe criminality's in the blood, so habitual criminals can be arrested on suspicion that they *might* go on to commit another offence. The Nazis'll execute a petty thief because they reckon he'll never become a useful member of the community. At the same time, members of their own Party literally get away with murder.'

'How do you know that?' asked Matty.

'You've got to know your enemy.'

Sara stifled a snort of derision, and continued to ball up the silk scarf in her left hand, which she trailed out of the window.

'If someone told me that I had the hand of a murderer, I'd kill them.'

'Too late, Matty,' said Nick. 'Guy de Maupassant's already written it.'

'Trust you to know that,' said Matty. 'So, who do you know with a double "N" in her name?'

'I'm trying to think,' replied Nick.

Sara released the scarf so that it streamed alongside the car. Ahead, a red and white pole descended across the road at the German checkpoint on the Old London Road.

'Hell.' Matty slowed down. 'Why do the Jerries have to man this place tonight? They haven't bothered with it for weeks.'

Sara pulled her arm back as the car drew up outside the converted toll-house.

The guards flashed the beams of their torches over the passengers' faces before collecting their identity papers and carrying them into the light. One returned holding an ID card. He identified Sara.

'You are from the *Warthegau*?' he demanded, using the *Reich*'s new name for western Poland.

'I was born in Breslau. It says so there.'

'This card has not been validated for residence in England.'

'But I have my residence permit.' Sara searched through her handbag. 'Here.'

The guard ignored her outstretched hand. Instead he opened the passenger door. 'Come.'

Sara moaned in protest. 'But surely . . .'

'I'll come with you,' said Matty.'

'No.' The other guard stopped him from opening his door.

'I'll be all right,' said Sara bravely. 'Everything's in order. Send in the cavalry if I'm gone more than an hour.'

She smiled uncertainly over her shoulder as the guard took her arm and led her into the small stone house, where until last November a widow had sold honey from her front door.

The house was redolent of stale bread and dust. In the front parlour, sagging armchairs had been pushed against a wall to allow room for a trestle table and chairs. Duty rosters and sheaves of orders, stamped with the ubiquitous swastika and eagle, were pinned to the floral wallpaper. Holding Sara above the elbow, the guard steered her down a passage. The only light came from a dim 40-watt bulb under a pink tasselled shade. Sara caught sight of herself as they passed a mirror – she thought she looked suitably pale. An SS man standing guard on a door at the far end moved aside to allow her to enter. The guard released her arm and closed the door behind her.

She found herself in the kitchen. A generator chugged unevenly just outside the window and a large fire was roaring in the grate.

SS *Standartenführer* Stolz rose from a rocking chair.

'*Heil Hitler.*' His right arm shot out like a piston.
'*Heil Hitler,*' replied Sara.

I lay in the drainage ditch with my nose pressed into
a dandelion, and cursed myself for ever wanting
to be a hero. Ahead, the German sentry stood stock-
still, his head turned into the wind. He must have
heard Cyril trip over that brick. They'd probably even
heard it in the officers' mess the other side of the airfield. I expected a professional burglar like Cyril to
be light on his feet – not to possess the stealth of a
shire horse. Finally the sentry resumed his leisurely
progress into the shadows of the hangars looming to
my left. Ahead, on the tarmac, I made out the massive shape of a four-engine Focke-Wulf Condor. It
was as high as a house, with the huge wingspan
that enabled it to cruise for hours over the Atlantic.
The Condor was one of the new 200C-3s possessing
revolutionary air-cooled BMW-Bramo 323R-2 Fafnir
engines with methanol-water injection. These engines
had increased the aircraft's operational radius by more
than 600 miles. Last week, one of these Condors had
surprised a Royal Navy submarine on the surface in
daylight because the sub's skipper thought that he
was far enough from land to be safe. Now the powers
in Canada urgently wanted to know more about the
new engine. Studying its maintenance manual seemed
an obvious solution.

I was being allowed to lead this raid on the coastal airfield partly because Matty had twisted an ankle, but mainly because I had nagged Angel until she finally gave in. Matty had tried hard to try to stop me, but I was determined. In the end he had given me his lucky balaclava to wear. I forgot to ask why it was lucky.

There were three of us: Trevor, who'd formerly worked as a carpenter on the airfield, to lead us to the maintenance chief's office; Cyril, to open the door and the safe; and me, to make sure we were not lifting the operating instructions for the CO's lawnmower.

I'd met the other two men for the first time that night. They were keen but clueless, and now Cyril had gone and fallen over the only stray brick on the vast airfield.

I cradled my Thompson gun and waved at Trevor to move up towards the administration block. The rising wind sang in the telephone wires over my head as I made out a Blenheim bomber with *Luftwaffe* crosses.

Trevor was up and off, his dark pudding shape lumbering over the grass between the hangars towards some lower buildings. Twenty yards on, he suddenly pitched forward. He was still in mid-roll when a klaxon began its banshee wail. A white flare went up away to our left as a searchlight clicked on, its orange beam probing around the area around the

Condors. There was only one thing to do – get ourselves out before they released the guard dogs. Trevor had been very strong in his warnings about the Alsatians the Germans had brought in. Shame he had said nothing about the trip wire.

I tapped Cyril on the shoulder and pointed back towards the shadowed gap between the hangars that led to our hole in the perimeter fence. I gave him a shove to get him on his way, and moved fast and low towards Trevor. He was up now but, instead of running, was pointing his pistol towards figures approaching through the gloom.

'No,' I yelled. Too late.

He fired once, twice. It was pointless. Trevor was out of range while the machine carbines of the guards were not. The searchlight caught him just as his head exploded.

I turned to see Cyril well ahead of me and legging it, his slighter figure covering the ground like a greyhound. Bright stabs of flame came out of the blackness surrounding the nearest hangar. Cyril staggered, his momentum still propelling him forward so he appeared to be running through quicksand, his body sinking lower and lower until he collapsed. I fired a short burst at the muzzle flashes and dropped down beside him. He was groaning, with one hand pressed to his side. I hauled him to his feet, ready to sling him over my shoulder in a fireman's lift, when a sledgehammer thumped into my chest. I was thrown backwards, the breath knocked out of my body. I put my hand up to feel for the wound. Instead I found the cigarette case my mother had given me now had a deep dent in its surface. The round had gone straight through poor Cyril, killing him, and exited with enough force to knock me over.

I rose unsteadily to my feet, put my head down and lurched into a run. I didn't stand a chance. It was two hundred yards still to the perimeter fence. Over the sound of my rasping breath, I heard dogs barking. Ahead of me bullets were sparking off the chain fence and rounds whistled over my head. I braced myself for the expected punch in the back. I didn't think I'd ever make it – but I did. Suddenly I was through the hole and belting across a stubble field to the lane on the other side where a car without lights coasted towards me. I tumbled into it.

'What happened?'

'A fucking disaster,' I gasped, forgetting myself.

'Another one,' sighed Angel.

I don't think I've ever felt more humiliated in my life than the first time I saw a British Jew wearing a yellow star.

A poorly dressed man in his fifties, with the bearing of a lifelong soldier, he passed by without a word as I sat in the municipal park's sunken garden, waiting for Angel. It was another minute before I could move again for the anger, pity and shame flaming inside me. Next to his yellow star the man was wearing the Military Medal for bravery.

The Germans had just decreed that all Jews had to buy themselves three stars costing a shilling each. These stars, to be worn over the heart, were deducted from their clothing ration.

The edict was yet another step in pushing the Jews further to the outer edge of society. It followed closely on the previous week's order that all Jews had to register at their local police station. It had also banned them from public places like cinemas and street markets. God only knew what was to come next!

The small garden was a blaze of colour at this time of year, with camellias and azaleas amid swathes of daffodils, but all I could see was that old soldier. The daffodils were nodding their yellow heads as if to beckon me. I picked one and put it in the buttonhole of my greatcoat.

'You'll get into trouble for doing that.' Jacob Jenner stood in front of me.

'At this moment, Jacob, I would welcome it.'

'I thought I'd come and sit here for a few minutes. I'm on my way to collect these new stars for me and Miriam.' He joined me on the park bench. 'Why are they doing this to us, Nick?'

'I don't know.' I was telling the truth. All regulations regarding the Jews came from the burgeoning

Office for Jewish Affairs on the second floor of the *Feldkommandantur*. The office was under the control of the *SS WVHA* – *Wirtschaftsverwaltungshauptamt* – the SS Economic Administration Department that dealt with concentration and labour camps, with a few officials from the *SS RuSHA* – the Race and Resettlement Department – and had nothing to do with Glass or the Anglo-German Friendship League.

'I'm not ashamed of being Jewish but I always think of myself as English. Does it really matter what race I am?' Jacob appeared diminished – a small, rather pathetic-looking man with tight grey curls and tiny blue veins along his nose.

'Of course not.'

'Simon is very concerned about Anna. There are rumours that all foreign-born Jews are going to be deported.'

I felt a stab of fear – the Jewish bush telegraph was usually accurate. 'How's Miriam taking this?'

'Worrying for the world. She's convinced they're going to confiscate our bank account. Not that there's much left in there.'

'Oi, what are you doing in here?' A youngish policeman stood glaring down at Jacob. 'Hop it before I nick you.'

'What are you talking about, constable?' I put on my best officer voice.

'Parks are public places so Jews are banned from

them.' He stepped towards Jacob. 'Hop it or I'll arrest you.'

'Oh, come on,' I said. 'We're having a conversation. What harm's my friend doing?'

'He shouldn't be here, and he knows it,' snapped the copper.

Jacob, usually so chirpy, so ready with an answer, said nothing.

'You see that plaque on the cairn there, in the middle of the sunken garden?' I asked reasonably. 'Can you read what it says?'

The policeman read aloud. '*This arboretum was created by the generosity of Miriam and Jacob Jenner for the pleasure of all.*' He shrugged. 'Yeh, so?'

'This is Mr Jenner.'

'He's still a Jew,' snarled the copper. 'Don't try to be clever.'

I leaped to my feet, the red mist descending over my eyes. Fuck it! I was going to beat the shit out of this copper.

'Nick, Nick, I will go.' Jacob grabbed my arm. 'I have to get to the police station, anyway.'

'No, you stay. You stay in this park as long as you like.' I held the copper's eyes with my own.

'Nick, no trouble, please. I must go, really.'

I shook hands with Jacob. 'I'll call in soon.'

The copper was still eyeing me up. I stared back. I wanted to know him in future. After an age, he backed down and skulked off the way he had come. I sat back down and thought of Jacob Jenner and his three yellow stars.

The distant sound of a muffled pistol shot broke my reverie. I glanced at my watch. Angel was running late. It was a fine April day but too cold to sit on a park bench for long. When she arrived, she did so in a rush, whipping off her beret and reversing her beige mackintosh so that it became deep green. She dropped down on the bench, glowing with excitement. There was a familiar smell about her that at first I couldn't place. Then it came to me: cordite. Before she could speak, we heard the hobnail boots of a German patrol approaching along the gravel path.

'Don't take this personally,' she whispered. Angel grabbed my waistband and dropped something cold and metallic down the inside of my trousers. Before I could react, she had unbuttoned her blouse and placed my hand over her brassiere.

'For Christ's sake, kiss me.' Angel pulled my face down onto hers. I tried to remove my hand from her breast but she kept her hand clamped over mine.

'Get on with it.' Angel began to moan.

It wasn't easy, knowing German soldiers were going to appear at any moment. Angel grabbed my cock. I opened my eyes to catch her gleam of amusement. Bitch! The footsteps had halted. Angel's nipple grew hard. She was enjoying this. Out of the very corner of my eye, I saw the Germans standing gawping on the edge of the sunken garden.

'They're looking at us,' I murmured.

Angel groaned and began fiddling with my fly buttons. Two could play at that game so I slid my hand under her skirt. She bit down on my lip. 'Another inch and I'll rip your balls off.'

'What's sauce for the gander is sauce for the— Ouch!'

We broke up as if startled at the sight of the watching patrol. Angel pretended to squirm with embarrassment as she readjusted her dress. I didn't need to pretend. The grinning corporal gave me a brief, mocking '*Herr Hauptmann*' and the patrol marched off, guffawing among themselves.

'Do you want to get out whatever you dropped down there?'

'You do it.' She giggled as I stood up and fished around. A small key dropped to the ground.

'What was that all about?'

'It's better if you don't know.' She scooped up the key.

'Why does everyone always say that to me?'

'You're not going to like it.'

'Try me.'

Angel thought for a minute before replying. 'I was helping someone commit suicide.'

She waited for her words to sink in.

'Sorry?'

'Arthur Holding, chairman of Holding and Branson Engineering, was about to give the Germans the blueprint of the sonic mine his company and the Royal Navy were jointly developing before the invasion.'

'Why?'

'Because he wanted the contract to build those mines for the *Kriegsmarine*. Instead he committed suicide in his library.' She was watching my face closely. 'Does that disturb you?'

'No. No, it doesn't.' I surprised myself. I'd have recoiled in horror from a murderess in peacetime, but in war patriots did not commit murder – they killed their country's enemies. 'Was that the shot I heard?'

'I expect so. His home overlooks the park.'

'You reek of cordite.'

'That's why I didn't want that patrol to get too close.'

'And the blueprint?'

'I burned his copy. The Royal Navy have their own.' Angel shivered. 'His butler almost caught me.'

'Why didn't you take someone with you as back-up?'

'There've been too many failures already. And now Madame Isadora has disappeared. The hoopla stall owner found her booth empty after the fair closed in Plymouth two nights ago. No one saw her leave, and there were no signs of a struggle. She's just vanished into thin air.'

'She should have seen it coming.'

'Be serious.' Angel kicked me. 'That's only the last in a number of set-backs. The Germans found an arms dump near Okehampton last week.'

'Do we have a traitor in our midst?'

'Maybe it's just coincidence,' said Angel shortly. 'Now I must go and wash away the smell of cordite. Holding pulled a gun from his desk and I grabbed it. I didn't intend to shoot him. Fortunately, it'll look like suicide.'

'Hang on.' I realized what she had just said. 'How do you *normally* kill people then?'

'You'll see. I might need your help with the next one.'

'The next one?'

'Holding is just the start. We have to convince those sorts of people that it really doesn't pay to deal with the Germans – or, rather, you'll end up by paying with your life if you do.'

'I can't see myself as a professional assassin.'

'You're not. I am. Now you can buy me a very large drink.'

'Tell me more about yourself.'

'Why?'

'I've never met an assassin before.'

'How do you know you haven't? There're more of us than you think.'

'But it's hardly a . . . vocation for a young English girl.' If Angel really was a killer she must have evolved from sixth-form schoolgirl to Resistance leader and assassin all in about six years.

'These aren't normal times. Anyway, I'm half American.'

We were sitting in the bar of the Great Western Hotel, surrounded by Germans, English businessmen and local girls hoping to do business. This was Angel's idea, not mine. It was perfect cover, she said, and besides they had the best washroom and the best brandies.

A waiter in a tight yellow waistcoat and shiny black trousers approached our table. The Great Western Hotel and the County, now the SS Officers' Club, had always been *the* hotels in the city. The Great Western had previously had a doorman in a bottle-green coat and top hat to open the door for guests. Now there were two doormen – to keep people out. If your face didn't fit, if your clothes were shabby, you didn't get across the threshold. My officer's pips and swastika armband had the doormen fighting with each other to let me in. The hotel was obviously thriving. Its Regency façade had just been given a fresh lick of paint, the public rooms had been newly

carpeted, and the reproduction period furniture recovered in red and gilt.

The waiter halted in front of us.

'*Was wollen Sie?*'

I recognized the bloody little pipsqueak. I'd been
teaching him German not two years ago. Now he
was putting it to good use.

'Asbacher and twenty Players.'

'I've not seen you in here before, *Fräulein.*'

Angel gave him a look that a basilisk would have
died for. 'It's none of your business but I only joined
302 this week. And you are?'

'Peter Pettigrew, *gnädiges Fräulein.*'

Peter hurried off to find a lavatory while I blinked
in astonishment at Angel's guile.

It had been brilliantly done. You nowadays
assumed that all restaurant and hotel waiters were
informers, but by telling Pettigrew she was a member
of *Geheime Feldpolizei 302,* the local security police
squad which investigated crimes by the English
against the occupying forces, Angel had not only
effectively choked off his curiosity but had also made
him terrified of her.

But that wasn't the only reason I was speechless.
Angel had spoken to him in perfect German, with a
muted Berlin accent. Her use of the language was
better than mine.

She saw the questions piling up in my eyes.

'You shouldn't even ask, Nick. You know what curiosity did to the cat.'

'But I've only spent two of my nine lives. Why did you never tell me you spoke German?'

She regarded me seriously, as if making a decision.

'At the outbreak of hostilities, I was training to join a secret government department. It was intended that I should be stationed abroad. Instead I found myself in a foreign land called England. With Mills and one or two others, I volunteered to stay behind to form the kernel of a resistance movement here.'

'I haven't seen Mills for a while. Is he around?'

'He's in Canada.'

The bar was filling up with its early-evening crowd. Horace Smeed, in a blue suit, sat at a prominent table, his head bent close to a *Kriegsmarine* captain. His daughter April had not returned after Roy's death. I'd heard she had been sent off to a secretarial college in Switzerland. Shame, as she was a good kid. Half a dozen *Luftwaffe* pilots were getting noisily and determinedly drunk. They were bound for the Eastern Front in the morning, whispered Pettigrew.

Angel leaned forward out of the deep armchair that shielded her from public view. She spoke gravely. 'Nick, you shouldn't be asking questions. We might have a traitor, and it could well be you.'

'It's not me, I swear.' Not half an hour ago, she had said the disasters could just be coincidence.

'How do I know for sure? See it from my position. You're in daily contact with the Germans. You could have been turned, suborned, blackmailed, bought. To be honest, you're the most likely candidate.' Angel held up her hand to still my protests. 'I hope you're not, but I'm worried that I'm allowing personal feelings to cloud my professional judgement.'

The brandy was making her loquacious. I felt there had been real chemistry between us on the park bench: a genuine tingle rippling through the make-believe. I told myself she wouldn't have acted that scene with just anyone – only with someone she fancied.

'Let's hope you're not a traitor, Nick.' Angel squeezed my hand. 'I'd hate to have to kill you.'

15

I dug David in the ribs to stop him hissing at Hitler on the screen as a sullen policeman strode up and down the aisle, scrutinizing the audience for signs of disapproval. Cinemas now had to keep their lights on for the newsreels, after the first pictures of German victories in Russia had been greeted with boos and catcalls. The SS had taken the whole audience of a Torquay cinema into 'protective' custody after one of them had fired a shot at the image of Hitler on screen. The four hundred people had never been seen since, and the cinema had been burned down. Now most folk kept their mouths shut and their views to themselves.

The newsreel began with Hitler himself, surrounded by respectful generals, pointing at a map. In the next clip he was awarding decorations to impossibly handsome young soldiers. Rapturous women wept for joy, white handkerchiefs with swastika borders pressed artistically to their eyes. My bowels loosened as the wail of Stukas' sirens on-screen sent me back to a shallow slit trench outside Ashford.

308

Images of infantry advancing through birch woods, swastikas rippling against the sky, flame erupting from the muzzles of heavy artillery. Angelic children throwing flowers to bronzed soldiers singing lustily on the march. Finally a close-up of the *Führer* smiling benevolently.

This wasn't a newsreel. It was a German propaganda film.

'Yeuk.' David pretended to be sick.

'Shush.'

The rest of the news was not much better. More British *Freikorps* were leaving Dover to join the SS Viking Division. The camera closed up on a belt buckle carrying the SS motto: *My Honour is Loyalty.* The announcer was trusting that in the months to come there would be sufficient volunteers to form a complete British *Waffen-SS* division.

It seemed a new Chair of Racial Studies had been founded at Oxford. Its first professor was a bespectacled rodent of a man I'd never heard of.

Göring, looking even more bloated and bemedalled than ever, gloated greedily over the display of the British Crown Jewels in Berlin. He looked as if he was about to try on a crown for size but then thought better of it, at least in front of the cameras. The collection was soon to be returned to Britain, proclaimed the announcer.

My ears pricked up. There were growing rumours that the Duke of Windsor would be crowned King

... And there he was, himself – visiting a hospital for the war-wounded at Colchester with his duchess. The camera followed them as they alighted from their train to be greeted by the station master wearing a top hat. Cheering crowds lined the route; nurses curtsied prettily to the duchess, local dignitaries bowed to the duke. It had all the trappings of a traditional royal visit – and there was not a German to be seen.

The next item also featured the royal couple. This time the duke and von Ribbentrop were opening a new blast-furnace complex together. They both waved to the camera, standing in front of a display of Union flags and swastikas.

I could recognize this as clever propaganda. Maybe the rumours of a coronation were not that fanciful after all.

The lights went out and we all breathed a sigh of relief. I hadn't wanted to take David to the cinema for a while, because the *Reich* Ministry of Information and Propaganda had insisted that every cinema show the film *The Jew Süss*. We'd voted with our bottoms to stay at home. After weeks of empty cinemas, Goebbels admitted defeat. Instead, the film was now to be shown to schools, factories and offices.

But Goebbels still had a trick up his sleeve. Instead of the opening credits of *The Ghost Train*, a squalid passageway with stained walls and oily puddles, shot from floor level, filled the screen. A high-pitched squealing and rustling grew and grew until the very air vibrated. Around the corner surged a swarm of rats, tumbling over each other in a heaving brown mass. As they were about to sweep over our heads, the shot dissolved. Instead there was a sunken lane, filling the screen exactly as the corridor had done. It was packed with terrified men stumbling straight towards us: Orthodox Jews from Eastern Europe, looking strange to our eyes, with beards and hooked noses and side-locks hanging from under their black hats. They crowded over us, panic-struck. Their mouths hung open but the only sound was demented squealing. As this torrent of men broke around the camera, they became rats again, a tumbling mass of vermin.

You could physically feel the shock in the deep silence that followed. There was a lone whistle, then the projectionist started running the Will Hay film. For the first time I couldn't enjoy it. I kept seeing those rats and the Jews and somehow I knew that every living person we'd seen on that screen was dead and that those driven men had been killed like rats.

Joan must have been listening for us because she came running out while I was still pulling the BSA back onto its stand. She looked pale and drawn.

'What is it?'

'There's a German inside, waiting to speak to you and David.'

'What's he want?'

'He won't say.'

'What's he wearing?'

'Civilian clothes.' That usually meant one thing: *Gestapo*. No wonder Joan was upset. 'He's talking to mum . . .'

'Mum's talking to a German?'

'He says he knows the Jenners.'

Bleicher. A weight lifted off my heart. *Anyone* was better than the Gestapo – even Bleicher. He had not been around for a while – but Bleicher was like that. He could be in my office every afternoon for a week, and then I would not see him for a month.

'What have you been doing, David?'

'Nothing.' The boy scuffed at the pavement.

I put my arm around his shoulders. 'Okay, let's go and face the music.'

As we entered, Bleicher rose from the armchair, a smile on his face. 'Your mother has been making me so welcome.' He indicated the cup and plate beside him.

With a Victorian sense of decency, my mother excused herself. We waited as she crabbed out through the doorway.

'I didn't know you were back,' I said to him, to break the ice.

'I've been back for a fortnight, working from

Corunna Barracks,' confessed Bleicher. 'I really must go and see the Jenners. It's a difficult time for them.'

He was obviously not in a hurry to come to the purpose of his visit, accepting Joan's offer of another cup of tea – if Mrs Pendleton was sure she could spare it.

Maybe Bleicher was telling the truth when he said he enjoyed spending time with local families; perhaps such occasions did remind him of home in Germany. And perhaps, somewhere, a pig was growing wings.

'So what brings you here?' I asked.

'This is not easy.' He appeared reticent about disturbing the family harmony. 'May I ask young David a question?'

Joan dropped a saucer. It rolled under the table.

'Do you know a boy called Andrew Baker?'

David said nothing.

'David!'

'He's a friend,' the youngster reluctantly admitted.

'In your class?'

David nodded.

I placed Andrew Baker now. Fair hair, almost white, and large ears that stuck out. His father was a prisoner of war and his mother worked in the drawing office of Smeed's armaments factory.

'You hang around together?'

'Sometimes.'

'You do things together.'

'Maybe.'

'In fact, you've been responsible for all those "V for Victory" signs painted on the walls of the barracks – and on the sides of our German Army lorries.'

'Not all of them.'

Bleicher let the words settle over the kitchen like a shroud. The genial atmosphere had already changed to be replaced by a sense of foreboding.

'Oh, David,' breathed Joan in dismay.

David stuck out his lower lip in adolescent defiance.

'Your friend Andrew Baker was caught red-handed this morning. He named you as his accomplice.' Bleicher took off his glasses and rubbed them on his tie. I felt he was waiting for me to play my part – so I did.

'What happens now?'

'Because young Baker was caught defacing army property, he's the responsibility of the *Abwehr*. I saw David's name on the report and remembered he was your nephew.'

Bleicher was telling me the *Gestapo* was not involved. 'Thanks.'

'Baker will spend a week at Corunna Barracks under military discipline, cleaning up the transport and the buildings. He might even enjoy it.'

'What are you going to do to my nephew?' I sensed Bleicher's cat-and-mouse game was driving Joan mad.

'Nothing. I've taken his name out of the statement but next time it might not be so easy.'

'I promise you there'll be no next time,' said Joan. 'David, you must say thank you to Mr Bleicher.'

'Thank you,' he barely mumbled.

It was rare for Joan to lose her temper. But she grabbed David and shook him as a terrier shakes a rat. 'Say thank you properly.'

'Thank you.'

'That's better. You'd be sent to one of those awful camps if it wasn't for Mr Bleicher. Go to your room now. I'll talk to you later.'

David shuffled out of the door, face glowing with shame.

'Children!'

'It's a difficult time for him. He's not a child,' sighed Bleicher. 'But neither is he a man. Go to him. He will be scared. He is probably crying.'

Joan got the message. She left us alone. Payback time?

'Thanks.'

'It was fortunate I saw the report. But what's the point of sending a thirteen-year-old to a concentration camp?'

'Stolz might not agree with you.'

'Stolz has bigger fish to fry. He seems to be having a run of successes at the moment, what with several foiled bank robberies, that airfield raid, *and* finding that arms dump on a farm near Okehampton.'

'A lucky run?'

Bleicher snorted. 'I wish *I* could be that lucky.'

'Don't you two work together?'

Bleicher ignored my sally. 'When you used to go to the Three Horseshoes pub, do you remember seeing a stocky man there, an outsider, late thirties, military bearing?'

He was describing Mills. I boxed clever, or so I thought. 'Bushy eyebrows, stern-looking?'

'Yes.'

'A few times, I suppose.'

'Did you talk to him?'

'Not really. The weather, the beer. He was never in the bar.' I caught myself in my contradiction. 'He used to be with Roy in the snug, and he'd leave when I arrived.'

'Did he have a girl with him? Around your age?'

'One night, in the passageway, I saw him leaving with a woman. She had a headscarf on. About this height.' I added three inches to Angel's height.

'No,' said Bleicher. 'She's shorter than that.'

16

'*Generalleutnant* von Glass, Miss Coral Kennedy.'
Nick introduced the two to each other.

Angel smiled gamely, and swore silently to herself. There were two hundred women in the *Feldkommandantur*'s great hall who would eat their corsages
to meet Glass and he had made a beeline for her –
even though she had stayed on the edge of the throng
assembled to celebrate Hitler's birthday the following
day.

The last thing she wanted was to be noticed. She
was acutely aware of the risk she was taking in
coming here but, if all went well, the result would be
worth it.

'May I offer you a cigarette?' Glass produced his
case.

'Thank you, but I'm trying to give up.'

'But the cigarette holder?'

Angel, in a plain frock with a single strand of
cultured pearls, was toying with a long black ivory
holder. 'It's just something to do with my hands.'

'Of course.'

Glass really was quite handsome, she decided. The missing arm and the scar across his forehead gave him a piratical appearance. Most women would be attracted to him but he lived a monastic life, said Nick, seldom socializing with the English unless he was called on to do so – like tonight.

She surveyed the elegant gathering. Even the waiters here were better dressed than most ordinary people. The last time she had attended a party this grand had been at the British Embassy in Paris in the last August of peace.

'Ladies and gentlemen.' A thin man with pince-nez was standing on the podium at one end of the room, sounding like a skeleton with a chill. 'Berlin radio has just announced that German forces have successfully crossed the Bersinen River. The Ukraine now lies open – a fitting birthday present for the *Führer*.'

There was a rousing cheer from the Germans and enthusiastic applause from the English contingent.

'Wouldn't you like to be fighting on the Eastern Front, general?' Angel turned to Glass.

'I'm a soldier, so I endeavour to do my duty wherever I am.' Glass gave a wry grin. 'To be honest, Miss Kennedy, I'd gladly drop a rank or two to get out there. A soldier's job is to fight, not to administer.'

'You speak excellent English.'

'I have a good teacher here.' He nodded towards Nick, who was now translating between Hauser and

Mrs Smeed. 'Don't let him get into trouble. I may not always be here.'

'I won't.' She remembered something Roy had once said: *Nick attracted decent people.*

'I've enjoyed meeting you, Miss Kennedy. Perhaps we'll talk again later.'

Angel caught an ugly little SS *Standartenführer* watching them through thick spectacles. Someone walked over her grave and she shivered. 'Yes, I hope so.'

Glass bowed, clicked his heels and turned to be enfolded in the verbal embrace of the waiting Lord Lieutenant.

Angel lifted a glass of champagne off a passing tray and took a moment to weigh up Nick. He wasn't one of your clean-cut fighter-pilot types nor did he have film-star looks, but there was something about him. He had a presence, and it was all the more attractive because he didn't know he possessed it. What would he say if he knew that her real name was Jennifer – with a double 'n'?

A plump blonde, expensively if flashily dressed, had begun to harangue Nick. By their body language it was clear she was asking him something and that Nick did not want to know. The girl stamped her foot in a pet and barged away into the crowd.

Angel drifted over to Matty's circle, thinking how Sara had pushed the boat out tonight. Her low-cut black frock was tight across her backside, and showed off a generous bosom that she was usually at pains to conceal. She was in the middle of telling Horace Smeed all about her mother's family estate on the Oder.

'She married my father because he was the most brilliant mathematician in Poland – the youngest professor ever to hold a chair in Breslau,' she was saying.

Drink had loosened Sara's tongue. Angel remembered the woman's boast that she refused to speak German because she hated them so much. Then why had she come to this reception?

Matty stood by her side, as courteous and reliable as ever. He had changed in the months since Roy's death. He was not so much fun nowadays, claimed Nick – but then, who was? Mills rated Matty very highly. He was training him up to take a major role in the growing Resistance movement.

Matty took Angel's arm and steered her a few feet away. 'The *Gestapo* have found that printing press in the oil refinery,' he whispered.

'I knew you should never have let Pip Cartwright look after it,' snapped Sara, suddenly materializing at their side. 'The boy's too young.'

'Have they got Pip?'

'No, only the press,' said Matty.

*

Percy Tickell had seen Penny curl his lip as he had announced the German success. It had been not something he had enjoyed doing, but as Secretary of the Province's Supreme Council, it had been his duty. Why couldn't Penny understand that – instead of making yet another show of dumb insolence? He could not understand why the *Kommandant* allowed the young man to get away with it. He hoped Stolz had witnessed Penny's reaction. He would bring Penny down a peg.

Tickell headed for Matty Cordington's group, frowning when he saw Penny also joining them. He did not know what a member of the gentry like Cordington was doing mixing with someone like Penny anyway.

'Cordington, how pleasant to see you,' said Tickell. 'Do remember me to your father.'

'Of course. How are you?'

'Kept busy. We're plagued by these silly "V for Victory" signs, foolish acts that accomplish nothing but which bring grave consequences in their train.'

'They're everywhere nowadays, aren't they?'

'Not for much longer. We're putting up a £100 reward for information leading to the arrest of any vandal responsible.'

'Shouldn't that be for their conviction?' demanded Penny, overhearing.

He really was going too far. 'Once they're arrested, they'll be convicted – have no fear of that.'

It was almost nine o'clock, time for the *Führer* toast. Angel slipped away to the lavatory. She locked herself in a cubicle and from her cocktail bag pulled out her lipstick. Unscrewing the bottom, she removed a very small phial. She uncorked the phial and, using a pair of fine tweezers, withdrew a sliver of cork. With infinite care, Angel loaded the cork into the cigarette holder, tamping it in until she was satisfied it was secure. In the middle of the cork was a tiny dart, hardly bigger than a bee sting.

Angel took a deep breath and steeled herself. The moment was approaching when she would kill a traitor – the moment of greatest risk to herself.

Sir Rufus Forty was the owner of the massive Western Electrics Company – entrepreneur, businessman, Tory Party benefactor, collaborator. He'd already held several meetings with the German giant AEG, which worked exclusively for the SS, about his company's work on a wireless without valves, which promised to revolutionize communications. Murmurs of disapproval about his trading with the Germans had been met by him with a blunt message to the effect that no one was going to tell him who he could or could not do business with. *The Times* had reported his speech at length.

Getting access to Sir Rufus had proved impossible. Since the death of Arthur Holding, his home had been turned into a fortress. SS bodyguards accompanied him everywhere, and when he visited his factory, the workers were shut inside so they did not even see him arrive or leave. Yet, as Angel rejoined the company, there he was just ten feet away, a portly self-important man.

Angel beckoned to Nick. 'Do you have a cigarette?'

Nick produced his case. Angel extracted a cigarette in her left hand. She was still too far from her target. She needed to be no further than four feet away to be sure of hitting Forty's neck with her tiny dart. Pretending to try to see the podium better, she sidled closer to the industrialist.

'Light?' She manoeuvred Nick between herself and her target and put down her glass.

He held out the lighter.

'Not yet. Don't move.'

The buzz of conversation died as *Standartenführer* Stolz climbed onto the podium.

'*Generalleutnant* von Glass, Lord Lieutenant, Sir Rufus, *Meine Damen und Herren*,' began Stolz.

Angel put the long cigarette holder to her lips. It paid to practise, her instructors had told her. Practice made the real thing easy. Angel had been practising an hour a day for the past four months.

'Tomorrow, the twentieth of April, is the birthday

of our beloved *Führer*, Adolf Hitler. I give you a toast . . .' Stolz raised his glass. *'Der Führer.'*

'Der Führer.' A thicket of glasses was raised aloft.

Sir Rufus Forty brushed away a sudden pinprick on his neck. Behind him a woman coughed. Angel shook out the fragment of cork onto the floor, inserted the cigarette and had it lit within two seconds. She lifted her glass from the nearby table and took a hefty gulp.

'Our leader,' said Nick softly, surreptitiously passing his glass over a jug of water standing on the table.

Angel saw Glass glaring at Nick with a look of exasperation.

I sat in the front of the *Gestapo* car, first thing on Monday morning, feeling Stolz's malevolent little eyes boring into the back of my skull and wished I was invisible. Stolz's Armstrong-Siddeley, flying swastika pennants on its wings, led three other cars packed with SIPO *Feldpolizei*. Anyone seeing this convoy would get out of the way fast – but not before they'd seen Nick Penny in the lead car.

I didn't know what I'd done to get in Glass's bad books but I must have done something, for he had never allowed Stolz to 'borrow' me as an interpreter before.

Mine not to reason why, mine but to cheat and lie.

'Next right,' I instructed the driver. Before the war, I'd often been to Sundial Farm to buy its famous Cheddar cheese which, in those days, had been sent up to food halls in London.

The convoy roared into the farmyard, scattering ducks and chickens before squealing to a halt. It was a dramatic entrance, intended to intimidate. The first *Feldpolizei* were already sprinting towards the wooden barn even before the cars had stopped rolling. Others ran into the dairy and milking parlour. Stolz hammered on the kitchen door. It was locked, which was unusual. It was Martha Copp's practice to leave some cheeses on the kitchen table if she was busy outside. Callers just helped themselves and left the money.

Martha's white hair appeared at an upstairs window, as half a dozen women were herded out of the dairy and into the courtyard.

'What do you want?' she called.

'Tell the old crone to open the door or I'll smash it down,' I was ordered.

'Please open the door, Martha.'

'Is that you, Nick Penny?'

'Yes, my love. Don't worry. Just do as they say.'

Martha took an age to come down. As soon as she opened the door, a couple of goons burst past her up the wooden stairs to the storeroom where she matured her cheeses. We listened to the clump of their boots over our heads.

'What be you a-doing with this lot, Nick Penny?'

'I've been ordered to come and translate for them.'

Martha had a round, merry face and apple-red cheeks. It was hard to believe such a face could show disgust, but she managed it. 'You should be ashamed of yourself.'

I was.

The kitchen smelled of freshly baked bread, and a huge cauldron of stew was steaming away on the old range by the corn dolly and last year's calendar. A pile of seven chipped bowls and a ladle sat on the scrubbed wooden table next to a large, partly eaten loaf and a slab of Cheddar. A tabby cat uncurled itself from behind the log basket, completely unmoved by the shouting, and padded across the flagstones. It leaped lightly up onto the deep window ledge and curled up again. An eighth plate and a spoon lay in the big square sink.

'What be they a-doing here, Nick Penny?'

'I wish I knew, Martha.'

Two sergeants came in at the double to report that they had found no one in the dairy or in the storeroom. Stolz ordered them to check again: search the stables, the hayloft, the barn, the chicken shed, the well. Search everywhere.

'*Jawohl, Herr Standartenführer.*'

'Is her cheese any good?' Stolz demanded.

'It used to be sold in Fortnum and Mason in London.'

'I know where Fortnum and Mason is. Tell her I want to taste some.'

I interpreted and Martha cut Stolz a slice and held it towards him on the point of the knife. As an afterthought, she carved off a larger chunk and cut it into squares. Then she sat down in the rocking chair by the range, and tracked the movement of the men overhead by the sound of their boots. One by one the men reported that their searches had drawn a blank. Stolz grew angrier at each report. Growing impatient, he slapped his riding crop against his black breeches. The cat opened one eye.

'He's here somewhere – I know he is. Tell her that if she doesn't hand him over, I'll take the women back to *Gestapo* HQ for questioning.'

'Who?'

'She knows.'

Martha swallowed once. 'I'm not hiding anyone. If I am, you'll find them. If you don't find anyone, it's because there's no one to find.'

Most Germans would have been taken in by Martha's serene indifference. When the farm-wide search drew a blank for the second time, they would have given up.

But Stolz knew.

Martha was quietly laughing at him. As each soldier came in to report failure, she gave him a piece of cheese.

'You can have some as well, Nick Penny.' There was only one square left.

'I'm not hungry.'

'No stomach for what you be a-doing, eh?'

Stolz stormed out of the farmhouse, unable to contain his impatience. He strode from dairy to stables and back again. He muddied his uniform by going down on his hands and knees to peer inside the hen house, worked up a sweat plunging a pitchfork into piles of hay, banged his knee slipping down the ladder from the apple store, splashed his shining black boots with cow shit, and still found nothing.

His men had lost heart for the search. Only Stolz was still convinced. He stormed back into the kitchen where Martha was now calmly stirring the stew. The dirty dish in the sink had vanished. Stolz knew he was being humiliated by this white-haired old woman and he was not going to stand for it for another minute.

'Tell me where you are hiding him.' Stolz pulled out an automatic pistol from his holster. It was a 7.63mm Model 1932 Mauser, the type favoured by the SS. There was nothing elegant about the Mauser: it was an angular workmanlike piece with a ten-round magazine and a muzzle velocity of 1575 feet per second.

Fear lit a dim flame behind Martha's eyes but she refused to give in. 'You tell that jackanapes that if he wants to shoot me, then to hurry up about it. I've got the chickens to feed.'

'She insists there's no one here.'

'I know there *is*, Penny. And I will find him if it takes me all day, or all night.'

He fired a shot into the low ceiling. The report cracked in my ears and echoed around the kitchen. The cat flew out of the door without touching the floor. Martha's hands were trembling as she strove to appear calm.

'I'd better take some cheese out to the girls if they bain't going to be allowed their dinner.'

She cut more pieces of Cheddar and slices of bread, before moving across to fuss around the Welsh dresser.

I didn't hear the first splash nor the second, but I caught the sound of the third. Stolz must have heard it at precisely the same time. We turned from watching Martha counting knives to stare at the platter of bread and cheese. A droplet of blood had splattered the golden Cheddar with pale red. I followed another drop descending all the way from the ceiling. It fell in slow motion until it landed – on the bread this time. Another drop, and another ... until the bread was speckled pink and the cheese blossomed with red roses.

Pip Cartwright was found lying between the false floor of the storeroom and the kitchen ceiling. Stolz's shot had, freakishly, entered his chest cavity and punctured the pulmonary artery. The boy bled to death outside in the farmyard.

And Stolz had known he was there.

Pip's death affected me more than I'd expected. It was a waste of a young, exuberant life. Matty, too, took it badly, blaming himself for ever introducing the boy into the Resistance. Martha Copp and all her girls were sent off to a women's punishment camp north of Berlin, called Ravensbrück. We never heard of any of them again. There was a story that Martha had been killed by lethal injection before she even reached Harwich. Matty wrote a letter to inform Pip's father in his prisoner-of-war camp – then petitioned for his release on the grounds that the estate urgently needed him. He did not succeed.

Pip's mother received a bill for three hundred *Reichsmark* to cover the cost of the petrol used on the raid and the price of the bullet that killed her only son. Matty paid it.

I heard about Sir Rufus Forty's demise the same day as the raid on Sundial Farm. His death in his sleep after the birthday reception on Saturday night broke no one's heart. Some said it was divine judgement on him for dealing with the Germans. The *Gestapo* decided it was suspicious and ordered a post-mortem.

Word quickly got out that I had been present at the raid on Martha Copp's farm and my standing in the city sank as low as the underbelly of a sewer rat. Even Angel seemed to find reasons to avoid me. By Thursday I was coming to the end of my tether.

But just as I thought things couldn't get worse, I was summoned to translate at a high-powered meeting inside the *Feldkommandantur*.

I squeezed into a seat behind Tickell, Detective Superintendent Bearup and the chairman of the Supreme Council, Sir Reginald Launcestone, in a small committee room. Opposite sat Stolz and two officials from the Office for Jewish Affairs. Another hard-faced bureaucrat presided at the head of the table. He wore the uniform of an SS *Oberführer* – one rank above Stolz. The meeting had already started.

'*Oberführer* Fest is the *Reich*'s expert on the Jewish Problem in Britain,' Tickell imparted in an awed whisper.

'I didn't know we had one.'

'He reports directly to *Reichsführer* Himmler himself.'

Fest put down a sheaf of papers to glare at the English delegation. 'These figures do not add up.'

'As we have said, you *have* to take the children,'

said Launcestone. From his barely concealed impatience, I gathered that they had been over this ground before.

'We do not have the facilities.'

'Surely, it's better if the children stay with their parents,' argued Launcestone. 'We don't want to break up families.'

'And we couldn't cope with a lot of Jewish orphans,' agreed Tickell. 'The orphanages here are overflowing already.'

'You're only trying to make up your quota,' Fest accused bluntly. 'You shouldn't have overestimated the number of Jews in your province.'

'Superintendent Bearup collated the figures,' said Tickell quickly.

'With respect, *Oberführer*, *WVHA* Berlin demanded to know the number of foreign and British Jews before we managed to finish the register,' protested Bearup.

'That is not *my* problem.' Fest held a pencil up in front of his face and snapped it in two in a convulsive movement.

I was struck by how ordinary Fest looked. He reminded me of nothing more than a small-minded clerk, or a storeman who would delight in sending back a form because some petty detail was wrong.

'We are trying to do as Berlin wishes,' oiled Launcestone. 'We have even widened our definition of a

Jew as being someone with just two Jewish grandparents. The *Reich* itself stipulates *three* grandparents.'

'Your zeal is commendable,' muttered Fest
sarcastically.

'We just don't have as many Jews down here as
Berlin assumed. It appears the *Juden-referat des SD*
overestimated the total number in Britain.' Bearup
would be back on the beat by lunchtime if he continued like this. Launcestone and Tickell kept their
eyes fixed firmly on the table.

'We could widen the catchment range from the
ages of sixteen to sixty for men and sixteen to fifty-
five for women,' murmured one of the *WVHA* clerks.

'Widening the age bands for men will make
hardly any difference,' said Bearup. 'You *have* to take
the children of foreign Jews if we're to fill our quota.'

Fest was still reluctant. 'There's a nominal transportation cost for every Jew. We have to ask ourselves if it is cost-effective to transport these children
all the way through Holland and Germany to Poland
and beyond?'

'As children are smaller, surely you can pack more
into each transport,' suggested Launcestone. 'That
way the unit cost per head would be less.'

'Fortunately we'll soon have an end solution
closer to hand,' said the *WVHA* clerk, a man who
clearly enjoyed the sound of his own voice.

It was his use of the word *Endlösung* that caught

my attention. I hadn't heard it before. It literally meant 'final solution'.

'What about broadening the round-up by nationality?' demanded Fest.

'Initially we only counted German, Austrian and Eastern European Jews resident down here,' explained Launcestone. 'But when we realized the shortfall in numbers, we included various other Western European Jews and even, finally, French Jews. The figure before you represents all the foreign Jews, who are not British citizens, in the Province.'

'No British Jews?'

'I thought we'd agreed to exclude British-born Jews,' said Tickell quickly.

Bearup rapidly added up a column of figures. 'If you include foreign Jews who only became British citizens *after* 1930, we can meet the quota,' he proclaimed. 'But you *must* take their children.'

'All right,' agreed Fest. 'Include the children, although I wish to put my reluctance on record.'

'Noted, *Oberführer*.' That same clerk again.

'You are satisfied that you can physically locate these Jews, Superintendent?'

'I have the address of every single Jew in the Western Province, *Oberführer*.'

'You understand the round-up must be an exclusively British operation. German troops will stay in barracks while it continues.'

There was a silence until Bearup admitted, 'We

don't have sufficient manpower, even if we drafted men in from neighbouring forces.'

'Then use auxiliary police.' The word Fest used was *Hilfspolizei*.

'We don't have any of those in Britain.'

'Swear in Special Constables, then,' suggested Launcestone.

'Where will I find them?'

'Use men from the British Union of Fascists,' said Stolz.

'Blackshirts!' Bearup clearly did not like that idea.

'The *Gestapo*'s been using them successfully in recent weeks. We'll soon have to recruit local auxiliaries to take the place of German personnel now needed on the Russian front, anyway. This could prove their first blooding.'

'Excellent idea,' enthused Tickell. 'The football stadium is already being prepared, and the Red Cross will be on standby. You may rely on us, gentlemen, to make this weekend's round-up of Jews a total success. A model for all those to follow.'

'I trust so.' Fest gathered his papers to show that the meeting was over.

Tickell pushed back his chair. I blocked his path to the door. 'Where are these Jews going?'

'They are being resettled in work camps in the East.'

'There's fighting in the East.'

'Not everywhere.'

'But you're selling out naturalized British citizens just because they are Jewish.'

'Sometimes you have to light a small fire to control a forest blaze,' snapped Tickell, pushing past me.

The BSA was coughing like an asthmatic donkey. Slowing down outside the Dower House, it gave an almighty backfire. Just as well there were no Germans around – they might have fired back. The explosion brought Bert Latcham out of the greenhouse.

'Master Matty's up at Home Farm, seeing to things.'

'What things?'

'Why, his father, of course. Been dead for two days, they say. Serves the old bugger right. If he'd been decent to people when he was alive, they'd have found his body sooner.'

With difficulty, I managed to get out of Bert that the Major had been found that same morning by his weekly cleaning woman. He was sitting bolt upright in the carver chair at one end of the dining table, empty bottle of malt whisky by his side and a picture of his wife in his hand. Yesterday's newspaper still lay untouched on the mat inside the front door.

I believed in the superstition that bad things come in threes. The Major's death was the third in less than a week. I hoped that it would be the last for a while.

'He drank hisself to death,' declared Bert.

'How's Master Matty?'

'Taking it hard that he didn't know the Major was dead. I told him it weren't his fault. It had got so the Major wouldn't even answer the door to him. There was nothing Master Matty could have done, anyhow. The Major's heart just stopped, says the doctor. Master Matty's got the estate to think about now.'

Indeed he had. Matty was now master of all he surveyed: over twelve hundred prime acres, a pedigree dairy herd, Home Farm itself plus four tenant farms, a dozen cottages, fishing rights and woods, together with another three farms around Merricombe, and God knew how many acres of moorland brought into the family by a good marriage forty years earlier. Matty had suddenly become a pillar of the community, complete with a family pew in the church. Poor old Matty.

'I didn't know he was dead,' Matty kept repeating later as we sat in the kitchen with a bottle of the Major's Inchgower malt whisky. 'I can imagine him sitting there alone for all that time. First there's the light from the lamp on the table in front of him. But then its oil runs out. Dawn breaks and a whole day passes, while we all went about our lives just a stone's throw away. And then a second lonely night in total darkness.'

Once he was dead, it didn't matter how long he sat there, I pointed out.

'But what will his friends say? What will the neighbours think?'

'Be honest, Matty, he didn't have many friends in the last few years.' And his neighbours would say good riddance to the bad-tempered old so-and-so. 'Everyone knew how difficult he'd become. You have nothing to reproach yourself for.'

After I'd told him the same thing in a dozen different ways, he seemed to buck up – or maybe the whisky was having its effect. To change the subject, I told him about the planned round-up of Jews.

'Are the Jenners affected?'

'Only Anna. She didn't become naturalized until 1936 so she's included in the round-up. On the other hand, Barbara's safe because she married a Kent farmer, so she's counted as British. It's paradoxical.'

'I don't understand.'

'The way the Department of Jewish Affairs has worked out who's to be taken is cock-eyed. Anna became a British citizen the year after arriving from Hungary. When she and Simon married, she was already naturalized. If she'd kept her Hungarian nationality and married a British citizen, as Barbara did, she'd be all right now. It shows how no one's thought it through.'

'Anna will have to go into hiding,' Matty declared. 'Hawthorn Cottage is empty and no one goes up Scotch Hill any more.'

'That's good of you.'

'If needs be, Anna can hide up in Merricombe but let's see first how she gets on in Hawthorn Cottage. We'll make sure she's warm and well fed.'

'I've been thinking about that raid on Sundial Farm,' I said hesitantly. 'Somehow Stolz *knew* Pip was there.'

'Don't worry about it.'

'Of course I worry about it. And I remember something Bleicher said when he came to talk to us about David, about the *Gestapo* enjoying a good run at the moment. I said perhaps they were just being lucky but he hinted it was nothing to do with luck. What if I was taken along on the *Gestapo* raid to make others think *I* was the traitor?'

'Why would they do that?' Matty topped up our glasses from the last of the bottle.

'To divert suspicion from the real traitor.'

'What does Coral say about it?'

'She's avoiding me.'

'You're not a traitor.'

'I know that but we seem to be in a minority of two.' For the first time I heard the tick of the old grandmother clock. 'When's the funeral?'

'This Saturday, if everything can be done in time. I just want to get it over. The Germans are hanging on to Forty's body for a post-mortem so we'll get in first. Wouldn't do to have two funerals on the same day. The mourners might lose out on their free booze. You'll come, won't you?'

'Of course.' It occurred to me that Sara should be here comforting Matty. 'Where is Sara?'

'In Meadow Cottage, I expect. She said she doesn't like dead bodies.'

'Are you two getting on all right?'

'Yeh.'

Matty was being unusually coy. Maybe their relationship wasn't what Roy and I had suspected. Maybe it was platonic after all. No, it was too intense – it had to have a sexual basis.

'I know,' Matty jumped to his feet and pulled another bottle of Inchgower from the dozen in the cupboard. 'Let's go up and visit our attic. I've something to show you.'

It wasn't really an attic – it was a single big room on the top floor, with windows facing south and east, possibly the domestic servants' dormitory in the old days. It had served as Matty's nursery until he had joined the local primary school. When the three of us became friends, Roy and I used to be invited back by Matty's nanny to play with him there after school and on Saturday mornings. It would have been a very lonely life for Matty without us. From the age of ten, Matty had dinner with his father two nights a week. The rest of his meals he ate in the attic with his nanny or, later, in the kitchen with the cook and gardener.

I think I was fifteen before I even realized that Home Farm had a front door – a grand white one with a massive iron knocker under a circular portico. I'd still never been through it. In fact, I couldn't remember ever seeing it open.

'I'm not sure it does open,' said Matty doubtfully.

'Shouldn't the coffin be carried out that way?'

He supposed so.

As we'd grown older, the attic room had become our den. Roy 'borrowed' flagons of cider, I nicked my sister Joan's cigarettes, and Matty smuggled up scuttles of coal for the fire. We'd spend nights on the floor in sleeping bags, telling each other ghost stories by candlelight and having midnight feasts. We were always a little scared because the old house groaned and creaked, but more scared that the Major would hear our laughter and come and tell us off. He never did.

If he was disappointed that his only son had taken up with town kids, he never said anything. I don't think he cared. We all passed the entrance exam for the High School, and so we all stayed together. There was the annual fear that Matty might get sent off to Clifton, where the Major had gone as a boy, but each year it blew over safely. As I said, I don't think the Major cared.

'Look, isn't he a beauty?'

'God! He's shrunk. He's a pony. He used to be the biggest horse in the world.'

Matty pushed down on his nose and Champion rocked back and to, as if pleased to be in human company again. 'I found him next door. I can't remember putting him there.'

When had we consigned the rocking horse with the white mane and tail to dusty oblivion? I remembered a time when he had towered above me and I'd had to be helped up into the saddle, where I'd cling on to the bucking bronco as we held Wild West rodeos.

We sat cross-legged under the naked light bulb, the bottle of whisky between us, inspecting mementos of our childhood. Everything had become smaller and shabbier. The air rifle that had once seemed so heavy and powerful was a feeble toy now that I had fought with a .303 Enfield. So many memories – the dented drum with its flaking paint; the posters of open roadsters and RAF biplanes; a home-made Punch and Judy show; toy soldiers in red jackets and blue trousers – not at all like the real ones in drab khaki.

I was becoming maudlin and the picture albums didn't help. Our lives between the ages of seven and eighteen were there between the covers. Right on the first page, we were who we were to become. We were dressed up as crusaders with cardboard swords. Roy, a barrel with a grin; Matty, slight and already good-looking, brandishing his sword aloft; me looking sheepish – but then, I never did take a good photo.

'I don't remember that,' complained Matty.

'Downton village fête. You insisted on being Richard Coeur de Lion – except you couldn't pronounce it and kept saying Richard Cuddly Lion.'

'I worry about your memory. Your head's so full of this stuff, there can't be any room for anything new. This one?' He held up a shot of us as teenagers in cricket whites.

'Easy. Playing for the Colts – I think against Bluecoats. I made twenty-five. It was my highest score to date. I think you took three wickets. I know Roy was out for a duck.' I could see Matty wondering how much I was making up. I wasn't.

'Here's our class photo from junior school.'

'Form three. There's Mrs Hubbard. How come you're right in the middle of the front row?' I stood at the end of the back row, looking as if I wanted to go to the lavatory.

'Where's Roy?'

'That must have been when he was off for a month with measles.'

In the whole album, it was the only picture taken by someone else that didn't include all three of us. The last one showed three young men in open-necked shirts and blazers, playing for the cricket First XI. We oozed confidence that the world belonged to us, and that we would live for a thousand years.

A tidal wave of sadness swept over me. Innocent hope is not extinguished by one blow, but is eroded over time until nothing is left but the barren subsoil of existence. I reviewed my life and its cast. My mother was ailing – if I was honest I didn't think she'd see the year out. David, lacking the father he needed, was starting to go off the rails. Joan was involved in some sort of relationship with a profiteer that left her feeling so guilty that she refused even to acknowledge it. Angel was clearly avoiding me. Even Glass, the one bloody German I'd grown to like, had gone off me. Only Matty stuck by me, good old Matty.

He seemed to read my mind. 'I'll never let anything happen to you, you know.'

I was embarrassed by this declaration of friendship. 'It gets to me at times. It'll pass.'

'How about an adventure to cheer yourself up?'

I guessed we were heading for the abandoned fishing village of Lostmaids when Matty bellowed into my ear to turn up a lane that led over the headland and down towards the sea. I slowed to allow Sara in the Chrysler shooting brake to catch up. Matty and I were troubleshooting ahead on the BSA, but she was driving infuriatingly slowly. I winced as she flashed her headlights to tell me that she had closed up. That beam could be seen for miles on a clear night like this.

Sara was driving a Danish scientist and his wife on the final leg of an underground journey that had begun two weeks earlier in Copenhagen. The operation had been sprung on Matty that afternoon, he said, when Angel had been suddenly called away. He had not told Sara until the very minute when we were about to set off. She did not hide her irritation at having her routine disrupted.

We coasted down the lane into the ruins, where rosebay willowherb sprouted in the doorless entrances of deserted cottages, and the church – a roofless shell of four thick stone walls – cast melancholic shadows in the moonlight.

The three of us had once camped here for a weekend when we were fifteen. Even in daytime there was something spooky about the place. Why had anyone built homes and a church on this lonely coast? And why had they all abandoned the place sometime around 1880, judging by the last dates on the lichen-clad gravestones?

The scientist, a giant of a man with a huge head and a mane of red hair, who towered over his dainty wife, felt it too. 'An unhappy place,' he kept murmuring as he waited.

Sara managed to drop one of the two powerful torches she was helping Matty position above one another in a cross-shaped gap in the church wall, facing out to sea. She seemed tense and unhappy.

'Are you all right?' I picked up the torch for her. Fortunately, it still worked.

'Fine.' She gave me a tight little smile.

'That's the spirit.'

If looks could kill, I'd have been dead. It was

difficult to be natural with Sara. I never knew what to say to her although I tried for Matty's sake. Maybe I tried too hard.

Matty began signalling out to sea. Dash dash dot. Dash dot dot dot.

Right on cue a light began blinking back through the darkness. I made out the dark shape of a conning tower out in the bay, and I was transported back to that terrible night when they'd taken Roy. For a moment I feared I was going to be physically sick.

Two marines with blackened faces knelt in the bow of the dinghy that loomed out of the night. I caught a rope as the marines leaped onto the crumbling jetty and sprinted to take up covering positions by the church. Sailors passed up two suitcases, cartons of Senior Service cigarettes and boxes of chocolates, before a lanky radio operator climbed awkwardly ashore and shook hands all round.

'It's good to be back,' he said in an Edinburgh accent.

The scientist and his wife stepped into the dinghy, the marines sprinted back to join them and then they were gone.

I'd assumed that I'd take Sara back to the farm, while Matty drove the radio operator to the safe house, but instead Sara climbed behind the wheel of the shooting brake and promptly drove off.

'That went well.'

'The old firm. Let's get back and have a nightcap.'

I kicked the BSA into life and set off. It was good to feel the night air on my face. I was exhilarated. I'd accomplished something at last. It wasn't going to alter how people thought of me – they wouldn't know – but I'd feel better. Perhaps I'd be able to put up with the insults and snubs more easily now.

Perhaps.

We moved Anna into Hawthorn Cottage early the next day. It was not easy persuading her to leave her husband and children, but in the end family pressure won. We concocted a story that she had gone off to visit friends in the south London suburb of Mitcham, deliberately chosen because it had been badly damaged in the fighting and most of its electoral rolls had been destroyed.

Even as we were hiding Anna under a blanket in the back of Matty's old farm Riley, she still had doubts she was doing the right thing.

'I will see the twins again, won't I?'

'Of course.'

'And you'll bring Simon up to see me?'

'If we can.'

The Chrysler parked outside the Dower House showed that Sara was back from her trip to the safe house. She emerged as we drew level.

'Damn!' Matty swore under his breath. 'Everything all right?' he asked her.

'Fine. Got back an hour ago. Didn't see a single German.' Sara was frowning at the back seat, where Anna's dark hair was peeping out from under the blanket.

'Good.' But I could tell Matty was not pleased that Sara had intercepted us. He was picking up Mills's paranoia about security. We drove up towards Scotch Hill, where Bert Latcham's wife Bessie was waiting with the kettle boiling and newly baked seed cake. Hawthorn Cottage had been cleaned from top to bottom and smelled of Brasso and polish. Vases of bluebells sat on the window ledge and the table.

I had to get off to the *Feldkommandantur* so we left Anna explaining that she didn't drink tea.

Jenner's Tea Rooms had been renamed Leech's Café. There was a big new sign: *Under Aryan Ownership*. I couldn't bring myself to go in any longer. It wasn't just that the prices had gone up or that the cakes had lost Miriam's magical touch, it was the principle. I was weighing up whether to spend my lunch playing hunt-the-mutton in a steamed pie or risk my teeth on a curling cheese sandwich, when Angel appeared alongside me.

'Hello.'

'Hello.' My stomach released a flock of butterflies.

She slipped her arm through mine. 'Did you make the rendezvous?'

I recounted the night's events. She scowled on hearing that Matty had allowed Sara to drive the radio operator to the safe house.

'He shouldn't involve her like that.'

'I gather she insisted. And when Sara insists . . .'

'I should have been back in time.' Angel didn't tell me where she'd been or what she'd been doing. 'By the way, I thought you'd like to know that Gown stumped up the money.'

'That's good. I hear the *Gestapo* have called for a post-mortem on Sir Rufus Forty.'

Angel shrugged. 'They won't find anything.'

It was an uncomfortable feeling: this pretty young woman with her arm through mine had killed someone in my presence. I suspected now that she had also been responsible for that outbreak of food poisoning at the Irish Club, and maybe those two boys who had died soon after I'd come back. The *Gestapo* had always insisted they had been poisoned, but who ever believed the *Gestapo*?

Angel broke into my thoughts. 'What are you doing tonight?'

'Um . . . I don't know.'

'You could take me for a drink.'

'I thought you were avoiding me.'

'Why ever did you think that? What a sensitive little soul you can be at times.'

*

I'd only been back in my office ten minutes when Hauser burst in. From the pinkness of his cheeks, I could tell he was excited about something.

'You'll never guess what?'

'Adolf's apologized? It's all a mistake? You're going home tomorrow?'

'Ssh ... One day someone from over there will hear you.' Hauser tilted his pomaded head towards the *Gestapo* wing.

'All right, then, surprise me.'

'The *Kommandant* has invited you to dinner at the Residence tonight. Seven-thirty for eight. Not black tie.'

'What!'

'With a guest.'

'What?'

'He mentioned the lady he met with you at the *Führer*'s birthday celebration. '

Angel! 'Why me?'

'You're in part exchange for Sir Rufus Forty, who can't make it since he's dead.'

'What if I have a previous engagement?'

'Just cancel it.'

'Why's Glass doing this?'

'Perhaps he likes you. Perhaps he's giving you a last chance.'

And I still didn't know what I'd done wrong.

17

Hauser did not understand why Glass had invited Nick Penny. He kept trying to winkle the reason out of his superior, right up to the time when it was announced that Sir Reginald Launcestone's car was arriving. But then Hauser did not get to see the weekly *Gestapo* digest.

Usually, it was not worth the paper it was typed on – the *Gestapo* did not share its secrets with the *Wehrmacht*. But this week it had been different. Stolz had slipped in something that he knew would hurt. Something for which, he said, he had irrefutable evidence.

Damn Stolz. And damn Penny, too.

Glass frowned at the two white tablets before popping them in his mouth and washing them down with brandy. His arm, his missing arm, had been aching all day. He couldn't face this evening without painkillers – and the brandy. The dinner in his Residence, a late-Victorian mock castle complete with castellated turrets and battlements, was in honour of *Oberführer* Fest. Last night the man had dined with senior SS German officers, tonight he was meeting the local Great and Good.

As he watched Launcestone's car draw up, Glass glanced towards the thicket of masts of impounded yachts anchored out in the middle of the wide river. For a fortnight, every year before the war, Glass had sailed around the Baltic by himself in his old twelve-metre boat. Perhaps he would try sailing here, now summer was on its way. The thought cheered him as he descended the stairs, working out how he could cope sailing literally single-handed.

Glass was pleased to see that Penny was accompanied by the same girl he had encountered at the *Führer*'s birthday reception. There was something about Coral Kennedy that appealed to him. She possessed a vibrancy, a mischievous impishness that juxtaposed with his inherent Prussian correctness. They did say opposites attract.

'Miss Kennedy, how pleasant to see you again.'

'And you, *Generalleutnant*. Or should I demote you to *Herr Oberst* in the hope that it brings you what you desire?'

'Ah, my wish to get to Russia.' Glass smiled, pleased she had remembered their previous conversation. 'I would answer to whatever rank you gave me. But why didn't you tell me you can speak German?'

'How do you know I do?'

Glass switched to his native tongue. 'There can't

be many young Englishwomen who understand German military ranks that well.'

'I confess, I grew up in Berlin.'

'How long were you there?'

'Almost ten years. My father worked for the branch of a New York bank there. We had an apartment just behind Leipziger Strasse.'

'Did you enjoy Berlin?'

'Who couldn't enjoy Berlin in the thirties, if you ignored . . .' She hurried on. 'I don't think I ever slept. It was a point of principle to be still partying at dawn to enjoy the free breakfasts in the Potsdamerplatz. And I fell in love with the *Anhalter Bahnhof*, with its trains constantly arriving and leaving for every capital in Europe. I wanted just to get on those trains and travel.'

'Travelling hopefully rather than arriving?'

'If you like.'

'I don't see you as a romantic, Miss Kennedy.'

'I'm not. But I was a traveller.'

'Yes.' Glass returned her slow mysterious smile. 'No doubt we'll find we have friends, and other things, in common. But excuse me – I have to attend to my other guests. We'll talk later, I hope.'

The moment he moved away Sir Reginald and Lady Launcestone descended on him. Bearup was muttering to *Oberführer* Fest about the details of the impending Jewish round-up – it seemed to be an open secret. Bearup's wife stood next to him, clutching a large handbag. From the way she flinched each time he gesticulated, Glass guessed that he was given to beating her.

A wave of depression swept over him as his gaze swept over the antechamber. God! He'd rather be freezing in some Russian forest than standing here in front of this unnecessarily large fire with people he despised. At the front, he'd be with men he respected but these people did not understand the meaning of respect – the mutual respect that bound you to your comrades through thick or thin. He would have died for his Brandenburgers just as he expected them to die for him. These English were only out for themselves, first, second and last.

How, for example, did that plodding Superintendent Bearup ever rise to be head of the CID? Perhaps stories about the power of Freemasonry were true after all. But their turn was coming – once the Jews had been dealt with.

Then there was Smeed: small, shifty and supremely self-important, with a smile capable of switching instantly into a snarl. A mistress installed near the harbour and a secretary carrying his unborn child, said the *Gestapo*. Glass could not stand the man yet he found himself fighting for *Kriegsmarine* contracts for Smeed's engineering company, to prevent the man's workers being shipped off to labour in Germany.

Sir Reginald Launcestone over there, with his gold

watch chain across his paunch. The King's representative in the Province. It was Berlin's policy to cultivate Lord Lieutenants as a way to circumvent the regional Supreme Councils if they tried to become independent. There was no chance of that down here, with Sir Reginald also the chairman of the Council. The man made the *Führer* sound like a social democrat.

The diners – the eight English guests together with Fest, Glass, Hauser and the English-speaking army doctor – filed into a baronial dining room adorned with fan displays of broadswords and with suits of armour lining the oak-panelled walls. Over the huge stone fireplace proudly hung the coat of arms of the original owner, a patent-medicine manufacturer.

Each diner had a printed menu card in front of them. The cuisine was German, the ingredients English, and the wines French.

Seezungerfillet mit Senfbutter
Fillet of sole with mustard butter

   Sorbet

Rehrücken mit Rotweinsoße; Himmel und Erde
Roast saddle of venison with red-wine sauce;
Heaven and Earth

Schwarzwälder Kirschtorte
Black Forest Cherry Cake

Glass had thought about setting an example and serving just a one-course meal until Hauser had pointed out that *Oberführer* Fest might take it as an insult, even though Berlin itself was demanding that everyone should have a simple meal one day a week, donating the price difference to the Winter Relief Fund. There had been newspaper pictures of the Duke and Duchess of Windsor sitting down to a tureen of humble soup. Even the Golf Club had followed suit last Sunday.

'I don't understand why our own bobbies have to conduct this round-up.' Lady Launcestone's braying voice resonated down the table. Glass realized she must have been drinking before she came out.

'It's in the treaty,' explained her husband.

That was not true. As far as Glass knew there was nothing in the Treaty of Surrender to say that the British police had to do the *Gestapo*'s dirty work.

'I've nothing against the Jews personally. My dressmaker is a little Jewish girl from . . .' Lady Launcestone flapped a hand in a vacuous attempt to remember. 'Somewhere.'

'You've nothing against them because you don't appreciate the harm they are wreaking on English society,' lectured Fest. 'Jews are like TB bacilli. They infect the whole body, suck its blood and leave it weak and enfeebled, while they get stronger.'

Glass did not think bacilli sucked blood but it was

not his part to correct *Oberführer* Fest. He willed Penny to stay silent.

'The Jew has no homeland, so like a leech he feeds off the work of others. In your goodness, Lady Launcestone, you do not see the poison they spread. On the work floor, they cripple industry by their verminous agitation. They start wars for the profit of international plutocrats.'

'They should be deported,' proclaimed Sir Reginald. 'England's for the English. We don't want any foreigners here.'

'Not even our German guests?' demanded Penny.

Glass stifled a laugh. Launcestone muttered something inaudible through a very small, resentful mouth.

'Well, Sir Reginald?' prompted Glass.

Launcestone shot Penny a look of pure hate. 'That's different. You beat us fair and square.' A thought occurred to him. 'May I remind you, Penny, that it was Britain who declared war on Germany. This war was none of their making.'

'They invaded Poland.'

Glass felt a sharp pain in the ankle. He winced, at the same time noticing Coral Kennedy looking daggers at Penny to shut up.

'Political necessity,' barked Launcestone.

Realizing her mistake, Coral Kennedy blushed, catching Glass's stare. Glass stopped himself grinning back.

'Everything's ready for tomorrow's round-up, *Oberführer,*' said Bearup. 'We've got enough arrest teams now that we've sworn in the Specials. The first families should be in the football ground by six in the morning.'

'Are you shipping them out straight away?' Lady Launcestone had finished her sorbet.

'No, we need to make sure all is in order first. We hope we'll begin transporting them the day after tomorrow. There'll be Red Cross feeding stops provided on the way.'

'Will it take that long?' asked Mrs Smeed.

'The railways are busy with material and troops going to Germany. The transports have a low priority. We hope to get them to Harwich in a day or two.'

Glass caught Nick's eye and dared him to speak. The silence seemed interminable until Mrs Smeed asked: 'What's "Heaven and Earth"?'

'Apples and potatoes,' replied Glass. 'As you are about to see.'

General conversation lapsed during the main course and Glass used the opportunity to ask Coral Kennedy more about her time in Berlin. He enjoyed hearing her sharp Berlin accent.

'Those free breakfasts you mentioned?'

'In the Excelsior or else in the Café Werner.'

'Not in the Hotel Adlon, then?' Glass picked at food already cut up into small pieces.

'A little too stiff and serious.'

'Full of Nazi Party top brass, you mean?' Glass smiled.

'I suppose so, yes.'

'I see nothing wrong with these corrective camps,' Sir Reginald was telling *Oberführer* Fest. 'It's about time the government was tough on crime. Teach these riff-raff a lesson. Military discipline will do them good.'

'Who decides who are riff-raff?' asked Coral mildly.

'Society. In Germany we rely on the people policing themselves,' replied Fest. 'Once the authorities declare a group like Jews or Gypsies to be outcast, we leave it up to the public to denounce them. Ninety per cent of all *Gestapo* cases come from denunciation. It means that our justice is popular justice.'

'Your justice is popular only in how you trade on people's prejudices,' Coral chipped in quickly. 'You took the edges of society and sliced them off instead of trying to fold them back into the middle.'

'The population was glad to see them go.'

'Only because the people were already predisposed to endorse discrimination.'

It was a central paradox that in wanting safer streets, orthodoxy and an end to political weakness, the German people had ended up with the most corrupt and vicious regime in Europe, although Coral did not dare say so at *this* table. There *was* no political debate in the *Reich*. There were no political opponents

– only deviants. And everyone knew where they ended up.

'Tell me, *Kommandant*, are these rumours about the coronation true?' Mrs Smeed wiped a dribble of cream from her mouth.

'I only know what I read in the papers.'

'We attended the last coronation – such a grand spectacle,' thrilled Lady Launcestone. 'Another one is just what the country needs.'

Glass's missing arm began aching again. He was growing bored. Fortunately, coffee and brandy came promptly. Unable to tolerate another half-hour of Launcestone holding forth, brandy balloon in hand, huge backside masking the fire, he gestured for Hauser to bring out the gifts as a signal that the evening was drawing to a close. Most of the guests received silver propelling pencils, but Glass had a special gift for Nick Penny – and for Coral Kennedy. He hoped that Penny at least would understand the warning.

18

The little girl in the blue dress and white ankle socks sat cross-legged at the foot of the angel. She was whispering to herself as she plucked petals from a daisy, one of a bunch she clutched in her small fist.

'She loves me. She loves me not. She loves me. She loves me not.' Her lower lip trembled, then she tossed away the flower and started again.

The mourners at Major Cordington's funeral ignored her.

'What are you doing?' I asked her.

She regarded me solemnly from huge brown eyes. 'Seeing if my mummy still loves me.'

'Where is your mummy?'

'I don't know. They put her on a bus.' The little girl started plucking a fresh daisy. 'She loves me. She loves me not. She loves me . . .'

'What's your name?'

'Daisy.' She held up the flower as if to explain.

'And what's your second name?'

'I don't know.' She swung her small legs over the edge of the tomb, refusing to look at me.

'Where's your daddy?'

But she had gone back into her game. 'She loves me. She loves me not . . .'

The graveyard was an oasis of peace and tranquillity in a town in chaos. The round-up of the Jews had turned into a shambles. While some of the victims allowed themselves to be herded, bewildered but compliant, onto buses, others resisted, refusing to leave their homes. At the bottom of Priory Road, I'd watched an old woman open her bedroom window and pour the contents of her chamber pot onto the heads of two policemen trying to break down her front door. The scene would have been funny if it had not been pathetic.

Everywhere there was an air of disbelief at the sight of English bobbies in their comfortingly familiar blue uniforms beating down doors and dragging away innocent civilians. The foreign Jews who had fled to England had always trusted the bobby – unlike the policemen they had encountered abroad. Then one Saturday morning the policeman who had previously greeted you in the street now arrested you for no other reason than that you were Jewish.

The cathedral church of St Augustine was full. Matty and Sara sat in a pew by themselves at the front; the only other members of his family – a couple of second cousins somewhat removed – sat behind them. There were other Cordingtons lurking off stage but they had decided not to bother travelling to attend. I hid at the back as the organist set off to win his personal race to the end of 'Abide with Me' ahead of the congregation. Then it was the bishop's turn to struggle as he did his best to find anything charitable to say about the deceased. He dwelt on the Major's love for his wife, and on his bravery. The bishop ignored his indifference to his son, his reclusive drinking, the way he had let the estate run down, and his general contempt for humanity.

The organist struck up again and the congregation cleared their lungs for another breathless gallop over four uneven verses of 'The day Thou gavest, Lord, is ended'. It had been Matty's fourth choice of hymn; his first three, 'Jerusalem', 'I Vow to Thee, my Country' and 'Onward, Christian Soldiers', were all banned. As the service droned its way through another reading, the twenty-third psalm and yet more prayers, I thought about last night's dinner party. I still couldn't work out why we'd been invited, unless Glass wanted to see Angel again. In fact, he had hardly been able to keep his eyes off her. Nor did I know why we had been given those long silver spoons. If it was a German custom, it was a new one on me. I told myself that I must ask Hauser about them.

I made sure that Matty saw me as he followed the coffin to the graveside, but then I stayed in the background. The little girl had vanished. On the grass were five daisy stalks.

The Golf Club set attended in force. Last night I'd dined with Launcestone and Horace Smeed. Today they ignored me, so I chatted to the estate workers.

'It's a sad old day.' Bert Latcham looked uncomfortable in the same suit he'd been married in forty years before. The cuffs were frayed and his tie had slipped to reveal a missing collar stud. But he'd tried – tried to keep up appearances.

'Things'll be better with Master Matty in charge,' I encouraged him.

'Ay, maybe as so. But I'm not sure about that woman he's got in tow.'

'Sara? What's wrong with her?'

'Aarrr, well . . . least said, soonest mended.'

'Come on, Bert.'

He hesitated. On the one hand he'd known me since I was a nipper. On the other, he felt he was being disloyal to his master. 'She got him around her little finger, she have.'

Bert shambled away, worried he had said too much. I was trying to work out exactly what he'd meant when Leech came up to me. There was nothing old or worn about his mourning clothes: a thick top coat, grey homburg and very shiny shoes. He was altogether too well dressed for a funeral.

'I didn't really know the Major,' admitted Leech as his eyes ceaselessly scanned the mourners. 'But I felt I had to come. How's Joan?'

Not *How's Mrs Pendleton?* Not *How's your sister?* But *How's Joan?*

'Fine,' I replied.

'She's a remarkable woman.'

At that moment, Trevellian, the property magnate, became detached from a nearby group and Leech was instantly by his side. I was surprised he had the temerity even to approach one of the richest men in the west – and even more surprised when Trevellian shook his hand warmly. The unctuous Leech was rising in the world – but why was he asking about Joan?

'Earth to earth. Ashes to ashes. Dust to dust. In the sure and certain hope of the resurrection to eternal life . . .'

A stick-thin teenage boy, with a skullcap on top of a mass of black curls, came hurtling around the side of the church. Snot was flying from his nose and he was obviously terrified. A police whistle blew shrilly behind him. The boy suddenly realized that he was in the middle of a funeral and he stopped, wild-eyed and panting like a cornered wild beast, before darting towards the church door.

Sir Reginald Launcestone stuck out his walking stick with cruel and precise timing. The boy went flying over the gravel to crash into a gravestone. With a moan, he began crawling towards the church.

'Sanctuary. Sanctuary.' The words rasped from his tortured lungs.

Launcestone pinned the boy to the ground with his stick.

'How dare you allow this ragamuffin to disturb a solemn ceremony,' he barked to two red-faced constables who had now lumbered around the corner.

'Sanctuary,' pleaded the boy.

'I'll give you sanctuary.' One policeman dragged the boy to his feet by his ear. 'I'm sorry to have disturbed you, sir.'

The policemen saluted Launcestone before frog-marching the boy out of the graveyard and into the road. When they thought they were out of sight, they began beating him around the head.

'Sanctuary, indeed,' muttered the Lord Lieutenant contemptuously.

'Thanks for coming back.'

'Don't be daft. You managed to get the front door open, then?'

'We had to force it. Bert thinks it was last used for my mother's coffin to pass through.' The heavy door creaked as Matty swung it back and to. 'By the way, don't bother to fight those vultures over the food. I've kept some things back for us to have later.'

The spread was everything the mourners had hoped for. A whole ham, a poached salmon, some turkey, cheeses, fresh-baked bread, pickles and preserves, farm-made butter and bottles of beer and whisky, port and sherry were laid out in the dining room where Matty's father had been found dead. Sara was very much in evidence. Invisible while the Major had been alive, now she was everywhere, keeping an eye on the servants, making sure everyone's glass was full, but somehow never far from Matty's side.

I poured myself a beer – everyone else was clustered around the whisky – and let the babble of conversation wash over me.

'I haven't set foot in this house for ten years . . .'

'Young Cordington'll have his hands full running this estate. The Germans are demanding more and more all the time . . .'

'There's a place on the bench for him, of course. What do you say, Cordington?'

'Um, I'll have to think about it,' replied Matty.

'He's looking forward to shouldering his civic responsibilities,' Sara cut in quickly.

When Matty caught my eye and sidled out through the door, I followed down a dim passage into a small room used as an office. He slumped heavily into a chair and poured us two large whiskies from a waiting bottle.

'Is everything all right, Matty?'

'I imagine so. No one can find a will so it all comes to me.'

'You didn't think . . .?'

'Nick, he was such a curmudgeonly old devil, he was capable of anything.'

Among the mourners, Matty had been careful to keep up an attentive mask but here in private his face sagged with tiredness. I was surprised he was taking the death of his father quite so badly.

'You look all in.'

'Nick, you don't know. It's not just the . . . Listen, I've something—'

Sara stood in the doorway.

'What are you doing in here?'

'Talking to Nick,' replied Matty with childlike simplicity.

'You're ignoring your guests.'

'I won't be long. I need a minute's peace.'

'You can't hide away in here. Mr Smeed wants to talk to you about joining the Food Committee.'

'All right. I'll be there in a second.'

'Come now. And you don't need that drink. That's how your father started.'

Embarrassed by the scene, I turned away to look out of the window. A police car was passing, heading up the dead-end lane that led towards Scotch Hill, Hawthorn Cottage – and Anna Jenner.

'Matty!'

He spun around just as the police car disappeared from view behind a drystone wall. Sara was still holding the office door open. The murmur of conversation drifted along from the dining room and in the kitchen someone dropped a plate. Something passed between Matty and Sara.

The punishment for harbouring an illegal alien, which Anna had officially become that morning, was imprisonment in one of the punishment camps sprouting up around the country.

'The police won't dare arrest you,' Sara said. 'Not with the Lord Lieutenant here. You didn't know she was there.'

'Fuck the police.' It was rare for Matty to swear. 'I gave my word to the Jenners. I'll get Launcestone to sign a reprieve. We'll stop them on their way back.'

Sara blocked his way. 'Don't be stupid. It's nothing to do with Sir Reginald. Let the police get on with their job.'

'Maybe Anna'll see them coming,' I said, for want of anything better to say.

But she didn't. I stood there in the window and watched, until five minutes later the police car returned with Anna's frightened face staring out from the back.

Matty saw the car from the dining room. He turned pale. Mourners commented how he was taking his father's death to heart and set about another round of ham sandwiches.

*

The round-up was still under way as I went to break the bad news to Simon. At the junction of Tinners Road and St John's, an ambulance was taking away the body of a woman who had jumped from a fifth-storey window with her baby in her arms. A crowd of stone-faced citizens had gathered to watch the Jews being flushed out of their Ex-Servicemen's Club onto the back of a lorry.

'Good riddance to you,' shouted one sharp-faced woman in a knotted headscarf.

'Hush,' said the woman next to her. 'It'll be us next.'

One or two policemen looked ashamed; most treated it as another job. They were just obeying orders.

Barbara opened the door to me, Hope at her breast wrapped in a shawl. She knew instantly what had happened.

'Anna?' she breathed.

I nodded.

'Oh, no.'

I thought Barbara was going to faint. Hope sensed something was wrong and began wailing. I helped Barbara to a chair as Miriam, Jacob and Simon came crowding round. I explained again what had happened.

'But how did they know she was there?'

'Maybe a walker out on Scotch Hill saw her.'

'But no one would know she was Jewish – that she was hiding,' objected Jacob.

'Poor Anna,' sobbed Barbara. 'Let them take me instead.'

'Hush now, dear,' comforted Miriam. 'Don't talk like that.'

'But I'm only here because of her kindness. And now she's gone . . .' Barbara dissolved in tears. Miriam took the baby out of her unprotesting arms and began soothing its screams.

Simon had gone as white as paper. 'How can I get to see her?' he demanded.

I said I thought I could probably get him into the football ground, but I wasn't sure if I could ever get him out again, not if he was wearing his yellow star.

'It doesn't matter,' he decided. 'Perhaps I can do some good in there. I'll take my medical bag and whatever drugs I've got left.'

'Take her some food. She might not have eaten.' Miriam hurried off and began making sandwiches as Simon went up to see the twins. I had the feeling that he was saying goodbye to them.

British *Freikorps* SS stood on guard at the peeling entrance to the Chapel Hill ground, where in the past local crowds had cheered on City. Now hundreds of distraught women, many with sobbing children clinging to their coats, waited in lines in front of trestle tables where teams of *WVHA* clerks sat with their card indexes and typewriters. There were very few men among the internees.

I recalled that the last time I'd been here Roy, David and I had watched City beat Bristol Rovers thanks to Otto Klein's brilliant performance. It seemed such a long time ago. Klein's unit was now stationed somewhere near Smolensk.

The notion of restarting the league never had taken off. The trouble that had flared on Merseyside and in Glasgow had put paid to that idea.

I recognized SS *Oberscharführer* Schmidt from the Office for Jewish Affairs.

He glanced at Simon's yellow star as we approached. 'Good. We need everyone you can find.'

'It's not what you think.'

'We're well short of our quota. Bearup and his bloody list! At this rate we'll be snatching prisoners out of the jail and cutting off their foreskins to get our numbers up.'

I explained that Dr Jenner had come to search for his wife, who had been arrested by mistake.

'She should be over on the west terrace, with the city Jews – but you won't get her out if she's already been registered.'

The ground had become one vast encampment. Groups of women and children huddled together on the terraces, some talking quietly, most sunk in mute

despair. Long queues stretched away from the lava-
tories and the Red Cross sick bay that had been set
up in the dressing rooms. Incongruously, small girls
were still skipping to English nursery rhymes, while
the boys fulfilled their fantasies by playing football
on a real pitch.

Simon and I were walking slowly around the
touchline, trying to pick out Anna in the crowds, when
a boy playing tag tripped and tumbled head over
heels down one of the terraces. Blood pumped from
his nose but it was the way the boy's thumb stuck out
at an obscene angle that caused the women nearby a
collective sharp intake of breath. Simon was there in
a second. He grasped the dislocated thumb and gave
a sharp jerk. The boy screamed, but the thumb went
back into its socket. He was trying to staunch the
boy's bleeding nose as the mother rushed up.

'Dr Jenner. Dr Jenner. Thank you.'

Other women recognized him now, and gathered
around all talking at once. A Red Cross nurse shoul-
dered her way through to ask him if he'd hold a
surgery in the sick bay.

'Of course, but let me find my wife first.'

'Mrs Jenner is already there. She's helping us with
the little ones.'

Simon turned to me. I already knew what he was
going to say.

'It seems I'm needed here, Nick. Explain to mum
and dad, and give the twins a kiss from me.'

'Will they be all right?'

'My family will look after them. We'll send for them, wherever we end up.'

We shook hands. The waiting women crowded round and carried him off like the tide bearing a prize out to sea – out of my reach, out of my depth.

As I rode back to the Jenners, Jews from nearby country towns were still arriving in buses and lorries. The streets were now deserted, apart from mobs of Specials carrying away loot from abandoned houses. Bearup's reservations about employing them had been justified: they were out of control. A plume of smoke rose above Touchstone Rise, where they'd torched the home of the Jewish pharmacist.

My heart sank as I pulled up outside the Jenner house. Half a dozen Specials were crowding around the front door. I recognized at least one from the scuffle outside the tea shop.

'What are you lot doing there?' I said in what I hoped was a commanding voice.

'Who the fuck are you?'

One yob pointed at me: 'He's a Jew-lover.'

I pushed through them till my back was against the door. For once I wished I was wearing my uniform.

Miriam's voice came from inside. 'Is that you,

Nick? Shall we open the door? They say they're policemen.'

'They're not,' I shouted to her.

'Yes, we are. We've been sworn in, and we'll fucking nick you.'

'If anyone's going to get nicked around here, it'll be you. So sod off now, or you'll answer to the *Kommandant* himself.'

My bluff did not work.

'Fuck off. We've got mates in the *Gestapo*.'

One of them hurled a stone at a bedroom window. The sound of smashing glass triggered a frenzy of violence. Others started throwing stones, too. As another window shattered, a shooting brake pulled up and Matty, still in his suit and black tie, began to climb out of the passenger side. Sara held on to his arm, but Matty shook himself free and ran up the drive.

As Matty pushed one of the thugs aside, a vicious free-for-all broke out. I kicked out at one and punched another, before going down under the weight of three of them. Finding a nose close to my face, I sank my teeth into it and bit like holy hell. The scream could have been heard a mile away. I struggled to my feet in time to get a whack on my ear, and reeled back, smashing my head against the wall. If only Roy had been there . . . but he was dead. I had a vague vision of Jacob Jenner wading out with a walking stick before being knocked to his knees.

A shot – reverberating loudly through my throbbing head. Then another. I opened my eyes to see Bleicher, pistol raised above his head.

'*Was is hier los?*' German officers from next door were crowding around the gate.

'*Abwehr,*' announced Bleicher. 'Get some men to take away this rabble.'

A minute later, the sullen Specials were escorted away by soldiers with fixed bayonets. The shooting brake, and Sara, had vanished.

Young David was filling the kettle as I got home. I swallowed the last aspirin left in the house and felt the duck egg coming up on one side of my head.

'I'm making Gran a cup of tea. Do you want one?'

'Thanks.' I couldn't ever remember him offering to make a cup of tea for anyone before. My antennae should have twitched then, but my head was throbbing too much.

But there was no mistaking Joan's anger as she stormed in through the door. She had not put down her shopping bags before she started laying into David.

'What's this about you being so rude to Mr Leech? He said he gave you a bag of aniseed balls but you tipped them down the drain.'

'I didn't ask for them.' David concentrated on spooning tea leaves into the pot.

'You accepted them from him, though.'

'He made me.'

'When did this happen?' I was astounded that any boy would throw away precious sweets, as things were now.

'This afternoon. Mr Leech has just told me.' Joan began unpacking her shopping with furious energy, pouring potatoes into the vegetable rack and banging a tin of rice pudding down on the table so hard that I winced.

'You should have brought them home for us if you didn't want them,' I said in a feeble attempt at jocularity. 'It's years since I tasted an aniseed ball.'

'He was only trying to smarm,' muttered David.

'David, don't be so ungrateful. It was very kind of Mr Leech to—'

'I don't want anything from him. Everyone knows he puts stones in the bread and keeps all the best things for the Nazis.'

'David, that's a terrible thing to say.'

'*Everyone* says it.'

'Who's everyone?' demanded Joan.

David weighed up whether he was going to get a friend into trouble. He decided he didn't care. 'Wilf Polherry.'

'What does he know?'

'And Arthur Stockman and Chris Dodd – they all say it. They reckon you're going out with him—'

'David!'

'—Just to get extra rations.'

Joan's eyes widened in horror. 'Get to your room this instant. This instant, I say, or you'll feel the weight of my hand.'

David opened his mouth to protest. I gave a tiny shake of my head and he ran out of the room, slamming the door behind him. I winced again.

Joan took over the tea-making. Her hands were shaking, and she did not seem aware that she was still wearing her outdoor coat.

'I've never heard the like, never. The ungrateful wretch . . . Ungrateful . . .' She continued to mutter to herself.

'Joan . . .'

She held up a hand to deflect any discussion. That was all right by me; my head felt as if it was going to fall off, anyway. She made three cups of tea with a compact ferocity, and carried away one for herself and one for mum, still wearing her coat.

I took my tea to the fireside chair and thought about the events of the past hour. Thank God Bleicher had turned up when he did. He had saved us from a kicking, and the Jenners' home from being ransacked. Miriam had ministered to our wounds while Bleicher apologized to her for not being able to take Anna's name off the list of detainees. Somehow, I doubted he was telling the truth. Secret police everywhere wield disproportionate power and influence. Miriam and Jacob had accepted Simon's decision to stay with his wife with almost biblical stoicism. Only Barbara could not help her tears. I had taken Matty home on the back of my bike. We'd found the Chrysler outside Home Farm. Neither of us had referred to Sara's flight.

I dozed off, thinking how Bleicher's presence did not bode well for the Resistance. I entered an unsettling and confused sleep, with dreams all in grey. Angel and I were together in a house or maybe a fort – the only ones left. Everyone else had been killed. Although we had surrendered, they were still going to shoot us. But who *were* they? Sara, certainly, and Bleicher ... They wanted to give us an award for bravery, but they were going to shoot us as well. I called them both hypocrites, and handed Bleicher a big old-fashioned Luger, saying: 'There's two fucking rounds left. Get on with it.'

I woke with a start to find Joan rattling the fire, complaining at me for letting it almost go out. I'd been asleep for over an hour.

'Sorry, sis.' I sat up and winced as the pain shot through my head. 'Ouch.'

'Are you all right?' She was suddenly concerned.

I explained about Simon and Anna, and the visit by the Specials.

'That's terrible.' She delved in her bag and produced a small bottle of aspirin. Painkillers were like

379

gold dust but she handed me three. 'Mum's asleep so wake her in half an hour. There's a tin of tongue and some beetroot for your tea.'

'Where are you going?'

'The Golf Club.'

The manner she turned away as she spoke made me suspicious. I struggled to bring her face into focus, noticing that she was wearing lipstick and powder. And a decent dress.

'Sis?'

She snatched up her handbag and inspected its contents. 'I won't be too late.'

She was by the door before I continued, 'Are you all right, sis?'

'Of course I'm all right. And it's no one's business but mine how I spend my time. No one in this house objects to eating the food I put in front of them.'

'Sis!'

'Nothing's for free any more. Just remember that.' Joan slammed out of the house, leaving me with an even worse headache.

19

Angel's note next morning was terse. I was to be at the first house on the right entering the village of Cross Hands, ten miles outside the city, by ten-thirty.

I set off in plenty of time. An unreal calm lay over the city after yesterday's upheavals. It had rained heavily overnight, leaving pools of water on the roads. I hoped that those locked inside the football ground had managed to find some shelter.

I arrived early, so I stopped outside Cross Hands and listened as church bells rang along the valley, calling the faithful to prayer. I wondered why the same bells had not rung in alarm yesterday, and why I had not seen a single Anglican vicar, Catholic priest or Nonconformist minister out on the streets, pleading for the Jews. Their bells had been silent yesterday. They had found their voice today – and I despised them for it.

The house was a pastel green box behind rusty wrought-iron railings. I hid the Empire Star in the stable at the back. Angel opened the scullery door as if expecting me to come that way.

'You missed the funeral,' I said in greeting.

'I was busy.' Angel was back to wearing her black slacks, leather jacket and the roll-neck sweater that accentuated her cheekbones. She touched my forehead. 'That's some bruise. Just as well Bleicher showed up when he did.'

'How did you know about that?'

'I called in at Home Farm earlier. Matty's covered in bruises, too.'

I was curious why she'd been at Home Farm so early on a Sunday morning but I knew better than to ask. I was getting the feeling this was not on a social visit. As if on cue, Mills emerged through a door leading to the rest of the house. He seemed to be passing himself off as a farmer in baggy old corduroy trousers and a sports jacket. But there was a noticeable lump pulling down his right-hand pocket. I realized I hadn't seen him for months.

'We were just saying it was lucky for Nick that Bleicher arrived when he did, yesterday.'

'Indeed. Please sit down, Nick.' Mills indicated a chair at the scrubbed kitchen table. 'How well do you know Bleicher?'

'I've met him socially at the Jenners' and spoken to him in the *Feldkommandantur*.'

'I hear he let your nephew off with just a caution when he was caught painting Victory signs. Unusual thing for an *Abwehr* agent to do, wasn't it?' Mills, squat and powerful, paced the room. 'What did he want in return?'

'Nothing. He was just being decent.' I knew it sounded odd. The *Abwehr* did not make a habit of being decent.

'Do you see much of him in the *Feldkommandantur*?'

'He's not been around for a while. When he's there, he sometimes camps in my office when he wants to see who's coming and going in the *Gestapo* wing.'

Mills crossed to the sink and filled a cup with water to drink. I was left sitting at the table while Angel leaned against a dresser looking worried. I knew the game. Create a vacuum of silence and someone will feel obliged to fill it. I'd been taught that technique in Intelligence, but the silence here suggested some sort of trial.

'Why do you ask?' Refusing to accept my role as wrongdoer, I rose from the table to see that Angel's hand was hovering near an open drawer. I had the feeling I'd find a gun in there. I took a cup off the draining board and copied Mills. That made him move across to the door to put the table between us. He clearly did not want to be too close if Angel had to shoot me.

'Didn't you think it strange that you weren't arrested after Roy's death?' he demanded. 'It's standard *Gestapo* practice to put family and close friends alike in detention camps. You were his best chum, yet that didn't happen. Why?'

'I don't know. Bleicher did question me but his heart didn't seem to be in it. Maybe Glass was protecting me.'

Mills changed tack. 'Where did Sara Burskin say her father was professor of mathematics?'

'Breslau. She claimed he was the youngest man ever to be given a chair in the entire history of the university.'

'I want you to meet someone.' As Mills disappeared through the door, Angel gave me a wink before dropping her gaze. Mills returned. 'This is Stan. He was reader in theoretical physics at Cracow University.'

Stan was a very sturdy five feet six inches, with the battered face of a booth fighter. Anyone looking less like an academic I'd yet to see.

'You are familiar with the members of the mathematics department at Breslau, Stan?'

'Of course. We'd meet at conferences, read each other's papers.' Stan's voice rumbled out from deep inside his broad chest. 'In Poland, the academic scientific world was a small one.'

'So you knew everyone?'

'Not everyone. I wouldn't know assistant lecturers or postgraduate supervisors from other universities but I was acquainted with professors and senior lecturers.'

'So you'd know the professor of applied mathematics at Breslau?'

'Of course. Anton Tula was my good friend.'

'Not Burskin?'

'I do not know a Burskin.'

'Hang on,' I said. 'Burskin's not her real name.
Matty said that was as close as he could get to
pronouncing it. It's Bureschatzetskin or something
like that.'

'Familiar?' demanded Mills.

'No,' replied Stan, firmly.

'Maybe Sara has got the department wrong.
Maybe it's pure maths.'

'That's Tscolosky.'

'How old are these men?' asked Angel.

'In their sixties now.'

'Perhaps she was boasting,' I tried. 'Maybe her
father's just a lecturer.'

'Why are you trying to defend her?' asked Angel.

'I'm only trying to be fair. Many refugees like to
inflate their pasts.'

'Let me meet her. I will know in an instant if she
is telling the truth,' rumbled Stan.

'Thank you, but that won't prove anything except
that she's been lying about her past and, as Nick said,
that's not unusual among refugees.' Mills escorted
Stan out of the room.

'You think she's a fraud?' I asked Angel.

She shrugged. 'Someone is.'

Mills returned to fix me with a cold stare. I felt my face redden. I was as innocent as a newborn lamb, so why was he making me feel guilty? 'What do you really know about her?'

'Only that Matty met her in Suffolk . . .'

'Where exactly?'

'I don't know.' That was strange. I didn't.

'Does she have any contact with the Germans here?'

'Not that I know of. She says she can't stand them.' A thought occurred to me. 'If she *is* an informer, that would explain how the police found Anna Jenner so quickly.'

'Do *you* think she is?' asked Angel in a gentler tone.

'It's not a nice thought.'

'Stop being *nice*.' She smiled and some of the tension left the room. Angel slipped the drawer shut and squeezed my arm in an affectionate gesture.

'Nick, I've a favour to ask. Two, actually.'

'Whatever I can do to help.'

'Will you give me a lift back to town via Dumonbury Hill?'

'Dumonbury?'

Dumonbury was one of two local Iron Age forts located on adjacent precipitous hills. Dogglesbury was the other one.

'A radio operator's coming down from Gloucester

this afternoon, to service a new underground circuit being set up in the west. He's going to lie up in the old cottage at the foot of the hill for a couple of hours while waiting for his escort. I just want to give the cottage a quick once-over first.'

'You wouldn't rather move him at night?' Mills asked Angel.

'I think it's too risky. If he's caught after curfew with the radio set, then he'd have a lot of explaining to do. No, the baker's van's collecting him at five.'

'You said *two* favours,' I reminded her as I wheeled the bike out of the stables.

'Pick me up from home later. There's something we must see.'

Sunday lunch was frosty. Joan had stayed out late last night, and she and David were not talking. Our mother did not seem to notice: she was drifting away from the real world. Instead, she embarked on a long, rambling account of some school outing which, from the names of teachers who had been dead for a decade, must have taken place just after the First War. At least her chatter filled the brooding silence that otherwise hung over the kitchen. Even the luxury of a slab of Cheddar cheese, after the sausage, mash and cabbage, failed to lift the oppressive atmosphere between us. David could not wait to get back to his room, and once mother had gone for her afternoon lie-down, Joan channelled her anger into the washing-up.

'I will not be made to feel guilty by my thirteen-year-old son. It's totally ridiculous.'

I could have pointed out that no one was *making* her feel guilty, but then she'd probably have thrown a saucepan at me. I said nothing.

'Yes, all right, I did see Leech last night,' she continued. 'Is that a criminal act? Why am I being treated like a leper? I don't encourage him, if that's what you think.'

'I don't think anything, sis.' I hoped she could see the olive branch I was waving.

'He did the Jenners a favour, buying their business. And you know he's promised to give it back if the time comes.'

The idea that Leech had done the Jenners a *favour* had not occurred to me. He had taken advantage of the situation to grab their business at a rock-bottom price. And I'd believe he'd hand it back to them when I saw Matty's herd of Tamworth pigs flying over the Shire Hall.

I did not reply, which drove Joan to further frenzies of activity at the sink.

'If *he* hadn't bought it, someone else would have done. I'm not defending him but . . .'

'That's exactly what you're doing.'

'All right, maybe I am, but he's not as bad as he's painted. Nothing like as bad as those silly schoolboys make him out to be.'

I believed Leech was a smug, greedy, greasy, self-righteous, Nazi-loving git – so I said nothing.

'The jam, the pickled onions, the eggs, that tin of peaches, our candles, soap, and even the Carnation milk we're having for tea today all come from him,' continued my sister.

'You're the one who said nothing's for free.'

When would I learn to keep my mouth shut? Joan spun around, soap suds up to her elbows, her eyes blazing.

'Yes, I did. But it's in my own time and no one else's. Hubert's very attentive. We have tea at the Great Western Hotel or go for drives in the country. It's all very innocent. You want me to take mum along as a chaperone?'

'No, of course not.'

'And to be honest, Nick, this last year has been unremitting hell. Believe it or not, it's nice to have someone to light your cigarette, to open a door for you.'

The trouble was that I still could not see the ingratiating little grocer as the right man for Joan. I didn't object to Joan going out with a man – what right had I? But Leech! I just couldn't imagine them together.

I buried myself in the *Sunday Express*, reflecting on how Joan's husband Ted had been dead for less than nine months.

Angel and I lay in the long grass up on the ridge and peered down at the railway siding in the cutting in the valley beneath. Directly across the valley rose the twin hill forts. According to archaeologists, the Iron Age folk had first dug deep ditches and erected their earthen ramparts on Dumonbury Hill, before finding they were still vulnerable to attack from the east. So they did the same again on the adjacent and even more precipitous Dogglesbury Hill. A hell of a lot of extra work for getting it wrong.

Identical white cottages sat at the foot of each hill. The two labourers' cottages, which had been abandoned at the start of the war, lay off short tracks either side of the lane leading to the farm beyond the hills. The radio operator was hiding out in the cottage on the right.

But we were not there to keep watch on this cottage half a mile away. Much closer to hand was a picture of hell.

Below us, out of sight of the rest of the valley floor, was the rail siding where in peacetime beef cattle had been loaded onto wagons to be transported up-country. But, on this fine late Sunday afternoon,

Jewish people had taken the place of cattle and the animal pens were crammed with a mass of frightened humanity. The milling throng below us contrasted starkly with the air of tranquillity that lay over the empty valley's sunlit fields and the ancient earthworks on the hills opposite.

A ragged line of detainees was being herded along up ramps to be loaded into cattle trucks by German guards with their snarling Alsatians. Forty Jews to each truck, I counted. Fifty trucks to each train. Three trains, in all.

Angel was making frantic notes, frequently glancing at her watch. A thin cigar tube peeped out of the top of her jacket pocket. She seemed unusually nervous. 'What's that brown uniform the soldiers are wearing?'

'They're *SS-Totenkopfverbände* – the Death's Head troops used to guard the camps in the *Reich*.'

One train on its spur line was already complete. Two tank engines were under steam, the wagon doors closed. As we watched, a soldier leaned out of the guard's van and waved a green flag. A thin cloud of steam escaped from the engines' funnels and slowly, imperceptibly slowly, the train began moving.

Secretly they went, like wrongs hushed up – no whistle to announce their departure, no friends to wave them goodbye. The train set off, then slowed, so that buffer clanked on buffer in a long metallic ripple. The cutting bent away to the left, and soon only a plume of smoke indicated where the cargo of human misery had reached.

'Look.' Angel pointed at two cars coming along the valley from the direction of the town. They were big black Armstrong-Siddeleys, the sort favoured by the *Gestapo*. Angel slid back a little behind me as we watched them head up the lane between Dumonbury and Dogglesbury hills.

'Betrayed.'

In close convoy, the cars sped towards the spot where short tracks branched off to the cottages. Straight on and they would pass between the hills and end up at the farm beyond. To the left was Dogglesbury cottage. To the right, Dumonbury cottage – where the radio operator was hiding.

Angel placed her hand gently on my collar, brushing up my hair with her finger. The convoy slowed. Angel squeezed my neck.

'How did they know?'

The cars accelerated away up the left-hand track towards Dogglesbury.

Angel gave a sharp intake of breath and a strangled, gulping laugh. Then she threw herself on top of me, kissing my face with the same joyful excitement as a puppy licks its master.

'Hang on, there.'

'I'm so glad. Oh, Nick, I'm so glad.'

'But the *Gestapo* . . .' I tried to rise to see what was happening.

'There's nothing for them to find. There's no one there.' Angel's eyes shone with happiness. She threw her arms around me, and this time I was ready. The kiss became something slower and deeper.

'Wow,' she said at last, laughing.

But then I saw the cigar tube again. It lay on the grass with the top off. My grin died.

'You would have . . .?'

She pulled a sad clown's face. 'It didn't come to that.'

'But you would have?'

That's why she had brushed away the hair on the back of my neck. So she could puncture my spinal cord with the hypodermic needle contained in the cigar tube.

If those Gestapo cars had turned the wrong way, I'd be dead by now.

She put her head on my chest and wept. My Guardian Angel had become my Angel of Death.

Angel held me very tightly as we rode back into town. Maybe it was her way of saying sorry. We were due to meet Mills in a room over a pub on the Exeter Road. The place contained a billiard table and some chairs, and had not been used for a long time, judging by the dust. Angel murmured something briefly to Mills, before he offered me his hand.

'We had to be sure,' he explained.

'Of course.' What else could I say?

'Will you fetch Matty Cordington here? But get him to come without Sara.'

'That'll be difficult. She sticks to him like glue.'

'If you have any problems, say I need to see him about an extremely hush-hush underground operation.'

Sara opened the kitchen door of Home Farm before I could even knock. She was wearing a tweed skirt with a fawn jumper and cardigan that made her look like a farmer's wife. Maybe that was her intention.

'Hello, I've come to see if Matty fancied a pint.'

'He's busy.' Sara folded her arms, blocking the doorway.

'Oh, I really wanted to talk to him . . .'

'Nick.' Matty hove into view. 'What are you doing out there? Come in.'

Sara marched to the far side of the room, her arms still folded.

'I wondered if you fancied coming out for a drink.'

'Nice idea,' he said tentatively.

'You haven't the time,' complained Sara. 'You've got the farm accounts to do and the Germans want our milk-yield figures.'

I dropped my voice. 'To be honest, Mills has turned up. He wants to see you urgently.'

'Why didn't you say so, Nick?' Sara's scowl miraculously lifted. 'Off you go, Matty. I'll have supper waiting. And don't forget your curfew pass.'

The bare wooden stairs creaked with our every step as we climbed up to where Mills was practising cannons on the billiard table. Angel locked the door behind us as Mills produced a bottle of whisky. He poured out four glasses.

'Matty, we need to ask you about Sara,' he began. 'You met her in Suffolk – but where exactly?'

'Near Woodbridge. Well, in Burgh, really.'

'How did you meet?'

'She was staying in the local pub where I used to stop for a drink after work. We got to talking.' He shrugged. 'We were both lonely, I suppose.'

'Whose idea was it for her to come back here?'

'Mine, I think. I don't remember. Why?'

'Are you sure it was *your* idea?'

Matty tugged at a lock of hair behind his ear, a sure sign that he was troubled. 'I'm not sure it was *anyone*'s idea. It just sort of happened.'

'Did you find it difficult getting permission to return home?'

'No, I was surprised it all went so smoothly. I

thought I'd be stuck in Suffolk for ever. Why are you asking all these questions?' Restlessly, he moved to the billiard table and began rolling the red ball against the cushion.

'Matty, you remember, when I came round to your house this morning, I mentioned a radio operator hiding out at Dogglesbury Hill?' said Angel.

'Yes.'

'The Gestapo raided the cottage this afternoon.'

'No.' He hurled the red ball down the table and caught it on the rebound. 'No!'

'It's all right,' said Angel. 'There was no one there. There *was* no radio operator. I made him up.'

'I don't understand.' Matty frowned.

'I told Nick here that he was hiding at Dumonbury, and you and Sara that he was hiding at Dogglesbury. We have an informer in our midst, and it seems to be Sara.'

Matty grasped the edge of the billiard table as if his own legs would not support him.

'I don't believe it,' he murmured in a voice from beyond the grave.

'It came down to two suspects,' explained Mills. 'I'm sorry, Nick, but we had to know. The Gestapo turning up at Dogglesbury was proof it was Sara. Exactly how much have you been telling her, Matty?'

'Everything,' whispered Matty. 'Everything. She was so enthusiastic about what we were doing.

She insisted that I get involved, fight back, hurt the Nazis she hates. Everything. I had no secrets from her.'

He was making little sense. I put my arm around his shoulders. 'Sorry, mate.'

'Why haven't they arrested us?' Matty was close to tears.

'Why should they?' asked Mills. 'You don't kill the goose laying the golden eggs. You protect and cherish her.'

'What happens now?'

'Sara must die.'

'No.' Matty's face had turned a putty grey.

'We don't have a choice, Matty.'

'Can't we use her?' I asked. 'Feed her false information, that sort of thing?'

'The Germans would soon discover we were lying,' replied Angel softly.

'She must die,' repeated Mills. 'But she must seem to die in an accident.'

'An accident?'

'If the *Gestapo* think we've killed her, they'll come looking for us.'

'But surely she'll have told them everything already,' I argued. 'Once she's dead, they'll pick us up.'

Mills sucked at his teeth. 'I don't think so. They don't know that *we* know she's an informer. If they

believe she died accidentally, without us having discovered her secret, then it's in their interest to leave
you and Matty alone.'

'What about you and Coral?'

'We both have to leave first thing in the morning.'

'I don't like it.' Matty was swaying as if drunk –
as if he wasn't taking in what was happening here.

'See it from the *Gestapo* side,' insisted Mills. 'You
two are their sure way into the Resistance movement.
The *Gestapo* will open your mail, tap your phones,
follow you around in the hope you will lead them to
others. You are one end of a long piece of string. If
they arrest you, then they'll lose that string.'

Mills went on to give more reasons why he
believed we would be safe. But his words were not
penetrating my brain. The revelation that Sara was a
German agent was too great to comprehend.

'I'll do it.' Matty was staring sightlessly at the
floor. 'It's my fault, my responsibility.'

'You don't need to.'

He hurled the red ball down the table again, in an
explosion of violence. It struck the white balls and
sent them careering wildly around the baize. 'Yes, I
do,' he insisted.

'Matty, I'm sorry, mate. I really am.'

He had become businesslike suddenly. 'It's easy
enough to have an accident on a farm.'

'Let me do it,' urged Mills.

'No. I brought her here so it's down to me.'

Angel regarded Matty with tears in her eyes. 'It's not like killing in the heat of battle, you know. It's much harder.'

'I'll do it.' There was cold steel in Matty's voice. 'I'll do it myself.'

PART THREE

With every dawn I expected the knock on the door.

Yes, General, I know the Gestapo could have picked me up any time they wanted at the Feldkommandantur, but that's not the Gestapo's way. Terror has to be seen to be done.

I wasn't worrying just for myself but for my mother, my sister, my nephew David. At first, the tension was unbearable. I would lie awake and the slightest sound in the early morning would make me retch. I was once physically sick when I heard the coalman's lorry pulling in at a neighbour's. But Mills had divined correctly: the Germans did nothing. And, as the days became weeks, inevitably I relaxed.

But it was a bizarre situation. I knew that the Gestapo knew I worked for the Resistance – but they did not know that I knew they knew. You could tie your stomach in knots just thinking about it.

Only Matty, Bert Latcham and I attended Sara's cremation. It was an odd affair. Matty never once mentioned how Sara was supposed to have died, and I didn't ask him. I knew nothing about her death although, from the way that her body had been taken to the German hospital, I assumed that the Gestapo had intercepted Matty's call for an ambulance.

As summer came, so the importance of the Anglo-German Friendship League diminished. Apart from helping to organize the indoctrination camps for sixteen-to-eighteen-year-old boys, I had little to do. The whole character of the Occupation was changing. The Eastern Front was devouring men, munitions and equipment at a headlong rate, and the Germans were squeezing their conquered lands ever harder to feed their war machine. They were becoming less concerned with wooing the English than wringing them dry.

In June, the Germans finally announced that the coronation of Edward VIII and Queen Wallis would take place at Westminster Abbey on August 6th, triggering a panic among the Friends of New Europe as they scrambled for invitations.

It was to be a glittering interlude in an increasingly grim time. For by now our conquerors had introduced the hated Compulsory Labour Act intended to force young men to work in factories and mines in Germany. Rather than be shipped abroad, thousands fled their homes to join the bands living rough. In our region they called themselves Moorsmen.

Almost all front line Wehrmacht units had pulled out, to be replaced by German police battalions. These were backed up by the British Militia: organized scum formed out of the fascist Blackshirt Specials, who were determined to out-Gestapo the Gestapo in their brutality and cruelty. I'd had to coach their leader Ricky Gregan so he could give his oath of loyalty to the Führer in German. I well remember his triumphant smirk at the ceremony.

It was exactly the same smirk he had on his face the second before I cut his hand off.

How come?

I'll tell you when my story reaches that point. As I'll tell you about the corpses that would hang in the street like some strange fruit – a sight I see nightly in the tortures that my dreams have become.

In the middle of July, Vee Harper returned from two months in London. She had put on weight. She did her best to get me into bed, but I wasn't interested. Anyway, her baby already had one father – even if he was currently en route to his death in the Ukraine.

Matty changed after Sara's death, becoming reclusive like his father before him. When I went to visit him, I'd inevitably find him drinking whisky by himself in the gloom of his small farm office.

Angel and Mills had disappeared the day of Sara's death. It was almost three months before I saw Angel again – the day of my birthday, in fact.

Yes, General, I was bitter that they'd abandoned me and Matty in the firing line. But I told myself it was important that they should survive to build up the Resistance.

We buckled down under an ever more oppressive occupation as food and fuel grew increasingly scarce and the Germans more brutish. It seemed as if it would go on for *ever. I didn't know at the time, but in fact it was the end of the beginning or maybe the beginning of the end.*

Besser ein Ende mit Schrecken, als ein Schrecken ohne Ende.

I'm sorry, General, I forget you don't speak German.

Better an end with suffering than suffering without end.

20

My twenty-fourth birthday confirmed my belief in the superstition that things come in threes. It was a beautiful July day, there was not a cloud in the sky, and the sea looked an inviting blue instead of its usual forbidding grey. So far that morning had brought the treat of a breakfast sausage, a red silk handkerchief from mum, and a family birthday card made by David out of red, white and blue paper. Surprisingly, there was nothing from Matty.

I was walking to the *Feldkommandantur*, wondering why Matty had not sent his ritual rude card, when Jacob Jenner materialized out of Turnpin Lane with a tray of gingerbread around his neck. Selling gingerbread and cakes on the street provided Jacob and Miriam's only source of income nowadays. The money they had received from Leech for their businesses had been blocked under the law banning Jews withdrawing money from their bank accounts.

'I was hoping to catch you,' said Jacob. 'Happy Birthday.'

'Thank you. I'm surprised you remembered.'

Jacob had aged noticeably since Simon and Anna had been taken away. His body had shrunk, hunching in a way that emphasized his narrow shoulders. The skin on his face was grey and loose, and only his eyes still hinted at the merriment they had once held.

'You know Miriam – she's a walking filing cabinet of birthdays and wedding anniversaries. She baked this for you.' He held out an extra large gingerbread man. I assumed it was meant to be me, with brown icing sugar for my hair and three pips for my captain's rank.

'Thank you. She shouldn't have.' I knew that Miriam must have used up precious ingredients baking this present.

Just then Miriam herself came bustling out of the alley, with the twin girls. Ruth held up her arms so I could give her a big kiss. She giggled so much that Rachel wanted the same.

'Jacob, look what came in the post after you'd left.' Miriam delved into her bag to produce a card. 'It's from Simon and Anna.'

'How are they?'

'It's the standard printed message saying they are being well treated and have useful work, but Simon's managed to add something in pencil.'

'What does he say?'

'*Just arrived at this camp. Don't worry about us. Lots of love to you and the children. God bless.*'

Jacob took the card from Miriam and a huge smile spread across his face.

'This is from your mother and father, girls.' He bent down to show it to the twins. 'They send all their love and say I must give you a special hug just from them.'

Jacob handed me the postcard, I examined the postmark under heavy German postal franking.

Auschwitz. The name meant nothing to me.

'How's Barbara?' I asked.

'The baby cries a lot. I think Hope senses her mother's unhappiness. I tell Barbara to be cheerful for Hope's sake but she doesn't listen. Still, she is a good mother. Her baby is her whole life.' Miriam gasped. 'There's that van again.'

I spun round as a black Morris van slowly crossed the road junction. Its windscreen and side windows were made from darkened glass, and not being able to see who was inside it imbued the van with infinite menace. Mothers warned their children against the bogeyman who lurked in the back while repeating the rumour to one another that the van was used to snatch babies off the streets for use in unspeakable German medical experiments. The sinister vehicle had first appeared maybe two months ago. No one knew where it came from – only that it emerged occasionally to cruise the streets like an omen of death.

The van disappeared. We breathed a sigh of relief but just then Jacob caught sight of a policeman.

'This is not a good district for me to get caught in,' he muttered, slipping out of sight.

I tucked the gingerbread man safely into my tunic and carried on towards the *Feldkommandantur*.

Glass was in a foul mood, as he was most days now that his efforts to be transferred to the Eastern Front were proving fruitless. But there was an added reason for his ill humour. His power was lessening as Stolz's grew, reflecting the increasing influence of the SS. I recalled Glass's warning on my first morning there, almost eight months ago. Then the *Wehrmacht* had been basking in Hitler's favour; now it was bogged down in Russia and the SS were becoming more powerful than ever before. Its Jewish department and its Labour Office had expanded to fill the whole second floor, while the *Führer*'s previous pet project, the Anglo-German Friendship League, had been quietly allowed to drift into still waters. Not forgotten exactly, but certainly no one's priority any longer.

I left the *Feldkommandantur* at one o'clock on the dot. The rest of the weekend was mine. I was on my way to the harbour to see if I could pick up a crab for our family tea when I received my second surprise.

I had just turned into Water Street when a deep voice broke into my contemplation.

'All right then, my 'andsome, don't talk to us.'

Fred and Hilda Worsnipp stood at my elbow. I hadn't seen them since before the war.

'What are you two doing in town?' Grinning with delight, I shook Fred's hand and kissed Hilda on the cheek.

'We've been trying to get to see Master Matty,' said Fred. 'We thought as how to pick up some household things while we're here, but all the shops are empty. We can't find a pail or a ball of string for love or money.'

Now in their sixties, Fred was wiry with blunt features in a face tanned mahogany while his wife Hilda was large and matronly with a mop of white hair. No one would ever mistake them for anything other than a farmer and his wife.

'Matty told me how you'd hidden the Crown Jewels,' I said quietly.

'It was nothing.' Hilda blushed. 'Mind you, if we'd known they'd lead to Roy's death, we wouldn't have touched them with a barge pole.'

'Hush now, woman, don't distress yourself.' Fred put a comforting arm around her.

'I'm sorry, Nick.' Hilda pulled a handkerchief from her sleeve.

'Ay. 'E were a good young chap,' murmured Fred.

'It seems like only yesterday you three used to spend time with us in Merricombe.' Hilda dabbed at her eyes. 'Right little tearaways, you were.'

'They were good times,' I said, recalling the summers at Pear Trees Farm: the crusty fresh bread, blackened sides of smoked bacon, home-made jams, sherbet fizzes and cool lemonade. I couldn't remember it ever raining there.

It had been the stuff of every boy's dream. Three young teenagers riding out over the moors, air rifles slung over our backs and accompanied by the farm collies, looking for adventure. We potted nothing more than a rabbit or a pigeon, but in our imaginations we were Western scouts leading a wagon train or blazing a trail for longhorn cattle out of Texas.

Then there had been the secret priest hole behind the panelled wall of the farmhouse hallway where we had spent hours on end, telling ghost stories by the yellow gleam of an oil lamp.

'How is the farm these days?'

Fred pulled a long face. 'We get by.'

We fell silent as two Militiamen in their new uniform of grey shirt, black trousers and khaki British army blouse strutted past. Their uniform summed up what they were – a ragtag mob of misfits.

'Four of those scum were up in Merricombe last week and nabbed two young Moorsmen who came down into the village for flour,' muttered Fred.

'But they got a bit cocky, didn't they?' Hilda took over the story. 'They made us all watch while they paraded those lads around the village in a halter and bit so by the time they drove off, Hereward was ready. Those Militiamen didn't get far.'

'Who's Hereward?' I was puzzled.

Fred took over. 'Don't know his real name but he's the leader of the Moorsmen. They say he was once a history teacher, which is why he calls hisself this fancy name.'

'He's a clever one,' added Hilda. 'He sent four of his lads dressed up in the Militia's clothes through the German checkpoint on the main coast road, so the Germans wouldn't blame their men's disappearance on the villagers.'

'That's really why we're here,' said Fred. 'I've a message from this Hereward for Master Matty himself.'

'Why Matty?'

'He's been up to talk to Hereward a couple of times.' Fred gave me an old-fashioned look. 'You telling me you didn't know Master Matty's the Resistance boss's right-hand man?'

It was news to me – but then, I had not been much involved over the past three months.

'Security,' I said.

'Oh, ay. Right.' Fred nodded sagely. 'Only it seems Master Matty's not around, and no one knows where he's gone. That's why I'm telling you, my dear. We've got to get back to Merricombe. The farm don't wait for time or tide. You tell Matty that Hereward is still waiting for the consignment. It's overdue. Master Matty'll understand.'

The last surprise was the nicest. I was approaching the bottom of the hill leading homewards, a boiled crab wrapped in newspaper in my pocket, when I made out the slender figure of a woman dawdling on a corner ahead. She seemed to be waiting for someone.

'Hello,' said Angel, as I drew close. She gave me a timid little smile as if uncertain about the welcome she'd receive. 'Happy birthday.'

'Thank you.'

She was wearing a thin summer dress that came down to just below her knees and her golden tan brought out her freckles. I'd forgotten her elfin cheekbones and the way her blue eyes could turn plaintive and vulnerable. She looked smaller than I remembered and even more lovely.

We stared at each other, not knowing what to say next.

'You're back?' I ventured at last.

She reached into the large bag over her shoulder and produced a bottle of champagne. 'This is for you. I thought maybe we could have a picnic.'

'What would we be celebrating?'

'Your birthday. And us,' she whispered.

'Us?'

'Nick, please don't be cross with me,' she said quickly.

'I'm not,' I lied.

'I know you think you have a right to be.' Angel sighed and let her head drop.

Conflicting emotions battled inside me. Part of me wanted to pick her up and crush her in my arms, the other half just wanted to walk away. My bitterness at the way I had been abandoned, every day expecting to be arrested by the *Gestapo*, while the Resistance professionals had fled to safety, threatened to boil to the surface.

'How did you know I'd even be here?' I asked.

'I have been thinking about you.' She swallowed back tears. 'It's not been easy for me. I didn't like leaving you, but I had to. Mills and I know too much. We can't afford to fall into the *Gestapo*'s hands.'

'But *I* can?'

'I'm sorry. If you don't want to see me again, I'll understand.' She chewed on her lower lip. 'Take the champagne anyway.'

Angel began walking away slowly. Then I had her in my arms, swinging her wildly off the ground. When I finally put her down, we kissed like lovers do.

'I'll do you a deal,' I said, producing my package. 'Your champagne for my crab?'

'You always knew how to tempt a girl,' she laughed, wiping away her tears.

It was a strange picnic. On a slab of warm rock by the water's edge in Seal Cove, we ate the crab and Miriam's gingerbread man, washed down by the champagne. Gulls screeched and bickered overhead as two oystercatchers grubbed on the shoreline among a flock of busy dunlins. There was no one else for miles.

There were so many questions I wanted to ask her, especially about Matty's burgeoning role in the Resistance. Seemingly, while I'd been hung out to dry Matty had been continuing to work for Mills as if nothing had ever happened.

'While I remember, there's a chap called Hereward who says his consignment is overdue.' I explained about bumping into Fred Worsnipp before rolling over on my back to gaze up at a few high fluffy clouds plying their way up the coast like proud Indiamen under full sail. 'Have there been any more leaks?' I asked after a while.

'No, none.'

'Good.' I could not stand the brightness of the sun any longer so I rolled onto my stomach to watch the ebbing tide gurgle and foam in a channel under the rock. A small crab was trying to scuttle to safety over the pebbles, only to be sucked back to sea with every wave.

'Did you know Hitler's supposed to be coming to London for the coronation together with many of the Nazi top brass?'

'Just hope someone takes a pot-shot at him. Why's it taken so long for the Germans to put Edward on the throne? There were hints back in April, then it all went quiet.'

'The Germans were trying to get King George to formally abdicate first. When Hitler failed, he decided to go ahead and crown the Regent anyway.'

'What do you mean, "crown the Regent"? Hitler's not going to do it himself, is he?'

'Not personally. The Archbishop of York's conducting the service. Canterbury refused.'

Angel brushed the nape of my neck and ran her finger up through my hair. Instantly, I was back on the downs, watching the Gestapo cars speed up towards Dumonbury and Dogglesbury Hills. I spun around and grasped her hands. They were empty.

'Sorry,' I muttered.

'It's only what I deserve.' She did not look at me for a while.

'No.' I was desperate to make amends. 'I'm just on edge. It's not been easy . . . every day not knowing . . . it gets to you in the end. I'm sorry.'

She met my eyes, a half-smile on her face. 'You're a strange man.'

'What?'

'Nothing. I'm not here to harm you. Relax and lie back.'

I closed my eyes as she began massaging my shoulders and the base of my neck. I murmured in pleasure until she dug her thumbs in sharply and I yelped.

'God, there's a sackful of marbles in here.' Angel worked away with her thumbs while I squirmed and wriggled. 'Just lie still.'

'That hurts.'

'Don't be a baby. You'll feel better once I've broken down these knots.' She continued kneading away. 'Mills doubted if you'd stand the pressure, you know. I always said you would.'

'Thanks.' I drifted away in a doze. A little while later I came awake and opened my eyes to find myself staring at a pair of slim brown legs. I was still blinking when a dress slid down over Angel's feet. A bra fluttered down next, then her knickers.

I opened my eyes wide in time to see Angel leap off our rock and run naked into the sea. She splashed in up to her thighs, then dived into the water, striking out in a powerful crawl before turning over and floating on her back. She beckoned to me.

The coldness of the water took my breath away. I swam over to where she was floating, forty yards away from the shore. The short hair, slicked flat against her head, made her look more like a mischievous elf than ever. I went to tread water and found I could stand on the sandy bottom, the sea only up to my chest. Angel flung her arms around my neck and wrapped her legs around my waist. She weighed nothing. My hands felt each rib before circling her waist.

There was a knowing wanton glint in her eye.

Angel made love ruthlessly and enthusiastically, until she leaned too far back in the water, and I lost my footing. We both went under, and the moment was lost in coughs and giggles. Angel led me by the hand back to the shoreline. We sank down onto a patch of wet sand.

'We should have done this four months ago.'

'So why didn't we?' she asked.

'You said it didn't work with men you worked with.'

'And you listen to everything a woman tells you?'

21

'Why not? The Coronation Ball will be wonderful. The Friends of New Europe certainly know how to throw a party. '

'I really don't want to, Hubert.'

'There's no need for you to be embarrassed about going back to the Golf Club as a guest rather than a waitress.'

Joan pulled up the sheet to cover her bare breasts, and wondered if Leech was being sarcastic. 'I'm not at all embarrassed by that, Hubert. There's nothing wrong with being a waitress.'

But she did not wait on tables any more. Those evenings she told the family she was working at the Golf Club were spent here at Leech's seedy little flat. What had begun as an innocent friendship had moved on. For a while they had gone to small hotels out in the country but Joan had been terrified she might bump into someone she knew, and she sensed that Leech resented paying for a room only to leave it after a couple of hours.

'Nothing wrong at all,' Leech was quick to agree.

'Look at me, for instance. Just twelve months ago I was just a small shopkeeper, and now ... Did I tell you I'm negotiating to buy the flour mill?' He wrapped a silk Paisley dressing gown around his sloping shoulders and held up the bottle of Angostura Bitters. 'In or out?'

'Out.'

'Have you thought seriously about my offer?'

'I've told you I don't want to go.' Joan stole a glance at her clothes, neatly folded on the chair by the washstand, half hidden behind the dividing curtain. Leech's wealth had not bought him good taste. The bed sheets were coarse winceyette, the walnut veneer was curling off the second-hand wardrobe, and the rugs were stained and threadbare.

'No, I mean you coming to live as my housekeeper at the manor house.' Leech swirled around the bitters in Joan's glass before pouring them into his own.

'I already have a house to run, thank you, Hubert,' replied Joan coolly, knowing this latest digression was just a bargaining ploy to get her to attend the ball with him.

Leech held out the drink just far enough away from her so that Joan had to drop the sheet to reach it. His eyes slid over her exposed breast and, despite herself, her nipples grew hard. She took a sip and pulled up the sheet to cover herself again.

'All right, but at least come to the ball. I need to have a partner.'

'That's very kind of you but . . .' Joan would rather be seen dead than go to the ball with Leech in what would constitute the public registration of the private bargain and sale between them.

Yet his regular gifts made all the difference – more than her family realized. At first they had been small luxuries. But then, as rationing had tightened, even items like soap, margarine, bacon, jam and eggs had become rare. Leech's weekly contribution had grown until he now provided most of her family groceries.

Rationing did not touch the rich. If you had money, you never wanted for anything. But for the poor the soaring cost of living – candles, for instance, now cost four times as much as a year ago – bit harder and harder. Even if you did find something scarce, you couldn't afford it.

Joan told herself she had never accepted anything solely for herself. Well, perhaps the odd pair of stockings or box of chocolates. No, what she did, she did only for her family. And, after all, life under the occupation was a compromise, as she had informed Nick when he'd first arrived back home.

After her first time with Leech, Joan had analysed her feelings and been rather shocked to find that she did not feel as soiled as she had expected to. She could even smile at her inversion of values that made it acceptable for her to sleep with Leech but not to be seen out with him in public.

'I ask you to do *one* thing for me and you refuse,' insisted Leech. 'After all I've done for you.'

'Don't go on, please, Hubert.'

'People are falling over themselves to get tickets. This'll be no different at all from the balls you used to attend with your husband.'

'Really, it's not my cup of tea – not any more.' She saw he was watching her keenly, trying to fathom her motives for refusing him.

'I've told you, don't worry that you once worked as a waitress there.'

'Oh no, it's not *that*.' As soon as she spoke, Joan knew she had made a mistake.

'Oh, I see.' Leech bristled. 'I'm not good enough for you, is that it?'

'No, not at all.' She tried to make light of it.

'Being escorted to a dance by a mere shop-keeper . . .'

'Don't be silly.'

But Leech was no longer listening. 'What makes you so bloody high and mighty? You're quick enough to accept things for that hoity-toity family of yours, but when I ask for one small favour in return . . . You're ashamed to be seen with me. That's it, isn't it?'

Joan felt her face flaming. To hide her embarrassment, she climbed out of the other side of the bed and wrapped a dressing gown tightly around herself.

'You've got it wrong,' she protested mildly.

'Have I? I don't think so. I'm not good enough to be seen with in public, but you don't mind fucking on the sly . . .'

Joan leaped forward and slapped his face hard. For a second, she feared he would strike her back.

'You bloody little whore.' He put a hand to his stinging cheek. 'You've had your last penny out of me.'

Stepping behind the curtain, Joan began dressing with furious haste. The silence grew like a wall between them.

Leech stood by the window, biting his lip, fighting between pride and expediency.

'I'm sorry,' he muttered. 'Please don't go. You know I care for you.'

Her face grim and set, Joan pulled her petticoat over her head, and smoothed it down with frantic movements. She buttoned up her skirt and blouse and stuffed her stockings in her pocket.

'You can't go. Not now, not like this. Sit down and have a drink. You *can't* go.'

'Just watch me.'

Leech's mood swung back to bitterness. 'You walk out now after all I've given you and your family and you'll be sorry. You see if you're not – I'm warning you. You'll see.'

Joan closed the door firmly behind her.

22

'So what was the only thing Sparta had to fear?' demanded Matty over his shoulder to Mills.

'Luxury,' he replied.

'They'd have been safe here, then,' said Angel, glancing around at the bare office with its dusty floorboards. She wiped at the grimy window-panes, trying to peer out over the derelict ship-repair yard.

'Good to see you again, Nick,' said Mills, shaking his hand.

'Sorry, mate, I was under instructions not to tell you.' Matty grinned guiltily.

'Your two situations weren't the same,' explained Mills briskly. 'You work under the very noses of the Germans, Nick. And you have a family while Matty doesn't.'

That was the only explanation Mills was prepared to offer. And not a word of apology.

'Did you apply for that leave?' he demanded in a businesslike way.

'Forty-eight hours beginning at midnight.'

'Will the *Gestapo* know you're absent?'

'Not unless they're checking up on me every day.'

'We'll have to risk that.' Mills had not changed in the months since the four of us had last gathered together in a similar dusty room. He was still the squat powerhouse radiating energy. 'Know anything about theoretical physics, Nick? No? Neither do I. But there's an Austrian scientist called Otto Frisch, currently at Liverpool University, who's just had a breakthrough with using atomic energy to make some sort of superbomb. The Germans overlooked Frisch, or rather *had* overlooked him, until he wrote to a former colleague, Niels Bohr, telling him about the breakthrough. You met Bohr, of course, when you put him and his wife on a submarine. Bohr is the father figure of Europe's atomic scientists.'

He handed me a single typewritten sheet.

As a weapon the superbomb would be practically irresistible. No material or structure could be expected to withstand the force of the explosion.

Owing to the spread of radio-active substances on the wind current, the bomb could probably not be used without killing large numbers of civilians, so this may make it unsuitable for use as a weapon by a responsible nation.

If one works on the assumption that Germany is developing this weapon, it must be recognized that, since no large-scale shelters are available, the only reply would be a counter-threat with a similar weapon.

'Rather naive of him to write this stuff,' I said when I'd read it through twice.

'Seemingly, scientists do things like that. The *Gestapo* intercepted the letter, but fortunately one of our chaps in the postal censor's office managed to make a copy. This is part of it,' explained Mills. 'As we speak, a scientist called Werner von Heisenberg is on his way from Germany to talk to Frisch.'

'They know each other?'

'They all know each other. Science knows no national boundaries – that sort of thing. Von Heisenberg will try to get Frisch to go back to Germany, so that they can work together.'

'What happens if Frisch doesn't want to go?' asked Matty.

'He won't have an option,' said Mills.

'Hang on, what exactly is this so-called super-bomb?' I demanded.

'In a nutshell, Frisch and others believe that a chain reaction in a radio-active substance called uranium can generate unimaginable amounts of energy within a fraction of a second.'

'Are the Germans also working on this super-bomb?' demanded Matty.

'We believe so,' replied Mills. 'The *Wehrmacht*

have commandeered all stocks of uranium in the *Reich*, and seized the Czech uranium mines. We don't know how far they've got in developing it.'

'So what's Frisch's breakthrough?'

'Not only has he found a simple way to detonate the bomb but he's also discovered it doesn't need as much uranium as scientists previously thought – which means the superbomb will be easier to build.'

'One of these dropped on Berlin could end the war?'

'So would one dropped on Toronto,' said Mills grimly. 'Nick, you and Coral have got to reach Frisch before the *Gestapo* do, and bring him back down here to hide until we can get him to Canada.'

'Me!'

No one had contacted me for three months and now I was expected to go and snatch this scientist from under the noses of the *Gestapo*. 'What if Frisch declines our offer?'

'I'll give you a message from Bohr as proof of your bona fides. Whatever happens, he must *not* be allowed to work for the Germans.' Mills glanced towards Coral, who gave the slightest of nods.

'You're not coming, Matty?' I asked.

'Afraid not. I've got something else on.'

Angel handed him a piece of paper. 'Here are the contact numbers and addresses for South Wales, the Forest of Dean and Bristol. Memorize them and destroy the list before you leave this room. Powell, in the Rhondda, will pass you on to the Beacons Group.'

Mills must have noticed me looking blank. 'I've been charged by His Majesty's Government with organizing a meeting, a conference if you like, of leaders of Resistance groups in England and Wales,' he explained. 'We're going to hold it in London on the same day as the Coronation. Matty is helping me set it up, and it's not easy. The Communists are proving bloody minded about cooperating with any non-Communist groups.'

'You can say that again,' smiled Matty. 'The Welsh mining valleys are Reds to a man, but the resistance band up on the Brecon Beacons is led by a viscount. They hate each other almost as much as they hate the Germans.'

So that was what Matty had been doing. With his blend of natural charm and authority, he'd be good as a fixer. Mills must trust him totally.

'So it's you and me for Liverpool,' said Angel.

I was only too happy to spend time with her. After making love on the beach, we had gone back to her new place – and had not got up till Monday morning. She must have read my thoughts, for a faint blush touched her cheeks.

'I don't know how some doddery old scientist is going to cope on the back of the bike for hours on end,' I said.

427

'I've made other arrangements to bring you back,' said Mills. 'Anyway, he's thirty-six years old.'

It took nine hours for us to reach Liverpool. We had set off well before dawn, refuelling at friendly garages that Angel knew. The roads were largely empty but my Empire Star did not like the poor-quality petrol and once I had to stop at the side of the road to clean the carburettor. By the time we arrived at the waterfront, I was exhausted, nearly deaf and my hands were shaking from the constant vibration.

The atmosphere in the city was tense. The Mersey-side dockers' strike had ended only two weeks before, with the massacre of fifty hostages, half of them shot in Liverpool FC's ground at Anfield and half in Everton's Goodison Park. The Germans feared open rebellion and were taking no chances, with machine-gun crews in full battle-dress holding strong points at street corners and with two Mark III Panzers dominating the waterfront.

Angel went to buy a *Daily Post* from the news-paper seller outside the Royal Liver building, now topped by a gigantic swastika and housing the *Oberkommando der Kriegsmarine West*. After a short murmured conversation she returned with Frisch's address and a street map of the city.

'He's staying at the home of a colleague who's in

Cambridge for the summer,' announced Angel. 'I'll navigate.'

Soon we were riding slowly through a leafy suburb full of detached Edwardian houses. Angel tapped my shoulder.

'That one on the left, with the low brick wall and the laurel bushes. Go past slowly.'

'Seems peaceful enough,' I muttered.

'That's what Custer said at Little Big Horn.'

We completed a circuit around the quiet streets, until we approached the house again. This time I rode up a short semicircular drive to the front door. The BSA cut out as soon as I throttled back. The only sound came from a rag-and-bone merchant half-heartedly touting for goods from an empty cart. His horse reflected his despondency, plodding past with a lowered head and the saddest clip-clop I had ever heard.

Angel pulled at the bell. There was no reply. While she knocked, I stepped over a border of pinks and carnations to peer into a pristine living room.

'There's no one in.' Out of the corner of my eye, I saw a bedroom curtain move in a house across the street.

Angel tried several keys in the lock until the front door swung open. I followed her into the hall and closed the door behind me.

'There's no one here,' I hissed.

'Then why are you whispering?'

Only the kitchen showed signs of habitation. The sink was full of dirty dishes, with four used saucepans sitting on the hob. The other rooms were immaculately tidy, if dusty. Upstairs, only one back bedroom seemed occupied. It was more of a library than a bedroom, with books in three-feet-high stacks cluttering the floor. I picked up a roll of wallpaper lying on the bed, and found that its blank side was covered with diagrams and scientific symbols.

Peering out of the window, I saw that every garden had a vegetable patch. In the one directly behind us a man in his shirtsleeves was resting his foot on a spade.

I wandered off into the front bedroom, to gaze across the road at the window where the curtains had twitched. As I watched, a small light flared and went out. Someone lighting a cigarette in a bedroom? Near the window?

A knot began growing in the pit of my stomach.

I thought again about the gardener at the back. He had not moved. He was still standing there with his foot on the spade, vaguely facing in our direction. It dawned on me that he was wearing highly polished black Oxfords. Either he was the best-shod gardener I had ever seen or I was getting paranoid.

'If it is a trap, they don't seem to be in any hurry to catch us,' muttered Angel. 'But better not to take the chance, eh?'

The BSA started at the first kick, and we were speeding away in seconds.

'What do you think that was about?' I called.

'Maybe the *Gestapo* are playing a waiting game. Perhaps they've lost Frisch. Park somewhere away from the university so we can do a recce.'

We rode along Mount Pleasant until we came to a long building in Victorian mausoleum style with a sturdy clock tower. A saloon car with two men inside was parked across the road from the Physics Building. We kept on going. The road ended in a T-junction, with a large pub, the Abercrombie Vaults, standing on the corner. Next to it was a short parade of the sort of shops you'd expect near any college: a bookshop, a stationer's, a café, and an outfitter's specializing in blazers and college scarves.

I parked at the side of the pub and five minutes later, wearing the dark blue striped scarves of the University science faculty and carrying a couple of textbooks each, Angel and I strolled back towards the physics department. She seemed to know where she was going. I followed her into the quad of a handsome red-brick building. Since this was the summer vacation there were very few students or staff around. In the broad hallway, an owl-like figure with thick round glasses and swept-back hair was wrestling to put up a green baize noticeboard.

'Excuse me,' I began. 'We're looking for Dr Frisch.'

'Take that side, will you – thanks. I want to make sure these holes are lined up. Sorry, who do you want?'

I lifted one end of the board against the wall.

'Dr Frisch,' repeated Angel.

'If you'd slot those brackets over the screws. There. He's probably downstairs in the bunker but I can't remember seeing him today.' The owl tutted. 'That's not level, is it?'

'No. You're about two inches too high on the left.'

'I knew it wouldn't be right.' He stepped back, shaking his head. 'I'm useless at this sort of thing, but there're no maintenance men any more. Is Frisch expecting you?'

'We've got a message from a friend of his.'

'The *Reich* Education Ministry's liaison chap was hunting for him earlier. Frisch hasn't got into any trouble, has he?'

'Not that I know of. Who's this liaison man?'

'Dr William Wessel – known as Willie the Weasel. He's the stool-pigeon put in by Jerry to make sure we all toe the Party line.' The owl squinted suspiciously at our scarves. 'But you'd already know that if you were students.'

'We're not,' I admitted. 'I apologize for the deception, but it's vital that we contact Dr Frisch.'

'And I promise you we're not Germans,' added Angel. 'God forbid.'

The owl broke into a smile. 'I'm Alistair Massie, assistant lecturer and general dogsbody.'

'Did this weasel say why he wanted Dr Frisch?'

'Some German VIP or other is arriving to see Frisch this afternoon. Wessel got into a flap because Frisch wasn't in his office. Frisch is *never* in his office. He lives in the basement with the cyclotron.'

'Did you tell Wessel that?'

Massie cleared his throat. 'I didn't deem it necessary.'

'Where exactly is this cyclotron?'

'Down the stairs at the end of the corridor. Chips'll be there, even if Frisch isn't.'

'Chips?'

'His assistant. It's a joke – Frisch and Chips.'

'We're only just in time,' said Angel as we descended the stone stairway. 'I reckon the *Gestapo*'s looking for Frisch but they can't afford to antagonize him until they see if von Heisenberg can persuade him to work for them. The heavy stuff will start if Frisch refuses.'

'But they can't *make* him work for them. Not even the Nazis can make a man *think*.'

'Frisch still has family in Austria so the Nazis can make him do whatever they want once they've got him.'

The steps ended at a wood-and-glass door opening onto a laboratory with mottled cream walls and blackboards filled with diagrams and mathematical symbols. On a plinth in the centre stood a roundish steel contraption, like a giant vacuum flask. It was about three feet in diameter and held in place by flanges.

A small man in a dark suit was in the act of removing papers from a drawer.

'Yes?' He blinked at them in surprise.

'We'd like to see Dr Frisch.'

'He's not here at the moment . . .'

'It's very important.'

'He's busy.'

'We have a message for him from friends abroad,' said Angel.

Chips's eyes became very alert suddenly; a muscle tensed in his cheek. 'Come back in an hour and you'll catch him then.'

'Can't you tell us where he is now?'

'He's busy, I said. Who shall I say called?'

'Tell him friends of Niels Bohr.'

'Niels Bohr,' the man repeated carefully. 'All right.'

Going back up the stairs, Angel said: 'We can use that time to have a wash-and-brush-up, and something to eat. Let's see if the refectory's open during vacations.'

Alistair Massie was still in the hallway, drilling another hole, his tongue protruding from the side of his mouth in concentration.

'Find Chips?'

'Yes, thanks. He says Frisch is busy but he'll be back in an hour.'

'Will you help me hold up this noticeboard again? I think I've got it right now. He didn't keep you down there long.'

'Sorry?' I struggled to hold the board up to the wall.

'Chips is very proud of his cyclotron. It's the only one in the country. He's kept visitors trapped down there for an hour or so talking about it.'

'He didn't even mention it.'

'Alistair,' said Angel thoughtfully. 'You've heard of Niels Bohr?'

'Heard of him! Bohr is the Pope to Einstein's God.'

'So if I said we were friends of Niels Bohr, how would you react?'

'I'd kiss the hem of your raiment.'

'What does Chips look like?'

'There, that's better.' Massie stood back to admire his handiwork. The noticeboard was now no more than half an inch out of square. 'Chips? You can't mistake him – tall, beanpole of a man.'

Angel and I stared at each other aghast. Before we could speak, there was the sound of footsteps pounding down the stairs from above us. Two breathless young men hurtled into view.

'Massie, get out quick. There's a lorryload of German police pulling up at the back.'

'What's happening?' I asked.

'Don't know. Could be a round-up. We're not going to wait to find out.' They darted past us, brushing against the noticeboard so that it promptly fell to the floor.

'Do you know where Dr Frisch is?' I hollered after the fleeing men. 'It's vitally important.'

'He finished his experiment yesterday,' cried one.

'He could be down the Vaults with the Poles,' shouted the other. 'Just get out.'

'Come on.' Massie led us through a door and started jogging down a corridor lined on either side with glass-fronted laboratories. At the end, he leaped down three steps to a rear door.

'Useful short cut to the pub,' he explained.

We found ourselves alongside a pile of coke in a small enclosed area behind the main building. German voices could be heard on the other side of a brick wall separating us from the main yard.

'What did he mean, "With the Poles"?' demanded Angel as we hurried after Massie.

'The Germans formed a labour battalion out of the Polish servicemen and sailors who fled here when their country fell. Their barracks are just up the road. They pile into the Abercrombie Vaults whenever they can.'

'Dr Frisch drinks with them?' Angel was astounded.

'He plays the piano for them.'

In its Victorian heyday, the Abercrombie Vaults had reflected Liverpool's mercantile prosperity, with its shining brasses, thick carpets, bold scarlets and golds, and its frosted-glass snob screens. But the Depression, the war and the occupation had all taken their toll. Paint was flaking off a once-proud façade, the cracked windows were filthy, and the doorway to the adjoining Jug and Bottle was boarded up.

We opened the door into the pub's back room to be hit by a wall of noise and heat. Through the haze of blue cigarette smoke, we made out a man with a mass of dark hair hammering away at the keyboard of an upright piano. I thought I recognized Beethoven's 'Emperor' Piano Concerto but it was difficult to tell in the hubbub. The Poles glowered suspiciously at us as we pushed our way through the crowded tables.

'Dr Frisch, some people to see you,' shouted Massie.

Frisch smiled up at us. I was struck by his heavy eyebrows and lofty forehead. There was an amused glint in his eyes and his shirt collar was frayed. Three half-pints of beer sat on top of the piano.

'Dr Frisch, I've a message for you from Niels Bohr,' said Angel, leaning forward to make herself heard.

'Niels! But he's in the United States.' Frisch had a strong Austrian accent.

'He wants you to join him.'

'In America?'

'Listen, the Germans intercepted your letter to him. They want you to make the device for them.'

Frisch ended the second movement with a flourish. 'Forgive me, but how do I know you are genuine?'

'I can tell you where Niels Bohr and the others hid their Nobel Prize medals in Copenhagen when the Germans marched in,' said Angel.

Frisch smiled. 'All right, where?'

'They dissolved them in a tank of acid in the university basement to stop the Nazis getting their hands on them, yes?'

'Yes.' Frisch absent-mindedly launched into the *Rondo*. 'I do seem to have stirred up a hornets' nest.'

'Professor von Heisenberg is due to arrive this afternoon to persuade you to continue your research in Germany.'

'I would never do that.'

'You won't have a choice.'

'Werner von Heisenberg is an honourable man.'

'But his bosses aren't,' argued Angel. 'There are *Gestapo* waiting outside your home and they're surrounding the Physics Department as we speak. They're desperate to find you.'

'And what do you suggest I do?'

'Get away to Canada.'

Frisch stopped playing. 'And you two young people can organize that?'

'I put Niels Bohr and his wife on a submarine to safety,' I said. 'I can get you away, too.'

Frisch burst out laughing. 'So I'm meant to just walk out of this room and jump on board a submarine, leaving everything behind. Just like that?'

'We can't risk you going anywhere near your home.'

Frisch looked down at the keys. He was clearly thinking hard; balancing his past against his future. The Poles, who had been watching us talk to their friend, began murmuring angrily among themselves.

Frisch turned to the room, held up a placatory hand and then struck a dramatic chord. Chopin's 'Grande Polonaise'.

As one, the Poles rose to their feet for the piece of music that Free Poles around the world had adopted as their unofficial anthem.

Frisch played it with gusto. At least two of the piano's keys were dead but it did not matter. The Poles, shabby, battered, defeated, grew taller under this music swelling with patriotism and nobility. The hairs on the back of my neck rose.

As Frisch ended the piece to a storm of applause, there was a commotion at the doorway.

'Germans,' someone yelled.

'They're after Dr Frisch,' Angel cried. 'Help us get him away.'

The Poles demanded no more explanation. Immediately, they began to barricade the door with

tables and chairs. Two men led us towards the lava-
tories at the back, as the banging on the door grew
more insistent.

The Poles punched out a plywood sheet filling the
window of the men's lavatory, and first Angel, then
Frisch, me and Massie were helped up through and
out into the backyard. Six feet away sat my Empire
Star. From the pub came the sound of a single shot –
followed by a ragged volley.

'They are shooting my friends,' cried Frisch. 'I
must go back.'

'No.' Angel grabbed him by the shoulders. 'They
are buying you time. Use it.'

There was the heavy rip of a sub-machine gun,
followed by a sharp explosion. I jumped astride the
bike and kicked it into life.

'Nick, a mile up this road there's a Mobil garage
with two petrol pumps,' cried Angel. 'Look out for a
bald man. Say, "Tomorrows that sing." He'll reply,
"And the days that weep." Then hide the bike and
wait for me. Now, for Christ's sake, go.'

'Can you really make this bomb?' I asked Frisch as I
changed gears to climb the long hill outside Shrewsbury. I calculated that we had perhaps an hour of
daylight left in that long summer evening and, tired
as I was, I was determined to put as many miles
between us and Liverpool as possible.

'It's possible in theory but it won't happen over-night. Maybe in three or four years,' he replied. 'We have to control the chain reaction.'

'And the bomb will be as powerful as you say in your letter?'

'More so. I've since calculated that a uranium bomb containing just twenty-five pounds of active material will be equivalent to 1,800 tons of TNT.'

'That's one hell of a bang.'

'In 1917, an ammunition ship laden with 5,000 tons of TNT exploded in the harbour of Halifax, Nova Scotia. It destroyed two and a half square miles of the centre of the town and killed four thousand people.'

'So, you'd only need about seventy pounds of uranium to achieve the same result?'

'Yes. And it's so scientifically simple – but then such things always are, once they've been thought out. We'll trigger the bomb by firing two masses of enriched uranium towards each other. When the masses meet, they'll go critical, and – bang ... Oh, dear.'

Ahead, German soldiers stood in front of a barrier across the road.

'It was inevitable,' I said, making myself sound calmer than I felt.

Frisch adjusted his *Luftwaffe* officer's cap and smoothed down his uniform. 'Don't worry, my young friend, I have not played in amateur dramatics since I was a little boy without picking up a trick or two.'

'*Jawohl, Herr Oberst*.' I was encouraged by his self-assurance.

We knew it would be impossible to travel halfway across England without being stopped somewhere en route at German checkpoints, so Mills had concocted a cover story based on recent stories of how Göring was ferrying lorryloads of looted art treasures to his new chateau on the Loire. Consequently, we were driving a *Luftwaffe* van with French-based registration plates. Frisch, playing the officer because of his perfect German, carried forged orders from Göring's personal representative General Schelling in the *Oberkommando der Luftwaffe* in Whitehall, giving us safe conduct across the country.

The van, which actually contained my motorbike and a new printing press, was secured with the imposing special seal of *Reichsmarschall* Göring himself – or what the Resistance guessed the seal might look like. After all, how many German troops had actually seen the real one? We hoped the guards would be so fascinated by the van's imaginary treasures that they would ignore its drivers. And so it proved.

We sailed through the checkpoints with knowing winks until I was too tired to continue. Then we pulled off the road to catch a quick three hours' sleep. At dawn, we filled up from our jerrycans, shared a flask of lukewarm tea and some cheese sandwiches, then pressed on. The false pass and the sealed van worked like a charm, until we came upon an officious *Feldgendarmerie* sergeant outside Bristol.

Frisch was brilliant. He did not try to browbeat the man, but pointed out instead, in a reasoned, world-weary manner, the consequences if he acceded to the sergeant's demands to open the van.

'*Feldwebel*, my orders are that the van must not be opened until we reach the *Reichsmarschall*'s chateau. If you wish me to break the *Reichsmarschall*'s personal seal, you will have to force me to do so at gunpoint, so that at my court martial I can argue that I had no option but to obey you. I will require your name and army number, and the location of the nearest *Luftwaffe* post, so that I can report the violation. I'd say you'll be serving as a private in a punishment battalion on the Eastern Front within a week, maybe sooner.'

And that was that. By nine o'clock that morning we were on the coast road outside the city, approaching our safe house – a pebble-dashed box of a bungalow built on a strip of reclaimed land between the marshes and the new sea wall. The house was the first one on the left, fronted by a pocket handkerchief of a lawn and a straggling hedge of fuchsia and pyracantha.

'There's something wrong.'

'What is it?'

'The curtains are open.'

'So?'

'One should be closed to show that everything's all right.'

'Perhaps they forgot.'

Frisch's casual approach to security annoyed me. 'And perhaps the *Gestapo* are waiting for us.'

'How can the Germans know we're coming here?'

'I don't know. But one curtain should be drawn.'

Once we were out of sight I pulled up to think through the implications. The all-clear signal involved making a deliberate effort to do something – like drawing a single curtain. So if the occupants were surprised by the *Gestapo*, they sent the warning by simply doing nothing. Perhaps it *was* an oversight – but what if the *Gestapo* were indeed waiting? But then again, how could they be? They couldn't know that we planned to hide Frisch in this safe house hundreds of miles from Liverpool. Maybe the elderly sisters who lived in the bungalow had just forgotten – yet something at the back of my mind nagged at me to be cautious.

I'd be stupid to ignore the signal – but what would I now do with Frisch? I couldn't take him home, or to Matty's. Those would be the first places the *Gestapo* would come looking if they had an inkling that Frisch was down here. The arguments whirled round in my tired brain.

'I'm not risking it,' I decided. 'We're not coming all this way just to walk into a trap.'

Frisch shrugged. 'Whatever you say.'

I turned round and drove steadily back along the road. The bungalow's curtains were still wide open. There was no sign of life. I accelerated away to my next rendezvous.

The scrapyard was tucked away in a worked-out quarry. Two workers directed me to a narrow gap between a high pile of wrecked cars and the rock face. They had taken off the *Luftwaffe* number plates and were preparing to repaint the van even before Frisch and I changed back into civilian clothes.

'Where are we going now?' he asked.

'To see someone I know,' I said as we set off on the BSA.

As Jacob Jenner opened the door, I pushed Frisch into the hallway.

'This is a friend of mine,' I told Jacob. 'Can you hide him for a week? He's a superb pianist.'

23

There was a note on my desk to report to Hauser as soon as I got in next morning. I'd spent most of the previous day, Wednesday, sleeping. I found Hauser in chaos. Piles of files and ledgers lay on the floor, and the waste-paper basket had fallen over, spewing more documents onto the carpet. When I walked in, he gave up struggling to rip a file in two and handed it to me to do instead.

'*Generalleutnant* von Glass has at last been given an army corps on the Eastern Front,' he announced. 'I'm going with him.'

'Congratulations.'

He gave me a rueful look and I could tell that Hauser was not anticipating the fighting quite as keenly as his master.

'We're leaving tomorrow to join von Paulus's Sixth Army. Stolz is assuming temporary command of the region, God help you.'

I picked up the waste-paper bin, which fell over again immediately. 'Why don't you empty this?'

'Because I personally have to make sure it goes straight into the incinerator.'

'Not leaving anything for Stolz to find, eh?' Hauser blushed as my sally found its mark.

Just then, Glass himself marched in. Hauser scrabbled among the papers on his desk.

'Your travel arrangements are confirmed, sir: 0800 train to London tomorrow, and direct flight to Berlin on the evening *Luftwaffe* flight from Hornchurch at 1800. You have seventy-two hours' leave before taking up command.'

'Well done, Hauser. How did you manage it?'

Hauser simpered with pleasure. 'I've a chum in *Luftwaffe* flight movements, sir.'

'Thank him for me. But from Berlin I intend to head straight for my command. You take your seventy-two hours' leave, you deserve it.' He glanced at me. 'Come in, Penny.'

There was a new-found urgency in the way Glass crossed to the map on the blackboard, now showing the current battle around Kharkov. 'I'm going to be just in time for the Sixth Army's offensive towards Stalingrad. Hopefully we can capture the Caucasian oilfields before the rains start.'

'Will you miss England, sir?'

'Yes, in many ways. I'd like to think I've made some friendships here.' He turned to face me. 'I have two farewell gifts for you, Penny. The first is to remind you of what I gave you that night you came to dinner. Remember, I gave you and your lady companion a couple of long-handled spoons?'

'Yes, sir.'

'Yet you continue to sup with the devil.' Glass put his head close to mine and whispered. 'Stolz knows about your . . . activities.'

I coloured. At first I thought he was referring to my recent Liverpool trip to rescue Frisch. Then I realized he was passing on Sara's betrayal of us. It was a shock to find that Glass knew about my Resistance work. For a moment I felt as if I had betrayed a friend – then reason reasserted itself. He was a friend in the enemy army occupying my country.

And he didn't know that I already knew.

'So why hasn't Stolz arrested me, then?' I whispered back.

'It crossed his mind, but I had to point out that as a member of my staff, you are answerable only to the *Wehrmacht*. He could have argued the point but I think he's content to know you for what you are. A plum waiting to be picked whenever he chooses to.'

'Thank you. I'll watch my step.'

Glass raised his eyebrows. 'I think you may have to do considerably more than that.'

His words made me wonder again about the absence of that safety signal. I'd told Angel the news when I met her at the station, after her long journey back from Liverpool. She insisted that until she had personally investigated the safe house, I was to tell no one, absolutely no one, where Frisch was hiding.

I came back to the present to find Glass eyeing me keenly. He pulled open the top drawer of his desk and produced a brown envelope.

'Open it.'

Inside was a single sheet of thick white paper, on which were written two sentences in soft pencil.

This is to inform you that Joan Pendleton regularly hides escaped prisoners of war at her home in Mountroyal. She also keeps a pistol and amunition there.

Some bastard had denounced my sister. My first thought was Mrs Harper. We'd certainly not seen much of her recently. Had Joan or my mother upset her in some way?

'It's not true. Neither accusation is true.'

'And I believe you.'

But who had sent it? Clearly someone who could not spell – not 'ammunition', anyway. Leech, maybe? But why should he denounce Joan? I had thought they were supposed to be good friends. Anyway, Leech should have been in a good mood as his bakery – Jenner's bakery – had just been awarded the contract to bake for the German garrison. But Joan had seemed especially grumpy this morning. When David complained about being allowed only one slice of toast for his breakfast, she had snapped his head off, yelling that he'd have to pull his belt in like everyone else. I'd thought it had just been one of

Joan's outbursts about current scarcities but perhaps there had been something more to it.

'Luckily Hauser recognized her connection with you,' Glass was saying. 'Don't do anything hasty – you can't know who sent it.'

Oh yes, I did. Apart from that telling spelling error, I recognized the type of pencil Leech used to write out his bills. And the cartridge paper looked like part of the stock he kept under the counter.

Stolz marched in and my stomach lurched.

'The Japanese have just bombed America's main naval base in the Pacific in a brilliant surprise attack, destroying the Yankee fleet,' he announced triumphantly. 'The Führer is about to pledge Germany's support for the Japanese Empire.'

'But that'll mean war with the United States,' frowned Glass.

'So?' replied Stolz.

'I assume the *Führer* expects Japan to declare war on Russia in exchange; forcing the Soviets to fight on two fronts,' said Glass. 'But if they don't . . .'

'They will. Your lily-livered generals believed the *Führer* had miscalculated when we reoccupied the Rhineland, when we marched into Austria, into Czechoslovakia, even when we conquered Poland. If we'd listened to the military High Command, we'd still be paying reparations for the last war instead of now ruling the world. When will you army people admit the *Führer* is a genius? He *knows* what he's doing.'

'I hope you're right,' murmured Glass.

'We'll have to mine the beaches and impose a coastal blackout. You're leaving us just as it gets interesting, Glass.'

'It'll be interesting in Russia, too, I imagine.'

Stolz ignored the jibe. 'I must go. *Oberführer* Fest is bringing the new camp commandant, Höss, to discuss the new round-up.'

'I don't wish to know about that,' said Glass coldly.

'No, that's the trouble with you army officers. You never do. *Heil Hitler!*' Stolz spun on his heel and marched out.

There was a silence before Glass spoke again. 'I fear your country's about to change, and not for the better. What with the sparks of rebellion within and the threat of American intervention without, England is going to become an uncomfortable place to live. The whole of Merseyside is already under martial law.'

'Why? What's happened there?'

'Three *Feldpolizei* and twenty Poles were killed in riots after a public house burned down.' Glass held out his hand. 'Take care of yourself, Penny, and remember what I said. Maybe we'll meet again when the world's at peace.'

I was by the door when Glass called out: 'You can take that denunciation if you wish.' As I'd already slipped it into my pocket, I could only give him an embarrassed grin.

I was walking past the door of Number One Committee Room when Stolz's bark cut through my thoughts.

'You, Penny – get in here and close the door.'

The scene reminded me of that previous meeting in this room. *Oberführer* Fest again sat at the head of the table, with Bearup and Tickell on one side and Stolz and the same hard-faced bureaucrats on the other. But now, next to Fest, was a heavy-jowled man in SS uniform wearing an Iron Cross.

Fest was saying, 'We're delighted that Commandant Höss has agreed to leave his former command at Sachsenhausen to run the new camp. He brings unrivalled experience to the application of the Final Solution in Britain.'

'We have found a more efficient way . . .' began Höss. He was in his early forties with a small scar on one cheek.

'We'll discuss that later,' Fest cut him short. '*Herr Sekretär* Tickell, you are confident you can provide the necessary numbers of Jews this time?'

'Yes, *Oberführer*, we have checked.'

'I hope so.'

Tickell cleared his throat and fingered his wing collar nervously. 'I must place on record the Supreme Council's disquiet at taking Jews who were born in this country, especially those who fought for Britain in the last war, and, most of all, those decorated for bravery. We were previously given to understand that they would be left in peace.'

I translated. A secretary took a note.

'I would have thought that playing a significant part in making your province the first Jew-free zone in Britain would constitute a source of satisfaction for any loyal servant of the *Reich*,' said Fest coldly.

Tickell dropped his eyes.

'Now let's move on,' continued Fest. 'The construction of the camp is on schedule?'

'Eight hundred prisoners are already working on it,' replied Höss. 'Tomorrow's draft will complete the buildings, then enable us to start up the clothing and signals factories. Station Z is complete and—'

'Wait.' Fest held up his hand. 'You English can leave now. These matters do not concern you.'

Angel was waiting under the statue of Sir David Frobisher down on the Ness. It was one of my favourite spots, although I'd often wondered why the city had chosen to honour an Elizabethan seafarer born in Yorkshire.

We sat together, gazing out to sea, sharing her

spam sandwich as I told her of Glass's departure and discussing Germany's declaration of war on the United States. Finally I asked, 'What's happened about the safe house?'

'You did the right thing,' replied Angel. 'The *Gestapo* were waiting. They eventually ran out of patience, and took away Elsie and Emily Tremayne early this morning.'

'But how would the *Gestapo* have found out about the place?'

Angel chewed on her sandwich for a moment before answering. 'I don't know, but we have used it before.'

'You're joking!'

'It's not so easy to find a reliable safe house,' snapped Angel. 'And we had to set it up in a hurry. It'd be better if Frisch could stay on with the Jenners. But no one, I mean *no one*, must know he's there.'

'The Jenners don't mind having him,' I said, then changed the subject. 'Do you fancy going out for a drink tonight?'

'Sorry, Nick, I'm busy.'

I knew better than to ask any questions.

Leech was not in evidence in his store, although all around me I spotted examples of his poor spelling. Ignoring a pimply shop assistant's protests, I marched round behind the counter where I found the stub of a soft-lead pencil. It matched the shade and thickness of the printing on the letter in my pocket.

'Where *is* Leech?'

'I don't know.'

I shoved my face up against the assistant's. 'Think.'

'Mr Leech may be over at the tearooms, sir.' The boy swallowed nervously. 'If I see him, who shall I say wants him?'

'Nemesis.'

'Is that your first or second name, sir?'

The tearoom was largely empty, the old dears who used to drop anchor there for hours on end in Miriam's days having now departed for ever. Instead, four Militiamen sat at a table in the corner, swearing loudly. I caught a waft of brandy as I walked up to the counter.

'Hello, Betty. Nice to see one familiar face still here.'

'I don't know for how much longer, Mr Penny. It's not the same, that's for sure.' Betty Martin adjusted her waitress's white-lace cap and scowled at the Militiamen.

'Do they make much trouble?'

'Mr Leech lets them get away with murder, but no one dares say a word.'

'They told me up at the shop that Leech might be here.'

'Have you tried upstairs?'

'What's up there?'

'There's a self-contained flat. It's the black door immediately outside on the left.' Betty sniffed loudly. 'He often spends time up there with his ... lady friends.'

I opened the street door onto a steep flights of stairs. At the top was another door. I knocked. A friendly knock, an intimate's knock. Leech answered. His face was full of eager anticipation until he saw me. I pushed him back and closed the door behind me, sliding its bolt into place.

'You should learn to spell correctly before you try to make trouble.' I backed him up against the edge of the table as his face erupted in sweat.

'I don't know what you're talking about.'

I shoved the denunciation in his face. 'You're a shit, Leech.'

'Get lost.'

I hit him in the stomach, once – very hard. As he doubled over, retching, I grasped his well-oiled hair and straightened him up, then hit him again. Leech staggered over to the door but I beat him to it, cutting off his escape. He reeled along the wall. Too late, I saw him press a bell button.

I hit him again, in the face this time. He squealed and spat out blood.

'Yeh, go on, hit me,' he gasped. 'But it doesn't alter the fact that your sister's a tart.'

I raised my fist again. Leech taunted me from behind his hands. 'Ask her how many times she's been up here with me, opening her legs.'

A red mist descended.

When it finally lifted, Leech was a crumpled mess against the wall. His face was a bloody pulp and my knuckles were aching. There was the sound of footsteps running up the stairs. Someone hammered on the door.

'Mr Leech. You all right, Mr Leech?' came a deep voice.

It must be one of the Militiamen from downstairs in the café.

'Help me,' croaked Leech. 'Help me . . .'

I was trapped, my options limited. Shinning down a drainpipe was not one of them. Not in my uniform and not in broad daylight.

Instead I ran into the kitchenette and found what I wanted. Back in the living room, Leech was struggling to open the front door. I grasped him by the collar and hurled him across the room to crash over a chair.

'Break the fucking door down,' shouted someone from outside.

I waited a second before slipping the bolt back and flinging the door open. The four men charged into the room. The hindmost made a grab for me but

I swayed backwards out of his reach. I knew they would not be armed since the Germans did not yet trust the Militia enough to give them guns, but it was pointless trying to make a break for it. They would use their whistles to set up a hue and cry and there were too many Militia out on the streets for me to make a clean getaway.

Instead I stood by the doorway and shouted at Leech. 'The next time you falsely denounce any of my family, I'll break your fucking arms, you understand. Don't even think of it – for I'll know. I deal with Stolz and the *Gestapo* every day, remember.'

It seemed politic for me to find a new friend – for the Militia's ears, at least.

'Get him. Get him,' gasped Leech.

The Militiamen weren't so sure. The nearest one took a step forward. It was my cue to whip out the six-inch kitchen knife I'd slid beneath the strap of my wristwatch. He took a step back.

'We're nicking you,' he blustered.

'Fuck off. You couldn't nick yourself shaving.'

I held the blade horizontally, aimed at his throat, while I backed out through the door and closed it after me. I descended the stairs quickly and lightly. As I expected, no one was in a hurry to come after me.

*

Needing a drink, I went into the George for the first time since those two IRA men had frightened the life out of me with their scheme to assassinate Glass. It proved a mistake this time, too. A member of the German police battalion was sitting at my old table, halfway through a pint of cider with a glass of brandy as a chaser. A lethal mixture. From the overflowing ashtray, it seemed he had been there for some time. I should have left then but, as I said, I needed a drink.

The German regarded me with bleary eyes and I realized that I'd seen him somewhere before. He'd asked me directions to the *Feldkommandantur* map room when his battalion had first arrived two weeks ago.

'Prost. Haben Sie schon gefrühstückt? Noch nicht.' He held up his mug of cider. 'Have you had your breakfast yet? I haven't.'

'How long's he been here?' I murmured to the landlord, who was spilling my beer in his haste to get away.

'All day. Even when we should have been closed. And that's a real gun he's got.' He disappeared.

The German was in his mid-forties, with a heavy, round face, receding fair hair and hard shovels of hands. He had missed a patch of bristles under his left ear while shaving that morning, and had spilled something down both lapels. His eyes were red as if from crying.

Suddenly he slapped the table. 'I know you.'

My heart sank. 'Yes.'

'See, I remember, you're the one who speaks German,' he blurted out. 'We were in the Ukraine, you know. It's better here – anywhere's better than the Ukraine.'

I made a vaguely interested noise and wondered how soon I could decently finish my drink and leave. He downed his brandy in one and slammed down his glass.

'I'm a skilled worker, a toolmaker from Bremer-haven. I joined up to be a policeman in 1938. I never thought I'd become a member of an *Einsatzkom-mando*.' He paused. 'Have you heard of us?'

'No.' *Einsatzkommando* meant 'task force'.

'Then you won't have had your breakfast yet?' He gave a demonic cackle, put his finger to the side of his nose and winked. 'The final solution.'

That word – *Endlösung* – again. The German clerk had used it at the meeting I'd attended before the first Jews were transported. And Höss had used the same word just only hours ago.

'The final solution?' I repeated.

The German beamed vacuously, happy for a chance to speak his mother tongue. 'It's not the same here. They don't shoot them the same. No breakfast.'

'Breakfast? I don't understand.'

His eyes filled with tears. He was in that dangerously volatile stage of drunkenness. One moment I'd be his best friend; the next he'd blow my brains out.

'That's what the hard men used to say when they hadn't any Jews to shoot in the morning. *I haven't had my breakfast yet.*'

'The hard men?' I coaxed.

'At the start we were all a bit weak. We'd get back from cleansing a village and we'd be literally shaking. That wasn't why we were in uniform. We were a police battalion and skilled workers in civilian life. Did I tell you I was a metalworker? From Bremerhaven?'

'Yes.'

'We didn't want to kill Jews,' he snorted. 'At first, we couldn't eat, couldn't even talk about it; about what we had seen, what we were doing. But then the jokes began . . .'

'A way of coping?'

'Yes, yes.' He banged his glass on the table in agreement. 'But we changed. Some were haunted by what they were doing, some were indifferent. Some called Jew-killing "eating breakfast", and the hard men began sneering at the cowards . . .'

'And you?'

He ignored my question. 'But we weren't all animals. If we knew a Jew personally, we tried to shoot him from behind so he wouldn't know what was about to happen.'

'Were *you* a hard man?'

He did not reply and I thought that I had lost him. It was as if he had gone deep inside himself. I didn't know even if he had heard my question. Then, holding his cider pot in both hands, he continued in a flat monotone . . .

'I tried to shoot only the children. The mothers led their children by the hand, my mate shot the mother and I shot her child. I reasoned that, after all, the child needed its mother, so I soothed my conscience by releasing the children who could not survive without their mothers . . .' His voice tailed away.

He used the word *erlösen* – to release. It also means to redeem or save. The one who 'releases' is *Der Erlöser* – the Redeemer. In his tortured logic, this man had made himself the children's saviour.

I left my beer, got up and walked out. I don't think he noticed.

Now that I wasn't going to see Angel that evening, I thought I'd go and collect David who was working at Home Farm during the school holidays. But first I had to see how Frisch was getting on in hiding.

I knocked on the Jenners' kitchen door. It was opened by a grinning Bleicher. My heart missed a beat – or maybe ten.

Bleicher had not been around much in the last few months. A fortnight ago, the reason had become clear. He had set up a ring of double agents in Southampton and Portsmouth, so efficiently that not only had it snared two wireless operators and a £50,000 war chest from Canada but also some of the best volunteers in the area. The only crumb of comfort was that three Germans had been killed in the shoot-out when the *Gestapo*, hoodwinked as much as the Resistance, had ambushed the leaders of the bogus ring. Now Bleicher had returned to the West Country again.

'You're just in time for a concert, ' he announced.

'Sorry?'

'We're having a small concert with Jacob's Austrian cousin,' replied Bleicher. 'Such a pianist! I cannot compete so I'm playing the violin. It is an honour to play with so talented a musician.'

I followed him into the living room where Frisch was sitting at the piano with Jacob by his side, holding his violin.

'Willem Krauss,' said Frisch, rising to shake my hand. 'We haven't met.'

'Willem is staying here for a week's break from the Royal Philharmonic Society,' explained Miriam.

Oh, Christ! I bit my lip. Mills had taken a lot of trouble to lay a false trail leading north from Liverpool to Fleetwood, culminating with the crashing of a car containing Frisch's diary near a German checkpoint. The ploy had prompted the Germans to send an entire police battalion to hunt for the scientist throughout Lancashire. It had made life difficult for the lads up there but Frisch was worth it. But now he and the Jenners were playing schoolboy pranks on one of the most astute *Abwehr* men in England. They'd soon find Bleicher was far too cute to fall for their inventions, and the slightest wrong word . . .

The nightmare got even worse when Bleicher took me by the elbow and led me over to the window.

'I bet I know why you're here,' he murmured.

I said a silent prayer that he didn't.

'You came to warn the Jenners about the new round-up. Don't worry, I've made sure their names have been taken off the transportation list. They're now under the protection of the *Abwehr*. They're untouchable.'

'That's wonderful,' I stammered as relief swept over me.

'I told you before they are my friends. And now to be allowed to play music with *Herr* Krauss . . . I don't know what to say.'

I didn't either. Frisch was being the life and soul of the party: flirting with Miriam, swopping jokes with Bleicher, even coaxing a smile from Barbara. I had to fire a shot across his bows before he got completely carried away.

'I heard a lovely story recently of the difference between an Austrian and a German,' I said, looking meaningfully at him. 'When things are going badly, the German says, "The situation is serious but not hopeless." The Austrian says, "The situation is hopeless but not serious."'

Frisch smiled back sweetly.

'That was a bloody stupid thing to do.'

'I'm sorry, I—'

'You know how she kicks. Putting that churn next to her was asking for trouble.' Matty's face was dark with anger as the last of the milk trickled down the grating. 'And you let the cows get into the mangel field.'

'I didn't know that fence post was rotten, Master Matty. I'm going to fix it first thing in the morning.'

Matty seemed about to reply when he turned sharply and strode out of the dairy. Bert hitched up his broad leather belt and looked after him more in sorrow than anger.

'He's got a lot on his mind at the moment,' I said to try to assuage Bert's feelings.

'Maybe he has,' replied Bert. 'But it don't hurt none to keep a civil tongue. That's not the first time he's snapped my head off recently. He's his father's son all right, make no mistake.'

'What d'you mean?'

'He's changed, he has, and not for the better.' The fact that Bert was even willing to talk about Matty was an indication of his disappointment.

'Maybe it's the responsibility of running the

estate.' And all the Resistance work – but I couldn't tell Bert about that.

'There's something on his mind, right enough but I be buggered if I know what it is.' Bert righted the churn. 'And he's away such a lot. That's why we're behind, even with young David to help.'

'How's David getting on?'

'Oh, he's a grand lad, very keen – can't do enough for Master Matty.'

'That's good, but why don't you get more help?'

'There's talk about us getting some Russian prisoners of war, but where's the sense in that when our own men are still being held prisoner? Whatever, there's no cause for Master Matty to act like he is.'

I could understand how the strain was getting to Matty. He was a born leader and fearless in battle, but it took an altogether different type of courage to be an underground agent. Battles were relatively brief events that made the body pump out massive amounts of adrenalin to get you through the moment. Working in the Resistance meant that fear was *always* present. At the back of the mind, you dreaded every dawn because it might bring that knock on the door. You could never relax. In the end your nerves became as taut as a cheese wire.

I left Bert to carry on with his milking and went off to find Matty. He was leaning on a rail, staring moodily down towards the spinney.

David came along, leading the two gentle shire

horses. Working out in the open air had given him a healthy tan, while the manual labour was putting muscles on his slim frame.

'We've finished cutting the grass down in Common Furlong,' he announced. 'The horses have had their feed, so I'm turning them out for the night. Is that all right?'

'Fine, thank you.' Matty still seemed distracted.

David paused, dwarfed by the horses either side of him. 'Shall I get the rods?'

Matty looked blank. 'Rods?'

David shuffled his feet. 'You said we'd go fishing after milking.'

Conflicting emotions crossed Matty's face. He was about to find a reason to cancel the promised expedition when he sighed. 'Why not? It's a beautiful evening. Get one for Nick, too, and my fishing bag from the gunroom. And some flagons of beer, while you're at it. Chop-chop, the fish won't wait all night.'

Matty was right: it was a beautiful evening. High in the pale blue sky, swifts dived and swooped like commas as they fed on airborne insects. As David disappeared, Matty and I set off over the stile and down the slope of rough pasture towards the broad stream running through the wooded valley below.

'You've a lot on your plate, Matty?'

'You don't know the half. The Resistance leaders' meeting is definitely on for next Wednesday. Mills reckons the Germans will be so busy guarding Hitler and the other Nazi big shots that they won't have time to bother about anything else. You wouldn't believe how hard it's been, persuading all the different factions to sit down together. You'd never think we were all supposed to be together in fighting the Germans.'

'So what's the problem?'

'The Communists take their orders from Moscow, and they're the most disciplined and best organized. There was even a danger they'd take over the Resistance, but that won't happen now the Yanks are about to enter the war.'

'Why not?'

'We'll have control of American money and arms to hand out to whoever we like. Either the Reds do as they're told or they're in for a lean time. At last we've a chance of victory, now the Yanks are in with us.'

'Perhaps it'll make some people think twice about collaborating with the Germans,' I said.

'What d'you mean?'

'Well, there's bound to come a day of reckoning when the war's over. There must be dozens of collaborators and informers wetting themselves at the thought of the Resistance getting their hands on the Gestapo files.'

'You'll have your pound of flesh, then?'

'I want to see the bastards strung up. Don't you?'

'Of course.'

David came trotting up behind us, fishing bag over his shoulder, his arms full of rods and a wicker frail containing three flagons of beer.

As we approached the river near the Cattle Drink, a kingfisher darted low over the water, a flash of iridescent blue and red. In the meadow opposite a heron took flight with slow sweeping wing-beats. The earlier wind had dropped and, through the fine high cloud, the evening sun was flooding the stream with rose-water light. A cob and his pen ushered their three cygnets away with reproachful looks at us for disturbing their feast of water crowfoot. Electric-blue damsel flies hovered over the small daisy flowers that covered the narrower channel to one side of Otter's Island.

'All right, David, what's the first thing we do?' asked Matty.

'Nothing,' replied David.

'Good lad. We'll set up the rods and wait to see what's on the water, see what the fish are scoffing for their supper. Then what do we do?'

'Match the hatch,' recited David.

'I was thinking more of opening the beer but, yes, you're right. Nice and slow and steady.' After a few minutes spent studying insect life on the surface, Matty demanded, 'What do you reckon?'

'Maybe a small dark sedge . . . Wow!' There was a splash in the pool beside the fallen willow. We all peered upstream to see ripples widening in a circle.

'The bigger the splash, the bigger the fish,' intoned David.

'Go and try for him, then. Nice and gently. Don't let your shadow fall on the water or you'll put him down.'

The boy jogged off, Matty already shaking his head indulgently. We both knew what was about to happen. David was in too much of a hurry to get his line out cleanly. His cast landed on the water in a limp tangle.

'Take your time,' called Matty. 'Remember, keep your thumb on top of the rod as if you're shaking hands. Hold the rod out in front of you at nine o'clock. Raise it quickly to eleven o'clock, now give it a quick flick back to half past twelve and stop. When you feel the slight pull on the line out behind you, cast forward with a flick down to ten o'clock. Smooth, not jerky. That's better . . . Oh, good cast.'

I popped the cork out of a flagon and started on the beer, before moving downstream to begin my own fishing. I'd never been very good, but Matty soon caught two brown trout, and David hooked a grayling, which pleased him. Then, as often happens, the river went dead. The fish either went to sleep or began feeding in the weeds. Nothing we could do interested them. After a while I gave up, while Matty instructed David on some of the finer points of casting. He was very good, very patient – and very funny. I wished that someone had taught me to fish that way. I flopped on my back on the bank of buttercups, smelling the fresh grass just becoming damp with the dew, and watched the ghostly white shape of a tawny owl drifting low in the field opposite, hunting for moles in the dusk. Matty left David to persevere, and joined me for a beer.

'I'm sorry I blew up at Bert,' he said after a long drink. 'I'll go round there and apologize when we're done here. My nerves are . . .'

'Don't worry.'

'I'm glad we came fishing. It's like the old days.'

'Yes.' Inevitably we fell to reminiscing about our fishing trips with Roy before the war and, as the years rolled back, I felt Roy was there with us on the river bank in the twilight. He was a clumsy buffalo of a fisherman, with little patience. If he failed to catch anything within a few minutes, he'd give up and get stuck into the beer instead.

'Do you remember that time Roy caught a cow?'

We bellowed with laughter at the memory.

'And he couldn't get near her to unhook the fly.'

'She gave Roy such a filthy look and trotted off with him running after her, holding the rod with the cow still attached on the end of the line . . .'

'And he tried to offer her a handful of buttercups . . .'

'And every other cow wanted them apart from the one he'd hooked'.

'And the time he caught that mallard.'

'Oh, God! That poor duck – trying to take off at the same time Roy was trying to reel him in . . .'

'We cooked two trout and a duck over the fire. We were camping just up the river from here.'

'It was this time of year – a night like this.'

The first stars were twinkling in the darkening sky. Matty and I fell silent, both reliving in our minds those magical times the three of us had shared.

'I'll miss you.'

'No, you won't. You'll be too busy playing soldiers.' Coral Kennedy raised herself on one elbow and traced an invisible pattern on Glass's naked chest with her fingertip.

'Will you write to me? Every soldier at the front likes to receive a letter.'

'I don't think that would be a good idea – do you?'

'Maybe not.' Glass knew he was taking a risk every time he brought her back here to his official residence. If the *Gestapo* ever found out, after Stolz had officially warned him of her role in the Resistance, Glass could be executed for treason within days. It made the affair all the more exciting.

He pulled her down so they lay side by side, their faces close, the stump of his arm hidden under him. A bottle of champagne sat on the table beside the four-poster bed.

Glass kissed her nose. 'Are you glad I'm going away?'

'No.' She kissed him back. 'I'll miss you, too.'

'At least you'll no longer risk getting tarred and feathered as a horizontal collaborator once I'm gone.'

'How do you know I won't take up with Stolz instead?' she teased.

'You dare and I'll come back and bring my whole corps with me.'

They had started seeing each other regularly soon after that dinner party. As Glass had suspected, Coral Kennedy was the type of woman who found power an aphrodisiac. They had made love on their second evening alone together.

They kissed slowly.

'More champagne?

'Why not?' said Coral. 'I'll get it.'

Glass shifted to watch her slim naked shape moving around the bedroom.

'We're an unlikely couple,' he said as she handed him a glass.

'Are we?'

'The Governor and the Terrorist.'

'The Oppressor and the Freedom Fighter,' she shot back.

They paused, both stunned that the unspeakable had been spoken.

Glass had told her *he knew*.

And Coral had said . . . so what!

Each of them was sleeping with the enemy.

The frisson of it drove them into a passionate embrace. Later, Glass reached for a packet of cigarettes, shook two free and offered them to Coral.

'Look after Penny,' he murmured.

'Nick?' Coral's tone intimated that it was bad form to mention Nick now. Glass had never actually asked her whether she and Nick were lovers. The German could be strangely incurious at times. She could not tell if it was self-confidence or indifference.

'There's an appealing naivety about him,' continued Glass.

'It's an act,' contradicted Coral, cross that this talk about Nick was making her feel guilty. 'Underneath he's as tough as old boots. Anyway, who's going to look after *me*? That should concern you more.'

'*You*'ll be all right. You're a natural-born survivor.'

'Thanks.'

'Penny's rubbed Stolz up the wrong way on too many occasions. He could get away with it in the past, but now Stolz'll be wanting to show him who's boss.'

'Couldn't he do that before?'

'I could always protect Penny – but now he's on his own.' Glass inhaled on the cigarette. 'I think it would be better if Penny left – and you too.'

Goose pimples rose on Coral's bare arms. 'But Nick's got a family here. If he disappears, Stolz will take it out on them. They'll end up in some camp.'

'I'm only warning you what I think *might* happen.'

'But what can he do about his family?'

'That's up to him.'

24

The second round-up of Jews, on 1 August 1941, was carried out with much greater brutality than the first. The iron fist no longer bothered to conceal itself inside the velvet glove. It seemed that the Germans had stopped caring what anyone thought of them. The Militia and the SS were out in force from early dawn, herding tearful Jewish families onto the backs of lorries amid a welter of curses and blows. As I passed, a mob of Militia was openly looting the home of Tuchmann the bookseller, one of them carrying out a canteen of silver cutlery and another struggling under a huge oil painting. A holding pen had been set up at the bottom of Pennyquick Hill, where dazed families sobbed white-faced at their calamity. I dropped my eyes, grateful that Bleicher had taken the Jenner family off the list.

All of a sudden I had the feeling I was being watched. The sinister van with the blacked-out windows was crawling along forty yards behind me. I ducked into a narrow alley where it could not follow, but its presence unnerved me and I kept looking over my shoulder the rest of the way to the *Feldkommandantur*.

The foyer was packed with the English clerks who worked there, queuing up to have their passes inspected by two SS troopers. A *Gestapo* man stood behind them, checking each name against a list. As I went to hand over my pass, he snatched it from me.

'Stand over to one side.'

I was forced to wait there as the others filed through, doing their best to look as though they did not know me. Finally, when there was no one else, the *Gestapo* man got round to scrutinizing my residence permit and identity card. He confiscated my security pass before handing me back a temporary one, valid for one week only.

'You are permitted access only to the floor on which you work. If you are found elsewhere you will be arrested.'

It was Stolz's first morning in power.

But the bigger shock was still to come. The door to my office now bore the name of *Leutnant Heidegger, RHSA*.

I was still staring dumbly at the door when Stolz himself strutted around the corner, followed by his humourless ADC, Abetz. He carried a sheaf of papers in his hand

'Penny, translate these new orders.'

'And where would you like me to do this?'

'There. You work over there, and from now on

you start work at 0700.' He pointed to a wooden table and chair crammed into an alcove at one end of the corridor. 'Get on with it. The *Reich* and its vassal states will be at war with the United States of America from noon today, New European Time. I want these new notices posted up throughout the region by nightfall.'

The first notice warned that, in the event of acts of sabotage against the occupying power, any prisoner already held in custody was liable for execution. In addition, Stolz reserved the right to nominate prominent British personnel to be executed in the event of hostile acts against communications, harbours, et cetera.

Under these new diktats, people were banned from walking on beaches and clifftops; isolated houses within sight of the sea were to be cleared, and communicating with vessels out to sea was an offence instantly punishable by death.

Word quickly went out that Stolz had it in for me. Most of the German clerks and Grey Mice who would normally pass the time of day now ignored me. One or two sneered openly. Tickell and Bearup found it possible to walk towards me down the whole length of the corridor and still not see me. Late in the morning as Stolz, with a smirking Gregan basking in his role as head of the local Militia, marched past, Gregan contrived to knock the papers off my desk.

But if this new location meant that my humiliation

was made as public as possible, at least I got to see all the comings and goings. Late that afternoon, I happened to glance up to see a lengthy procession heading towards me. At its head were Stolz and an even shorter man in SS uniform, with sticking-out ears and heavy pebble glasses that failed to conceal his pronounced squint.

I recognized him from a recent article in the *Daily Mail* – and my heart stood still. SS *Oberführer* Professor Dr Franz Alfred Six, formerly holder of the chair of political science in Leipzig University and currently head of the *Gestapo* in Britain. He passed by without so much as a glance at me. I made a mental note to tell Angel of his presence.

That evening, I trudged home up the hill, worrying about my future – or lack of it. The round-up appeared to be over. Here and there, wide-open doors told their sad story of an abandoned home. On the pavement by one front gate, a suitcase had burst open to spill its contents on the ground, where its owner had been forced to abandon it.

I learned that David was at the farm and my mother had gone to visit the Jenners. This was a good opportunity to ask Joan if Leech's accusation about her hiding a gun and ammunition was true. I couldn't take any chances now that Stolz was being so openly hostile.

Joan continued to grate a carrot. 'Why do you ask?'

'The way Stolz has got in it for me, he could send his goons to search our home any day. If they find anything here, we'll *all* end up in a camp.'

'I'm wondering why you're asking me about a gun just now.'

'Christ, sis, I've just explained.' I wanted to shake her.

'There's a small automatic upstairs that I was given when Ted and I were stationed in China. It was a gift from the Shanghai Bund.'

'Joan, I don't care who it was from. Please fetch the gun and any ammunition, and I'll throw them in the sea.' I saw the reluctance in her eyes. 'Sis, *please*.'

'All right, all right.' She put down the carrot and left.

She reappeared carrying a beautifully made lady's pistol with mother-of-pearl inlay on the grip and intricate chasing on the barrel. I was examining it when the door burst open.

We froze.

Our mother stood there, looking dishevelled and on the verge of hysteria.

'They're going to take them. They're going to take them away. Oh, those poor children.'

'What's wrong, mum? Who's taking who?'

Mum dragged her twisted body over to her chair and sat down heavily. Her hat was crooked and she had lost her walking stick. 'They smashed their way in.'

'Mum, what are you saying?'

'Something's happened to the Jenners?' Joan was kneeling before her.

Mum just stared at the empty grate, her mouth working soundlessly. Finally she spoke. 'They're evil. Evil.'

She seemed to be slipping into a trance. Joan managed to get her out of her coat.

Mum's eyes were glazed, her mouth working ceaselessly away. But the only sound was a whispered, 'Evil, evil.'

'I'll put her to bed and give her a sleeping pill,' said Joan.

'I'd better go and see what's happened.'

The Jenners' home had been ransacked. The front door gaped open, with windows smashed and the curtains torn down. Dining-room chairs lay splintered on the lawn.

'Hello?' I stood in the hall, my voice echoing round the empty house.

Coats, their linings ripped out, were strewn around the hall floor. Jacob's violin, broken in half, lay in the doorway to the living room. In the room itself, the carpet was covered with shards of glass. Every chair and table had been kicked over. The sofa and the sideboard lay on their sides. Cushions had been slashed, their stuffing hanging out like obscene entrails. In the kitchen, a trail of blood led over Miriam's smashed jam jars to a thickening crimson pool by the back door.

I kept calling as I made my way upstairs. There, mattresses had been ripped open and drawers emptied onto the floor. In the twins' bedroom, dolls and teddy bears had been pulled apart in the orgy of destruction. Even the mattress on Hope's cot in Barbara's room had been shredded.

On the landing, a smear of blood ran along the wall towards the bathroom. The door was closed and when I reached for the handle, it was wet and sticky. My palm came away covered with blood. I kicked open the door – and almost threw up in relief to find the room empty.

The brooding silence closed around me. I had to get out of there. Fighting the panic rising inside me, I dashed down the stairs, across the front lawn and out onto the pavement. I was still gasping for air when the bent figure of old Enoch Copples appeared from out of his house opposite. He peered nervously up and down the street before shuffling over.

'You just missed them, Nick,' he wheezed. 'They were after the hidden fortune.'

'Who were? What hidden fortune?'

'The Militia. It was that Gregan hisself. They

kicked your mum out and then started on the Jenners, trying to make them tell where the jewels were hidden. The bastards tortured Miriam. She was screaming something rotten. It got so bad even *they* had to do something.' He nodded towards the German officers' club housed in my old family home.

So Bleicher's generosity in taking the Jenners off the round-up list had been in vain. The Militia had chosen their own victims. Poor Jacob and Miriam – all for a groundless rumour. I knew there were no jewels.

But then I realized that it was not just the Jenners who had been snatched. The Germans now had Otto Frisch.

I tried the football stadium, where the Jews were again being held, but I couldn't find anyone I knew there. This time the captives were being guarded by the local Militia and the SS. My British Army rank counted for nothing with them. My efforts were met with derision – and the threat that if they let me in I'd leave in a cattle truck with the rest.

I rode up to Corunna Barracks to enlist Bleicher's help, but he had done one of his disappearing acts again.

That left Angel. I found her at home – but not particularly welcoming. I relayed what had happened to Frisch and the Jenners.

'Find out where they've gone,' she said.

'I've been trying,' I told her.

'Keep trying,' she said.

Not everyone in the Jenners' home had been captured, however. When the Militia forced their way in, Barbara had been out in the back garden rocking seven-month-old Hope to sleep. The angry shouts, the hammering on the door, the hoarse commands had brought her worst memories back to life.

Barbara had slid deep into the laurel bushes, crooning softly to her baby. When she closed her eyes, she saw again those terrible times in Cracow – the times she never spoke of. The English thought they were suffering under the Nazis, but what did they know? The Germans basically respected the English and wanted them for their allies. They despised the Poles and only wanted their land. Polish Jews like Barbara were held in particular contempt as being *Untermenschen* – the 'under-people'. Immediately after Germany had conquered Poland, the Jews had been banned from all public transport. They'd even had to step off the pavement into the gutter if they met a German coming towards them. Her father, a surgeon, was made to scrub the floor of the local German barracks; then their own maid claimed that the family had insulted the *Führer*. She was rewarded with the family apartment while they themselves were forced into the ghetto. Life there behind the high walls, segregated from the rest of the world, was unreal. No news, no sense of time, just survival and work – and the constantly revised lists of those no longer able to work. The children, the old, the sick, the useless were taken away – and never came back.

Then Barbara and her sister and her husband were put on one of the lists. They had tried hiding but they had been discovered, and transported to Plaszov camp. There, in retrospect, the ghetto seemed like heaven. Barbara slaved in the camp's clothing factory, washing, mending and patching the filthy blood-stained clothes that constantly arrived by the lorry-load. Then came the day when her sister and her husband were caught smuggling food into camp. They were made to dig their own graves and were shot on the spot. Barbara was forced to gather the wood to burn their bodies.

Life was cheap, but still so precious.

The Militia mob had gone upstairs now, hurling Miriam's possessions out through the shattered windows.

And still Barbara's memories flooded back to her. The fourteen-year-old boy, who the guards heard singing to keep his spirits up. After three unsuccessful attempts to hang him in front of his mother, the Germans finally shot him. Murdered for trying to be happy.

The lorryload of priests, closely followed by one

of nuns. They were shot as soon as they arrived. Barbara had to clean and mend their bloodstained clothes.

The female SS guard they called *Hlopka*, meaning 'riff-raff', grabbing a girl's hair, beating and kicking her, while a fellow inmate was made to sing a sentimental Polish song.

She heard Miriam scream – and Barbara's blood turned to ice water. Miriam screamed again. A piercing, prolonged scream as if they were torturing her. Clutching Hope even more tightly, Barbara fled. At the garden gate she met German officers on their way to investigate the disturbance. Terror drove her blindly along the neighbouring streets until she paused, panting, at the corner of Mill Street and St Saviour's Vale. As if in a dream, a Jewish woman appeared from the doorway of the disused bakery and quickly led her up the outside steps to the granary loft above. Welcoming hands gathered her in to join about twenty women and their children already hiding there. Barbara slumped down tearfully in the loft with its covering of fine flour dust and rich smell of yeast, and offered Hope her breast.

But later, when night had fallen, and Barbara could make out one star through a chink in the ancient slate roof, Hope awoke and began to grizzle. A Militia patrol was passing, swearing drunkenly and chanting obscenities. A woman nearby tried to offer Hope a biscuit soaked in milk, but the baby screamed in fear of the stranger. Barbara clamped a hand over her baby's mouth and they all held their breath, but the Militia thugs were making too much noise of their own to have heard the infant's cries.

Scarcely an hour later the fugitives recognized the ringing hobnailed boots of an SS patrol. Shortly afterwards they heard a shot from the direction of the city centre.

Barbara, in her dark space, tucked her daughter's head deep inside her blouse and wrapped the shawl around them both. After the town clock struck midnight, Hope's grizzling remained the only sound.

Just minutes later the women froze as they heard a German soldier calling softly just outside. For the first time the Jews realized how clearly sound travelled on that still summer night. Just then Hope began wriggling, fighting against being constrained. Her head came free and she managed to let out one hefty bawl before Barbara could stifle her.

The women whispered furiously among themselves. The one who had earlier offered Barbara shelter crawled up to her as she sat with her arms wrapped protectively around her baby daughter.

'You're going to have to do something about the child. Can't you keep her quiet?'

'I'm trying to, but she's scared.'

'It's not right that she should endanger all our lives.'

Barbara had hidden once before, in the Cracow

ghetto. The Germans had found her then, and she had ended up in that camp of terror.

'She'll be quiet, I promise,' Barbara pleaded.

She slid lower against the wall and kept her promise. Silence fell again over the darkness where the women and their children huddled for safety. At first light, one of the women went to offer Hope another milk-soaked biscuit but the child had fallen asleep at Barbara's breast. Barbara herself sat awake and unblinking, transported back to another place where life had been so cheap and at the same time so precious.

When the SS troopers came for them with fixed bayonets shortly after nine o'clock that morning, the women were made to file down the outside wooden staircase one by one. Barbara brought up the rear, still holding Hope to her breast. On a landing, some nine feet above the ground, she paused. The guard behind prodded her to move on but she was measuring the distance. Right beneath her a soldier stood watching the assembled fugitives, his rifle slung over his shoulder. Barbara slipped under the rail and launched herself onto his bayonet. Her aim was true – the bayonet pierced her heart.

But by then Hope had been dead for eight hours, smothered by her mother to keep her quiet.

*

'So where are the Jews being taken?' I repeated to Tickell, blocking the corridor in front of him.

'It's no concern of mine.' He tried to brush past but I grabbed his thin arm.

'You *must* know where they're going,' I insisted. 'They're not being transported abroad this time, are they? They're going to that camp Fest was talking about. Come on, they're your people.'

He jerked away as though he had been stung. 'They are not *my* people. I have nothing to do with them.'

'But these are not foreign Jews like last time. They were all born and brought up here, English to the core. They fought for this country. You knew them, you visited their homes. Of course they're *your* people.'

Tickell's Adam's apple was bobbing up and down like a monkey on a stick. He glared at me, his eyes red-rimmed and watery.

'*Your people*,' I insisted.

He glanced around in what was known as the *German look* – everyone in the *Feldkommandantur* did it now. 'They've set up a work camp at some deserted village called Imber in the middle of Salisbury Plain.' Tickell told me in little more than a whisper.

'When will the Jews arrive there?'

'Early tomorrow morning, I'd guess . . . I'm sorry, Penny.' He closed his eyes as though saying a prayer.

They were moist when he reopened them. 'We thought they'd be safe after we sacrificed all the foreign Jews last time.'

'You were always very keen to help the Germans,' I accused him.

'I am a public servant. I was wrong to trust them.'

It was the first time that I had ever heard Tickell find fault with his German masters.

I watched him walk away along the corridor, a skeletal upright figure in a morning coat, high collar and striped legal trousers – like a heron in mourning, clinging to the last vestige of its dignity.

25

The dawn came slowly, a pink smear through the lattice of tree trunks over to our right – an imperceptible lightening of the sky as the twinkling stars turned golden and went out one by one. It was going to be another lovely summer's day. Somewhere ahead, a cock crowed, to be answered by another. Two pale moths began playing above the rosebay willowherb at the edge of the stand of elms and oaks where we were hiding. In the valley below, a generator fired up, running roughly at first. The first column of Jews would be here soon. I snapped the head off a dandelion, inspecting the white juice from its stem, and settled down to wait. Next to me, Matty remained motionless.

The fact that we were here above Imber was testimony to how extensive and efficient the Resistance had become. I had told Angel about the camp as soon as I'd left the *Feldkommandantur* Saturday lunchtime. Within three hours I had been briefed by Mills, collected Matty, and set off towards Salisbury Plain. Approaching the ten o'clock curfew, we had phoned

Mills from the outskirts of Warminster. He directed us to a house six miles away, in the village of Chitterne right on the edge of the Plain, where we were surprised to find Angel already waiting with a rather grand old woman she introduced as Lady Mary Stowe.

In the study of her Queen Anne mansion, Lady Mary produced whisky and a large-scale map of the Plain.

'The British army took over Imber as a training ground in December 1939,' she explained. 'It was an absolute disgrace how the villagers were given just six weeks to pack up and leave. Now the Germans have moved in. They've been very busy up there for the past two months or so.'

'Why there?'

'There's an old rhyme,' said Lady Mary. '*Imber Imber on the down. Seven miles from any town.* If you want to keep something secret, Imber's as good as you're going to get in southern England.'

'So what *is* going on there?'

'We've heard rumours that they're building a camp. They've certainly constructed a railway spur as far as Berrils Down – about a mile from Imber.' She pointed out the spot on the OS map.

'Our problem is to reach the camp, find Frisch, spring him and then get away again,' explained Angel. 'There's only one road leading into Imber. It's got two checkpoints and is patrolled twenty-four hours a day.'

'So using the road's out,' said Matty.

'Yes, and it's not feasible to try to get to and from the camp on foot. If the balloon went up, we'd be there for the taking.'

'Are we going to try to bluff our way through, then?' I asked.

'No,' smiled Angel. 'Lady Mary's come up with another solution.'

'Come,' said Lady Mary. 'Let me introduce you.'

We followed her through the house and into the backyard, where four horses regarded us incuriously over their stable doors.

'They hunted regularly over the Plain before the war, so they know the terrain. They're sure-footed and well-schooled, although Chancey will live up to his name if anything startles him,' explained Lady Mary.

Being the tallest, I was given Chester, a sturdy cob. Matty settled for Musket, while Angel, being the best rider, took Chancey. We kept Nelly, the docile one, for Frisch, not knowing if he had ever ridden before.

'Which leaves us the problems of finding Frisch and getting him out,' I reminded Angel.

'We need to be there as the Jews arrive so we can try to pick him out of the crowd. Then we'll have to play it by ear. If the camp's still being built, security can't be that tight.'

Lady Mary produced two SS Death's Head uniforms.

'You *have* been busy,' I said in admiration.

Angel obviously had a good eye, for both uniforms fitted well. I became the officer because of my German, while Matty was a lowly corporal.

After a late supper of Wiltshire ham and eggs we set off at two a.m. Matty led the way with map and compass, then Angel with the spare horse, and myself bringing up the rear. We trotted across the village street and through a brook, before climbing a long track up Breakheart Hill. We then headed north, smelling the fresh dampness and listening to owls hooting. Somewhere a dog fox barked.

For almost an hour we rode over broken countryside amid treacherous peat pits and tussocks of coarse grass, grateful for the three-quarter moon. We were crossing a series of spurs, the terrain rising and falling steeply, when the moon disappeared, leaving us in blackness. Within seconds I began to suffer motion sickness. I slackened the reins and allowed Chester to make his own way. Progress was worryingly slow. Just as we reached Fore Down we caught the faint sound of a railway engine away to our right. Just then, the moon re-emerged and we speeded up, trotting whenever we dared, until we reached a stand of trees. The village of Imber lay just over the next ridge. We dismounted. Angel stayed behind with the horses while Matty and I went off to scout ahead.

Imber must have been very pretty once. There was still a single curving village street of whitewashed thatched cottages, with a conduit running to one side. There was even a small pub. Directly beneath us sat the solid tower of the village church, the headstones in the graveyard luminescent in the moonlight. But at the far end of the village, behind a high barbed-wire fence, new wooden barracks stretched away out of sight beyond a steep bank.

Matty and I set off in the direction of the railway. We were only just in time. We were still in sight of the camp when the sound of shuffling feet reached us on the still air.

In this last remnant of the night, a long column of Jews was approaching, shawls and blankets over their heads and shoulders. It was a pitiful, timeless scene that could have stepped out of the Book of Exodus. Some of them carried sleeping children, others gripped sons and daughters by the hand. Each clutched a suitcase or a bundle of belongings.

The column was made to halt at the start of a narrow wooded defile opening at a right angle to the track. Death's Head officers began moving among the ranks of prisoners, handing out slips of paper. Behind them came guards who pushed those who had received papers out of the column. It soon became clear that the old, the sick and the very young were being separated off.

As the light increased, I spotted Miriam and Jacob with the twins at the very rear of the column. Miriam's face looked bruised and swollen. Frisch stood in front of them. By now the segregation was becoming more perfunctory. Miriam and the children were pushed out of the column. Jacob went to follow them but a guard beat him back with his rifle butt. As he tried again, Frisch grabbed his arm and pulled him back into line.

Those weeded out were prodded into a loose column and herded towards the defile. As they went shuffling away, a small band of women fiddlers appeared from nowhere and began playing sentimental European music. It was bizarre, but we did not have time to dwell on it; we were too intent on not letting Frisch out of our sight.

The remaining column was marched into the camp itself under a makeshift wooden archway, the women being ordered to one side, the men to the other. We could see that several of the huts were still being built.

The men were made to form ranks for roll-call on a cleared area of scrub. The parade was just ending when whistles blew furiously. Guards erupted from everywhere, flailing with whips and rifle butts at prisoners who'd arrived earlier to make them run to join the newcomers. Some of the former wore a uniform of blue shirt and trousers with black markings, but most were still dressed in their own clothes.

A teenager with a mop of curly hair was dragged struggling to the front of the parade. Commandant Höss, the SS man I'd previously seen at the *Feldkommandantur* meeting to discuss the Jewish round-up, strode into view. As he halted, his hands on hips, the boy was forced to his knees. Höss began shouting at the assembled Jews, while gesturing angrily towards the boy. Matty and I were struggling to hear what he was saying when a guard stepped up and casually put his pistol to the back of the boy's neck. Höss nodded and the guard pulled the trigger. As the shot echoed around the valley, the boy slumped face down in the dirt, twitched once, and lay still.

'Shit,' swore Matty softly.

The parade was dismissed as whistles blew to set the prisoners scurrying around like nervous ants. The boy's body was left where it was, forcing prisoners to step over it in their haste to join their working parties. Frisch and Jacob were assigned to a gang of men loading timber onto two old farm carts.

We watched closely as their group was made to haul the carts by rope out of the camp gate and along an earthen track, accompanied by two guards with rifles slung over their shoulders. We kept pace with them under cover until, a quarter of a mile on and well out of sight of the camp, the work party halted by a wooden derrick and began unloading.

'Now or never,' murmured Matty.

We skirted around in a semicircle until we came to the track. There we shook hands. Each of us took a deep breath and then we marched confidently towards the prisoners.

'Two men – you and you.' I pointed at Frisch and Jacob. 'Follow me.'

Jacob's eyes opened wide in astonishment. A podgy corporal with a Hitler moustache and round glasses stepped forward. 'Excuse me, captain, but these men are already on a work detail.'

I looked at him as though he was something nasty I'd just stepped in.

'Yes, corporal – mine.' I had to keep it short. My German was good, but it wouldn't fool a genuine citizen of the Fatherland for long.

'These men were detailed back in camp, captain. If you wish to countermand the orders of the duty major, I will need it in writing.'

Matty was offering the other guard a cigarette – two soldiers getting on with it while their superiors settled their dispute.

'I need two men to hold my surveying instruments.' I pointed vaguely to the left.

'But that area has already been surveyed.'

'Not to my satisfaction.'

Jacob Jenner broke the impasse. He picked up a large stone, casually walked up behind the corporal and brought it down on the back of the German's head. The corporal sank to his knees with a groan. As his eyes rolled up into his head, Jacob hit him again. The other guard fumbled to unsling his rifle. Matty pulled out his bayonet and stepped in close. The soldier screamed as the blade pierced his stomach. Matty stabbed again and this time he got it right. The bayonet slid under the guard's ribs and into his heart.

Jacob was kneeling down to smash the rock into the corporal's head for a third and final time. He straightened up with a wild triumphant look.

'I've been wanting to do that for days,' he panted. 'Thank you for coming.'

'Jacob . . .'

He must have seen something in my expression, for he dropped his eyes.

'Jacob, I'm sorry.' My guts had tied themselves into a knot. Even as I spoke I knew I couldn't leave my friend here.

The other Jews had drawn together in a huddle, muttering among themselves.

'What have you done to them?' demanded one, staring down at the dead Germans.

'Only what they planned to do to you,' replied Matty evenly.

Incredibly, some of the Jews were actually starting

up the track leading back to the camp. We had to stop them.

'Anyone stupid enough to go back will be instantly punished for the murder of the guards,' I shouted. 'The Germans will kill you just as they killed that boy not half an hour ago. This is your chance to escape. Go, get away while you can.'

'He's right.' Jacob addressed them. 'Get away from here.'

'Can you ride?' I whispered to Frisch.

'Sort of,' he replied.

'We'll come with you,' called out one of the Jews.

'No.' Matty stepped forward. 'You must make your own way. Head south until you come to the Wylye Valley, where you'll find a railway line and a trunk road.'

It was also the opposite direction from our escape route.

'I will buy you as much time as I can,' announced Jacob, picking up the corporal's rifle and beginning to fill his pockets with cartridges.

'Don't. We've horses hidden beyond the ridge,' I whispered. 'You and I can double up.'

'I'm staying, Nick.' He raised his voice for all to hear. 'Once I had a family. Then the Germans came. Now I have no one. I will be avenged. I will remain here and kill Germans.'

Another Jew, in his fifties, with a bruised face and

short grey hair, stepped forward to pick up the other rifle. 'And I will fight with you.'

'No one's going to die on my account,' exclaimed Frisch. 'I'll stay.'

This was no time for heroics. 'You're the reason we're here,' I told him. 'You're coming with us.'

'I'm not leaving Jacob behind.'

'I'm an old man,' said Jacob. 'Dying is no big deal to me but before I die I'd like to think I'd done something to help win us the war. Now go.'

Frisch hesitated. Then he and Jacob embraced.

'I'm sorry . . .' I stammered. 'I thought Bleicher had made sure you were safe. We didn't know . . .'

'It is God's will.' Jacob took my hand. A serene calmness emanated from him as he gazed up to where two lapwings tumbled in the morning sky. Nearer, a skylark was fluttering with desperate wing-beats, drenching the air with its song. 'It is a good day to die.'

I've never felt so guilty in my life as I did then, abandoning that good, kind, brave man. A cloud passed in front of the sun, casting its shadow over the valley. We had to leave. We hurried to where Angel was waiting with the horses.

As we were about to mount, Frisch hesitated again. 'It's not right that other men should die for me.'

'I'm afraid that's what war is all about,' I said.

Without another word, he mounted. We set off at a trot, heading south-west until we were well out of sight, then swung west-north-west. If anyone saw us from a distance, we were German soldiers out for a morning ride. As the ground improved, we settled into an easy hunting canter. Frisch had been modest. He was an excellent rider and we soon ate up the miles. We were at the edge of Salisbury Plain, above the village of Bratton, when we heard the first shots – two together, then a fusillade followed by silence. We pressed on until we came to White Horse Hill. There we paused to listen again, as individual shots, then the rattle of heavy machine-gun fire and finally a series of explosions carried on the breeze.

In a barn at the foot of the hill Lady Mary and some local Resistance men were waiting for us with our civilian clothes. Within minutes, we were climbing into the back of a local water company van, and were on our way to Westbury station. The Plain was silent again.

26

'The *Gestapo* have been here, looking for you.'

Joan's words of welcome sent a shiver down my spine. 'When?'

'There were two of them here yesterday afternoon, and again this morning. I told them you'd gone to stay with friends near Newquay for the weekend. I kept it as vague as I could.'

'Good girl.'

'Luckily, your motorbike didn't arrive until ten minutes after they left. I don't suppose you want to tell me where you've been?'

Matty and I glanced at each other. 'It's better if we don't.'

The journey home had gone remarkably smoothly. Angel had hurried Frisch away to a secret hideaway while Matty had come home with me – but Joan was not making us particularly welcome. In fact, she had greeted our arrival with something like resentment. Not long ago she would have visibly brightened in Matty's presence but today she remained flat and irritable. Her hair looked as if it had not been washed for days, her blouse was fastened at the neck by a safety pin where a button had come off, and her slippers had holes where her toes showed through. All in all, my sister had become a little threadbare.

Matty and I flopped down in chairs by the empty fireplace while Joan poured tea and left to take a cup to our mother, who was in bed, where she'd been ever since she'd returned from the Jenners' home.

'What do you think the *Gestapo* were doing here?' murmured Matty once we were alone.

'I don't know. I wasn't supposed to be on duty over the weekend. I just hope Stolz is being bloody-minded.'

'Don't worry. He won't do anything to you – or your family,' Matty reassured me with what I felt was misplaced confidence.

'I'm too tired to worry about anything at the moment.'

Matty excused himself to go to the outside lavatory as Joan returned.

'She's asleep. I'll leave her until lunch is ready.'

'What are we having?'

'Tripe and cabbage,' she answered shortly. 'That's all I could find.'

'Is there enough for Matty, too?'

'He won't want tripe.'

'Why not? Tripe's good for you. Isn't it, Matty?' I added, as he came back in.

'Absolutely. I like tripe.'

'There's nothing in the shops,' continued Joan defensively, dropping a yellowing cabbage into boiling water.

'You should have said. I'll make sure David brings some things home for you from the farm.'

Joan battled with her emotions. Her pride lost. 'Thank you, Matty. I'm sorry, I'm a bit on edge. Sometimes I let it all get on top of me.'

'No one goes hungry on a farm,' smiled Matty. 'Really, you should have said earlier.'

I went upstairs to see if I could persuade mum to get up for dinner. She was still asleep, her lined face lying sideways on her pillow, puckered mouth sagging open.

'Mum.' I gently touched her shoulder. 'Mum?'

She opened her eyes, washed-out, almost colourless, and regarded me with absolutely no sign of recognition or even curiosity. After a moment, they closed again. I left the room.

Matty was commenting on how few pages the Sunday newspaper now contained.

'And it's all about that wretched coronation,' objected Joan. 'I wouldn't cross the road to see that traitor and his hussy. No one with an ounce of moral decency would.'

Matty began reading aloud. 'In the first part of the ceremony, called the Recognition, the sovereign is presented to the people. Once acclaimed by them, he then takes the Oath . . .'

'What, to serve his master Hitler?' mocked Joan, getting out knives and forks.

'He is anointed with oil, then robed in the Pall of the Cloth of Gold, and invested with the Regalia – the Orb, the Sceptre with the Cross, the Sceptre with the Dove, the Coronation Ring, and finally the Crown of St Edward.'

'He'll have his hands full by then,' I suggested.

'As the archbishop places the crown on the king's head, all the peers present put on their coronets,' Matty continued to read out. 'The Archbishop of York is the first to pay homage, followed by the Princes of the Blood Royal and representatives of each order of the peerage ... I wonder how many of those will turn up.'

'They'll turn up,' Joan muttered darkly. 'They know which side their bread's buttered on.'

'The sovereign then proceeds to St Edward's Chapel to prepare for the triumphal return journey to St James's Palace. The sovereign's escort will be drawn from the Household Cavalry and from Prussian *Uhlans*. The Life Guards and *SS Leibstandarte Adolf Hitler* will provide the guard of honour at the Abbey.'

'I don't know why Hitler doesn't just have himself crowned,' said Joan, bringing warm plates out of the oven. 'The food's ready. Nick, are you sure mum doesn't want anything?'

'I'm not even sure she knew who I was.'

There was a knock on the door and Mrs Harper's head appeared around it. 'Hello, it's only me.'

'Yes, Mrs Harper, what can I do for you?'

Mrs Harper was dressed in a new-looking light beige coat trimmed with fur, and a summer hat with artificial cherries around the brim. 'I've just been to lunch at the Golf Club and I brought your mother back a piece of Madeira cake.'

'Thank you,' said Joan, as if chewing on ash.

After lunch Matty and I went out into the garden for a cigarette.

'I'll sort you out with some supplies as soon as I get back to the farm,' he said.

'There's no hurry.'

'No, I will. I'm off on my travels tomorrow. I'm driving to Merricombe to see this Hereward character.'

'What's he like?' I was curious.

'A strange cove. He was previously a grammar-school headmaster, who'd been unscathed by the war until a German army lorry ran over his only daughter – she was just eighteen. It unleashed a monster in him. I've never known anyone hate the Germans with such intensity,' replied Matty, drawing on his cigarette. 'Now he's a brilliant guerrilla leader and utterly ruthless. If he had his way, he'd kill every single German on these islands. He's not interested in surrender, only in extermination.'

'Strange what demons we have lurking inside us all.'

Matty shot me a keen glance. 'After seeing this Hereward, I'm going on to talk to our people in Bristol, Southampton and Reading. I'll be ending up in London for that meeting on Wednesday, if all goes well.'

'You'll get to see Hitler,' I joked.

Matty blew a perfect smoke ring. 'Who knows, I might.'

I gave Matty a lift back to the farm where I found David, happy as a sandboy, helping with the milking. I chatted to Bert as Matty filled my haversack with eggs, potatoes, kale and a slab of bacon.

'Master Matty apologized to me for his hard words,' Bert revealed when we were alone. 'Came round to my house and said sorry like a gentleman.'

'I told you he had just too much on his plate.'

'Is he all right? Not sick or summat is he?'

'Why?'

'It's only that he's just had me witness his will. I'm wondering as to why a healthy young man would suddenly want to make his will?'

'It's good practice when you own a large estate like Matty does,' I replied. 'That way the government doesn't get its sticky fingers on too much of your money.'

I didn't share Bert's perplexity about *why* Matty had made a will, but I was puzzled why he hadn't asked me to be an executor – and why he had not even mentioned it.

On the way home, I decided to visit my father's grave. I had not been there for months.

The clifftop cemetery was deserted under the late afternoon sun. I walked through the graveyard amid the heavy hum of bees and insects. Peacock butterflies were playing on the buddleia bushes and damsel flies hovered over an old green-stained tap that dripped. But the cemetery had been neglected; the dead forgotten in the ongoing struggles of the living. The grass sprouting between the graves had grown very long, with clumps of dandelions at the side of the gravel pathway, while part of the drystone boundary wall had crumbled away. At first I could not find my father's grave in all the grass. Then I discovered his plain wooden cross, leaning at an obscene angle. It had been daubed with a swastika.

Stolz was playing a cat-and-mouse game, with me as the mouse. He made no mention of the two *Gestapo* men he had sent to my home over the weekend, but every time he walked past my small table I caught him eyeing me sideways. By the time I went to meet the schoolboys back from Germany, my nerves were screaming. I stood by to translate, as the newly appointed Hitler Youth leaders in their brown shirts and black shorts goose-stepped past Stolz with Guards-like precision.

'What did you do in the Fatherland?' inquired Stolz of their leader.

'Fired rifles and machine guns and once marched through the night singing, sir. We helped the war effort against the Bolsheviks by loading railway trucks with ammunition.'

'What was the best part of your trip?'

'Meeting the *Führer*, sir.'

'That's a privilege very few German boys ever enjoy,' agreed Stolz.

'I told him I was going to join the SS St George Division to fight the Russians when I was older, sir. The *Führer* actually patted me on the cheek and said I was a good boy.'

I remembered Glass, on our first meeting, quoting Hitler's words: 'I will corrupt the countries I occupy.'

After the parade, I was glad to get away to breathe some clean air. I had not got fifty yards from the *Feldkommandantur* when a ragamuffin in a tattered pullover tugged at my jacket.

'Mister, mister, there's a man wants to talk to you. You gotta come with me.'

'What sort of man?'

COLLABORATOR

But the boy was already scuttling away. Uncertainly, I followed him down Sea Coal Lane into Caulkers Row where we ducked in and out of several back alleys before arriving at the Sea View fish and chip shop. It was open for one of the three days a week allowed, and was offering a penny's worth of chips with two slices of swede in batter for a half-penny. The lad skirted the queue stretching out of the door, lifted the counter flap and nodded towards a back room. The chip shop's owner and his wife both ignored me.

'In there, mister.'

As my eyes became accustomed to the dim light in the storeroom, I made out Mills standing in the corner, next to a solitary sack of potatoes.

'Thanks for coming. We've a crisis on our hands. That lunatic headmaster who calls himself Hereward is planning to ambush the Militia in Merricombe today, the damned idiot.' Mills could not conceal the anger in his voice. 'He's trying to raise the stakes before the meeting, so he can haggle for a bigger arms allotment.'

'Wasn't Matty heading up there this morning?'

'He left before I became aware of Hereward's plans.' Mills brought out his cigarette case and offered me one.

'What's so wrong with ambushing some of the Militia? It's about time they were taken down a peg.'

Mills gave a deep sigh. 'Firstly, Nick, this Hereward should have the wit not to rock the boat so close to the crucial meeting. Secondly, what he does *not* know is that part of the SS Regiment *Germania* has just arrived on his doorstep.'

'Shit!'

'Quite. They moved down from Aldershot overnight. I assume they're on anti-invasion exercises now that the Americans are in the war, but the timing couldn't be worse. Hereward and his irregulars don't stand a chance in hell against them. The regiment is the best the Germans have left in Britain and some of their units are less than ten miles from Merricombe.'

'Matty's going to walk into the middle of this scrap?'

'I'm hoping you can catch him before he gets to Merricombe.'

'Me!'

'Cordington had to go and see someone else first, so you still stand a chance of overtaking him on your bike. Maybe you can reach Hereward before he springs his ambush. I've written him a note.' Mills produced a buff envelope.

'How can *I* go? I'm expected back at the *Feldkommandantur* in half an hour.'

'I'll send the boy back to explain that you've been taken ill.'

'With what?'

A spasm of irritation crossed Mills's face. 'Stomach upset, bad headache – I don't know.'

'They'll check up on me. The *Gestapo* have already called at my home twice while I was away over the weekend.'

'Nick, you're the only one who can help us. Apart from trying to prevent Hereward and his Moorsmen being massacred by the SS, it's imperative that nothing happens to Cordington. He has a vital part to play in setting up the meeting.'

I thought swiftly. Stuff the meeting; stuff Hereward too, but I couldn't let Matty run into the middle of a pitched battle. 'I suppose I could say my mother has suddenly been taken ill. She's actually been in bed since Friday, but they won't know that.'

'Good man!' Mills began pacing the room, new energy radiating from him. 'I'll get a friendly doctor to visit her this afternoon, to make it look authentic.'

'But what happens if the *Gestapo* call at my home and find I'm not there?'

'You've gone to get medicine, fetch a relative. Anything.'

Mills clearly could not be bothered over such fine detail. He was thinking of the events now unfolding in Merricombe.

'I'll have to go home to get my bike,' I said.

'It's waiting outside. Forgive me but every minute's precious. Here, take this.' He handed me the envelope, and with it a Sauer 7.65mm automatic pistol. 'Fired one of these before?'

'No.'

'Double action, internal hammer.' Mills balanced the pistol on the palm of his hand. 'The thumb safety blocks the hammer. Once you've cocked the weapon, pressing this lever lowers the hammer safely so you can carry a round in the chamber. Simply pull straight through on the trigger to fire. Or push down on the lever to recock, if you need to take more deliberate aim. Mag holds eight. Here's a spare clip.'

'Thanks.' I put the pistol into my side pocket and scribbled a note to Stolz's ADC, explaining my absence. I hoped it would satisfy them.

I mounted the Empire Star – now with a full tank of petrol, I noticed – and set off along the coast road.

It was just over an hour later, as I turned inland, that I rounded a bend to find a convoy of brand new AEG lorries drawn up along the roadside. In an adjoining field, hundreds of SS troops were bivouacked, while SdKfz. 231 armoured cars and a dozen half-track armoured personnel carriers each hauling a light anti-tank gun were drawn up under a row of tall beech trees. The Germans were packing considerable fire power. Hereward's irregulars would be annihilated.

Feldpolizei stood across the main road ahead, ready to stop any passing traffic. I swung aside into a narrow sunken lane, hoping the Germans had not spotted me. I kept tacking north until I came to a crossroads I vaguely recognized, then headed straight on until I halted on the top of a long ridge lying less than a mile from Merricombe. As soon as I cut the engine, I caught the crackle of gunfire on the afternoon breeze. I was too late, it seemed.

From the top of an oak in the hedgerow I could clearly make out the village climbing up the side of its hill. There was Pear Trees Farm, and there the thatched roof of the Red Lion pub. Among the rows of white cottages I picked out the grey-stone school, the post office and the village shop. The slate roof of the other pub, the Packhorse, peeped out of the dip. As I watched, a Union flag was unfurled from the Norman tower of St Michael's church, and a cheer rose on the wind. I could see men running away from the outskirts of the village and over the fields towards me. From their khaki battledress I knew they were Militia. As my eye followed their route, I spotted the Chrysler shooting brake with Matty standing on its running board, peering towards the shooting.

At least four of the Militiamen were heading directly towards him but he could not see them for the hedgerows. I climbed down and kick-started the bike. It was going to be touch and go to reach Matty before those men did. As I rounded the last bend, I saw they had got there first. Three were dragging Matty from the car, while Ricky Gregan was beating him over the head with a starting handle. I pulled out my pistol and opened the throttle.

I was eighty yards away and closing fast before they saw me. As I fired twice over their heads, Matty broke free of them and dodged around the far side of his car. That gave me a nice solid target. I kept the gun rigid in front of me, sighting along my arm and the barrel. The group grew bigger and bigger. I aimed low and pressed the trigger. The man next to Gregan staggered away. I saw the flash of Gregan's pistol as he fired back. God knew where the round went. I fired twice more, then the thugs scattered and fled through the hedge. I leaped off the bike and fired at them from the bank. I didn't expect to hit anyone – I just wanted to make sure they'd keep running.

'God! The sight of you coming down that hill! I couldn't decide if you were Sir Lancelot or the Seventh Cavalry. I just knew I was really glad to see you.' Matty was pressing a handkerchief to a bloody wound on his forehead. Blood was trickling down the side of his face. He looked pale but managed a grin.

'You all right?'

'Yeh. The bastards wanted revenge and I happened to be in the wrong place. From what they said, I gather they've been ambushed.'

'I'm here to try to prevent that ambush – and keep you out of trouble.'

'You're a bit late on both counts, old chum.'

'Hereward doesn't know the half of it.' I told Matty about the SS troops just a few miles away and repeated Mills's message that once he had spoken to Hereward, he must get away from here as soon as possible.

We drove on to the village in convoy. The first person we saw was Fred Worsnipp standing in the gateway to Pear Trees Farm and holding a double-barrelled shotgun. I hid the BSA behind some hay bales in the barn, out of sight of light-fingered Moorsmen, while Fred's wife Hilda fussed over dressing Matty's wound. Once his head was bandaged, Matty and I went to search for Hereward among the villagers still gathered along the main street. The children who had been in school when the shooting had started were already reliving the battle amongst themselves.

We found Hereward inspecting five Militia corpses lying outside the church. I recognized one as a member of the gang we'd fought outside Miriam Jenner's tearoom that night. Hereward reluctantly came over to acknowledge our presence. He was a slight man in his early fifties with thinning grey hair and stooped shoulders. He seemed every inch a schoolmaster – until you saw his eyes: unblinking eyes that crackled with a coruscating intensity. Here was a man with hatred burned into his soul. Matty introduced me.

As I handed him Mills's letter, Hereward regarded me with unalloyed suspicion.

He read it quickly, glancing up at me just once,

before ripping the paper into small pieces. 'I will not be instructed by the eunuch in the harem.'

'Colonel Mills doesn't want the Germans alarmed this close to the meeting of Resistance leaders.'

'It was time those Militia scum started to get their come-uppance. But then, Mills wouldn't know that from where he sits.'

'Well, from where he sits, he knows that you have units of the *SS Germania* positioned not ten miles away. That was the other thing I came to tell you.'

'I don't believe you.'

'You will, when they arrive here to avenge their Militia chums.'

'We'll be long gone before then.' He gave me a superior look. 'That's the essence of guerrilla warfare – strike quickly and then get away, so the counter-attack falls on thin air.'

'Leaving the villagers to bear the brunt of the German anger.'

'How dare you!' The man who called himself Hereward spun on his heel and marched off. I pointed out to Matty our old adversary lying among the corpses.

'God, doesn't that seem a long time ago,' remarked Matty. 'Roy was colossal that night. Remember how he rammed Gregan's head into that wall?'

'That was only back in January.'

'It seems a lifetime since Roy died.'

'It's what? Six months? So much has happened. And nothing for the better.'

Matty gripped my shoulders with an unexpected fervour. 'But it will get better, Nick. It will. Nothing lasts for ever – you'll see.'

'I hope so.' I was surprised by Matty's unexpected intensity.

He went off to make his peace with Hereward. The Moorsmen were preparing to pull out. A line of men was passing sacks of tinned meat, tea and flour out of the village shop to be strapped onto a string of hardy ponies, while young village lads searched for cartridge cases in the gutter. I was inspecting the bullet holes around the church door when Matty rejoined me.

'I hope I've sorted that out,' he said with a wry grin. 'Now I must get on or I'll never reach Bristol tonight.'

'Are you all right to drive after that knock on your head?'

'I've had worse playing rugby.'

'Which way will you go?'

'Back south, then around by Warleggon Cross.'

'Back towards the Germans?'

'I'll be fine if I leave now. If I head north I'll have to go right round the moor, and that'll take me for ever.' He moved slowly, I thought reluctantly, towards his shooting brake.

'Take care,' I said.

'I will, and thanks again, old friend.'

'That's what mates are for.'

He gave a melancholy smile. 'Yeh, that's what mates are for.'

Matty hesitated at the driver's door. 'Sometimes we do things we don't want to do. But one big, really big, good deed wipes the slate clean, yes? What do you think?'

'I think that if you don't go now, you're going to run slap bang into the Germans.'

'It'll work out for the best, you'll see.' Matty lowered himself into the driver's seat and closed the door. He wound down the window. 'One last thing. If anything does happen, get your family away immediately. Don't let the *Gestapo* get them or you.' There was a note of desperation in his voice. 'Promise me that.'

'I promise. Are you sure you're all right?' Before I could say anything else, he slammed the Chrysler into first gear and drove off, an arm waving out of the window in farewell.

I also had to think about leaving. To make sure that I wasn't about to ride into the arms of the Militia or the SS, I set off to climb the church tower from where I could see over the surrounding countryside. I emerged through the trapdoor to find that Hereward had failed to set a lookout there. I peered over the stone parapet in the direction Matty was heading.

There he was, in the distance, making good time. I scanned the surrounding countryside, then looked again. A black Morris van was parked beside a fork in the road half a mile ahead of him. I remembered the sinister van that terrorized the city. As I watched, Matty rounded the corner before the fork and seemed to slow down. Was he heading into a trap?

The blast hurled me back across the roof of the tower to crash into the rear parapet. Forgetting all about Matty, I slowly picked myself up, my ears still ringing from the explosion.

I peeped over the side. Christ! SS troops were running across the fields towards the village. Behind them I made out the barrel of an armoured car's gun protruding from a sunken lane, pointing in my direction. There was a sharp flat report and masonry was blasted from the tower not twenty feet beneath me. I dashed down the stairs.

Out in the village street, men were desperately struggling to calm the ponies that were rearing in panic. The first mortar bomb burst in the school playground. I grabbed Hereward and made him listen as I described the German axis of attack. He coolly set about deploying his men.

The position was hopeless: the Moorsmen were outnumbered and outgunned. They had nothing to stop the armoured car, or take on the mortars or the heavy machine gun that now began tocking away. In theory, their best chance was to hold out until dark, and then melt away towards the hills. But dusk was still a long way off.

At Pear Trees Farm, now at the apex of the village defence, I found two men filling milk bottles from cans of petrol, as Fred ripped up old shirts to act as fuses.

'Where's Hilda?' I shouted.

'Inside, rolling bandages and boiling water, ready for the wounded.'

'The pair of you should get out now, while you still can. The road to the north's still open.'

'Don't be daft, lad. We was born here, we stop here.'

I ran into the farmhouse and up to what used to be our room when the three of us had stayed as boys. From there I could see the armoured car creeping along the lane towards us, a rifle squad deploying in extended order along the field to its right. They were making no effort to seek cover. The Germans clearly did not take the Moorsmen seriously. They were about to receive a lesson. First one volley, then another rang out. The Germans toppled over like ducks at a fairground. Even before the handful of fleeing survivors had reached cover, two teenage boys were already collecting rifles and an MG34 light machine gun from the fallen.

The din of battle was growing. The crackle of rifle fire played above the deeper *crump* of 81mm mortars and the flat crack of the armoured car's gun, interspersed with sharp bursts from light machine guns. The defenders had now realized that the greatest threat came from the armoured car itself, and set about tackling it with fanatical bravery. As I watched, a man rose out of the ditch and hurled a petrol bomb towards it. He was too far away and the bottle burst harmlessly on the lane. As he went to throw again, a bullet hit him. He spun around and fell. The petrol ignited, turning his body into a blazing torch.

Remorselessly the armoured car crept forward. And now, sheltering behind it, came two half-tracks packed with troops.

A teenage boy appeared out of the tall bracken at one side of the lane to lob a smoking petrol bomb under the very wheels of the armoured car. He was just ten yards away – and he was committing suicide. His body jerked as several rounds thudded into him. With his last breath, he found the strength to fling a second bomb. First one, then the other exploded directly under the armoured vehicle. The hatch flew open and a German began to climb out. He was hit instantly. The rest of the crew trapped inside struggled to clear his body out of the hatchway. They had just heaved him head first down into the lane when there was a muffled explosion and a cloud of black smoke shot out of the hatch.

The church bell pealed for the victory – but it was short-lived. A shell from an anti-tank gun in the woods half a mile away slammed into the base of the tower and the bell fell silent.

The Germans were regrouping. They had expected to simply walk into the village. Instead they'd been given a bloody nose – and now they were going to do the job properly.

It was about time I either played my part in the defence or left. Logically I should get out when I still had the chance, but I couldn't leave Fred and Hilda behind. Head and heart fought – heart won.

I was just about to quit my vantage point when I noticed something moving in an overgrown ditch alongside the barn on the edge of the farmyard. The barn was probably the oldest building on Pear Trees Farm and that was saying something. It was dilapidated and crumbling in parts, but its walls were still a good yard thick, and pierced with the defensive arrow slits of centuries past.

From the way the nettles swayed, someone was crawling along the ditch itself. They would emerge by the gate, from where they would have a perfect field of fire right across the yard to the orchard wall, now lined with Moorsmen. In short, they would soon enfilade the cornerstone of the village's defence.

I hared back downstairs and into the cobbled yard, throwing myself flat as machine-gun rounds thwacked into the wall above my head. Ducking low, I ran into the barn and up to the first floor, to peer down through one of the slits. I had judged well.

There, not ten feet below me, was a lone German trooper in a camouflage smock. He was crawling forward, pushing an MG34 with a saddle drum of ammunition ahead of him.

I could have killed him then but that machine gun and its ammunition were too great a prize to be passed up, especially when I saw he had another two drums strapped to his webbing. I slipped away down the stairs, out past the dungheap, to dive flat in the long grass at one end of the barn. The battle raged above my head as I thumbed the safety off the Sauer and waited.

After an eternity the flash suppressor at the end of the long barrel inched into my sight.

Then the German's left hand extended the bipod rest, before the barrel was pushed forward under the gate. The soldier's head, smeared with earth, began to appear from the nettles. He was a big man with a broad beak of a nose and heavy eyebrows. That was all I saw of him.

He must have sensed my presence. It all happened in slow motion.

An eyeball swivelled in my direction and his head turned towards me, his mouth opening. Then bloody craters appeared on his face. His eyeball vanished back into its splintered socket and his lower jaw shattered in a spray of blood. I stopped firing only when a neat hole appeared in his temple.

I took a deep breath, pulled open the gate,

grabbed the machine gun and dragged the German's body around the side of the barn. His comrades must have been watching, because a storm of rifle and machine-gun bullets ricocheted off the old stonework. They didn't bother me. The Germans would run out of ammunition before they penetrated those walls, but it wouldn't be long before mortar shells started crashing down.

I ripped the two extra magazines off the trooper's webbing and weighed the MG34 in my hand. I could hear the other captured machine gun firing in short bursts from near the Red Lion. There was only one place to go – back up the church tower.

I commandeered two volunteers and we puffed up to the second landing. I propped the machine gun on the trestle table there, and peered through the narrow cross-shaped window, careful not to let the barrel show. The first thing I saw was the 81mm mortar team inside the wood. I had handled an MG34 during my Intelligence duties. I remembered that you pulled the trigger at the top for semi-automatic fire, and at the bottom for fully automatic. I began by pulling at the top – not wanting the gun to run away with me. I fired three shots and saw the mortar team duck. I adjusted my aim and then let rip.

The noise inside the tower was deafening, the chamber thick with cordite fumes – but the mortar team was dead. Encouraged, I spotted four German officers in a dip in the road in front of a scout car, obviously reckoning that they could not be seen. I pressed the trigger, feeling the stock judder and thump into my shoulder, until the four of them lay still.

We dragged the table to the adjacent side of the tower just in time to see the two half-tracks charge side by side up the hill towards a lightly defended quarter of the village. The APCs had a fatal defect: their open tops left them vulnerable to grenades or, in this case, a high-sited machine gun. I raked the nearer half-track until the men inside were dead or dying. Soldiers tried desperately to climb out of the second one while it was still moving. They didn't stand a chance.

At last I was doing my bit to win the Battle of Merricombe.

Pear Trees Farm was getting a battering from German mortars but the SS were making no effort to attack under the covering fire. With an uneasy feeling, I crossed to the far side of the tower. There I found the reason. The mortars were merely a blind to tie down the farm's defenders while outflanking them. Fighting groups of SS infantry were approaching along hedgerows half a mile away. I upped the MG34's sights and fired burst after burst, until the drum ran out.

I managed to get the empty one off, but I had no idea how to reload the gun with new twin drums. I began fiddling; pushing this lever and pulling that until the short dark-haired man who had been holding the bipod said, 'Put the drum directly over the magazine holder, ahead of the trigger guard.'

'What?'

'Push down the dust cover with the centre piece. There's a spring catch . . .'

'Hang on, how do you know all this?'

'I was an armourer, sir. Duke of Cornwall's Light Infantry.'

'Right.' I had to go and warn Hereward that he was being outflanked. I turned to the man. 'There's one hundred and fifty rounds left, so choose your targets well. And move from here before the Germans work out your position.'

'Trust us, sir.'

'Best of luck.'

Back at the farmhouse, I found Hilda on her knees inside the porch, tending a young lad whose face had been laid open by a jagged piece of mortar casing.

'Where's Hereward?' I demanded.

'I've not seen him, my dear.' She wiped away the blood oozing from where the fellow's mouth had been.

'Listen, Hilda, you must get away now. The Germans are working their way around the back.'

'I can't leave the young man in this state, now can I?'

So much for Hereward's guerrilla leadership. He'd been caught out by the speed with which the *SS*

Germania had reacted. He was now about to be trapped, forced to fight it out to the last man – and woman.

'Hilda, please. Everyone involved with the Moorsmen should get out of here.'

'Just put your finger on this piece of lint here, will you, Nick, dear? I'll try to fix a bandage around . . . There, my handsome. Rest easy now.'

I bent down over the man lying on the flagstones as Hilda reached for a pair of scissors from the medical kit she had assembled on the stone bench inside the porch. The next moment I was pitched forward head first. A blast of hot air rushed over me; a brilliant white light and then a deep gentle sea rolled over my head and all was quiet.

I opened my eyes on a deep deep blackness framed in crimson. There was a solid quality to that darkness. Phrases whirled around my head: jet black . . . as black as Newgate's knocker . . . black as pitch, as the ace of spades, as coal. Coal would be the best, I decided, because it possessed a solid quality – just like the darkness enclosing me now. I was trapped in a seam of coal, preserved in time – waiting to be found by future generations when the war was over.

I moved my head and winced in pain. I realized that I was lying on my back with my hands folded over my chest.

Had I been buried alive? Panic flashed through me. I pushed up against an imaginary coffin lid, but my hand touched nothing more than cool damp air. I sobbed in relief.

The movement sent blood clots weaving across my eyes in an amazing kaleidoscope of purples, royal blues, deep burgundies and rich browns. I closed my eyes to gather myself. I must have fallen asleep, for when I opened them again I felt well enough to sit up. As I did so, a wave of sickness swept over me – but then I saw the tiny flame of a night light. It dawned on my aching brain that I must be in the priest's hole at Pear Trees Farm. Next to the light was a pitcher of water and a chunk of bread. I couldn't face food but the water was welcome. I splashed some on my face and felt a tender lump above my right eye. Slowly, it came back to me: I had cracked my head when a mortar bomb had exploded behind me. Fred and Hilda must have hidden me in here.

My bladder was full, which meant I was going to have to move. Gingerly I rose to my feet, putting out a hand to steady myself as the world lurched and swayed. Once the giddy spell passed, I picked up the night light and took a step towards the door. I eased it open a fraction and listened hard. Silence. I stepped into the hall, thinking how the house felt unoccupied.

Through the open front door I saw a faint red glow in the sky. I reckoned it must be dusk.

It was only when I reached the porch that I found it was night and there was something on fire beyond the barn. I smelled acrid woodsmoke and, amid the distant crackle of burning timber, there came the deep rumble of a roof collapsing. A firestorm of sparks rose up into the darkness.

There were no voices to hear. No sound of gunfire. Where *was* everyone?

As I emptied my bladder in the garden, something hanging from a pear tree, dark and solid, caught my eye. It was turning slowly. I buttoned up and moved towards the tree. I had begun to reach up when I realized it was the body of Fred Worsnipp. Oh, God!

Hilda hung from the next tree, staring at me, her open eyes bulging and her tongue lolling out of one side of her mouth. She had suffocated to death slowly.

I fell to my knees and threw up, vomiting until my stomach ached with the effort of dredging up bitter juices. Finally I wiped my eyes and felt a terrible coldness descend over me.

Revenge.

An unearthly clarity of vision and purpose: revenge on the scum who had done this. Revenge without mercy; without consideration or cost.

Revenge.

But first I had to do the decent thing by my friends. I fetched a short stepladder and a carving knife, noticing that Hilda's bandages and the bottle of witch hazel were still sitting on the porch shelf. There was no sign of the wounded Moorsman.

It was not easy to lower the two bodies. I tried to take Hilda's weight as I cut the rope, but it snapped suddenly, and sent me tumbling back onto the grass with her corpse on top of me. My mouth set in a silent screaming rictus, I lowered Fred and laid him next to Hilda, on the land that had been theirs. Then I freed their necks from the terrible knots. Fred and Hilda had saved my life. They had hidden me away safely and then gone back to face the German onslaught.

I thought for a moment that I should say a prayer over their bodies, but I found I couldn't remember one – and anyway, it would have been a profanity in my state of bloodlust.

My Sauer pistol had vanished. I went to look in Fred's gun cabinet but it was empty. Surprisingly, the house had not been looted. In fact it had not been touched at all. I slipped a kitchen knife, whetted over the years until the blade was concave and razor-sharp, into my belt. As an afterthought, I lifted a sickle off the barn wall. Then I crept out round the orchard wall, through the wicker gate – and stepped into hell.

The whole village was ablaze, red and yellow flames shooting from its thatched roofs. Fiery displays of sparks erupted as each roof collapsed. Glowing pieces of straw floated in the dark smoke clouds rolling up the slope from the blazing cottages lower down the hill. The air smelled heavily of cordite and sulphur.

And everywhere bodies were hanging like obscene fruit.

My mind refused to register them at first; it simply refused to admit what I was seeing. But now that my brain had acknowledged the nearest body hanging from the chestnut tree on the green, I saw all the others. I screamed again: a primitive scream that shook my body and left me trembling and drenched in sweat. By the flickering light of the burning cottages I made out corpse after corpse, hanging from branches, out of bedroom windows, from telegraph posts and even from the awning of the village shop. Men, women . . . a child hung from the milepost.

The good folk of Merricombe had been massacred.

I stumbled on with no thought of concealment. Every step revealed new horrors. Mrs Carkeel, the teacher, suspended from the gateway that led into her school playground; old Luke Skitgate, with his one leg, lynched from the window of his tiny cottage. Four men swung together from the wrought-iron balcony of the Red Lion.

The sickly-sweet smell of roasted human flesh came from where the body of Mrs Treburley, the widow, cooked in the flames licking out of her living-room window. Outside the Packhorse, the landlord,

Wally Wishbourne, a gentle giant with a bushy grey beard, swung from his own pub sign.

There was no sign of the Germans, but from inside the pub I heard the bizarre sound of shouting and laughter. At first I couldn't believe my ears but I peered through the window and my heart lurched at the sight of Ricky Gregan and his Militia cronies crowded into the small public bar, drinking heavily.

It was a simple rectangular room with mismatched chairs, some settles and tables, and lit by two oil lamps under a low ceiling. The drinks were fetched in from the taproom at the rear, and although Wally had officially held only a beer and cider licence, he boasted a fine array of malt whiskies available to those who knew to ask.

Three iron bars had been welded across the street window after someone – Wally swore it was gypsies – had taken out a pane of glass one night and stolen most of that prized whisky. This had happened back in 1920, but to have heard him talk you'd have thought it was last week. With a stab of sorrow I realized that Wally would never tell that story again.

The Militia must have plundered his stock, for there were bottles of whisky on every table. I saw Gregan guzzling greedily from the neck of a bottle of Glenlivet.

I stole around to the back of the pub, and stopped dead at the sight of one Militiaman crossing the yard towards the lavatory. I gave him a minute and then followed him, making plenty of noise so that he'd think I was one of his comrades. The man, a deep shadow in the darkness, was chuckling drunkenly to himself.

'We've shown those bastards, eh?' he slurred as I entered. 'We strung the fuckers up good and proper.'

I stood close behind him. 'Yeh,' I whispered. 'But you're dead, too.'

'What?'

I slapped my left hand over his mouth and drove the knife into his belly, turning it this way and that before wrenching it out. Then I yanked the man's head back and stabbed upwards into his throat. As he slid to the floor, his face ending up in the trough of piss, I could only think it a shame that he had died so quickly.

It was also a shame that he wasn't carrying a gun.

Outside I noticed, for the first time, that lights were moving about up on the moors. I assumed it was the SS pursuing the last of the Moorsmen. At least it might mean that some of them had escaped.

The clarity that had possessed me when I had first found Fred and Hilda's bodies returned. I could not kill all the Militia in the bar with just my knife and sickle – but there were other ways.

I knew the pub and its outbuildings well. I knew that in the garage I would find a 1928 Bentley Tourer, raised up on bricks, and behind it Wally's stock of petrol. Empty beer bottles were stored in the outhouse behind the taproom so I just needed rags. I slashed the dead man's shirt into strips before carrying a crate of empty flagons to the back of the garage and setting to work. I filled the first four bottles with petrol and left their tops off. The next two I stuffed with strips of cloth before pouring in the petrol.

As I emerged with the crate, I made out another Militiaman pissing just outside the back door. He was only a yard from where I had left the sickle. If he glanced down, he was bound to spot it. Instead he looked over at me.

In his eyes I was just a comrade fetching another crate of beer to the party.

In my eyes he was dead.

'More booze? That's the stuff.'

'Yeh.' I walked right up next to him, put down the crate, then picked up the sickle. 'Look.'

He glanced down to his left as I swept the blade upwards in a backhanded sweep. The sickle was sharper than I'd thought. It sliced through his throat to leave his head hanging by a flap of skin. I leaped back to avoid the fountain of blood.

I left the body there and went back to check out the blazing street. No one was visible: the inhabitants were dead and the Germans were still out on the moors. That just left the Militia – and me. I placed the petrol bombs ready under the public-bar window, making sure the cloth wicks in the bottles were well saturated with petrol. I tested that my lighter worked, and then found a heavy stone.

A passageway ran right through the inn from the front door to the back yard. The public bar was on the left, an unused parlour on the right. Both had solid doors that opened outwards. In summer, Wally used to leave all the doors open, securing them with a couple of wooden wedges under the bottom of each door. As naturally as I could, I strolled into the passageway to check those wedges were still there. They were.

Now all I needed was luck.

I closed the bar-room door and quickly slipped the two wedges under it.

'Hey. Don't do that. It's too bloody warm in here,' protested someone from the bar.

'Don't fuck about.' A Militiaman rattled the door-knob. 'Open up.'

Everything now depended on speed. I heeled the wedges firmly into place and ran outside to peer in the window. The Militia had clustered by the bar-room door. I smashed a glass pane with the stone and pushed two of the open flagons through the window. Petrol sloshed out of them over the floor.

I put my lighter to one of my improvised wicks. For a second the cloth would not catch, then a tiny blue flame appeared; it hesitated and almost went out before spreading so quickly that I only just had time to hurl it through the window before it exploded. There were shouts of alarm from inside as I threw in another open bottle, neck first.

There was a whoosh and I saw the dancing flames reflected on the bar ceiling. I didn't really need the other petrol bomb – but I lit it and chucked it in anyway.

A chair crashed into the window, smashing away the rest of the glass but making no impact on the metal bars. As Gregan's head appeared, and he recognized me, sheer hatred filled his face.

'You bastard,' he yelled.

Gregan thrust an old British army revolver through the bars and leaned out to get a shot at me, leering in triumph as he saw that I was trapped between the window and the porch. It was an unpleasant grin, a smirk of anticipation.

I swung the sickle down in a fast arc, slicing cleanly through his wrist. Before Gregan could scream, his hand landed on the ground still clutching the gun. But when he *did* scream, it was a scream such as I had never heard before, rising up from his belly until it emerged from his throat in a piercing howl of pain and terror. It seemed to go on and on. I picked up the severed hand, pulled its warm fingers off the revolver, and hurled the hand back into the room.

More screams from the inside. The door was now rocking under the assault from within. I fired one shot through it at chest height and another at an angle, then leaped aside as a volley of shots came back.

At the window, three pairs of hands were trying desperately to work loose the top bar. I stood flat against the outside wall and slashed at them with my sickle. My aim was a bit off, but I severed three fingers and cut deeply into a few more. Out of the pandemonium, a fusillade of shots flew harmlessly into the night.

Retreating to the safety of darkness on the far side of the road, I saw that the bar room had turned into a Dantesque vision, with grotesque fiery shadows dancing wildly on the ceiling, accompanied by hideous screams and the stench of burning flesh.

It was time to go.

I emptied the revolver into the room. I missed the men but shattered one of the lamps hanging from the ceiling so that its paraffin spilled over their shoulders. An even better result.

Up the hill, I paused and looked back at the Packhorse. By now flames were roaring out of the bar window. I remember I smiled.

Hilda's favourite white and gold lilies were in bloom along the path leading up to the farmhouse, together with some delphiniums and blue hollyhocks. I picked a few of each and laid them on the bodies of my friends. I didn't know what else I could do.

My BSA was still safe in the barn. As I wheeled it

out into the lane, a wave of utter tiredness washed over me and I realized my head was throbbing fit to burst. My clothes reeked of petrol and I was splattered with blood. Altogether I felt hollow and sick. Under a canopy of stars, and the emptiness of heaven, I set off back to town – at that moment not caring if I made it or not.

27

I rode back in a daze. There wasn't another traveller to be seen on the roads – or, if there was, I didn't notice them. On the edge of the city I headed through the back streets towards Angel's current home, near the Ness. I left the bike in an alley and rang her doorbell. A faint light came on upstairs and then the house returned to darkness. I was about to pull the bell again when Angel called out softly.

'Who's there?'

'It's me, Nick. I need to—'

The door was already opening.

I waited at the entrance to her living room while Angel, in a blue Chinese silk wrap, checked that the curtains were tightly closed. She switched on a standard lamp, took one look at me, and exclaimed, 'God! What's happened to you? You should see yourself.'

She gently manoeuvred me in front of a mirror. She was right. I almost scared myself at the sight of the amount of dried blood and grime over my face.

Angel sniffed loudly. 'You need a shower.'

'I'm sorry. I shouldn't have come here . . .'

'Don't be silly. Get into the bathroom and out of those clothes. I'll fetch you a drink.'

'Have you heard about Merricombe?' I asked.

'No. Let me make a pot of tea, then you can tell me.'

'Anything stronger?'

'Whisky?'

I had a fleeting vision of Gregan raising the Glenlivet to his lips. 'Whisky's fine.'

The shower was only tepid but I did not care. Angel put a glass of whisky within reach and scooped up my soiled jacket and trousers. I stood under the trickle, feeling both the dirt and the tension wash away. It was only when I started shivering with cold that I turned off the water.

In the living room, I found Angel sponging my trousers with a damp cloth. She handed me a blanket. 'You shouldn't really be drinking whisky. I think you're suffering from shock. So, tell me what happened?'

I flopped onto the sofa. 'How much do you already know?'

'Only that you set off yesterday to try to persuade Hereward to call off his ambush – and keep Matty out of trouble. We know Matty's all right. He's arrived safely in Bristol.'

'Thank God! The last time I saw him, he was about to run into what looked like that Morris van with the blacked-out windows. Just then they attacked. But if he's okay, it must have been some other van. It was a long way away.'

'Why don't you start from the beginning?'

I did as she said, and Angel interrupted only once. 'Was Hereward among the dead?'

'I didn't see his body but there were so many.'

After a while I dried up. The night weighed heavily upon me. My exhaustion must have shown, for Angel urged me on.

'Who do *you* think was responsible for the massacre, the Militia or the SS?'

'There certainly weren't any Germans in the village and I did hear that Militia bastard say, "We've strung the fuckers up good and proper."'

'That's enough now. You're worn out. Come on.' In the bedroom she pulled back the covers. 'In you go.'

I climbed between the cool sheets, giving a huge sigh of contentment as Angel slid in besides me. It was all so innocent. She kissed my forehead before turning out the light and guiding my head to her breast. I was asleep in seconds.

Angel woke me with a cup of tea at seven o'clock. She must have been up for some time, for my trousers and jacket lay neatly pressed on the chair by the bed.

As I sat up, she said seriously, 'It's probably not the right time to say this, but I need your help to put Frisch on a submarine tonight. There'll be more German coastal patrols out now that they're at war with the United States, so I'd appreciate it if you rode ahead of us.'

'Of course.'

'What would I do without you?'

My sister Joan gave me a frosty glare as I walked in. 'Were you responsible for that doctor calling in to see mum yesterday afternoon?'

'Sort of. Was he any good?'

'He told me what I already knew: that she's suffered an intolerable shock to her system and this is her way of coping with it.' Joan cut a thin slice off a grey loaf and slid it under the grill. 'He gave her some sedatives – though God knows where he got them from. He said he'll be back this afternoon. Who is he, anyway?'

'I've never even met him,' I answered truthfully. 'Sis, has anyone else been here?'

'If you mean the *Gestapo*, no – not this time.' Joan scraped up some dried-out tea leaves from between two sheets of newspaper and put them in the pot. Her movements were conducted with barely suppressed anger. 'You'll playing a very dangerous game, Nick, dashing off here, there and everywhere on that motorbike. They'll get you sooner or later, you know that, don't you? They *will* get you in the end.' She slammed a butter dish down next to the toast. 'I don't know where you are from one day to the next.' Joan slumped into a chair, put her head in her hands, and began sobbing. *'It's not good enough, Nick.'*

I jumped up and put my arm around her. 'I'll stop. I promise.' But even as I spoke I remembered agreeing to accompany Angel on an operation that very night.

Joan pulled a handkerchief from her sleeve and dabbed at her eyes. 'Eat your toast while it's hot. You don't want to waste that lovely butter.'

I cut the slice in half and offered her a piece. 'I'm being thoughtless.'

'No. I'm sorry. It's just one thing after another. If I'm not worrying about mum, I'm worrying about you. It's always a struggle to get enough to eat. I seem to spend my life queuing. Sometimes it all gets to me.'

Her life had clearly got harder since she'd broken with Leech. 'Listen, sis, it's not going to last for ever – not now the Yanks are in the war.'

'How long? Two years? Five? And will you be alive when it's all over?'

Remembering Matty's strange words of warning, I took Joan's hand. 'Let's talk about what you *must* do if the *Gestapo* get me, all right?'

Joan's hand shot to her mouth. 'Nick, don't even think it.'

'Are you still in touch with Ted's sister in Wales?'

'Yes, I had a letter from her last week. She suggested we go and stay there next month. Apparently, there's a self-contained cottage at the back that she doesn't use.'

'Right. If anything happens, take mum and David there. I'll get you false identity papers. Keep a bag packed and make sure you've set money aside for the train tickets.'

'You're serious, aren't you?'

'Very.'

I paused as I heard a sound in the passage and a second later David entered, yawning his head off. I explained that I was going to organize false identity papers for his mum, gran and himself and that he had to remember his new name. He took it all in his stride.

We agreed a code word – Churchill. If someone phoned the farm when he was working there, and left that message, David was to leave immediately and go the maritime station where he would meet up with his mother. I would make sure that Bert Latcham's wife Bessie, who now normally answered the farm phone in Matty's absence, was in on the secret.

'You listening, Joan?'

She repeated my orders verbatim. I'd forgotten how good a mind she had – when she chose to use it. But then she added, 'Nick, be real. I can't afford even one rail ticket, never mind three.'

'Sis, that is not a problem.' I took her two hands

in mine and looked her in the eye. 'I promise you, money is not a problem.'

I meant it. If I was putting my neck on the line for the Resistance the least they could do was to take care of my family. I was getting a funny feeling about the future. And it was not funny as in ha-ha.

Angel was surprised to see me back so soon. From the way she was unpinning a small hat, she looked as if she had just got in herself.

'I remembered something Matty said at Merricombe, about me making sure my family were ready to disappear if anything happened to me,' I told her.

'Why would he say that?'

I shrugged. 'He said a few things I didn't understand. But can you arrange false ID papers and residence permits for Joan, my mum and David? I've written down their dates of birth and descriptions, and where they'll be staying. And rail tickets for two adults and a child to Shrewsbury? And they'll need some money – say £100.'

'You don't want much, do you?'

'By teatime.'

Angel was about to protest. Then she saw I was serious. 'The money and the tickets are no problem but I'm not sure we can get the documents done in that short a time.'

'Try, please.'

'You're a hard man, Nick Penny,' she said in a mock Irish accent before giving me a kiss on my cheek. 'Take care of yourself. I don't like the mood you're in today.'

'It's called surviving,' I replied.

My excuse for being absent from duty the day before was met with sneering disbelief from Abetz. But then the first whispers of the Merricombe massacre began filtering through. The abrupt arrival of a dust-covered SS colonel with *Germania* on his cuff sent the rumour factory into overdrive.

Five minutes later, a grim-faced Stolz and the colonel marched past me towards the *Gestapo* wing. The colonel was saying, 'They were still alive when we left . . .'

By mid-morning Sir Reginald Launcestone and Horace Smeed were closeted with Tickell and Bearup.

The Germans were clearly rattled. An SS goon came running along the corridor with a leaflet in his hand, to disappear into Stolz's office. Seconds later Abetz slapped the leaflet down in front of me.

'Translate this.'

German troops have massacred more than one hundred men, women and children in the peaceful village of Merricombe, in an act of shame and infamy that will ring down the centuries.

Units of the SS regiment Germania attacked the defenceless villagers who were going about their everyday business. Whole families were lynched outside their own homes. Others were locked into the public house and burned to death. Every inhabitant of Merricombe has been killed. Every house razed to the ground.

We shall not forget these horrific murders. One day – and that day is fast approaching – those responsible will be called to answer for their crimes against the English People, and against humanity.

The United States has joined our fight for right and justice. There can be only one result. We shall conquer the dark forces of evil that now infest our land.

Have courage. Keep Faith.

God save the King.

I guessed this was what Angel had been doing earlier that morning, using the new printing press from Liverpool. I wrote a translation and handed it to Abetz. Launcestone and Tickell had already requested a meeting with Stolz, but he was keeping them waiting. I was finally summoned to the conference room at lunchtime. Stolz sat on one side of the table next to the dour SS *Germania* colonel. But I was struck by the different reactions of the Englishmen present. Tickell looked flushed and angry, Launcestone stern and magisterial, while Smeed seemed embarrassed even to be there, an apologetic look on his shrewd face. Bearup was Bearup – weighty and immobile.

Stolz began speaking. 'We are still trying to establish exactly what happened yesterday . . .'

'We know what happened,' said Tickell shortly. 'You Germans were responsible for the deaths of a hundred innocent people, including women and children.'

'Do not interrupt me,' shouted Stolz, eyes blazing. 'You do not *know* they were killed by Germans any more than you *know* they were innocent. You know *nothing.*' He slammed his fist down on the table. 'Colonel Galen, tell us what *you* know of yesterday's events.'

Galen was a no-nonsense professional soldier with a lean sunburnt face and cold eyes.

'We first learned of an incident involving the Militia and a terrorist band when retreating members of the Militia came upon our advance units. The Militia had been ambushed, losing five men killed and another three wounded. The terrorists had taken over the village of Merricombe and illegally raised the Union flag.'

'What did you do?'

'Initially, I dispatched half a company to retake

the village. Unexpectedly stiff resistance meant that we had to commit a much larger force. We drove out the terrorists only after a considerable battle, losing a number of officers and men. The village was secured around dusk and SS units immediately set off in pursuit of the remnants of the terrorist band that had withdrawn towards the moors.'

'Terrorist casualties?'

'We counted fifteen dead. These were the only dead English I saw. The terrorists also left behind three seriously wounded men, who were treated by our medics.'

'If you did not kill the villagers, who did?'

'I assume it was the British Militia following on our heels.'

Tickell cleared his throat. 'Why don't you ask them?'

'They are all dead.' Colonel Galen pointed to the Resistance leaflet. 'Those burned to death in the local inn were in fact all Militiamen. It appears that a breakaway group of terrorists circled round back into the village and trapped them. The bodies of two other Militiamen found near the inn had been mutilated.'

'Are all the Militia dead?'

'Two of them were still alive when I left, but they won't last long. Both have ninety per cent burns.'

'According to this leaflet, the whole village has been razed to the ground,' said Tickell.

'One or two houses were on fire when my men passed through, but we did not torch the village. Neither do my men make a practice of murdering civilians.'

'Your men did not assist a third party to lynch anyone?' continued Tickell in his dry legal way.

'I have already said so.' The colonel bristled. 'And as an officer in the SS, I am not accustomed to having my word doubted.'

'Quite so,' rumbled Sir Reginald. 'The chap's given his word. That's enough for me.'

'The villagers would have been involved in the ambush of the Militia and then in resisting our attempt to retake the place?' demanded Stolz.

'Inevitably,' replied Galen.

'If Merricombe had been illegally aiding and harbouring terrorists, then it got what it deserved,' declared Smeed.

'One more question, colonel,' persisted Tickell. 'You would categorically deny on oath that your men were in any way responsible for the murder of the villagers?'

'Sometimes in the heat of battle ... There may have been the odd incidents where innocent people were shot in error. These things happen.'

'But your men did not hang any of the villagers after the battle?'

'For the last time, no.' Galen was growing impatient.

'Quite, quite. Very decent of you to explain matters,' murmured Sir Reginald.

'It's clear that the village people were in league with the Moorsmen,' summed up Stolz. 'They were summarily dealt with by the British Militia, who were then murdered in turn by returning terrorists. There will be a press blackout on the whole incident. The SS will bury the bodies and level the village. The area for ten miles around will be declared a prohibited zone. That is all.'

'But you can't just draw a line under it and say that's that,' protested Tickell, ignoring Launcestone and Smeed's frowns. 'The Supreme Council cannot condone the arbitrary deaths of the villagers . . .'

'I don't give a damn what your Supreme Council can or cannot condone.' Stolz rose to his feet. 'This meeting is closed.'

Once the Germans had stalked out of the room, Smeed turned on Tickell.

'You overstepped your authority, Tickell. Remember you are merely the secretary of the Supreme Council, you do not speak for the Council itself. It was impertinent, the way you cross-examined that colonel as though you didn't believe him.'

The Lord Lieutenant grunted in agreement.

'Damned shame this all had to happen so near to the Coronation,' murmured Sir Reginald to Smeed as they left the room. Bearup followed silently behind them.

'This is a bad business, Penny,' said Tickell when we were alone. He removed his pince-nez and pinched the top of his nose with a thumb and forefinger.

'At least you tried.' I felt an unaccustomed sympathy for the old man.

'I am a lawyer. I obey the law.'

'And if that law is rotten and corrupt?'

But he merely shook his head sadly, and walked away.

I left the *Feldkommandantur* at five to go and meet Angel.

'Do you know an abandoned fishing village called Lostmaids?' she asked.

'Of course. That's where we saw off Niels Bohr. A radio operator landed at the same time.'

'He was one of those betrayed by that bitch Sara,' said Angel bitterly. 'Here's your new ID and curfew pass. Frisch will be posing as a doctor on his way to see a sick patient. I'm borrowing a car to pick him up so I'll meet you at Hayrick Crossroads at nine-thirty.'

'You want me to ride ahead?'

'That's the idea. Now look what I've got for your family: three train tickets to Shrewsbury and one hundred pounds in fivers. And – tarrah – three new identity cards.'

'You're brilliant.'

'Yes, aren't I,' grinned Angel.

Joan was not as delighted with Angel's gift as I had expected.

'I don't care for the name "Joyce Gubbins",' she complained as she inspected the identity cards. 'It makes me sound like a parlour maid.'

'What's wrong with that?'

Joan was silent for a moment before blurting out, 'It's all right for you to talk about moving to Wales at the drop of a hat, but this is my home. You can't expect me to just walk out of the front door and hand the key to the nearest stranger.'

'Sis, you may *never* need to move from here. Let's hope you don't – but it can't do any harm to be prepared. Can it?'

'All right,' she conceded ungraciously. 'I'll try to sort it out tomorrow.'

I went upstairs to our mother's room. She was propped up in bed, staring straight ahead and unnervingly still.

'Hello, mum.'

She did not answer. I thought again how frail and wasted she looked. The flesh had left her face, setting her cheek- and jawbones into sharper relief against her parchment skin. I took her hot dry hand and squeezed it gently. There was no answering pressure.

'How are you feeling?' She did not answer. 'Mum, mum, can you hear me?'

Feebly, she turned her head. The corners of her lips rose in a semblance of a smile. I kissed her forehead and left.

Downstairs, Joan cocked an interrogative eyebrow. 'Well?'

'I don't know if she's still in there.'

'Quite! And you want me to take her off to mid-Wales. I'll be lucky to get her downstairs.'

28

I arrived at Hayrick Crossroads precisely on time. Within thirty seconds, Angel arrived in a small car. I set off in front, remembering that the last time I had driven this route, Sara had followed infuriatingly slowly and had kept flashing her headlights. Now I realized that she had been trying to attract the Germans' attention.

Angel had warned that the Germans had been stepping up their patrols since the declaration of war on the United States, so I was glad when I began the descent down the winding lane towards the ghost village. As we approached it, the moon came out from behind the lamb's-tail clouds to bathe the crumbling cottage walls in silver light. The trees seemed to have closed in even tighter around the ruins since I was last there. I pulled up in the moon-shadow of the church, and listened to the sea murmuring in the stillness.

I went over to Frisch. 'Ready for the last part of your adventure?'

'Absolutely. I've been kept a virtual prisoner since

I last saw you.' He took my arm and we strolled over to the quayside as the moon disappeared. 'I can't stop thinking about Jacob Jenner. Have you heard any news?'

'No. Angel would know more than I would.'

'She says she doesn't know, either. The Germans have sealed off the whole of Salisbury Plain.' He sighed. 'You know, Nick, I can't come to terms with the fact that men have died for my sake. The weight of their sacrifice is too much.'

'Just get that bomb built.'

Angel joined us. 'Rendezvous in twenty minutes. We'd better get the lights in place.'

'You won't need them.'

We spun around at the sound of the new voice. A woman's voice. From the deep shadow of a derelict boathouse Sara emerged, a pistol in her hand.

'But you're dead.' I gawped at her stupidly.

'No. I'm very much alive,' said Sara with a smirk.

'Won't you introduce me?' inquired Frisch mildly.

'She's a *Gestapo* agent,' said Angel coldly. 'I don't think we know her real name.'

Sara stepped forward. '*Herr* Frisch, I have come to escort you back to the Fatherland.'

'That's very kind of you,' he replied evenly. 'But I'd rather go to Canada.'

I admired his calmness. I was still rooted in shock.

'That is not possible. The *Reich* needs you.'

'But I assure you I do not need the *Reich*.'

Sara had not changed: her eyes still searched restlessly under her arched brows; her dark brown hair reached to her shoulders. But maybe there was an added hint of cruelty around the mouth. Maybe it had always been there.

'Where are the rest of your *Gestapo* friends?' inquired Angel.

'On a wild-goose chase to the north coast. I knew if there was a rendezvous it would be here.'

'But you didn't tell Stolz?'

'Why should I?' Sara shrugged. 'If they chose to be stupid . . .'

Angel began fiddling with the cigarette holder that had appeared in her hand. 'May the condemned be allowed a last cigarette?' she asked.

'Oh, you're not going to die – not yet, anyway.'

'I don't understand.' I finally found my voice. 'I went to your funeral.'

'I know. I watched you from a distance. I was most moved.'

'But how did you ever fool Matty?'

'Are you really that stupid! We faked my death as a cover for Cordington. You owe your lives to him – or, should I say, your lives so far.'

'How come?'

'Cordington insisted that Stolz leave you alone. It was one of his bargains. He was always making bargains.'

'But I thought Glass—'

'He could have done absolutely nothing if Stolz had really wanted to arrest you.'

'But why did Matty turn traitor?'

Angel had the cigarette holder in her mouth now, as natural as anything. Frisch was standing as if spellbound.

'He's Jewish – on his mother's side. After he was taken prisoner, he was given the option of being transferred to a special camp for Jewish officers, in Germany, or coming back home as a *Greifer*.'

'A claw?'

'That's what we call those we turn. It was a wise decision on his part. They work Jews literally to death in Germany's labour camps. Your Matty is a true survivor but, in a way, he's loyal to his friends.'

'He betrayed Roy.'

'No, that was a separate *Abwehr* operation. Cordington was fortunate not to have been caught that night.'

'So Matty's been a traitor from the start?'

'We brought him back here to insert him into the Resistance. We couldn't believe our luck when we found that the local leader was one of his closest friends. Cordington almost pulled out then. He wasn't expecting you and Roy Locke to be involved. We had to remind him firmly of the alternative awaiting him in Germany.'

'You bastards.'

'Cordington tried to mislead Stolz over Dr Frisch's

embarkation point, but I sensed that he was trying to protect you, Nick, as always.'

'You could not have known that Dr Frisch was anywhere near here,' countered Angel.

'The descriptions of the man and woman who called at Dr Frisch's home and the Physics Department matched you two. The *Luftwaffe* van was traced as far as Bristol, and you sent that other scientist to Canada from here. It all added up.'

Angel coughed, put a hand up to cover her mouth and coughed again.

Sara slapped a hand over her right eye.

I leaped forward and knocked the gun from her hand. Even before I could scoop it up, Angel had a pistol pointed at Sara.

'Quick, Nick. Set up the torches.'

Frisch and I ran across to the ruined church.

As I switched on the torches, I was rewarded by a distant light signalling back in Morse. Within minutes I heard the sound of an outboard motor approaching. Frisch and I shook hands.

I went to guard Sara as the dinghy swept alongside the old jetty. Frisch was helped on board while Angel spoke urgently to the officer in charge.

Sara seemed unperturbed by her plight. 'So what are you going to do now? Shoot me in cold blood?'

She took a step forward, then another. I gripped the pistol tighter.

'One more step and you're dead.'

'I don't think so.'

'I do.' Angel now stood at my side as the sound of the outboard faded out to sea. 'Anyway, you're dead already.'

'I have a habit of coming back to life,' mocked Sara.

'Not this time. That thing that hit you in the eye was a poisoned dart. You'll be dead in ten minutes.'

'I don't believe you.'

'You should,' I said. 'Remember Sir Rufus Forty. The *Gestapo* suspected that he'd been poisoned. Now you know. He was.'

'You . . .' Sara spat at Angel.

'How much did Matty tell you?'

'Everything. He told us *everything*. But he was sentimental in his friendship. He even gave you that balaclava you wore on the airfield raid so that the guards would know to miss you.' Sara rubbed her eyelid as her voice grew desperate. 'Help me and I won't tell anyone I've seen you. Just give me the antidote.'

'I don't believe Matty betrayed Pip Cartwright,' I said.

'That was down to me,' admitted Sara. 'Please do something.'

'There isn't an antidote,' said Angel.

Suddenly, Sara hurled herself at me, going for my eyes with long fingernails. I flung up my left arm to protect my face, and pulled the trigger with my other hand. Nothing happened. I staggered back under the onslaught – realizing that I had neglected to thumb off the safety catch. As I fumbled to locate it, Sara scratched at my face.

'Get away from her, Nick,' yelled Angel.

With an effort, I pushed Sara away. Angel fired, twice. Sara gave a surprised look and slid to the ground.

'Why didn't you just shoot?' demanded Angel.

'I couldn't find the safety catch,' I confessed breathlessly.

I knelt by Sara's body. One bullet had gone straight through her heart. 'She's dead,' I announced needlessly.

'A speedier end than she would have given us,' murmured Angel as she began searching Sara's coat pockets. She found a *Gestapo* identity disc and a warrant card in the name of Gertrud Daranowski Klink.

'Shame you don't look a bit more like her,' I said as Angel pocketed them.

'It'll do. No one's going to risk inspecting a *Gestapo* ID too closely.'

'Except other *Gestapo*.'

I scouted the surrounding area as Angel continued to search through Sara's pockets. A hundred yards away I came across the Morris van with the blacked-out windows that had recently terrorized the town. So Sara had been spying on us from inside it all the time. I kicked out at it in my anger.

'We'll return my car and use her van,' Angel decided as we carried Sara's body into an old underground crypt. 'I'm afraid you're going to have to dump your bike in the sea.'

'How am I going to get around?'

'Nick, love, this is the end,' said Angel softly. 'Once the *Gestapo* discover that Sara's really dead, they'll hunt us down. We can't ever go back. Not now.'

'Why didn't we just get on the submarine with Frisch, then?' Even as I spoke I realized that to have done so would have meant abandoning my family. I couldn't do that.

'Because we've got to warn the others of Matty's treachery. We've got to get ourselves to London.'

'Why?'

'To stop Mills telling Cordington where the Resistance meeting's being held.'

'Why would he tell Matty?'

Angel sighed impatiently. 'Mills believed it'd be impossible to maintain security if the twenty or so Resistance leaders knew in advance where they are to meet. Instead, they're being picked up individually as they arrive in London by a handful of trusted officers. They'll take the leaders to the safe house –

once they've made sure that they're not being followed by the *Gestapo*. Cordington is one of those escorting officers. Mills is briefing him and the others just after midday tomorrow. We plan to have all the Resistance leaders assembled by the end of the Coronation, three o'clock at the very latest.'

'Why don't you phone Mills?'

'He's in transit at the moment. I know where he's *due* to be tomorrow morning. I'm meant to phone him just after noon, but if his plans change and I miss him, then it'll be too late for me to set off.'

'Can't you leave a message at the safe house?'

'Nick, sweetheart. That's the whole point. Mills is not going to reveal the location of the safe house until the last minute so no one can betray its location. *I* don't know where it is.'

'I can't just desert my family like this.'

'I'll make sure that, first thing in the morning, they are all put on a train to safety. I'll organize someone to meet them in mid-Wales and take them to wherever they're staying. Does that put your mind at rest?'

'I suppose so.'

'Nick, I *need* you.' Angel gripped my arm.

'All right.' I wheeled the Empire Star out to the end of the jetty, took a deep breath of remorse and consigned it to the sea. As the bike disappeared beneath the water, I remembered that it really belonged to Matty. I couldn't bring myself to think about his treachery. Just to begin to do so brought a sick ache to the pit of my stomach.

A logbook identified the van as belonging to the *Gestapo*. The vehicle was going to be a godsend to us, until the *Gestapo* discovered it was missing – then it would become a death trap. I just hoped we would know when to dump it.

Angel led us in convoy back to a house in the new suburbs where the car's owner turned out to be the local Resistance quartermaster. Within minutes, Angel had organized new identities for the pair of us while I dashed off a note to Joan instructing her to leave immediately with the bearer of this letter. I promised to write more fully later.

I did, but I don't know if she received my letter before she was murdered.

29

It was 1.15 a.m. when Angel and I set off in the blacked-out van, with a thermos flask of tea and half a packet of digestive biscuits for sustenance. We hoped it would take us no more than ten hours to reach London. There was little risk of getting lost, even though the road signs had been taken down at the outbreak of war and never put back up. We simply followed the A30. If all went well, we should be in London before midday.

We drove in silence as I struggled to come to terms with the enormity of our recent discovery.

'What if she was lying?' I suggested at last. 'What if Matty's not a *Gestapo* informer?'

'And what if Hitler had been killed in that *Bier-keller* in 1939 and the invasion had never taken place?' Angel covered my hand, resting on the gear lever, with her own. 'I'm sorry, Nick. I truly am.'

'But I've known Matty ever since I was a nipper.' I shook my head helplessly. 'He's my best friend. He saved my life . . .'

'Nick, you're going to have to face the truth. Sara's supposed death was a perfect cover for him.'

'But you said yourself that there have been no leaks recently.'

'That's because the *Gestapo* have been after the *big* prize. God! They'd be prepared to turn a blind eye to anything to get their hands on Mills and the leaders of every circuit in England. We'd have to start all over again from scratch.'

'But—'

'No, the timing's right. Mills began organizing this conference just before Sara "died". The *Gestapo* have just been biding their time. I bet that's why Dr Six was down here last week – to be personally briefed now that things are coming to a head.'

'You've got an answer for everything, haven't you?'

'Nick, why should the *Gestapo* bother about destroying the odd arms dump when they can now break the whole Resistance movement? This is a godsend for them. The Germans need Britain docile so that they can concentrate their efforts on conquering Russia before the Americans really get into the war.'

I tried to absorb Angel's words but my mind was in a whirl.

'You mentioned there were twenty or so Resistance leaders attending this meeting,' I said after a while. 'But I remember Mills talking about only three or four escape lines.'

'That was at the beginning. Things have happened since then that you don't know about but which Matty does.' Angel sighed and paused to collect her thoughts. 'Since the New Year, local resistance groups have been springing up all over the country, while simultaneously we've been bringing trained leaders back home to set up and run their own circuits. Then, once Hitler invaded Russia, Moscow ordered British Communists to join the fight. About the same time, armed bands of fugitives began roaming the country-side, fleeing the Compulsory Labour Act. Resistance to the German occupation has mushroomed out of control. It's grown too quickly. We're like a lot of headless chickens pecking at one another in our own backyards.'

'Headless chickens can't peck,' I objected, slowing to swerve around a rabbit transfixed in the headlights.

Angel ignored me. 'The Resistance needs an over-all direction. This meeting is to make sure that we all sing from the same hymn sheet.'

'And you're sure Matty will be there so we'll come face to face with him?'

'Undoubtedly.'

'What will you do?' I already knew the answer.

'Find out exactly what he's told the Germans – and then I'll kill him.'

*

The weather started to break. The light drizzle thickened into a steady downpour. I drove on as fast as I dared, trying to put as many miles as possible between us and the coast. My eyes began aching with tiredness and, after I'd almost driven into a ditch, Angel demanded to take a spell behind the wheel. In the passenger seat, I closed my eyes and dozed off.

I was jerked out of my dream to find myself pitching forward, my head cracking against the windscreen. I opened my eyes to find that dawn had broken. In the raw early-morning light, I saw we were skidding sideways down a steeply winding hill. Everything was happening in slow motion. At the bottom of the hill, a lorry was climbing up towards us through the rain. We were revolving so that the van's rear end was threatening to overtake our front bumper in our headlong descent. I could see the other vehicle clearly now – a big flat-bed Foden – and we were closing on it with every second. Imperceptibly at first, the van began to respond to Angel's frantic turning of the wheel. Too slowly. I braced myself for the inevitable collision. The lorry driver's frightened white face stared out at me from his cab. Then we flashed past, missing the Foden by inches.

Angel gradually brought the van to a halt. She sat silently, gripping the steering wheel with both hands, before letting out a huge sigh.

'What was that about?' I asked mildly.

'I must have fallen asleep,' she confessed. 'I've no idea what we hit.'

We climbed out to inspect the damage, the rain sheeting down on us in a cold icy blanket driven on an easterly wind. You would never have thought it was August. The van's nearside wing had been crushed in so far that it was rubbing against the tyre. I used the wheelbrace to lever it away. Only then did I spot the real damage – the wheel itself was leaning inwards at an angle.

'I think the whole axle's bent,' I told Angel. 'How far are we from the nearest town?'

'We're somewhere between Chard and Crewkerne. Can't you fix it?'

'No chance.' I suddenly realized what she had said. I looked at my watch. It was seven o'clock. 'God, have I really been asleep that long!'

'You even slept through the checkpoints outside Exeter and Honiton.'

'No!'

'The *Gestapo* pass worked wonders. The Germans couldn't wait to wave us through and get out of the rain.'

'How are we off for money?'

'I've got £300 in fivers.'

'How much?' That amount would have bought a spanking new tourer before the war. 'What about taking a train to London?'

Angel thought briefly. 'No. It's too easy to get trapped on a train.'

'We'll be pushed to get to London by midday now.'

'We'll just have to try,' she insisted.

We limped on very slowly to Crewkerne, the van shaking itself apart every time we exceeded ten miles an hour. There we drank mugs of weak tea from a roadside caravan while we waited for the town to wake. Yes, the caravan owner told us, there was a second-hand car dealer but he couldn't honestly recommend him.

Beggars and choosers, I thought.

Standartenführer Stolz was frustrated and tired, but most of all resentful that he was still here at the *Feldkommandantur* when he should have been in London, waking up in Brown's Hotel – set aside for senior *Gestapo* and SS officers – to enjoy a pot of coffee while his valet shaved him.

He was bitter that *Reich* Security Berlin had suddenly decided that a scientist called Otto Frisch must be prevented from getting away to Canada at all costs. They hadn't bothered to put him into protective custody while he had been working in Liverpool only a week or so ago, oh, no! But now that he'd disappeared, he seemed to have become vitally important. The trail had led to the West. Cordington had said that he believed Frisch was being shipped out to Canada through a bay on the county's north coast. And then Cordington had departed for London – where Stolz himself should be. Last night's dragnet, which had involved the *Gestapo*, a company of *SS Germania* and two corvettes, had proved fruitless. If Frisch did manage to slip away to Canada, Stolz was in no doubt who would get the blame.

Abetz came to attention in front of him. 'The corvettes have been stood down, *Standartenführer*. Do you think Cordington lied to us?'

'Why should he? He only said *where* Frisch would be leaving from, not *when*. The tides will be right for the next three nights. Make sure those corvettes are back on station by 2100.'

The sight of a sheaf of overnight *VOBIES* in Abetz's hand reminded Stolz that he had decided to deal personally with Nick Penny's recent absence without leave.

'Where is Penny?' he demanded. 'He knows he should be here at seven o'clock.'

'He's not in yet,' replied Abetz.

It crossed Stolz's mind that Penny might be involved with Frisch in some way. Cordington denied that he was, but Stolz knew he had covered up for his friend before.

'Send someone to check his home.'

Cordington was going to be in for an unpleasant surprise, once the senior Resistance leaders had been captured. His importance would be at an end – and all deals would be off. That included the understanding that Penny and that Kennedy woman be allowed their freedom. Stolz was looking forward to interrogating them both.

'I can't remember seeing *Fräulein* Klink last night.'

'No, sir. Nor this morning.'

Stolz frowned. That woman was too ambitious by half. It would be just like her to go off somewhere on her own.

'Find her and tell her to report to me immediately.'

Angel dropped me a short distance from the second-hand car dealer, where half a dozen vehicles were parked on a patch of ground under a fading sign boasting Best Prices and Trade-ins. I didn't like the look of Honest Charlie Hall from the moment I laid eyes on his pencil moustache and oiled black hair. But we had no choice. Most garages and sale rooms had closed down. The fact that Honest Charlie Hall was still in business implied that he had another source of income – like the black market.

He saw me coming, literally and metaphorically. 'Can I help you, guv?'

'Can I have a look at the Ford van?' Angel had decided that a van offered better opportunities for an alibi if we were stopped somewhere.

'A wise choice, if I say so myself.'

The van smelled strongly of fish. A thin coat of paint failed to mask the sign proclaiming *P. W. Trundle High Class Fishmonger*. Honest Charlie practically ruptured himself cranking the engine, while keeping up a stream of sales patter. Finally, the engine coughed reluctantly into life and he trotted around to push in the choke before the carburettor could flood.

'You'll find she's a sweet little runner,' he said as we pulled off for a test drive.

'Fifty thousand on the clock,' I observed.

'That's nothing to one of these motors. Last for ever, they will.'

I knew practically nothing about cars but even I thought the knocking sound from the engine was an indication that all was not well.

'Don't worry about that. I put in new tappets a couple of days ago, and the rocker-box cover is still bedding in,' reassured Honest Charlie, blinding me with gobbledegook. 'Can I ask what you're wanting the vehicle for?'

'Me and my brother are breeding rabbits.'

'You what?'

'There's good money in rabbits,' I said defensively. 'You know everyone wants meat. Think how quick rabbits breed. We had just six when we started, now we've got almost five hundred. We're going to start selling them, and that's why we need a van.'

I beat Honest Charlie down to £27, because not to have haggled would have made him suspicious, and drove away. The knocking in the engine was worrying me, but I didn't want the Ford for life – just to get us as far as London. After that it could self-destruct as far as I was concerned.

Angel and I drove in convoy out into the country. In a hollow that had once housed an old gypsy encampment, we transferred our spare petrol into the Ford, then poured half a gallon over the *Gestapo* van and set it alight.

It was almost 8.30 a.m. We would not now reach London until well after midday.

Angel decided to hang on to Sara's *Gestapo* warrant card – a decision that was to prove almost fatal.

Stolz sat at his desk, listening to the extended eight o'clock news on the wireless about that afternoon's coronation. From overnight intelligence digests, he knew that British forces were claiming a major victory in the northern Atlantic, but the naval battle was not even mentioned. Instead the bulletin concentrated on mounting excitement in the capital where special overnight trains were arriving carrying friends of the *Reich* anxious to see the *Führer* with his puppet king and queen. Few would actually get to see Hitler, though. His only public appearance would be to accept the homage of the newly crowned king outside

Westminster Abbey, in front of a carefully vetted crowd.

Abetz entered. 'There's no one at Penny's home. His motorbike isn't there, either.'

'What do you mean, there's *no one* at home? Where are his family?'

'His sister and mother left there half an hour before our man arrived, according to a female neighbour who is known to us,' replied Abetz. 'She said they had a suitcase, and they left by car. Mrs Penny appeared very shaky. Maybe she was going into hospital.'

'What about the boy?'

'The neighbour, a Mrs Harper, believes he's working on the Cordington estate.'

'Bring him in immediately. He'll tell us where the others have gone.'

'Yes, sir. And there's no sign of *Fräulein* Klink anywhere. She left her quarters before nine o'clock last night and hasn't been seen since. Her bed has not been slept in and the van's missing.'

Stolz thought for a moment. '*Fräulein* Klink was involved when the Resistance shipped out that scientist through an abandoned fishing village called Lostmaids on the south coast, if my memory serves me. Send two men over to search the place.'

Angel and I were worrying about the knocking sound from the engine, and watching the petrol gauge fall before our eyes, when we rounded a bend to find two young *Wehrmacht* soldiers standing at the road-side, hitching a lift.

'Pull in,' ordered Angel.

'What?'

'No one's going to stop us if we're giving a lift to two Jerries, are they?'

It made sense.

'Where are you going?' I asked them.

'To our base on the other side of Yeovil,' replied the one with glasses.

The soldiers scrambled into the van. Keen to prac-tise his English, the bespectacled one, called Fritz, introduced his comrade Konrad, who handed round *Kapstan* cigarettes – the old Capstan Full Strength now made exclusively for the German Armed Forces – and insisted that we keep the packet. The two boys were only eighteen or nineteen years old, and looked like poor physical specimens. I was intrigued that the youngsters carried pistols. Normally only officers wore side arms.

'It's a new order that everyone leaving barracks must carry a gun. There are many bad men in the country,' explained Fritz. 'Where are you going?'

'To Shaftesbury to collect some rabbits.'

'Rabbits?'

Angel did a silly mime, all teeth and floppy hands for ears.

'*Kaninchen*,' chorused the boys.

They were still chuckling when we came to the roadblock. The four Militiamen lounging against the barrier looked bored – and itching for trouble. One held up his hand for us to stop. As soon as we drew to a halt they pulled open the front doors.

'Get out.'

'Why?' I demanded, reasonably.

'Because we tell you to.' One Militiaman made a grab for Angel's bag on the floor in front of her. 'What's in here?'

My heart sank. Angel's gun was safe in her jacket pocket, but the handbag contained not just a small fortune in cash but Sara's *Gestapo* warrant card.

Angel snatched back her bag. She and the Militiaman had a tug-of-war over it before I leaned across and bent back his fingers to dislodge them.

'Let go of that,' I snarled.

'Fuck you.' He grasped Angel's arm and began to drag her out of the car.

If the Militia got a look in the handbag, we were goners. It was about to become a shooting match, when the German boys came to our rescue.

Fritz shoved his pistol in the Militiaman's face. 'Let her go. Open the barrier,' he commanded.

The man released Angel and eyed his patrol commander uncertainly.

'Open the barrier,' repeated Fritz, waving his gun. I noticed that the safety was still on and doubted if the boy had ever fired a weapon in anger.

'We're only doing our duty,' muttered the Militia leader, reluctantly raising the barrier.

'Pieces of shit,' murmured Konrad in German.

'*Ja, Scheiße*,' I agreed and we all laughed again.

We dropped off the boys near their records depot and took stock. The petrol gauge had stopped falling so dramatically, the rain had ceased, and we had negotiated a difficult checkpoint.

It was not yet nine o'clock.

Angel and I shared the last of the tea from the thermos while we set fire to Sara's *Gestapo* card. But no sooner had we set off when the sky ahead began to grow darker by the minute. Suddenly there was a thunderclap directly overhead and the storm was on us. The windscreen wipers crawled ineffectually into life but I was forced to pull in as the world disappeared in a cascade of water. It was like sitting under a waterfall. Rain dripped inside the van from all around the windscreen. I spent the next ten minutes mopping up with my handkerchief while swearing revenge on Honest Charlie Hall.

No sooner had I pulled back onto the road than the engine began coughing and spluttering. Soon we were firing on three cylinders, sometimes just two and a half.

'What's wrong?'

'The points and plugs are wet. If it gets any worse, I'll have to stop to dry them out.'

We drove on, listening nervously to the engine

grinding and churning as if it was lubricated by grit. At this rate, we were never going to make London.

We were hiccuping our way through a pretty village when Angel spotted a newspaper billboard on the pavement outside a small general store.

England welcomes the Führer, it said.

'The officers have found a woman's purse in the graveyard at Lostmaids, *Standartenführer*,' reported Abetz.

'So?'

'The purse contains money but no papers. It is of German manufacture.'

'Hell.' A thought struck Stolz. 'Where is that Resistance woman Kennedy now?'

'I assume she is at home.'

'You assume?' Stolz's face darkened with anger.

'With respect, *Standartenführer*, you gave instructions that she should not be kept under closer surveillance, in case she became suspicious and vanished. We know she was at her home at six yesterday evening.'

'Put her under twenty-four-hour surveillance immediately. Once we hear the Resistance leaders have been arrested in London, then pick her up for questioning.'

'Yes, sir. By the way, the boy David was not on the Cordington farm although we found his bicycle there. The foreman, Latcham, refused to answer our men's questions so they've brought him in. They're interrogating him now.'

'Let me know as soon as he talks.'

'He's an old man. It won't take long.'

Angel ran into the newsagent's shop to return with a *Daily Express* and a roll of sticky tape.

The front page was filled with a picture of Hitler waving as he emerged from his personal Junkers aircraft at Croydon airport. It reminded me of another picture taken at the same spot three years ago next month. Then the British Prime Minister, Neville Chamberlain, had waved a piece of paper over his head and promised Peace in Our Time. The Germans had invaded us less than two years later.

The top half of page three was taken up by a picture of the present Prime Minister, Samuel Hoare, bowing to Hitler outside Buckingham Palace.

'Hoare by name, whore by nature,' muttered Angel bitterly.

There were further pictures of Hitler inspecting an honour escort of Coldstream Guards, and smiling at schoolchildren waving swastika flags. According to the *Express*, cheering crowds had lined the streets all the way to the palace, where the Führer would stay as the guest of the Protector, von Ribbentrop. Göring, Himmler and Hess had arrived later but there were no photographs of them – Goebbels was making sure nothing would distract the focus of public attention away from the *Führer*.

Hitler, we learned, had been escorted over the white cliffs of Dover by a special flight of the RAF flying Messerschmitt Bf109s. The afternoon had been spent meeting English cabinet ministers and senior administrators, before a formal dinner at St James's Palace with the Duke and Duchess of Windsor.

The *Führer*'s visit would cement the cordial relationship between our two great nations, said the official communiqué: his presence at the Coronation bestowing the blessing of the Third *Reich* on the new king and his American-born queen.

The other big news was the British SS St George Division's victory in its first battle as a distinct fighting unit, spearheading the breakthrough that brought German forces to within thirty miles of Stalingrad. The *Führer* had sent his personal congratulations to General Fuller, and awarded him the Knight's Cross – the first English officer to receive the decoration.

Angel threw down the newspaper in disgust. Outside the town we halted briefly while I taped Sara's gun to my ankle, then helped Angel tape her weapon to the small of her back.

The rain had cleared away leaving a few fluffy white clouds scurrying across a pastel-blue sky. We passed through a patchwork quilt of fields, with here and there the steeples of ancient churches rising amid soft-stone villages. We had braced ourselves for another checkpoint in Shaftesbury but we had a clear run through. We were just starting to relax, chugging up a long incline towards Salisbury, when I first noticed the steam coming from the bonnet. The sinking feeling in my stomach returned. It was 9.47 a.m.

'Oh, no,' wailed Angel. 'We'll never make it now.'

I changed down, feeling the van losing power by the yard. Just before we stalled, I double-declutched into first gear and managed to kangaroo our way over the crest of the hill. Ahead, a small town lay in a dip. Two things caught my eye – the massive swastika flag flying high over the church tower, and a roadside garage blazoned with pre-war adverts for Fina petrol, Castrol oil and John Bull tyres.

I coasted down to the garage workshop. From inside his glass-fronted office, a man with a ginger moustache watched our arrival but made no effort to come to our assistance. I lifted the van's bonnet, reeling back from the cloud of steam.

'Wait a second.' A grey-haired mechanic in greasy overalls appeared from beneath a farm tractor at the rear of the workshop. He tapped the radiator cap with his spanner. It flew off high in the air. 'Can be dangerous, that.'

'Thanks. Can you help us?'

'I can't spend too long.' He jerked his head towards the office. 'Or His Nibs will be demanding to know why I've not fixed old Rib-and-Tripe's tractor.'

'You mean that tractor belongs to Protector von Ribbentrop?' In my surprise, my words came out sounding stiff and formal.

The mechanic shuffled his feet. 'I didn't mean no harm.'

'Don't worry, we've heard him called worse than that,' said Angel. 'But what do you mean, it's his tractor?'

'This is his country estate. The village, the garage, everything you see belongs to him.'

'Not for long, we hope. And don't worry too much what you say in front of us.'

'Well, be careful in this village: it's sold out completely. It must be the only place in England that organized a street party for Hitler's birthday without being told to.'

'George, what are you doing there?'

The man with the ginger moustache stood in the doorway, hands on hips. He wore a sharp double-breasted suit with a golden swastika badge in the lapel. The mechanic cringed as though he had just felt the lash fall across his shoulders.

'I was just going to have a quick look at this gentleman's van, Mr Packer, sir.'

'Don't take long. You know your priorities.' Packer went to return to his office, but turned briefly to peer at our van. His brow furrowed. He cast me a sideways glance before spinning on his heel and vanishing without a further word.

'Friendly soul, isn't he?' murmured Angel.

'He's seen something,' muttered George.

'What sort of thing?'

'I don't know.'

The mechanic circled the van, scratching the back of his head. Then he stepped back. 'There, those number plates are false, and he's spotted it.'

'What do you mean, false?' I inspected the registration number: KWO 96.

'WO is used for private cars registered in Monmouthshire. This van should carry a plate for a light commercial vehicle.' George looked me sternly in the eye. 'You ought to have been more careful.'

'I only bought this bloody wreck this morning to get up to London on business, and it's been nothing but trouble.'

'You were done,' he said, shortly. 'Mr Packer will be getting on the phone now to the police, to show what a good little Nazi he is.'

'No, he won't,' muttered Angel, hurrying towards the office.

I turned back to George. 'Can you fix the radiator?'

'Depends. If it's the radiator itself that's gone, then no, I don't have a spare one. But if it's just a hose or a loose connection . . .' He refilled the radiator with water, cranked the van into life and peered underneath the engine. 'The hose to the block's completely rotten.'

'So you can fix the leak?' He nodded. Then I spotted a half-ton Morris van in a corner. 'Would that number plate over there be right for our van?'

'Oh, ay. That number's light commercial for Hampshire. But Mr Packer . . .?'

'Don't worry about him.'

'It's easy for you to say.' George started to replace the damaged hose while glancing nervously towards the office. 'He'd sell his own mother if he thought it would get him in further with the Nazis.'

George had almost finished the job when a grim-looking Angel reappeared.

'I don't know how to tell you this,' she began. 'But Mr Packer's just suffered a heart attack.'

'You mean he's dead?'

'I'm afraid so.'

I hurried after George into the office where Packer lay on the floor behind his desk, his eyes wide open. A grin spread slowly across George's face.

'There's a history of dicky tickers in his family.' George glanced shrewdly at Angel before rubbing his hands together. 'Good riddance to bad rubbish, that's all I can say. There'll be few around here who'll mourn him.'

George set to changing the number plates, humming cheerfully to himself. When he had finished, he asked us: 'What do you want me to do about Mr Packer?'

'Leave it until your lunch break before you "discover" him.'

To celebrate his boss's death, George gave us two gallon cans of petrol and a plug spanner, all for free. It was now 10.20 a.m.

'I had to dart him,' confessed Angel as she drove off.

It had become a funny old world, I thought. George had not turned a hair at the cold-blooded murder of his boss – but then, neither had I. And what was more, I was sitting beside his killer, and thinking how marvellous it was that we were in love. Yes, a funny old world.

'They've found *Fräulein* Klink's body in an old church crypt, *Standartenführer*,' said Abetz. 'She's been shot.'

'Shit! How long has she been dead?'

'Don't know, sir. A doctor's on his way there now. There's no sign of her van but the men say they can make out something lying in the water off the jetty. It could be a motorcycle.'

'That's Penny's bike, I'd bet on it,' exclaimed Stolz. 'Get divers on to it straight away. The registration number will be on file.' He slammed his fist on the desk. 'That stupid bitch has jeopardized everything. She should never have gone there alone.'

'So now Penny and the Kennedy woman know that *Fräulein* Klink did not really die back in May?'

'And they know that Cordington is a double agent,' stormed Stolz. 'They'll try to warn their chief in London. Send both their descriptions to *Reichssicherheitshauptamt London* and put out a red alert for Klink's van. Search Penny's home and Kennedy's too. Cut all civilian trunk lines and get me a list of all calls to London from ten o'clock last night. Shit!'

Abetz returned some time later to report that only a dozen trunk calls had been made to London from the region – three to Mr Smeed at the Dorchester Hotel, two from the hospital, and three from the local newspaper to its London bureau. All others, from private subscribers, could be discounted.

A sergeant suddenly burst in to hand Abetz a message. 'The van passed through a checkpoint outside Exeter at 4.35 this morning,' he announced.

'So they're definitely heading for London,' declared Stolz.

He could not put off alerting Dr Six any longer. Five minutes later Stolz replaced the receiver and wiped the sweat off it with his handkerchief, his hands shaking. His commanding officer had left him in no doubt whom he held responsible for the whole fiasco. It was Stolz's fault that the Klink woman had gone off by herself, his fault that Penny and Kennedy had remained at large. If they did manage to raise the alarm, not only would the Resistance leaders scatter, but the *Gestapo*'s chief agent would be exposed. If that happened, Six would personally see Stolz shot in the courtyard of his own *Feldkommandantur*.

Meanwhile Six would sever all the capital's civilian phone links with the rest of the country, and turn out every available policeman to block all roads leading into the city from the south and west. Every train and every station would be watched. Stolz had better hope the pair were caught in time.

Ten minutes later came a report that Klink's Morris van had been sighted earlier in Honiton.

Stolz was on his third cup of black coffee when Abetz returned to the room.

'Latcham's dead, sir. He died of a heart attack when they increased the electric current.'

'Get his wife and start on her.'

30

Our day was going backwards. Each time we encountered another band of fierce rain sweeping across southern England, the engine faltered. Twice it came within a beat of dying but at least the rain kept the Militia off the streets. In Salisbury we passed the checkpoint men sheltering in a road menders' hut. We ignored their shouts for us to halt and kept on going. We passed through Basingstoke and then Hook without any problems until, fifteen minutes later, we came upon a transport café where we topped up the van from our petrol supply before pressing on.

'We're not going to get to London before half-past one at the earliest now,' said Angel. 'I'm going to have to start looking for a phone box soon. Let's just hope I can get hold of Mills.'

I found myself wondering if Sara had been missed by now. I prayed that Joan had managed to get mum out of bed and onto the train, and that my nephew David had not disappeared off to some inaccessible part of the farm. If all had gone well, my family should be well on their way to Shrewsbury by now.

I looked at my watch. It was almost midday. The time Matty was due to make contact with Mills.

'Good day, Charlie, and how's business?'

Honest Charlie Hall smiled nervously at the detective sergeant, but his eyes kept drifting over to the black-uniformed German who had remained in the passenger seat of the police car.

'Slow, Mr Potticary. You know how things are. You can't sell a motor for love or money nowadays. Not that I'm complaining. I've some good bargains, if you fancy anything. Special rates to you, of course.' Charlie became aware that he was gabbling.

'You haven't sold a motor to a young couple today, by any chance?'

'Hand on heart, Mr Potticary.'

Detective Sergeant Potticary surveyed the vehicles on the sales lot. 'What's happened to that wrecked Ford you had here?'

'Ah, the van.'

'Don't try to be clever, Charlie. We're hunting for a young couple heading towards London. Talk to me or talk to the *Gestapo*.'

Charlie went white. 'It wasn't a couple, just this one bloke. He said he needed a van to knock out rabbits he's breeding.'

'What did he look like?'

'About your height, fair hair, average sort of build – average sort of bloke, really. Maybe a bit of a West Country burr about him. He wore a sports jacket.'

'What time was this?'

'As soon as I opened, at eight this morning.'

'What's the van's registration number?'

'KWO 96.' Charlies shrugged in embarrassment. 'Look, Mr Potticary, I didn't know he was a wrong 'un. I'll tell you what, though, I don't reckon that van will get as far as London. Proper knackered, it is.'

'For your sake, Charlie, you'd better pray it doesn't get there.'

Matty Cordington stood outside the only green phone box in London, listening to martial music blaring from the loudspeaker on the lamp-post nearby. Two *Feldgendarmerie* were eyeing him suspiciously. Security was tight on the Victoria Embankment, less than half a mile from the cordon now encircling Westminster Abbey. Matty stole a glance at his watch – his call was due in three minutes. Mills had drummed into him the dangers of arriving early for a rendezvous, but Matty had ignored that in his haste – and now could have paid the price.

The Germans stepped over to him. 'Papers.'

Matty pulled out a single folded sheet of heavy paper, and opened it up in front of them.

'Go away,' he said coldly.

The two Germans paled. Matty smiled at their retreating backs, congratulating himself on having ensured that he was untouchable. It hadn't been easy . . .

The first-class restaurant car stood by itself alongside an inspection platform in the furthest reaches of the vast marshalling yard outside Southampton docks, a soft light shining through its curtained windows. Nearby, an imposing 4-6-0 King-class locomotive was taking on water, wisps of steam rising from its funnel to disappear in the night air. In the distance, under a battery of arc lamps, busy little shunting engines were fussing to put together a long train of empty trucks for return to the mines in South Wales; their previous load of steam coal already on its way to the Ruhr. Matty Cordington climbed out of his shooting brake, stiff after the long drive. He heard the clunk of buffer on buffer and smelled the salt tang of the sea in the damp wind before stepping into the warmth.

'You are late.' Professor Dr Six picked his teeth with the nail of his little finger.

'I was held up at a Militia checkpoint.'

Dr Six pointed to the seat opposite him, as a white-coated steward stepped forward to take away the remains of a pork chop.

'Well, where exactly is this Resistance meeting being held?' Six poured the last of a bottle of Julienas into his glass and snapped his fingers for another.

'I don't know yet. As I've told you, Mills is not going to reveal the location of the safe house until the day itself.'

'I find that hard to believe.'

'I promise you that it's true. You know how obsessive Mills is about security. He's going to tell only a handful of escort officers literally hours before the conference. The officers will then meet each Resistance leader individually as he arrives in London, make sure no one's being tailed by the *Gestapo*, then take each one to the safe house. I'm one of those escort officers. I'll call you as soon as all the leaders are safely inside.'

'No, you will tell me as soon as you know where the meeting's being held. Fetch him a glass,' Six instructed the steward, who brought the new bottle of Julienas.

'How am I going to phone you without arousing suspicion? Others will be watching us all the time. That's the whole point of the operation.' Matty Cordington leaned forward into the pool of light cast by the table lamp. 'Even if I could slip away to call you, you still wouldn't know *when* they were all assembled. And don't even think of trying to put the safe house itself under surveillance. Mills will have teams of watchers and lookouts all around. I swear he has a nose for the *Gestapo*, and at the slightest hint of something wrong, he'll call the whole thing off.'

'I don't like it.'

'Remember, their meeting will go on all evening, maybe all night. You'll have all the time you need.'

'And how do you propose to tell us they're all assembled?'

'It'll be no problem at that stage. I'll volunteer to go out on lookout patrol. That way I can easily duck away and contact you.'

Six weighed up the proposal. 'I still don't know . . .'

'It has to be done my way, or it won't work.' Matty Cordington insisted. 'And I want some kind of special pass to get me through the London checkpoints.'

'I rather assumed the Resistance would give you a forged pass,' said Six sarcastically.

'And what if one of your men spots it as a forgery? If I get arrested then, that's the end of the whole operation.' Matty took a large gulp of wine. 'You were the one who told me how success in intelligence work comes from an obsession with detail. I'm just trying to think of everything that could go wrong.'

'Let me worry about things like that.'

'You don't know what it's like out there,' exclaimed the Englishman, raising his voice. 'Every time I come upon a checkpoint, I worry about being arrested and questioned, especially by those Militia thugs. Look at this.' He pointed to a purple bruise on his forehead. 'This came from a Militia gun butt, and where were you then? It would be ironic if I was arrested by your colleagues in London as I was going to meet a Resistance leader.'

'I'll give you a pass,' Six reassured him. 'One that will get you everywhere.'

'Once I've made that phone call, that's it, you understand?'

'Of course. Just phone us with that address and then use your pass to get through the inner cordon to my office in Great Scotland Yard,' replied Six smoothly.

He rose to head down the dining car, to where a *Gestapo* officer sat behind a typewriter. Six dictated a short order, then signed it with a flourish. He handed the sheet of heavy embossed paper to Cordington.

'Here, direct from the office of the *SS Oberführer des Reichssicherheitshauptamt England*. If anyone challenges you, show them this.'

'And you're sure this will get me everywhere?'

'This will even get you into Westminster Abbey, if you want to watch the coronation.'

Matty remembered Six's words as a laughing party of high-ranking *Luftwaffe* officers appeared from the river entrance of the Savoy Hotel, all clutching their coronation invitations. He checked his watch, and slipped into the telephone box.

He was staring down at the receiver, willing it to ring, when the door opened behind him and he felt a tap on his shoulder.

'Glad you could make it,' said Mills.

'I was expecting you to phone,' gasped Matty.

'I came in person. Follow me.' Mills led the way across the Embankment towards Cleopatra's Needle. 'There's something very strange going on,' he said to Matty. 'The Germans have set up roadblocks all around London, hunting for a young couple.'

'Is that going to affect our plans?'

'Inevitably, but I hope we've built in enough time to allow everyone to assemble before the end of the coronation.' Mills halted alongside a Thames pleasure steamer, decorated from bow to stern in swastika flags. *The Maidstone Castle.*

'This is the meeting place?' exclaimed Matty. 'I was expecting it to be somewhere miles away.'

'That's the point,' smiled Mills. 'We'll be setting off downstream as soon as everyone's on board.'

'Brilliant.'

Mills, who Matty now noticed was wearing a naval uniform under his raincoat, marched straight up the gangplank and past a sign that announced *Nur für ranghöhere Offiziere der Kriegsmarine* – Only for senior officers of the German Navy. Two sentries in sailors' uniform saluted him briskly.

Down in the saloon, Mills handed Matty a time-table detailing the arrival of each of his Resistance leaders. His first rendezvous was with the Welsh Valleys leader Brynmor Powell at Paddington station; the last would be with Hereward at Waterloo.

'I've been hearing stories of a pitched battle and massacre at Merricombe,' said Matty. 'It happened after I'd left, and I know Hereward survived. But is Nick Penny all right?'

'Absolutely. He was responsible for the deaths of all those Militiamen,' said Mills. 'I'll tell you more later, but now I need you to speak to another old friend.'

'Sorry?'

'Coral Kennedy's due to call that same phone box where I met you at ten minutes past twelve, to confirm that Frisch has left the country safely. Maybe Penny will be with her.'

Matty Cordington hurried back to the phone box as Mills prepared to intercept the next briefing officer. Matty looked forward to speaking to Coral – and maybe Nick – but the phone remained silent. At twelve minutes past twelve Matty even lifted the receiver, to make sure it was still working.

By 12.20 Matty was wondering what to do. If he stayed much longer he would be late in meeting Powell's train. His dilemma was solved by a man tapping on the glass.

'Message from Mills,' said the stranger. 'Don't

wait any longer. The Germans have cut all phone lines into London.'

'We're going to have to find a phone box soon,' urged Angel. 'Mills is expecting a call from me at exactly ten past twelve. The news will be a terrible shock to him. Mills really liked Matty.'

'And you'll find out where this meeting's going to be held?'

'I know that already.'

'But you told me Mills wasn't going to announce the safe house until this morning.'

Angel grinned. 'That's what Matty, and everyone else, believes. In fact, Mills and I selected the place a month ago.'

'Why did you lie to me?'

'What would have happened if we'd been captured and tortured?'

'You think I'd talk and you wouldn't?'

Angel scooped a small pendant on a silver chain from under her blouse. The front of the locket opened to reveal a rubber-coated capsule. 'Cyanide,' she explained briefly, closing the locket. 'Now you see why I didn't tell you.'

I placed my hand over hers and squeezed.

'One day, Nick, this will all be over.'

'Do you think we'll be together then?'

'That'll be nice,' she murmured. 'Although I'm

never going to trust you to buy a car by yourself again.'

I opened my mouth to reply when, from nowhere, a big Armstrong-Siddeley suddenly filled the rear-view mirror.

'Get down out of sight,' I hissed at Angel.

There was only one sort of person who drove such a vehicle – *Gestapo*. The car roared up behind us, then slowed to stay on our tail. I was getting really nervous as it pulled out and accelerated to drive alongside us. I held my breath as the men inside it gave me the evil eye. Then the driver put his foot down and off they sped.

Slowly Angel rose from the floor.

A mile or two on, I stopped at a telephone box on a country crossroads. Angel hurried over, clutching a handful of coppers and threepenny bits. She piled up the coins, lifted the receiver and began speaking to the operator. A frown grew on her face. By the time she returned to the van, she was looking very worried indeed.

'All the lines to London are down,' she announced.

'Did the operator say when they'll be working again?'

'No. All she said was, "It's not up to us."'

'Have the Germans cut the lines?'

'I don't know but we're going to *have* to get up to London to warn Mills now.' Her brow furrowed in thought. 'The first arrivals are due around one o'clock, and the last of them around three. We've just got to get there by then. If we're forced to split up, make for a steamer called *The Maidstone Castle* moored near Cleopatra's Needle.'

'Is that where they're meeting?'

'Yes.'

I was just about to pull away, my foot lifting off the clutch, when the same black Armstrong-Siddeley came hurtling back around a bend towards us. At the last minute it slewed sideways to block the road ahead.

'Shit!'

There were still the side roads so I heaved the steering wheel around and bumped over the grass verge to swing into the lane leading off on our left.

'Why did they come back?'

I concentrated on coaxing every last bit of power from the clapped-out old Ford. We could not hope to win a race with the Armstrong-Siddeley but if I could just get sufficiently ahead for a moment, I hoped I might be able to lose them in the cobweb of lanes.

Some hope. The big saloon had closed up on us before I reached the first bend.

The Armstrong-Siddeley rammed us, sending our frail vehicle careering across the lane and almost into the ditch on the other side. The lane was growing narrower between tall hedges, scarcely wide enough to allow two cars to pass.

Angel worked free her pistol, and slid down her side window.

The black saloon rammed us again.

The lane ahead swung sharply to the left.

'I'll get a shot at them as we take the bend,' gasped Angel.

'No, don't let them know we're armed. See that gateway into that field ahead – I'll try to get us in there. Hang on tight. Here we go.'

I hit the brake and wrenched the wheel round. The van clipped the gatepost, then we were bouncing across the field. We leaped out and ran back towards the gateway. The saloon had overshot the opening. The driver was reversing back, tyres spinning on the mud in the lane.

'I'll take the driver,' said Angel as we crouched ready behind the wall, guns poised.

The black car leaped forward into the field and stuck fast in the narrow gateway. Angel and I rose.

The windscreen exploded as Angel's first round struck. She fired again.

I approached within six feet of the Germans' car and pulled the trigger of my gun. By the time we'd finished, the stench of cordite hung in the air, and in the front of the Armstrong-Siddeley sprawled the bodies of two very dead *Gestapo* men.

*

'This is Mrs Harper, *Standartenführer*,' introduced Abetz.

'I think they've gone for good, sir,' said Mrs Harper.

'Why do you think that?' demanded Stolz.

'Mrs Pendleton's wedding photograph has gone, sir.'

'You saw them leaving this morning?'

'I noticed a grey car parked outside their house real early. A man carried a big suitcase out to the car, then returned to help Joan with the old woman. She's very frail now.'

'Did you recognize this man?'

'I've never seen him before, sir.'

Abetz cleared his throat. 'We've checked, and the mother's not in any local hospitals or nursing homes.'

'Any idea where they could have gone?' Stolz turned back to Mrs Harper.

'They're not a large family. Mrs Penny's got an older brother in Swanage but he's not been well for years. The only other relative I know of is Joan's late husband's sister in Wales – near a place called Machynlleth.'

'How do you know about her?'

'She came to stay with them just before the war. Gave herself airs and graces, I can tell you. But the whole family's like that.'

'Do you know her address?'

'No, sir. But she's never married. There can't be

many Pendletons in that part of Wales. She's probably in the phone book.'

'What the hell aroused their suspicions?' I drove away, grasping the steering wheel tight so that my hands did not shake.

'The *Gestapo* car had a wireless aerial. They must have picked up a message about us.'

The engine coughed, spluttered and died for a second.

'What now?' wailed Angel.

My eyes scanned the instrument panel. 'We're out of petrol. They must have holed the tank when they rammed us back there.'

We were approaching a village green with a large pub in need of a coat of paint at one end. The engine finally expired. I coasted to the side of the pub. We sat in silence for a moment.

'Who's going to have a car to sell us around here – wherever "here" is?'

'I don't know, but this pub's as good a place as any to find out. Come on.'

Just then we heard the bell of a police car approaching. A second later it flashed past, heading the way we had come. If the Armstrong-Siddeley – and its dead occupants – had already been discovered, then all hell was about to break loose. We had to get away from the area.

The publican's name was Stanley Alfred Onions – or that's what it said above the pub's locked door. I knocked a few times with no reply, then we walked around to the backyard where a washing line of sheets partly masked a large greenhouse. Chickens clucked around our feet in protest.

'Hello,' called out Angel. Through the open back door we could see a scrapbook and a pile of photographs lying on the kitchen table.

A severe-looking woman with steel-grey hair swept back into a bun appeared.

'Mrs Onions?'

'What do you want?' she snapped.

'I'm sorry to trouble you,' began Angel.

'We're closed.' Mrs Onions folded her arms.

'We were wondering if you knew anyone around here with a car or van to sell,' continued Angel. 'We need to—'

'I don't want to know.' She went to close the door.

'Are you the slightest bit of a patriot?' whispered Angel fiercely.

Mrs Onions halted. 'I'm a true Englishwoman if that's what you mean.'

'Then you'll help another Englishwoman being pursued by the *Gestapo*.'

'For the love of God, why didn't you say so? Come in. Come in.'

I decided it was better if the van was not visible

from the road so I went off to push it round the back, next to the greenhouse. I returned to find Angel holding the scrap book.

'Mrs Onions's elder son is serving on HMS *Hood*,' she announced.

'The Pride of the Navy,' the older woman proclaimed. 'Here's a photo of him and his shipmates being inspected by His Majesty the King. The *real* king, not that thing in London. The news from Canada last night said there's been a big naval battle off Iceland. Our lads have sunk the German heavy cruisers *Hipper* and *Scheer*, and the French battleship *Clemenceau*. Other German warships are badly damaged. They've taken a real beating.'

'I hope your boy's safe.'

'He's doing his duty.' A look of concern swept over Mrs Onions's face, then she rallied. 'Now, what were you saying?'

I explained that we had to get to London quickly but the *Gestapo* were after us, and our van was damaged beyond repair.

'Let me think ... There's not that many people with cars, or vans, nowadays. No petrol, you see.'

'There must be some laid up.'

'We've got a Sunbeam but it's on bricks. It'll take ages to get it going again. When do you need to be in London?'

'We should be there by now,' said Angel, almost in tears.

'Don't you fret,' said Mrs Onions, 'we'll think of something.'

But Angel was staring horror-struck out of the window into the backyard, where a German army lorry was pulling up. Angel and I looked at each other.

I felt for my pistol.

'That's only Josef.' Mrs Onions saw our fear. 'He's a sergeant at Sandhurst military college, just up the road. Josef sells what we grow here. He called in not half an hour ago to say he has to drive to London on the hurry-up, so he's going to take some of our eggs and tomatoes up with him.'

A melancholy–looking man with a downturned moustache emerged from an outhouse with a stack of egg trays as the German began to unfasten the lorry's tarpaulin.

'You see, the Sandhurst officer cadets from the SS St George Division are forming the honour guard at Buckingham Palace tonight,' continued Mrs Onions. 'At the last minute the *Gestapo* insisted the firing pins were removed from their rifles. It shows the cadets aren't trusted *that* much,' she sniffed. 'The boys travelled up this morning, but their rifles were left behind to be doctored. Josef's taking them to Wellington Barracks now, and he'll drop our things off on the way.'

Out in the yard, the two men had finished loading the lorry.

'They're coming in here so you'd better go and hide in the snug,' Mrs Onions advised. 'Josef's a friend of ours but he's also a German and at the end of the day you can't trust them.'

We followed her to stand silently behind the door of a smaller bar. After a moment we heard a deep voice speaking in accented English. 'They are putting up roadblocks everywhere but my travel orders are signed by the adjutant so I shouldn't have too much trouble. Now, just a quick beer and then I must be off.'

The voices faded as the two men headed into the public bar.

Mrs Onions flitted in, wiping her hands on her apron. 'Sounds as if you wouldn't get through even if you did get hold of a car.'

'Would Josef take us?' I asked desperately. 'We'd pay him well.'

Mrs Onions shook her head vehemently. 'Don't think of asking him. He'd take the money, then hand you over at the first roadblock, but ... what about hiding out in the back of his lorry?'

Angel and I looked at each other.

'It's worth a try,' she murmured.

'We might have problems getting out at the other end. We don't want to end up in Wellington Barracks.'

'We'll have to risk that. It's our only hope,' decided Angel. 'Where's Josef going first?'

'He'll drop off our eggs and tomatoes at a lock-up near Kennington Oval – where they play cricket,' replied Mrs Onions.

'What about our van?' I asked.

'Don't worry. We'll hide it as soon as you've gone.'

'Bless you,' said Angel. She gave the woman a hug.

We slipped out and ran to the back of the lorry. I helped Angel up first, and then scrambled in after her. I noticed that the farm produce was carefully concealed behind the racks of rifles. We managed to create another hiding place for ourselves right behind the cab.

'Best of luck,' our saviour whispered. Then she was gone.

Minutes later, we felt the lorry tilt as Josef climbed into his cab. The luminous dial on my watch told me it was 12.23.

Despite the tension I dozed off. Angel told me later that we'd passed through four checkpoints as I'd slept. I finally woke as the stopping and starting became more frequent, and I guessed we were entering the capital. My waking thought was how would I face Matty; what would I say to him? Would I be able to let Angel execute him? If I had to choose between my friend and my country, I hoped I'd have the courage to choose my friend.

'You don't have to kill him,' I whispered, my

mouth next to Angel's ear. We both knew who I meant.

'Nick, you should be thinking about what's happening to you, not worrying about Matty. You haven't come to terms with the fact that you can never go back home, have you? You're a fugitive now.'

Angel was right. It was too terrifying to think about. 'So are you.'

'I'm used to it. I'll get away to Canada till the heat's off.' She paused. 'I hope you'll come with me.'

The lorry jolted to a halt again. This time Josef jumped out. He pulled aside the rear flap and I heard him grunt as he picked up several boxes of tomatoes from their hiding place. The sound of his boots receded on the pavement.

I scrambled out of hiding, hopped over the tailgate and jumped to the ground. A second later Angel landed in my arms, light as thistledown. We found ourselves in a deserted road lined with warehouses. Over the rooftops, Angel pointed out a massive gasometer flanked by two smaller ones.

'That's the Oval, so the river's that way.'

I looked at my watch: 1.50 p.m. Matty had known the meeting's location for almost two hours by now. I only hoped that Angel was right in guessing that the *Gestapo* would not make their move until all the leaders were fully gathered together.

It still meant that we would have to put our necks into the noose to get the others out.

31

The colourful display of swastika flags alternating with St George crosses over Westminster Bridge was lost on Dr Six as he stared impatiently out of the window of his turret office in Great Scotland Yard. He brushed away his valet's efforts to rearrange the silver braid on his dove-grey uniform and glanced compulsively at the phone yet again.

He should have set off for Westminster Abbey ten minutes ago. Most of the congregation had been there for at least an hour by now but Six was waiting for Cordington's call.

Throughout London, squads of Gestapo backed by SS élite troops were on standby for that call. Why didn't the telephone ring?

And why hadn't those two terrorists been captured yet? The biggest manhunt of the occupation had been launched to intercept them. They had been tracked as far as a transport café in Hampshire, two *Gestapo* officers had been found shot dead in their car just over the border in Surrey, then the trail had gone cold. Six comforted himself that not even a mouse could get through the security screen that he had thrown around the capital.

He decided that he could wait no longer. His valet gave the silver death's head on Six's cap one last buff, then opened the door for him. Downstairs a Mercedes was waiting to take him on the short journey across *Reichsplatz* – as Parliament Square had been renamed – to the Abbey.

The phone suddenly rang. Six leaped to answer it.

'Oberführer Dr Six? This is Stolz.'

'Yes, yes. You've got them?'

'Um, no, sir, but we know where Penny's family are headed—'

'So why tell me?' Six exploded. 'Will that help me capture the terrorists?'

'No, sir—'

'Then get off the line, you idiot.' Six slammed down the receiver. Purple with fury, he marched out of his office and almost collided with a young officer.

'We've found the terrorists' van in the garage of a public house near where the *Gestapo* officers were shot, sir,' he announced. 'The publican and his wife are being questioned.'

'We need quick answers.'

'The local team are aware that extreme interrogation is not only permissible but necessary.'

*

Angel and I hurried on towards the Thames. The tree-lined road was empty apart from two women pushing a handcart loaded with pieces of rusty metal, and a solitary tram rumbling towards Brixton. Narrow terraces of soot-blackened houses, many with their front doors open, ran off the main road at right angles. The few locals we saw appeared shabbier than people in the West Country and they had a pasty, pinched look about them.

After ten minutes we came to the Elephant and Castle, where loudspeakers, bedecked with swastikas, were blasting out a commentary.

The expectant crowds . . . the hum of anticipation . . . just waiting for the moment when the Duke and Duchess of Windsor will begin their journey into history. And here comes the royal coach, preceded by a troop of the sovereign's personal guard, the Household Cavalry – and followed by a troop of Prussian Uhlans . . .'

We were only twenty yards from the red-tiled entrance to the Underground station when a man in a long leather coat and trilby appeared from inside, glanced up the road and disappeared again. Obviously *Gestapo*! That put paid to our plan to use the Tube. Instead we strode on even faster. There were more people on the streets around here, drifting in the same direction; spurred by curiosity rather than patriotism to see the coronation procession.

Neither Angel nor I knew this part of London well but we continued towards the river. As we neared

Blackfriars Bridge, we made out a checkpoint ahead where German sentries stood watching Metropolitan Police officers inspect identity papers and search bags.

'*Listen to the cheers as the* Führer *himself arrives at the Abbey in his personal Mercedes. The Leader is wearing a simple brown tunic with a gold swastika. He raises his hand in acknowledgement of the cheers.*'

To avoid the checkpoint on Blackfriars Bridge, we turned left into Stamford Street – and straight into a trap. Just beyond, outside the imposing frontage of the London Nautical School, lay another checkpoint.

'Hell. I've still got Sara's identification disc in my shoulder bag,' whispered Angel.

My blood went cold. We had destroyed the dead woman's ID papers but totally forgotten the small metallic disc with her *Gestapo* number stamped on one side.

Five yards ahead was a drain in the gutter. Angel hobbled a few paces to halt on top of the grating. She stood on one leg, running her finger along the rim of a shoe – and let the disc slip through her fingers.

A tall man in a double-breasted suit and bowler hat materialized beside us.

'Did you just drop something, miss?'

'No.' Angel straightened up, smiling disarmingly. 'My shoe was pinching. It feels better now.'

'Are you sure you didn't drop something down the drain?'

'Positive . . . er, who are you?'

'Inspector Trotts, miss. Metropolitan Police.'

A woman in a tattered straw hat decorated with faded red paper roses swayed in front of us. I could smell the drink on her breath.

'She did, you know. I saw her. With my own eyes.' The woman cackled. 'Something silver, it was.'

'May I see your papers, miss?' Trotts turned to me. 'Your papers as well, please, sir.'

My mind performed its terrible trick of going totally blank. Who was I pretending to be? Certainly not Nick Penny, but who was I meant to be?

'The duke and duchess are being received outside the Abbey by the Archbishop and the Bishop's assistant in their copes. Behind them stand the Lord Chancellor, the Lord Great Chamberlain, the Lord High Constable . . . Now the procession moves slowly into the Church as the choirs begin Psalm 122. "I was glad when they said unto me: We will go into the house of the Lord." Edward and Wallis enter as the Duke and Duchess of Windsor but they will leave as rightful King and Queen of England . . .'

'You two are together?'

'Of course.' Angel threaded her arm through mine. 'We're getting married.'

'I see.' He inspected my residence permit. 'You're from Salisbury, sir?'

'Both of us are. We came up for the coronation.'

'You're leaving it rather late, aren't you, miss . . .?'

'Carmichael, Emily Carmichael,' Angel said for my benefit. 'It took us longer to get here than we'd thought.'

The discovery of £270 in Angel's bag produced a soundless whistle. 'Lot of money to be carrying around, miss.'

'We want to live in London when we're married and we've been to view a house we wanted to buy. This was going to be a deposit. But the owner's changed her mind. Shame, really. That's why we're late.'

Angel was a wonderful liar.

The detective turned to me. 'Why aren't *you* carrying this money, sir? Surely, it's the man's . . . ?'

'Um . . .' I gulped.

'Inspector, Peter here would lose his head if it wasn't screwed on to his shoulders.' Angel smiled fondly up at me. 'I wouldn't trust him to carry threepence, never that much money.'

With slow deliberation, Inspector Trotts pulled out a piece of paper and began to read, aloud. 'Man aged twenty-four, about six foot, average build, fair hair, brown eyes . . .' He looked me in the eye.

'Could be anyone,' I said.

'Just what I was thinking myself, sir – could be anyone.' He referred again to the paper. 'The lady's description is rather more detailed. Aged around twenty-three, five feet five, slender build, blue eyes, short blonde hair, freckles, small features.'

I winced. That described Angel to a T. Trotts let his words sink in as we continued hearing the loud-speaker broadcast. A reedy voice was intoning. '*Sirs, I present unto you King Edward your undoubted King: wherefore all of you who are come this day to do your homage and service, are you willing to do the same?*'

A moment's silence, then the acclamation. '*God save King Edward.*'

'I'm going to have to ask you both to come back to the police station,' said Inspector Trotts as a fanfare of trumpets blared out over the loudspeaker.

'Oh, really, officer, we'll miss the procession.'

'I'm sure we can soon clear up any misunderstanding at West End Central.'

Inspector Trotts lifted his arm and a Black Maria police van rolled up alongside. Angel climbed in first.

As I was getting in, the detective called out, 'Nick.'

I ignored him.

The door slammed as Angel and I sat down opposite each other on the wooden benches. A key turned in the lock. The van pulled off, only to stop almost immediately while the driver spoke to someone. Then it moved off again.

'We can't allow them to get us into a police station,' announced Angel. 'As soon as that door opens, we're away. I don't want to shoot a bobby but I will if I have to. If we get split up, make straight for the boat.'

We swayed as the Black Maria turned a number

of sharp corners. We seemed to be driving through a series of backstreets. After a short time the vehicle halted and the driver switched off the engine. We heard him walk away.

'What's happening? Where are we? This isn't a police station.'

Through the tiny barred windows, I made out that we had stopped in semi-darkness. 'I think we're parked under a bridge. It must be part of the new Waterloo bridge.'

'Can you see what the time is?'

I held my watch up to the patch of light from the window. 'Quarter past two,' I said.

Hereward's train had been searched from end to end at Andover and again at Clapham Junction, so it was late arriving at Waterloo. Even then, every passenger under forty years of age was herded away to have their papers inspected yet one more time. Hereward, with his thinning grey hair, was allowed straight through the security cordon. Outside the station he caught sight of Matty Cordington.

Hereward set off after Matty, walking some distance down Waterloo Road, past the fire station, where he crossed over, and up the road alongside the Old Vic Theatre. Matty took the first left turn, strolling slowly until he came to the White Swan pub, where he headed into Alaska Street. Halfway along the terrace of houses displaying Union flags, he switched to the opposite pavement and halted to kneel and tie his shoelace. Then he sauntered back to the White Swan. All the time Hereward kept fifty yards behind. He found Matty ordering two halves of bitter. The coronation service was being relayed on the pub wireless although few of the drinkers present seemed to be listening.

'Is your Majesty willing to take the oath?'

'I am willing.'

'Will you solemnly promise and swear to govern the Peoples of Great Britain and Northern Ireland, Canada, Australia, New Zealand, the Union of South Africa, the Empire of India and Ceylon and all peoples of the Empire wherever they be, according to their respective laws and customs?'

'I solemnly promise to do so.'

'The watchers confirm that you're clean,' said Matty, handing Hereward a glass.

Hereward thought Cordington had aged in the few days since they'd last met. An air of jagged tiredness now overlay his dark good looks; he looked nervous and drawn, his eyes wide open as if only raw adrenalin was keeping him going.

'Why are the Germans so edgy?'

'Don't know. At least two of our leaders haven't turned up yet. But I see you survived the battle of Merricombe.'

'Some of us managed to get away up onto the moors. We lost the Germans in the darkness.'

'It's a shame the villagers weren't so fortunate,' said Matty.

'They knew the risk. We'll never win the war without sacrifices.'

'I had friends in Merricombe. As a kid, I spent my summers there on Pear Trees Farm.'

Hereward saw anger growing in Cordington's eye. He adopted a softer tone. 'I didn't anticipate the Militia were going to run amok. But I gather they got their come-uppance.'

'No thanks to your Moorsmen.'

A cold silence settled between them until Hereward leaned forward to whisper, 'I have what you asked for – if you still want it.'

'More than ever.'

'I don't know how you expect to get it through all these security checks . . .'

'Let me worry about that. Well?'

'We're five minutes' walk away.' Hereward registered the surprise on Cordington's face. 'Mills isn't the only one capable of organizing things.'

Five minutes later Hereward was knocking on the door of a lock-up workshop under the nearby railway arches. A man in a brown overall opened it a fraction before stepping back to let them enter.

Inside the brick cavern, hundreds of clocks were

ticking, whirring or chiming simultaneously. Tall stately grandfather clocks and slimmer grandmother clocks stood in groups, while rows of shelves heaved with mantelpiece and table clocks of every sort. The cacophony was deafening.

The clock mender reached under a workbench and proudly presented them with a bulky black leather briefcase.

'A work of art, even if I say so myself.'

'Looks genuine enough,' said Hereward, inspecting the silver swastika on the flap.

'It *is* genuine,' chortled the man. 'We took it off a dead German courier.'

'And it'll work?'

'It'll work, have no fear. See this switch under the handle, here? Five minutes at this side; one minute here. Ingenious, if I say so myself.'

Matty picked up the briefcase. 'It's heavy.'

'What do you expect?'

The man seemed in a hurry to get away. Outside in the street, Matty ordered Hereward: 'Stay fifty yards behind me but keep me in sight at all times. Don't worry if the Germans spring a surprise check, I'll get you through.'

Matty led the way through grimy streets towards the Thames. On every corner, loudspeakers were relaying the scene inside the Abbey where someone was now reading from the Gospel of St Matthew.

Near Waterloo Bridge, he was confronted by a five-man German patrol advancing purposefully towards him. He managed to appear unconcerned as the corporal eyed him closely before marching on. They passed a Black Maria parked under the bridge. Two hundred yards later, he came out on the riverside, where a boatman was tinkering with the engine of a stubby launch tied up to a derelict wooden pier. Matty strode straight towards him.

Angel threw down the bent hairpin and swore. 'I can't get this damn lock open.'

'It's a police lock – what do you expect?'

'I expect to be able to open it.'

Thanks to a loudspeaker on the bridge above, we had been forced to listen to the coronation service as we examined every inch of the Black Maria for a way of escape – short of shooting off the lock, which would only attract unwanted attention.

The reedy voice, which I had come to recognize as that of the Archbishop of York, was intoning: *O God the Crown of the faithful: Bless we beseech thee this Crown, and so sanctify thy servant Edward upon whose head this day thou dost place it for a sign of real majesty that he may be filled by thine abundant grace with all its princely virtues: through the King eternal Jesus Christ our Lord. Amen.*

Angel paused at the unmistakable tramp of a passing German patrol. A minute later English voices approached.

'Get ready,' warned Angel.

I grasped the pistol in my pocket as the Black Maria's door was flung open to reveal the police driver herding two handcuffed men.

'A couple of dips to join you,' he announced.

I went to pull my gun, and froze. Not twenty yards away the German patrol stood watching proceedings with interest. Angel gave a minute shake of her head.

'Why are we still here?' she demanded of the driver.

'Change of plan, miss. The chief inspector's decided to use the van as a holding pen. We'll take it to West End Central when we're full.'

The two pickpockets had their handcuffs removed and squeezed past us into the van. The door slammed and we were left in the gloom again.

'And now the Archbishop is reverently placing the great crown of St Edward on the sovereign's head. As the cry "God save the King" goes up, all the assembled nobility put on their own coronets. The royal fanfare sounds. In the distance we can hear the guns of the Tower of London begin to fire a one-hundred-and-twenty-one-gun salute.'

*

As the salvoes echoed across the capital, the launch set off across the Thames towards the pleasure steamer flying an outsize *Kriegsmarine* flag. A ladder was lowered as they approached and Matty scrambled up. Sliding the bulging briefcase under a bench, he escorted Hereward down the companionway.

'Welcome. You're one of the last to arrive,' said Mills, shaking hands. 'The Germans' manhunt has thrown a spanner into our works.'

'I trust no one's run into any trouble,' said Hereward.

'They could still be trying to get here. Help yourself to a cup of tea and a sandwich.'

An aide escorted Hereward into the saloon, where the other Resistance leaders were already gathered.

Mills turned to Matty. 'We'll hang on another fifteen minutes for the two who are missing and then we'll cast off. Can't wait any longer.'

'I'll go and warn the lookouts of our impending departure, sir.'

'Make sure you get back in time. I need you here.'

On deck, Matty retrieved the briefcase and set off down the gangplank.

'What'd they nick you for, then?' demanded one of the pickpockets.

'Just a mix-up with our papers,' I replied.

'Oh yeh? That's what they all say.'

'*Hear our prayers, O Lord, we beseech thee, and so direct and support thy servant King Edward that he may not bear the Sword in vain : . .*'

'We've got to get out of here, come hell or high water,' murmured Angel. She turned to the pickpockets. 'Next time they open the door we're going to make a break for it. Are you with us?'

'You're not some of those Resistance people, are you?' demanded the thinner one.

'So?' I met his look.

'Nah, fair enough,' said the other. 'We're with you, then.'

It was said too quickly and I made a mental note to keep my eye on him. Two minutes later the door swung open again. This time a handcuffed man with a shiner of a black eye stood pinioned between the driver and a younger copper.

'Here's your mate,' called the driver to the two pickpockets inside. 'Bit of a naughty lad – resisting arrest.'

'Now,' said Angel.

A number of things all happened at once. Drawing my gun, I started to leap out. One pickpocket yelled "Look out" and threw himself on Angel. I grabbed the handcuffed man and hurled him out of the way as the young constable went to draw his truncheon.

'Don't,' I warned him. Out of the corner of my eye, I saw the pickpocket wrestling for Angel's gun. I stepped back and cracked him over the head with my pistol butt.

Then I was facing the policemen again. Neither had moved but the younger one was staring at me intently. There was another crack, and a grunt, from the van and then Angel was beside me.

The driver glowered at us. 'You're terrorists.'

'No, mate. We're patriots.'

I pushed the police driver into the back along with the crooks and kept them covered.

'You stay with us,' I told the younger copper. 'Any tricks and I'll kill you.'

'I'm on your side,' he whispered. 'I swear it.'

I took a gamble. 'We need to get to Cleopatra's Needle,' I told him.

'The Germans have sealed off the Embankment beyond Charing Cross. We'll have to go over Blackfriars Bridge.'

'But there's a checkpoint there.'

'Trust me.'

'We're going to have to,' murmured Angel.

She climbed into the back of the van to cover the pickpockets and the driver with her gun. I locked the door, put on the driver's tunic and cap and sat in the passenger seat, my own pistol aimed at our new friend.

'You don't need that gun.' He started the engine. 'I only joined the police because I failed my RAF medical. If you're doing the Germans down, I'm with you. They killed my kid brother when he tried to escape from a PoW camp. I owe them.'

We were emerging onto a main street running parallel to the Thames.

'What's your name?' I asked him.

'John Godwin.'

I was thinking how the name was vaguely familiar as we turned left into Blackfriars Bridge Road. German troops with rifles were still watching the checkpoint. So too was a man in a foreign-cut suit. A bobby stepped forward, his hand up for us to stop. I ran my finger around the high collar of the strange tunic and tried my best to look like a genuine copper.

'Out of your way a bit, aren't you?' said the policeman, taking in John Godwin's divisional letter on his tunic.

'Tell me about it,' complained Godwin. 'This lot should have gone to West End Central, then it was Holborn, now it's Snow Hill. God knows what the City lads'll have to say when I turn up.'

'Tell you to bugger off like they usually do, I expect. What've you got there?'

'Bunch of toe-rags. Three dips, a smart alec knocking out hooky kettles and hobs and a couple of drunks. Feel like I'm driving a human dustcart.'

'I'll tell you what, mate, it's better than being stuck out here with these smiling Jonahs and their ruddy guns.'

'Yeh, watch they don't use you for target practice.'

John Godwin let in the clutch and pulled off, the Germans dutifully moving aside to let him through.

'Thanks,' I breathed, as we drove over the bridge. 'What now?'

'I'll drop you off, then dump the Black Maria and disappear,' replied Godwin.

'Will you be all right?'

'Yeh – no one knows how to disappear like a copper.'

Once over Blackfriars Bridge, he headed along the Embankment, past the Temple and Somerset House, which now housed the *Reich* Racial Purity Programme, before turning up Savoy Street and coming to a halt.

'This is as close as I can get. Any further and people will start asking what I'm doing there,' said Godwin.

Through the loudspeakers, the congregation inside the Abbey began acclaiming: '*God save King Edward. Long Live King Edward. May the King live for ever.*' There was a pause, then the organ began playing the hymn 'All People that on Earth do Dwell'.

We made sure no one was watching before letting Angel out. We shook hands briefly. Once Godwin and the van were out of sight, Angel and I headed to the river. Under shady plane trees we passed a bronze memorial: *To the British Nation from the grateful people of Belgium 1914–1918*. I was just thinking how we hadn't done much to help them this time round when Angel abruptly crossed the road, heading towards a steamer bedecked in swastikas: *The Maidstone Castle.*

As the assembled choirs in the Abbey sang the 'Te Deum Laudamus', the commentator explained in sepulchral tones that the king was descending from the throne.

'*Now carrying the sceptre and rod in his hands, the king, accompanied by Queen Wallis, moves down the south side of the altar into St Edward's Chapel, the four swords being carried before him. Following comes the full pageantry and panoply of centuries of English heritage, the Groom of the Robes, the Lord Great Chamberlain and the Lords carrying the regalia and finally the Dean . . .*'

Angel murmured quietly to a road sweeper who had been giving her the hard eye.

'You're only just in time,' he said. 'They're casting off soon.'

'Have you seen Matty Cordington?'

'He went off towards Westminster a couple of minutes ago.'

32

Matty Cordington gravitated towards the Abbey as if drawn by the force of destiny. The first phone box did not work. The second was occupied by a German soldier with a pile of coppers. Matty grasped the heavy briefcase and waited, listening to the service on the loudspeakers.

'*In this small chapel, one of the holiest places inside the Abbey, the king delivers the sceptre and rod to the Archbishop, waiting at the altar. The Archbishop receives also the great crown of King Edward. The king is disrobed of the Robe Royal and is arrayed in his Robe of purple velvet . . .*

'*Meanwhile, in the body of the Abbey, the guests, headed by the* Führer *himself, wait patiently, aware that they are part of a precious moment in the history of this sceptred isle . . .*'

The man finally pushed open the door of the kiosk and barged past. A cloud of cigarette smoke billowed out after him. Matty put down his bag and lifted the receiver, feeling the German's sweat still on the bakelite handle. He inserted two pennies, and pressed button A.

'I can't believe it.' Mills stared out over the Thames, his normally strong features sagging with disbelief.

'John, I swear it's true,' insisted Angel.

It was the first time I'd heard Mills addressed by his first name, and it sounded odd, as if I was eavesdropping on family matters.

'The guard said Cordington was heading for Westminster.'

'He volunteered to go and tell the lookouts that we were about to leave.' Mills had taken the news of Matty's treachery like a physical blow. Now he shook his head violently, as though to clear it. 'Tell the skipper to cast off immediately. Make for the pier at Wapping.' Mills spun to face Angel. 'If he's heading towards Westminster, that means he's gone to link up with his *Gestapo* controllers. He knows too many faces here.'

'I understand,' said Angel.

With ice in my heart, so did I. The boat began trembling beneath my feet as the engines started up. Angel ran down the gangway onto the pier. The boat was inching away from the side. I dashed across the deck, took a flying leap and sprinted after her. She was not pleased to see me.

'What are you doing here?' she demanded as she jogged along.

'I'm coming with you.'

'Nick, you haven't the sense you were born with.' She halted briefly to grasp me by both arms. 'With all these Germans around, do you really think I'm going to be able to shoot Matty Cordington and then get away? It's a one-way street, my lover.'

It was only then that the full horror of our situation dawned on me. Angel was going to sacrifice herself. Not only was I about to lose my best friend, but my love as well. My brain went numb – which left it easier to hurry alongside her than to make the decision to do anything else.

SS *Oberführer* Six fidgeted restlessly as he waited with the others for the king and queen to return from the Chapel. The 'Te Deum' had ended and the congregation was shifting in their seats, murmuring to one another. Six squinted towards Reinhard Heydrich, Head of the *Reich* Security Head Office in Berlin, and wondered what he was making of all this religious mumbo-jumbo – with his well-known pathological hatred of the church. Six's gaze drifted back yet again to the north cloister, where his man would give the signal that Cordington had telephoned. There was no sign of him yet. Six bit his lip and inspected the

English lords and ladies stooping beneath the weight of their crimson robes. It struck him how the women were all of two sorts – the younger ones pale and plain with long faces; the grey-haired older ones haughty and severe. He supposed that the younger women would transmute into the older, but he liked their tiaras with their long icicle points – especially the Victorian ones with jewels on springs so that the gems quivered.

His gaze alighted on a block of King's Scholars wearing black knee-breeches, white capes and buckled shoes, with mortar boards under their arms, sitting next to a contingent of Hitler Youth in brown shirts. The old and the new. The past and the future.

He suddenly spotted his aide trying to attract his attention and turned towards him. The man nodded and Six felt a great weight lift off his shoulders. Cordington would now be on his way, to put himself under the protection of the *Gestapo*. His usefulness was at an end. Six almost smiled.

This was the moment, the irrevocable moment.

As he passed under Hungerford railway bridge, Matty Cordington slowed down and took a deep breath. He knew there was not much time left.

Just ahead, occupying troops were manning a barrier across the road, marking the inner security cordon. Beyond the barrier lay a veritable army camp: *Wehrmacht* lorries, armoured cars and scout cars drawn up across the width of the Embankment. An SS crowd-control vehicle was parked under the trees outside Great Scotland Yard. Nearing the barrier, Matty attracted the attention of a man in a long leather coat. Matty held up Six's pass in front of his face. It was good to see a *Gestapo* man turn pale. Without further hindrance, Matty stepped through into the German area.

'There he is. Up ahead, at the checkpoint.'

I caught sight of Matty showing something to a man in a leather coat. He was immediately waved through. Three senior officers gathered around him. They seemed to be welcoming him. I closed my eyes. My last shred of hope that this was all a misunderstanding vanished. I saw Matty was carrying a bulging briefcase – no doubt full of Resistance secrets.

'What are we going to do now? We can't get through there.'

Another barrier lay across Horseguards Avenue, stopping pedestrians from getting into Whitehall itself, but Whitehall Gardens had been turned into a rest area for British police and ambulance men, with a mobile canteen dispensing tea. Angel hesitated for just a second and then headed into the gardens, which extended from the Embankment itself to a massive new government building that backed onto Whitehall and up towards Parliament Square.

King Edward VIII and Queen Wallis emerge from the chapel in a moment of majesty. The king, wearing the Imperial Crown, carries in his right hand the Sceptre and in his left the Orb. He progresses along the choir, his radiant queen a few steps behind. For the first time in over a hundred years, the king will leave the Abbey by the North Entrance.

Members of the noblest families in the land bend the knee as their rightful and lawful king approaches. Dukes, earls, viscounts, barons, baronets, the Lords Lieutenant of the counties, the aldermen of the City of London and the ordinary people, all hail King Edward, their sovereign.

From a small doorway set into the ministry's huge white façade a constant stream of German party workers and English civil servants was taking advantage of the tea stall.

'It's worth a try,' whispered Angel, almost to herself.

'What is?'

'Look how this building extends beyond the German cordon. If we can only get inside, maybe we can outflank the barriers and come out inside the security zone. If we hurry we might still be able to intercept Matty.'

'All right. As you say, it's worth a try.'

Following Angel's example I bought three mugs

of tea and shuffled towards the door guarded by a middle-aged Ministry of Works policeman with a walrus moustache. Angel started a lively exchange in German with a Nazi Party official. By the time she reached the doorway, it appeared as if she had known him for years. The Nazi showed his pass but Angel made a play of finding it difficult to juggle with the three mugs while reaching into her handbag.

'You go on,' she called out gaily, as she contrived to spill tea over herself. Then she switched back into English. 'Oh dear! Would you mind holding this mug, officer?'

'It's all right, miss,' reassured the Ministry of Works policeman. 'Go on in.'

'John will vouch for me, won't you, John?' she called to me over her shoulder.

'Hang on. I've got my hands full, too. It wasn't even my turn to fetch the tea.'

'Oh, don't complain. Hurry up or it'll be cold by the time we get back.'

'Wait a minute. I'm trying to . . .'

'That's all right, sir. Enjoy the procession.'

'Thank you. But you're going to miss it, stuck here.'

'To be honest, sir, I don't mind.'

Inside the building more loudspeakers continued to describe the coronation.

And as King Edward and Queen Wallis take the loyal obeisance of their people, the Führer *leaves to go to the*

dais outside the North Entrance, together with Reichsmarschall *Göring and* Reichsführer *Himmler and Hess.*
Here the Führer *and his party and the King and Queen*
and their attendants will wait separately while the bands
play the three great anthems 'Deutschland, Deutschland
Über Alles', 'God Save the King' and the 'Horst Wessel
Song'.

A long high corridor ran away towards Whitehall,
not the direction we needed in order to head off
Matty. I went to put down the tea mugs but Angel
stopped me.

'Hang on to two of them. No one ever suspects
someone carrying a cup of tea. It shows you belong
here.'

After a pair of internal doors the corridor suddenly widened out, still heading in the wrong direction. We hurried on through another set of doors.
Not ten paces ahead, two policemen looked up from
a security checkpoint commanding a junction of
major corridors running in four directions.

'Hell!'

Everyone passing the checkpoint was holding up
an identity card for scrutiny.

One of the policemen at the desk was beginning
to take an interest in us. The hunters were at risk of
becoming the hunted.

'Look, there.' The faded sign over a green door
said *Whitehall West. Foreign Office. Colonial Office.*

Treasury. A newer one above it announced *Rasse- und Siedlungshauptamt. Wirtschaftsverwaltungshauptamt. Commission for Reparations.*

'Come on,' hissed Angel.

One of the guards yelled, 'Hey, you, come back. Only German personnel are allowed down there.'

We put down our mugs and took off, running down flights of ill-lit steps. Down and down we went, until finally, deep underground, we came into a vast vault of brick and stone, its arched roof rising up into the gloom.

Angel took my arm and pulled me behind a blind brick wall. Beyond it, a low tunnel lit by a series of dim bulbs stretched away from us.

'Where are we?' I asked.

'Before the invasion, this was the Ministry of Aviation Supply. The vault's known as Henry VIII's Wine Cellar,' explained Angel. 'From here, tunnels lead all over Whitehall. If I can find the right one, we'll come up well within the security cordon. If we hurry we can still catch Matty.'

'How do you know all this?'

'I told you, I was going to be a civil servant.'

An angry policeman came puffing down into the vaults. 'Where've you bastards gone?'

Angel pushed me into view.

'Let's be having you.' The copper lurched over to take hold of my arm. Angel crept from behind the end of the brick screen and hit him over the head with her pistol. I caught his body before it hit the ground.

'I could have done that,' I told her, as I laid him on the floor.

'You'd probably have fractured his skull.'

We paused to listen as more heavy footsteps came pounding down the stairs towards us. We darted towards a large tunnel that seemed to run parallel to the Embankment but no sooner had we reached its entrance than we saw a group of black-clad SS men goose-stepping towards us, fifty yards ahead.

'Shit.' We backed away from them and slipped into the next tunnel.

'We'll have to go this way. Let's hope it links up somewhere.' This tunnel was much lower, with heating pipes attached to its roughly rendered roof, so I had to duck my head as I ran. Just as we reached a T-junction, the whistles began blowing shrilly behind us. The tunnel suddenly forked to the right and left, while a staircase opened out ahead of us.

'Westminster must be that way.' Angel pointed to the left fork.

We ran over old flagstones, ducking past swinging light bulbs, men's voices echoing behind us. The winding tunnel narrowed and grew warmer. We rounded a bend to find that it ended abruptly at a locked steel door. A flight of stone steps, worn with age, headed up through an archway to our right.

There was only one way now – and that was up. Our pursuers were drawing closer. As we climbed, the steps changed from stone to concrete. Breathlessly, we emerged through a doorway to find ourselves just off the vast lobby of some grand ministry. Over the loudspeakers, we heard the Massed Bands of the RAF playing the final chords of 'Deutschland, Deutschland Über Alles'.

From the staircase below us came more whistles and shouting.

Our position seemed hopeless. To our left, the main door out onto Whitehall was guarded by two SS troopers wearing polished coal-scuttle helmets and white gloves. No way out there.

Through a broad window, across the lobby, we made out an internal courtyard crammed with German troop carriers and SS troops in full battle order. The German military lining the streets outside were for show. The soldiers concealed here were for real, in case trouble broke out.

The only way left to us was up the marble staircase, under the massive portrait of the *Führer*. We forced ourselves not to run up it.

Brass plates on the doors of the first-floor offices told us that we had surfaced in the SS Economic Administration Department. Glancing into the rooms, we could see Nazi Party officials crowding around the windows to get a view across the square towards Westminster Abbey.

Our pursuers had now reached the lobby below. Angel and I climbed up the next flight, ignored by others hurrying past to get a glimpse of their *Führer*. Breathless, we finally reached the top floor. Most of the office doors there were closed. We tried the first one. It was locked. So was the second, but the third gave to my touch. The key was on the inside so I locked the door and slipped the key into my pocket. Avoiding the four clerks' desks pushed together into the middle of the cramped room, I crossed to the window and, bending down, found that I could see right across to the Abbey, about a hundred yards away.

The bands outside were just finishing 'God Save the King'. After a short pause they struck up the 'Horst Wessel Song' – the anthem of the Nazi Party itself.

'We're trapped,' gasped Angel.

'Let's get our breath back and then find a fire escape. Once the procession has passed, there's bound to be masses of people on the move. We should be able to melt into the crowds.'

It was said with more conviction than I felt. We had become rats in a trap. The last ten minutes had gone terribly wrong. Maybe it was our exhaustion, maybe it was an indication of the pressure we were under, but every decision we had made had been the wrong one. We had pushed deeper and deeper into the very heart of Nazi government until now we were stuck on the top floor of an SS ministry with no way out. If our pursuers ever realized who we were, they'd tear the building apart to find us.

I wiped at the grubby window panes with a piece of paper and called to Angel. It was obvious why no one had bothered to watch from here. Only two at a time could peer through the tiny window, and then only by half kneeling.

As the last strains of the 'Horst Wessel' died away, the commentator began again in hushed tones.

The Führer *waits on the low dais. Behind him stand the leaders of the Fatherland –* Reichsführer *Hess,* Reichsmarschall *Göring, leader of the* Luftwaffe*,* Reichsführer *Himmler. Besides them is the Protector von Ribbentrop who has done so much to bring about this great day; this symbolic union between two countries. Field Marshal Busch . . .*

Looking down at the scene, I reflected bitterly on how we had failed so completely. We had failed to prevent Matty Cordington from informing on the Resistance meeting: we had failed to prevent him from reaching the *Gestapo* headquarters with his secrets. The Resistance leaders had been forced to flee and now, under our very eyes, Hitler and his Nazi cronies were lording it over a puppet king of England. Not only had we failed – we were about to be captured. Angel had her cyanide capsule. But what did I have?

I stared intently at the distant figure of Hitler, focusing my anger and desperation on this evil incarnate who had wrecked all our lives. He was standing with both hands clasped in front of him. I wished him dead with every fibre of my being.

Outside the door, I could hear heavy boots pounding up the stairs towards us.

Angel gave me a crooked smile and drew her pistol.

'I'll not let them take me alive,' she whispered.

'Nor me.'

'Fight together?'

'Yes.' I pulled out my own gun. 'I love you.'

'I love you, too.'

'Of all the words ever spoken and the songs ever sung, the saddest are these – it might have been.'

'Nick, it was.'

We crouched behind a desk, listening to the loud German voices and the sound of office doors being thrown open.

'. . . as splendid a sight as this Abbey, so redolent with English history, has witnessed. King Edward, holding sceptre and orb, and his queen now wait to begin the procession between the honour guard of Grenadiers and SS Leibstandarte Adolf Hitler towards the dais. What a thrill for those in the crowd. Those present are privileged today because they will, for the rest of their lives, know that in a tiny way they have stood on the stage of history. Each and every one is a loyal member of the Anglo-German Friendship League. Now the king and the queen approach the dais . . .'

A hand rattled the doorknob. *'Wo ist der Schlüssel?'*
'Weiß nicht.'
'Find the people who work here, now.'
'The king bows graciously; Queen Wallis curtsies. The
Führer *responds by raising his right hand in his now*
familiar salute . . . Oh, dear, a woman has fainted just in
front of the dais. The majesty of this moment was too much
for her. A young man presses forward to help. He has a
bag; perhaps he is a doctor . . . The ceremony continues.
From the ranks of the Führer's *personal bodyguard, an*
officer steps forward to raise the cry "God Save the King".'

We heard the crowd echo 'God Save the King' as
our pursuers moved off down the corridor. I knew
they would be back. Angel squeezed my hand.

'And now the officer in charge of the Grenadier Guards
steps forward to give the Führer *salute. "Heil Hitler".'*

The crowd edges forward, their hands extended in the
Hitler salute, joyously proclaiming their Führer; *their*
Leader. One young man dashes forward between the
guardsmen. It's the doctor with his bag. He wants to shake
the Führer's *hand. No. People are wrestling the man to*
the ground.

The panes in our window shook as the explosion
echoed and reverberated around the square.

For a second there was an unearthly silence.
Then the first scream rose to rend the heavens . . .
Screams that still continue to this day.

Epilogue

So that's it. The rest you know – or think you do. Matty Cordington's nail bomb wiped out not only the Nazi leaders but the false English ones as well. Hitler and Himmler, Göring and von Ribbentrop, Edward and Simpson – all dead. It took the Gestapo until the next day to discover who the assassin had been – there was nothing left of Matty – but when they did, they razed his estate to the ground, took his workers into slavery, slaughtered his cattle and burned his crops.

They say that one hundred thousand perished in the reprisals, the uprising and the massacres that followed. I'm told the Gestapo were waiting for my own family when they got off the train in Shrewsbury. I don't know how they ever found out where they were going.

I grieve for them and for John Mills. He stayed behind in London when Angel and I fled, and was captured two days later. He took his suicide pill.

Matty Cordington hadn't betrayed the Resistance Movement after all. He gave the address of the meeting's safe house as Gosling Way in Stockwell, in south London. Sending the Gestapo on a wild-goose chase there was his way of showing that he kept his sense of humour to the last.

Angel – or perhaps I should call her Coral Kennedy now – and I escaped easily. Everyone in the building forgot about us once the bomb went off. We lost ourselves among the crowds, and used the escape route set up in case the Resistance leaders needed to flee. By the time the Gestapo sealed off the city we were well away. We hid in Lowestoft for a week, while the flames of rebellion flickered. Then we made good our escape thanks to the crew of a drifter and the bravery of the captain of HMS Alliance who was willing to risk his submarine to pick us up in shallow waters.

This is my story, General. I'm sorry if it was not what you expected. It contains few heroes, for it's hard to be a hero under German Occupation.

Those who suffer to live under an Occupation are cowards and compromisers and collaborators. Those who don't are dead.

Now if you'll allow me to return to my cell, I'm tired.